DIVITA

A Novel

Other books by Justin Cristelli

Red Knight: A Knight Without a Sword, Volume One
Caprice and Other Stories

DIVITA

A Novel

JUSTIN CRISTELLI

Edited by *Lindsay Cristelli*
Cover design by *Jeff Hewitt*
Interior layouts by *Lindsay Cristelli*

For Dominick and Norma Jean Cristelli, my parents.
They will always be immortal to me.

PROLOGUE
ROME
1955

Lucia's long, powerful legs wrapped around Dominic Divita, nearly squeezing the life from him. Her orgasms were slow and intense. He knew better than to touch her at these moments. If he did, the feeling would be overwhelming.

Her breathing went short. Her muscles seemed to lock. What Lucia hated most about sex was how vulnerable it left her.

Dominic's knees still felt numb as he clumsily rolled off of her. He lay next to her as she came down over the next few seconds.

"I love you," he said.

"Of course you do, you pervert," she chuckled.

Dominic laughed as he got to his feet. His broad, six foot tall frame bounced around the cramped hotel room.

"What are you doing?" she asked.

"I'm going to wash us off of me."

"That's disgusting."

On his way to the bathroom, he noticed the view of Vatican City out the window. He was quite pleased that, even though this suite was cheap enough to rent with a week's pay, he could see all the way to St. Peter's Square.

Lucia turned over to see what he was up to. The red light from the hotel's neon sign came through the window and shined on the man she loved; this naked man looking longingly at the church. She thought it was an odd sight, to say the very least.

"Are you thinking of confessing, or are you hoping the Pope can see your dick from over there?" she asked.

He backed away from the window and tried to pretend like he didn't care. Dominic made his way to the bathroom. He jumped into the dirt-stained tub and washed himself free of sweat. The water took forever to warm up. Dominic quickly stepped out to towel off. He shut the door behind him and began talking to her as he urinated.

"My parents would kill me if they found out about us," he said from behind the door.

"Don't talk to me when you're peeing! I hate it!" Lucia cried.

"Okay! Okay!" Dominic laughed, but inside he was terrified of what was to come.

His parents had indeed disliked Lucia, to the point of cursing her name and damning her to Hell. They had been willing to look the other way, however, hoping he would get tired of her eventually. In their hearts, they believed that God would forgive him.

Everything had come to a head earlier that day when Dominic was preparing for his evening with Lucia. He'd stopped by the pawn shop, just down the street from his father's restaurant, to buy a ring. He had been saving for weeks in order afford it. He'd felt like an adult for the first time in his life.

This feeling lasted for all of ten seconds. That's how long it took for him to feel a firm tug at his arm. It was Dominic's father, Sergio, a large, hairy man. Even though Dominic had become taller than him at the tender age of fifteen, his old man could still frighten him.

"What were you doing in that store?" He spoke to Dominic as if he owned the young man.

"Nothing! Let go!" Dominic was embarrassed as everyone passing by watched the scene. Some people suspected that he had been caught stealing from the store.

Sergio didn't believe him and dragged him back to their restaurant where Dominic's mother, Bella, was cooking in the kitchen. The round, gray haired woman stopped chopping carrots when she noticed the two men enter from the front. She demanded that Sergio explain himself for pushing around their oldest boy.

"Tell her! Tell your mother what you've bought!" he yelled as he shoved Dominic into the kitchen counter. He slowly pulled a box out of his pocket. Bella cupped her hands around her mouth in shock.

"Is she with child? Did that Gypsy trick you into marring her?" Bella gave the sign of the cross over her chest.

"No, I love her!" Dominic was hurt that his mother would think such a thing.

"No Dominic! It's lust, not love. That Gypsy will drag you down into Hell with her." Bella had suddenly become very frightened for her son.

Sergio, his arms crossed over his wide chest, stood silently to let Dominic to know how angry he was.

"Don't say that about her! I love her! You just don't understand her!" he snapped back at his mother.

Sergio stepped in and backhand his son. The blow knocked the young man down. This only made Bella more upset.

"Do not talk to your mother that way! She only wants to protect you! You are never to see that whore again! If you marry her, you are dead to us. You'll no longer be welcome in this family! You understand?"

Dominic knew he meant it. He held back his tears and looked his father square in the eye. As scared as he was of his father, Dominic was holding down his anger. He hated them for their willingness to cast him out over the woman he loved.

"All right, Poppa. I'll tell her tonight that it's over."

"Do whatever you want! Just don't come back here if you propose to that whore!" Sergio exited the kitchen. It was his way of ending fights.

Bella put her arms around her son and cried quietly so her husband wouldn't hear.

"It's all right. Just tell her it's over. That's the right thing to do. She probably won't care anyway."

When Dominic returned from the bathroom, Lucia had already pulled the covers over her, looking like nothing had happened.

"Now, you were saying?"

"Oh, just about my parents..." Dominic let the sentence wander off. It was a habit of his that never failed to piss off Lucia.

"Your parents...they..." she responded, hoping that he'd pick the thought back up.

It was a statement that Dominic didn't want to say out loud. It was a truth that they both understood, but they had never addressed. They had been seeing each other for months, and it was time to think about Dominic's folks.

"They know about us." He stood by the wall across the room, seeming as if he were too ashamed to be close to her.

Lucia listened very carefully. She waited for the exact words, the ones that ended affairs and broke hearts. She didn't make a sound as he stumbled to get the words out.

"My mother, she cried. My father he...he became angry. You know, that silent anger he gets."

Dominic looked away. He pretended that something had caught

his attention. She wasn't fooled by this ruse.

He took a breath and looked back at her. Dominic finally moved forward from the wall. He avoided looking directly into her dark brown eyes. If he did, he wouldn't have been able to finish what needed to be said.

"I've seen a lot of girls because of my family's restaurant, but when I saw you dancing that day I fell in love with you right away. My folks, my friends, say that you're a no-good Gypsy, but I don't know what they're talking about. You're so beautiful. I see a woman who knows who she is and doesn't give a fuck about what anybody else thinks."

Lucia moved to the edge of the bed. She fought back her tears. Just because he knew her soft side existed didn't mean she had to show it.

He pushed back a bit of his black hair that had fallen in his face as he brought himself down to his knees.

"You make me feel like a real man. If people think that you're a bitch, then maybe it's just because you care too much. Maybe you're angry that others are too lazy to think, or at least give a shit. I see them through your eyes now and they all look asleep to me."

Lucia was afraid. He was building up to something. Life had taught her that men who start speeches with love end it with heartbreak. Men need to let themselves off the hook. They need to feel like the good guy. Lucia hoped that he hadn't noticed her heavy breathing.

"My parents are Catholic. They don't trust Gypsies. They told me yesterday that if I remain with you, I'm out of the family." Dominic began to tear up. He sniffed it back. Lucia moved forward to comfort him, but he edged away from her.

"I would be out of the family. I won't take over the restaurant when Poppa retires. They won't even welcome any of our babies into the world. I'll be dead to them." Dominic rose up without looking at her.

Lucia knew what this night meant – goodbye. He was going to

have one last fuck and then walk out of her life. He was the first boy she'd ever know who wasn't afraid of her. Now it seemed that he was more afraid of his parents than any Gypsy magic she could produce.

He picked his pants up off the dresser and dug through the pocket. He removed a small, dark object. He turned back to her and kneeled once more.

"Lucia, I know we're just kids, but I know I love you. I want to be with you forever."

To Lucia's surprise, he opened a small box, revealing a tiny ring inside. It was nothing amazing; Simple white gold with three tiny stones that sparkled in the city lights that came through the window.

"Will you marry me? Will *you* be my family?"

Lucia exhaled. Dominic could now hear her rapid breathing. He had been too wrapped up in his speech to notice her hardship.

"What? I thought...I thought you were going to leave me!" she wept.

"No! Oh my God! I'm sorry!" Dominic dropped the ring and climbed into bed with her. Lucia rested her head on his chest.

"I thought you were building up to saying goodbye. I would have understood. Your parents aren't being fair to you." Her voice had shrunk to a whisper.

A smile had developed on his face.

"No, I'm sorry. I talk too much. I should have just come out with it. Will you marry me?"

"Are you asking me because we just did it?"

"No!" he answered in mock disgust.

Lucia lifted her head from his chest and looked him in the eye.

"Yes! Of course I'll marry you!" she answered as if this were the dumbest question in the world.

He kissed her. Lucia's body was warm and soft. There was no fear in her lips or in her body. Her face was still wet from her tears. She dried off her face with the bed sheet, trying to hide her embarrassment.

"Oh, God! Here I am crying. You must think I'm a pussy."

Dominic laughed.

"You're not a pussy! You're the strongest girl I know." He collected a tear in the corner of her right eye.

For the first time in her young life, Lucia didn't mind feeling vulnerable.

PART ONE

CHAPTER ONE

ROME
1963

Dominic and Lucia weren't speaking to each other. All that could be heard was the sound of their children playing outside. She did not want to see her husband. Lucia remained in the kitchen preparing dinner.

Dominic dressed for work. Buttoning up his shirt, he wondered when he and Lucia had gone from teenage lovers to a struggling couple with three children, both working at a restaurant to make ends meet.

"Three children..." he whispered to himself. Dominic broke away from this train of thought almost as soon as it popped into his head. He would die for his children. He didn't want to blame them for his and Lucia's troubles.

Dominic tied his necktie on the first attempt. This made him smiled, for he had a silly superstition concerning his tie. If he could tie it on the first try, he was in for good luck.

Maybe, he thought, after he leaves the bedroom Lucia wouldn't be angry with him any longer, or perhaps he'd get a nice tip at work. Dominic bet it would be the latter.

The Divita family's apartment was a small one. The kitchen and the living room were one and the same. Dominic and Lucia slept in one bedroom, while all three kids shared the other. The shared bathroom was down the hallway.

There were two bathrooms in the three-story apartment building that were shared among all of its inhabitants. There were signs posted in the bathrooms that everyone was supposed to clean up their own messes, but this didn't prevent Lucia and Dominic from having to clean other people's puke, semen, piss, and shit from time to time.

From the bedroom, Dominic could hear the clanging of spoons against pots as his wife worked diligently on dinner. She didn't slow down when he entered the room. Lucia acted as if she didn't notice him, but he could tell that she knew he was there by the way she'd tensed up. Her long, curly, black hair was tied up, so as not to fall into the meal. It made her seem angrier.

They stood near each other, neither of them saying a word. He wanted to say something...anything. Dominic hated that they had begun fighting all of the time. Lucia used to smile and laugh when they talked. Lately though, he had no idea how to speak to his wife without feeling her animosity.

"What?" Lucia was tired of him just staring at her. This outburst startled him.

"I...I'm...going to work now..." he stumbled.

She kept stirring the sauce. He stood in the doorway another minute, hoping that one of them would say something that would put an end to this fight. She didn't turn around. He exhaled, praying that something brilliant would follow it. Nothing did.

"Have a good night!" Lucia said in a tone normally used when damning someone to Hell. Dominic exited without a word.

Roberto sat on a trash can, watching his siblings kick their beat-up football back and forth. The twins, Vincenzo and Isabella, were only two years younger than him. He always seemed to forget that he was older than the pair. They had always been there for as long as he could remember. The twins had such a connection with each other; he felt more like a third wheel than a big brother.

Dominic needed to change his mood before saying goodnight to the children. He practiced how he would greet them as he neared the building exit.

"Poppa!" Roberto shouted.

Dominic jumped in between the twins and kicked the ball away. As they chased after him, he did his best to keep the ball from them, but he was no match for the five-year-olds. He quickly picked it up and examined it. The faded black and white ball looked to be enjoying its final days.

"Whose ball is this?" he asked.

"Mine!" Vincenzo and Isabella answered in unison. They giggled mischievously, as if they knew more than they were letting on.

"I don't remember buying you a ball." He tried to be stern, but even the young kids noticed the smile forming in the corners of his mouth.

"Did your mother buy you a ball?"

"No," they said.

Dominic looked them in the eye. He attempted to convey a message to them, hoping they would pick up on it.

"Did your mother buy you a ball?" he asked one more time, hoping that they would get the hint.

"Yes!" the twins replied. They laughed, knowing full well they their Poppa was in on the crime.

Dominic let them have their ball back. Vincenzo and Isabella playfully ran back to the small courtyard in front of the apartment building. Roberto never moved from the trashcan.

"Roberto! While I'm gone you're the man of the house, so do what your mother tells you!"

Lucia could hear him through the kitchen window. She smiled. Lucia knew that this was his stupid way of saying that he was sorry. Her husband always seemed to turn everything into a joke.

Dominic always walked to work. The restaurant was only two blocks away, so it simply made sense to travel by foot.

The neighborhood they lived in was known around the city as Jewish Rome. It was a section that had been populated by Jewish refugees after World War II. They'd had nothing left in their homeland and they weren't exactly welcomed with open arms in Italy. These German Jews had found themselves in this quiet ghetto, still littered with burnt out buildings from the war.

He made his way into Caesar's Restaurant. It was a small building with no sign. This didn't matter to the owner, because everyone in Jewish Rome knew it was the best place for Italian and Jewish food in town.

Caesar Ginsberg was, as always, behind the bar. He liked to run his place with a "hands on" style. The paper work was his wife's job. He enjoyed talking with his regulars. Caesar was a short, dumpy fellow and, even though he was sixty-one, his hair was still jet black. Seated at the bar were Irving and Sal, two of Caesar's most regular customers.

The restaurant was nearly empty, which was normal for a Tuesday night. Caesar knew it wasn't the lack of tips that was bothering his young waiter. He could tell from the moment Dominic stepped in that he and Lucia had been fighting. Caesar waved him over to the bar and asked him what the trouble was between them.

"It was nothing, boss," Dominic answered without even looking in Caesar's direction.

"Hey! Look at me!" Caesar shouted with a smile.

Dominic faced his boss. His mood was lightened a bit at being caught in the act of trying to avoid the issue.

"You two are a couple of good looking kids, why you fighting all the time?"

"Women are forgetting their place!" Sal interjected. "First, they pass that bill letting them work everywhere, now they think they can tell us what to do!"

"What the fuck do you know? You're not even fucking married!" Caesar turned his attention back to Dominic.

"Don't listen to this piece of shit. You got a good woman. She works here every day and she brightens up the room. It breaks my heart to see you two fighting. Why do you fight?"

Dominic didn't say anything for a minute. This question had plagued him for the past year and he was certain it was something that Lucia wondered as well. Suddenly, he said something that surprised even him.

"I guess...I guess we're just tired."

The three older men thought about this for a moment. Caesar was the first to speak.

"Tired? You kids are still in your twenties. What do you have to be tired from?"

"Well, they do have three children, Caesar," Irving answered.

"And when they're not taking care of them, they're here," Sal continued.

"Would you like someone to take the kids off your hands, you know, for a couple of days?" Caesar asked.

In the corner of Dominic's eye, he saw someone sit at one of his tables. This conversation would have to wait. He tied a white apron around his waist as he excused himself from the trio of wise men.

Lucia sat on her bed. She prepared her tarot cards for a reading. Before shuffling, Roberto knocked on the door. He and the twins were finished with dinner and wanted to see what she was up to.

She told him that she was going to do a tarot reading for her and their Poppa. This excited Roberto, for he had only heard stories about her Gypsy days. Now he wanted to see for himself how she could see the future. He asked if they could watch, and she told him if he washed the dishes afterwards, then they could watch her give a reading. It was a deal. He shouted for Vincenzo and Isabella and they stomped into the bedroom like a pair of drunken horses.

The three kids hopped up onto the bed with their mother. Isabella made her way to Lucia's lap. Roberto and Vincenzo sat at the foot of the bed giving her just enough room to lay out the cards.

"How do you see the future, Mamma?" asked Isabella.

"Like this." Lucia shuffled the cards and set the deck down. Roberto wanted to pick up the top card, but Lucia quickly grabbed his hand.

"No! You can't disturb the cards," Lucia snapped. Roberto carefully drew his hand back to his side.

"I'm going to ask the cards a question, a question about your Poppa and me."

"What's the question?" Vincenzo asked.

"She can't tell you! It's a secret!" Isabella answered for her mother.

Lucia was pleased by her daughter. She also didn't want to tell her children that she was worried about her marriage.

"That's a good girl! That's right. I can tell you that this is a three card reading. The first card will tell me what has lead up to this point in time; The second will help me see the present issues and what actions to take; The last card will tell me the possible outcome."

"Draw the first card!" cried Roberto.

Dominic neared the table in the far corner of the restaurant. A tall, blonde woman sat there. She was dressed in a black suit that was normally worn by men, the white shirt buttoned down low enough to see her impressive cleavage. She was still wearing sunglasses even though the sun had gone down an hour earlier. Her hair was short and spiked. She didn't look local.

"Hello, is this your first time here?" he asked.

"I've been around," she coldly answered.

Dominic could detect a German accent in her voice. She gave him a quick once over and smiled.

"What is your name?" the woman asked as she took off her sunglasses. The hair on the back of his neck stood up on end.

"Dominic..."

Lucia pulled the first card from the deck. It featured an illustration of ten arms, each holding a sword.

"Ten of Swords..." Lucia read out loud.

"What's it mean?" cried Vincenzo.

She thought for a moment on how it applied to her, and then about how to explain it to the children in a way that wouldn't upset them.

"It means...that I have a lot on my plate. I'm feeling weighed down."

"By what?" Roberto asked.

"What does 'a lot on my plate' mean?" Isabella whispered into her mother's ear.

Lucia took a second in deciding how to explain her feelings to her children without giving up too much information.

"To have a lot on your plate means that you are very busy and you're trying to do too many things at once. Feeling weighed down is to have these things cause you to worry about them," Lucia replied.

The children didn't speak for a minute. They were in awe of the great power of the cards. Isabella did ask if there was anything else about the card. Lucia looked down at it. She wasn't sure if she wanted to answer her daughter.

"It says that I feel alone."

The blonde German gave Dominic the once over. Her eyes almost seemed to change color in the light. One moment they were blue, the next they appeared gold, then red.

He felt awkward as she leaned forward and looked deeply in his eyes. He tried to think of Lucia and his children.

"May I take your order?" he asked, attempting to sound as nonchalant as possible. This just made her chuckle. She found it cute that he was pretending he wasn't attracted to her.

"Dominic, wouldn't you care to know my name? You're not afraid of me, are you?" the blond German asked.

He laughed, suddenly feeling silly. She is just some pretty tourist who wanted to flirt with the locals. It wasn't often when a woman could take him off guard like that.

"What is your name, pretty lady?" he asked.

"My name is Ursula."

Lucia pulled the second card. It had an old man painted on it. He resembled a prophet. It pointed away from Lucia. All four of them stared at the card. Roberto demanded to know what it meant. Lucia thought long and hard about the meaning.

"It's the Hierophant. It's reversed -- that means it's facing away from me. So, it's telling me that I think I'm in control of what's going on, but I'm being controlled by the situation." Lucia felt a tear roll down her cheek. Isabella noticed it and wiped it away so her brothers wouldn't see it.

The children were quiet, they knew that their mother was upset by the news the cards were giving her. However, they were all too scared to ask for any details at this point. Roberto surprised himself when he asked his mother to take another.

She reluctantly reached for the last card.

"Ursula? What a strong name. Your man must be proud of you," Dominic said.

"I have no man, just a series of men," she replied.

He tried to return to the business at hand, taking her order. Dominic laughed and he asked her again.

"Well, what would the lady like tonight?"

"Come closer, Dominic, and I'll tell you."

He leaned in close to her. She moved toward his left ear as if to whisper something, but instead she bit his earlobe.

Dominic didn't jump away as he felt the blood drip down his neck. It actually excited him. Dominic's blood rushed through his veins, his breathing was suddenly heavy, and all he knew was he never wanted it to end.

Lucia drew the final card. Nobody said a word. The image worried Isabella and she held on to her mother a little tighter.

"Mamma, what's it mean?" Vincenzo asked.

Lucia didn't answer. She simply stared at the card. It was the Death card and she knew that a change was coming.

CHAPTER TWO

"Mamma and Poppa are not going to die," Roberto whispered to Vincenzo and Isabella.

All three were lying in their single bed, the same bed they had shared since leaving the crib. The twins had been crying off and on for the past hour. They were trying to keep quite so they wouldn't disturb their mother.

"Then why was there a Death card?" Vincenzo asked.

"Mamma told you. It means change, not death," he assured them.

"What's going to change? Are they going to take us away?" Isabella asked.

"Who's gonna take us away?"

"Is Poppa going away?" Vincenzo shot back.

Roberto didn't have an easy answer for them. Being two years older, he had heard the fights between his parents more often than his younger siblings.

"I don't know," he told them.

Their bedroom door was cracked open so that the light from the hall could sneak into the room. Lucia had been sitting in the hall by the doorway. She had listened to their worries and thought about how she shared them.

Lucia remained sitting by her children's room all night. She was awoken by the occasional neighbor loudly passing by, or shouting, drunken rants, or both.

Nearly an hour after dawn, Dominic attempted to enter the apartment without waking his family. The loud creek of their door made that impossible in Lucia's case.

The first thing he saw were Lucia's eyes, glaring at him from across the room. She was furious.

There were two reasons why she didn't scream at him at this point; their children sleeping in the next room and the bandage that he was wearing over his neck.

"I was worried. I thought you were dead." She jumped up off of the floor and headed in his direction.

His clothes had a certain scent. Under the usual smell of food and smoke there was an odd, damp odor coming from his shirt. She was unable to pinpoint what it was, but it almost made her forget about being angry.

Dominic didn't stop. He grabbed a towel and a bar of soap from the kitchen and made his way toward the bathroom. She followed him.

"I'm sorry. I stopped at a bar after work and I lost track of time," he reported without even looking at her.

"What bar?"

"The bar near work," he answered.

"Oh, that's fucking descriptive. And what happened to your neck?"

He said nothing, shutting the door behind him.

He later climbed into bed beside her and fell asleep without saying a word. Lucia didn't sleep. She knew that there was something he wasn't telling her. She stared at the ceiling and listened to Dominic's snoring.

The next night was her turn at work. Caesar's Restaurant was busy enough to keep Lucia's mind off of Dominic.

She smiled and flirted with some of the better looking customers, as always. A band of five French boys, traveling the countryside, were most pleasant to her. They tipped her well and offered her a couple of marriage proposals. She politely turned them down, but it touched a nerve and she excused herself.

Caesar's wife, Rosa, had just finished cutting her husband's hair in the back office. She stepped into the kitchen to wash her hands free of all the oil that had collected on them.

Upon entering, she was hit with the smell of tomato sauce, cheese, and lentil soup. The kitchen was a busy mess, as usual, as the three cooks and the members of the wait staff scrambled to serve the food as soon as it was ready. The room was always clouded in man-made fog, created by the steaming pots of food and the dishwasher, trying to keep up with the plates coming in.

Rosa wiped her hands clean on her apron, leaving it stained with greasy black streaks. She turned around to head back to the office so she could sweep up and found Lucia sitting on a box. The young waitress was in her own world, staring into space.

"Lucia?" Rosa called to get her attention.

"Lucia?"

She noticed her boss's wife talking to her the second time.

"Oh, Rosa! Um...I'm sorry. I was just thinking. I'll get back to work." Lucia felt embarrassed that she had been caught off guard.

"Lucia. Let's talk for a minute."

"Thank you, but I already took a break, if your husband--"

"My husband cannot take a shit without me. I think I can convince him that you need another break."

Lucia liked Rosa. She admired how she held her large family together, while at the same time running her husband's business for him.

The older woman's black, shoulder length hair was interrupted by a white tuft at the beginning of her hairline. When asked, Rosa would say that it was the fault of Caesar and their seven children.

They sat at one of the unused tables. The lighting had been dimmed and candles were lit on each table to increase the romantic mood in the room. It was an ironic setting for Lucia to admit to Rosa that she and Dominic were having some difficulties of late.

"I had hoped that it would get better when money wasn't a problem or when the children were a bit older, but something happened last night. Something permanent. I..." she paused. "I don't know what to do."

Rosa took a deep breath. There was something she wanted to tell her, but she wasn't sure if it was her place to do so.

"Dominic left the restaurant with a woman last night."

The two women were silent for a minute. Lucia was stunned. She tried to decide if she felt angry or heartbroken. Instead, she realized that she just felt numb.

"He's out of the house. I never want to see him again."

"Oh, Lucia! Don't be like that! Men sleep around, but they always come back." Rosa already regretted telling her.

"That's because divorce is illegal! Because the fucking Pope says so. I'm not Catholic, why do I have to do what he orders? Fuck him!" Lucia shouted.

The outburst drew some notice from the other patrons and employees. An old woman at the next table had spit out her matzo ball. A middle aged Catholic couple stopped eating and stared at the two women.

Rosa ushered Lucia toward the office. Even though she respected her younger friend, there were still some things a woman should not say in public.

They passed Sal, who was enjoying his usual beer. He had been at the bar for hours. His beard and his dark suit stank of spilled booze.

The old man smiled at Lucia and raised his mug to her.

"I agree about the Pope," he cheered.

"Fuck you, too!" Lucia snapped.

Rosa sat Lucia down on the old couch by the huge, oak desk. She paced around the room until Lucia calmed down.

"Why the fuck do people want to share their stupid thoughts with me? They think that they are so special! I don't care what you think! Everyone is so fucking stupid!" Lucia shouted.

"You need to figure out what you're going to do. You can't just curse at everybody. What are you going to tell Dominic?" Rosa interrupted.

"I'm going to tell him to leave," she answered.

"What about your children? How are going to take care of them with less money coming in?"

"I will figure out a way. If I have to dance again, I will. Maybe I'll find my parents and we'll travel with them," Lucia said.

Rosa didn't like the idea of exposing the children to their mother's Gypsy lifestyle, but she knew now was not a good time to say so.

She sat beside the troubled young woman and took her hand. Neither of them spoke. Rosa broke the silence.

"Caesar cheated on me, if you must know."

"Go on." Lucia was hardly surprised.

"He would go out with his friends for nights out on the town. I had a feeling, but I chose to ignore it. We had started a family and a restaurant at nearly the same time, so I needed to keep it together. Maybe seeing other women helped him keep it together. Who knows?

"Finally one night, he went off and left the phone number of his friend I could reach him at. They were going to play cards with the usual gangs of local business owners. That night, our daughter went to the hospital to have her baby.

"I called his friend and he had no idea what I was talking about.

When Caesar came home, I told him that he was now a grandfather and I asked him where he was the whole time. He never answered me, but he hasn't been to another card game since."

The two women didn't speak at first, but after a few seconds they began to laugh. The laughter was interrupted by a polite knock at the door. It was Caesar, which only made the women laugh more.

He thought it would be a good idea not to ask what they were talking about.

"Um, Lucia? It's a phone call for you. I think it's one of your kids." He quickly stepped back out of the office.

Lucia picked up the phone on the desk.

"Hello?" Lucia could only hear the soft hum of the phone line.

"Mamma...?" whispered a small, frightened voice.

"Roberto? Baby, what's wrong? Where's your father?"

"There's a scary woman here."

Lucia couldn't speak. She could no longer hear the people and movements of the restaurant outside the office. She felt a tingle run down her arms and legs so intense that moving was not an option. Her heart was beating so strongly she could hear it.

Lucia listened to every knock and bump on the line, hoping that her son wasn't going to get cut off. She began to imagine that the phone line's buzz was what decay must sound like. She thought she was going to vomit.

"Mamma?"

"I'm here, honey! What scary woman?"

"She says she's gonna take Poppa away..." Roberto cried.

"Where are your brother and sister?" she asked.

"They're hiding..."

"I'm coming, honey! Mamma's coming!"

Lucia dropped the phone and ran out of the restaurant. Rosa was right behind her. She wasn't perfectly clear on what was happening, but she knew a mother's fear when she saw it.

They took Caesar's car and were at the apartment in minutes, arriving just in time to see Dominic and a blonde woman get into a black car. Lucia told Rosa to go in and check on the children so she could continue following them.

"Lucia? Are you sure you want to do this?" she begged.

"He let that whore in my home and scared my babies. Yes, I'm sure," Lucia answered.

Lucia pushed her out of the small, red Fiat 500 and wiggled her way into the driver's seat. She sped away after her husband, faster than Rosa had ever seen the sedan move.

It struck Rosa all of the sudden that this might be the last time she would ever see Dominic and Lucia alive as she watched the taillights of her car shrink into the darkness.

CHAPTER THREE

Cesar Ginsberg's rusty Fiat 500 sat in front of a large, old house on Via Veneto, which was known as the most glamorous street in Rome.

Lucia had driven past the outdoor cafes and restaurants vomiting the rich and famous out onto the sidewalks. Even though she was parked at a lonely end of the road, she could still hear their drunken shouting.

Lucia hated them. She hated all people. In Dominic, she had hoped that she'd found someone in this whole selfish world worth trusting. Now she found herself sitting in her boss's car, waiting for the right moment to confront him and his mistress.

Lucia tightly gripped the steering wheel and wondered if she should simply leave. She could get the children out of the apartment and be halfway to her mother's by the time he woke up the next morning.

Then she noticed the bedroom light switch on. While she was agonizing over their marriage, he was having sex with that woman. She opened the door and stepped out of the car. She had to make Dominic see what he was going to lose.

The blonde woman's house was a large, four-story building. The yard had been recently cut and there was a fountain with a statue of a naked woman pouring water from a bottomless bowl.

Lucia had never felt so tense. She could feel the drops of sweat roll down the curves of her body. She delivered three solid knocks on the front doors. A butler opened the doors a moment later. The young man was quite tall, with a head of white hair. He displayed a pleasant smile that wasn't the least bit sincere. It seemed forced and almost fearful.

Lucia didn't bother to explain her presence, she simply demanded to see her husband. Two teenage maids with English accents came in from the next room to see what the commotion was all about. Despite being late in the evening, the three members of the staff seemed bright, tidy, and a bit more alert than she would have expected. They tried to be polite, but were profoundly confused over Lucia's shouts for Dominic.

"May I help you?" asked a calm, German voice that seemed to caress the back of Lucia's neck. If it were possible for a voice to be tangible, this one certainly was.

Ursula was taken aback when Lucia turned to face her. She hadn't expected her to be so beautiful. Even dressed in her sauce stained waitress uniform, she stood out from all the tired bores that infected her senses night after night. Lucia had a voluptuous body that enjoyed all of life's pleasures. Ursula was so smitten with this new arrival that she failed to see Lucia's fist.

She punched Ursula in the face with all her anger behind it. Lucia could feel the woman's nose break and her teeth fold back and snap under her knuckles. The smaller woman fell to the black and white marble floor. Lucia's hand was wet with Ursula's warm blood, which sent a tingle up her arm and throughout her body.

The blonde German sat on the floor and choked on her own teeth. The staff appeared horrified at the scene. This all helped Lucia find the nerve to continue.

"Dominic!" Lucia shouted up the stairs. "I just made your new girlfriend less beautiful! Come down here so I can show you!"

It took Lucia a moment to notice that the butler and the maids hadn't budged. They were still focused on their boss. A puddle had formed between one of the maid's ankles and all three shook with fear. It suddenly dawned on Lucia that it wasn't her that they were afraid of.

Ursula spat out her front teeth and was laughing before they landed on the floor.

Lucia found herself as incapable of movement as the staff. The blonde walked toward her as if nothing had happened. Her nose no longer appeared broken and new front teeth had replaced the ones currently lying on the floor. The only evidence of what happened was the blood on her tuxedo.

Lucia had been taken in at the age of three by a Gypsy woman when her parents died. Her adoptive mother had taught her the ways of their culture and warned her of many dangers. Lucia instantly knew what she was facing -- a vampire. She was frozen, and she had no idea what to do next.

"Oh, shit!" Lucia exhaled.

"I take it you're Lucia Divita?" Ursula asked.

"Ye...yes..."

"I understand now why it took so long to seduce your husband." Ursula was pleasant almost to the point of giddiness.

Lucia didn't understand the statement. A question nearly left her lips, but the woman continued.

"The moment I want a man, he's mine. Women can take a few minutes longer. Even priests take half an hour.

"Your husband has yet to give in to me. He keeps moaning 'No! No! Lucia! Lucia!' The longer it takes, the more I want him. I thought you were some dominating shrew of a wife that he would have been happy to be freed of. Now after meeting you, I know why I couldn't shake your hold of him."

Lucia needed to get back in touch with her anger. She threw another punch toward the vampire, but this time it fell short. Ursula snatched her wrist before she could connect the blow. She squeezed with such strength that it felt like her hand was going to pop off.

In the blink of an eye, the vampire took Lucia by the throat with her other hand and slammed her up against the wall. Despite the fact that she wasn't tall enough to look Lucia in the eye, she had the power to lift her off her feet. Lucia was pressed against the wall so hard that she could hear the wood crack behind her.

She wondered if her husband and children were still alive. After all, she hadn't checked on their safety, they might be dead already for all she knew.

"What did you do to my babies, bitch?" Lucia growled.

Once again, Ursula was surprised by this woman. She was hardly in the position for making demands, but she did so anyway. Dominic's wife was so much more than she had assumed.

"What babies?"

"My children! Did you touch them?" It was amazing, Lucia sounded even less patient with her.

"I saw only the boy. He ran into the other room when we made eye contact." The vampire was startled that she even felt that she owed her an explanation. This woman was most impressive.

Lucia couldn't take her eyes off of her as she drew closer. She was inches from her face. There was blood still dripping from her mouth. As frightened as Lucia was for herself and her family, she was surprised at how beautiful she looked.

"Do you love with as much passion as you hate?" the woman asked. Lucia glanced at the staff and they cheerfully egged her on to answer.

"I don't understand..." Lucia let the sentence trail off.

"I have not been struck that hard in quite some time. You must love your family deeply. I thought Dominic was the strong one, but I had no idea that it was you. The two of you have so much untapped power. I can smell it. I can see it in the eyes of your husband and you. I wonder if I can taste it." She caressed the rim of Lucia's ear with her middle finger.

Lucia wanted to resist. She wanted to punch her and run, but her touch sent a ripple through her body unlike anything she had ever felt. Every touch put her on the verge of an orgasm. Her will was falling away piece by piece.

"Who are you?" is all Lucia got out.

"My name is Ursula Orlock. You can trust me. I want to make you and your husband an offer."

Ursula lowered Lucia down and let go of her neck. She smiled and took her by the hand. Ursula's small hand was soft and reminded Lucia of silk. She motioned to her to follow her up the staircase.

"Would you like to see Dominic?"

Lucia could only nod at this point. The staff was still standing in the middle of the lobby, awaiting some sort of order. They were all displaying uncertain smiles. Ursula addressed them without looking in their direction.

"I want that mess gone by the time I'm back or there will be more blood to clean up."

The butler and maids quickly got to it. Ursula escorted Lucia up the stairs and down the dark hallway. They passed a bedroom door that was cracked open. A small, desperate whisper came from behind the door.

"Help me...help me please..." the voiced begged.

Lucia heard the call, but she didn't acknowledge it. There was a certain unreality that had taken over and all she could do was follow the lovely woman.

They finally reached Ursula's bedroom door. Before entering the room, Ursula paused and flashed Lucia a wicked grin, hoping to convey the fun they were both about to have.

Lucia squeezed her hand a bit tighter and the two walked in. The lights were out, but the moonlight was bright enough for Lucia to see Dominic lying on the bed.

His shirt was missing and his arms were spread out across the mattress. He was asleep, taking deep, short breathes. The bandage from his neck had been discarded, revealing a noticeable bite mark. He appeared frightened and vulnerable. This man, who was a father of three, had suddenly become the boy that had proposed to her in that seedy hotel room so long ago.

Ursula giggled like a schoolgirl. She let go of Lucia's hand and hopped on the bed beside Dominic. She called to him in a half whisper.

"Dominic."

He didn't answer. She tried again. This time she tickled his nipples as she spoke in the tone of a domineering mother.

"Dominic!"

The second time was the charm. He woke from his deep sleep. Dominic was still unsure of his whereabouts until he saw Lucia standing at the foot of the bed. He instantly snapped out of the trance he had been in since first meeting Ursula.

"Lucia! Please forgive me. I couldn't help myself!" Dominic begged his wife. Ursula put her fingers to his lips.

"Hush! It's okay. She understands now."

Ursula slid off the bed and guided Lucia to sit next to Dominic. The couple sat on the edge of the bed as she stood above them. They felt like they were coming down from a drug.

"Allow me to ask both of you a question and I want you to answer honestly. What do you think of other people? In general?" she asked.

Dominic and Lucia each thought about the question for a moment. It wasn't the first question that either had expected to hear.

"I find them...disappointing," Dominic answered. He sounded as if he was finally admitting that to himself.

"I hate them." Lucia passionately stated each word like gunshots. She was happy that her husband was beginning to see things the way that she always had.

"Why do you hate them?"

"Because they're stupid!" Lucia answered without hesitation.

Dominic smiled in agreement. Ursula was pleased. She felt confident enough to make them an offer.

"Even though I can have anyone I desire, the problem is that most people are dead inside. I know you two see it. You see all the others walking around with that blank look in their eyes. Their tiny minds focused on their little worlds. They appear soulless.

"To become a vampire, a person needs to enjoy life -- someone who isn't an animated bag of meat that dies in fifty years."

She turned to Dominic.

"That's why I chose you Dominic. It would have broken my heart to see a creature such as you held down by this pathetic world. You are a brave, passionate man among sheep. I fell in love with you at first sight. You were even able to resist me. No one else could be as strong as my wonderful Dominic."

Ursula smiled at Lucia.

"Then you walked into my house. I should have known that his wife was the more powerful one. You're where he gets it from."

Ursula's words caused Dominic to let out a boyish chuckle.

"Lucia, nothing scares people more than a strong woman. You would be a perfect vampire. The two of you can spend the rest of forever enjoying your lives with me. You will no longer have to worry about bills, growing old, or feeling powerless. Will you join me?"

Ursula could feel them shake, not from fear, but with excitement.

Dominic and Lucia looked at each other in order to gauge their reactions. They didn't speak. There was no need for apologies or explanations. He could read in her eyes that she wanted it as much as he did. She grasped his hand tightly as they both faced Ursula and nodded "yes" to her offer. Ursula licked some blood from her lips in anticipation.

Lucia could see fangs where there hadn't been any before. She pulled back her long black hair so the vampire would have a clear path to her neck.

"Taste my blood."

Ursula leaned down and kissed her. The vampire's lips were smooth, soft, and covered in her own warm blood. Lucia felt as if something inside of her soul had just opened up. She wondered if sex would be this way forever, without boredom or routine.

Dominic was excited to watch the two attractive women kiss, knowing that he would be next. When his turn finally came, there was no guilt.

Lucia and Dominic welcomed this new woman into their lives. He was free to just be himself. He did not have to please the Pope or his parents anymore. It was like being born again.

Ursula stood up and studied her new mates. The lower half of Dominic and Lucia's faces were covered in her blood. It was running down their chins. She almost laughed, but she didn't want to ruin the mood.

"Do you still want it?"

"Yes!" the Divitas answered simultaneously.

Ursula carefully climbed onto Lucia's lap. The vampire wrapped her slender legs around Lucia's much rounder torso. Once her feet locked themselves into position, she leaned in to the left side of Lucia's neck. Ursula's upper fangs dug deep into her jugular.

Dominic was momentarily worried for his wife when he heard the blood squirt and felt her tighten her grip on his hand. The expression in her eyes eased his nerves. The look on Lucia's face was that of pure ecstasy, it reminded him of the night he proposed to her. That night was the last time she had allowed herself to be vulnerable in order to acquire some form of happiness.

Lucia's hold grew limp after a few minutes. He looked into her eyes to discover that life was quickly fading from her. Ursula gently laid her down on her back and crawled over to Dominic.

She was almost drunk from his wife's blood. Without speaking, she tore off her blood soaked tuxedo shirt and ripped into Dominic's neck.

He could feel the sharp throbbing of Ursula's powerful tongue lapping up his blood. The rush of retreating blood was more of a release than any sexual climax he had ever encountered. The lights, the sounds, and the feeling faded into darkness as if he was dozing off to sleep.

Ursula set him down next to his wife and stepped into the bathroom to clean up. After putting on a simple black blouse, she phoned downstairs to prepare the bodies.

A hulking, gray man in gray overalls, with all the grace of a robot, stomped into the bedroom. He was the groundskeeper, and he had spent the last hour digging a grave in the garden.

Dominic and Lucia were placed inside of a rather large coffin. There still wasn't enough room for two six-foot-tall people so Dominic was laid down first with his wife draped over him. They looked like they were in a lovers' embrace.

The groundskeeper nailed the coffin shut and lowered it into the earth. The garden behind Ursula's house made the perfect setting for the makeshift funeral. It was the middle of the night and the high bushes and fencing made it nearly impossible for any spying from the neighbors. The groundskeeper piled the dirt onto the coffin.

The only mourners in attendance were Ursula, the white haired butler, and a maid. Ursula said a few words in their honor.

"They make a lovely couple. I'm glad I kept them together."

CHAPTER FOUR

The voice in the dark kept repeating her name. It was a familiar voice and it sounded slightly panicked. Another sense joined in, the smell of blood and sweat combined with wood and dirt. The voice continued its desperate struggle to reach her.

Lucia's eyes fluttered open. It took a few moments for her to realize where she was. She was lying on top of Dominic's chest. She tried to lift herself up, only to bonk the back of her head on the lid of their coffin.

"Oww! God damn it!" Lucia shouted.

After taking stock of her pain, she noticed Dominic laughing. This didn't really improve her mood. Lucia was tired, hurting, and wasn't sure where she was, and Dominic was laughing at her. She hit him in his side under his ribs.

"Shut up! Don't laugh at me!" she snapped.

Dominic fought his laughter and the tears running down his face.

"I'm not laughing at you...it's...that you're alive!" he stated as he looked into her eyes with the most honest love she had felt from him in a long time. Dominic ran his fingers through her hair despite the fact that it was matted from dirt and dried blood.

Suddenly, Lucia didn't feel like being angry anymore. She just wanted to hold him, and rest her head down on his chest once more. They said nothing for a while. The Divitas laid together and listened to each other's heartbeats.

The seriousness of their situation began to press on them. The dirt above them was settling and caused the wooden casket to creak every few minutes.

"Are we vampires?" Dominic asked.

Lucia thought he sounded like an excited child asking if it was Christmas yet.

"We can see each other in this dark coffin, can't we?" She found his question unnecessary.

"Are they going to dig us out?"

Lucia wasn't certain. She just held on to him for a little while longer.

The question plagued them for another half hour until their patience ran dry. Instinctively, Lucia turned over onto her back and they pushed together on the lid of the coffin.

Dominic and Lucia were both surprised at how easy it was to break through the lid. Dirt rushed into the box, covering them in the freshly dug soil. They fought to get up on their feet as they crawled out of the coffin.

Dominic guessed that this was what being born must feel like. Lucia could smell manure from the nearby garden. They could feel the worms brushing up against their bodies, who must have been quite surprised about their supper's exit.

The second the Divitas' hands hit air, they heard a strange noise explode above them. It sounded like rain, as if a huge downpour had suddenly begun without warning. However, the ground had not turned to mud and their hands weren't wet.

The couple carefully pulled their heads free from the ground. When they cleaned the dirt from their eyes, Dominic and Lucia found that Ursula and her staff of thirty were giving them a huge standing ovation.

The puzzled pair looked around the garden. The young, white

haired butler, the maids, cooks, and the groundskeeper were cheering their arrival.

The applause went on for ten minutes. Even though it was obvious that some were getting tired, no one wanted to stop clapping before Ursula. Finally, she finished applauding and the rest quickly followed suit. She was proud of her two new mates.

"Happy birthday," she declared.

A couple of Italian servants walked over to the young vampires. They were both dressed in black and white. The man was wearing a simple button down shirt and pants, while the woman wore a black dress. They positioned themselves next to Dominic and Lucia and waited for Ursula to continue.

"Come! Let's get you cleaned up! We have much work to do in so little time."

The servants put their arms out for the couple to take. Dominic wrapped his arm around the girl's, while Lucia looked at the male servant as if he was insane. She chose to follow everyone into the house rather than be guided.

The staff filed in as Ursula took the white haired butler to one side. She whispered a question in his ear.

"Lane, who is that new maid?"

"The American?" he asked.

His mistress nodded yes.

"I believe her name is Karla. Why do you ask?" Lane asked, though he already knew what her answer might be.

"She stopped applauding before I did. I want her prepared for my bath."

The servants escorted Dominic and Lucia to separate bathrooms. They each stripped off the last of their dirty work clothes. Maids collected the rags and threw them away, as they had been ordered.

The bathrooms were large, at least half the size of their apartment.

Lucia marveled at the painted walls that depicted wolves playing in a forest. These fearsome predators seemed like happy puppies enjoying themselves.

The use of color was captivating to Lucia. The painter had used red sporadically throughout the piece; it appeared to make the painting come alive.

One wolf was sniffing a rose in the foreground and Lucia found herself drawn to it as well. The smell of the deep red rose stood out from the other colors in the painting. Lucia reached up and touched the rose with a single finger. It wasn't red paint. The bloody rose sent a warm sensation throughout her body. Lucia's nipples grew hard and goose bumps popped up and down her limbs.

The male servant knocked on the bathroom door, startling Lucia, who pulled her hand away quickly.

"Mrs. Divita? Is everything all right in there?"

"Yes! Thank you!" Lucia faked normality.

"Are you sure? You sound out of breath? Do you need me to come in?"

"I. Am. Fine. God damn it! Now leave me alone, I'm naked in here!" she shouted back through the door.

The young man didn't say another word.

Dominic and Lucia both took their time in the shower. The water was hot and stayed that way for as long as they were in there.

This was something alien to them. They shared their old bathroom with the whole first floor of their apartment building, so the water was often cold. They each decided to enjoy this luxury for as long as they could.

Lucia stepped out of her bathroom first. She was wrapped in a bulky white robe. She was instantly shown the way to a bedroom by three women. They wore simple black skirts and blouses.

The women smiled and giggled at Lucia, which didn't exactly put her at ease. They shut the bedroom door and one of them yanked off her robe. Before she'd had a moment to complain, Lucia noticed the dresses that the other two were holding for her. Each of the young women held a pair of dresses for Lucia to choose from.

"You're a size 56, right?" the girl with short hair asked.

"Yes. How did you guess?" Lucia was taken aback by the four beautiful and expensive looking outfits that were before her.

"We measured you and your husband while you were at rest," said the blonde holding her robe.

The other two women giggled when she mentioned "husband." Lucia knew that meant they'd had a good time measuring every inch of Dominic.

She decided to carry on with picking out her dress for the night. Though they were all beautiful, a long, black, strapless dress impressed Lucia the most. She playfully slid into the outfit and the girls had no trouble zipping it up. The black dress not only hugged the curves of her body, it accentuated them.

"This is nice." Lucia admired herself in the mirror. It had been some time since she'd dressed up for a night on the town.

"Thank you. We worked on them all day for you." The blonde spoke with a rare display of pride, a trait not seen in the rest of the staff.

Lucia was humbled that someone would go to all that trouble for her. She looked at the other two girls, who nodded back at her in agreement.

"You made this dress today?"

"No, we made all four dresses today," the youngest girl said.

Lucia let it sink in how much work these three women had done over the last twelve hours. The only thing she could add was "thank you."

The blonde girl asked if she would like them to apply her make up. Lucia politely declined. The three dressmakers all lined up together by the door. The oldest one spoke.

"Then unless there is anything else you need, we are finished Mrs. Divita."

"Thank you. I do have a question. If I'm a vampire, how can I see myself in this mirror?" Lucia asked.

"The mistress will explain," the oldest girl answered.

They turned in unison and exited. Lucia decided to get started with her makeup.

Dominic passed the three dressmakers in the hallway. He wondered why they were giggling at him as they walked by him. He decided not to give it a second thought; his only wish was to see Lucia. He carefully knocked on the door so as not to startle his wife.

"Are you decent?" Dominic asked.

"I'm never decent."

Dominic took that as an invite into the room. He found his wife working diligently in front of the mirror.

"Look away! I'm not done yet!" she cried out.

He quickly turned and placed his attention on a row of shoes Lucia had dug through earlier. After another minute, she told him that it was okay to see her.

Dominic watched Lucia twirl around in front of the mirror. This was the first time they had seen each other after returning from the grave. The wonder of that experience paled in comparison to how glorious they looked. Dominic first noticed Lucia's soulful eyes, accented by a smoky effect created by her makeup. Her long black curly hair matched her new dress, which highlighted her impressive cleavage.

Lucia was surprised that a simple haircut could make Dominic seem ten years younger. His new black suit was perfectly tailored, displaying his wide chest. He knew he looked good. Dominic flashed her that boyish smile that had won her over back in their teens.

The Divitas each thought to themselves, wondering if the tired, old grownups they'd become had been sacrificed the night before.

"Lucia, you're so beautiful. I have no idea what I did to deserve you. I love you."

There was a brief pause between the two. She momentarily worried over what he was going to say.

"I'm sorry I was laughing at you in the coffin earlier," he said.

"Why were you laughing?"

He thought for a moment about how he was going to explain it without sounding corny, but it was impossible.

"I woke up first and you felt lifeless. For a few minutes I was scared that I was going to have to live forever without you."

"Don't be a pussy," she smiled.

Laughter filled the room, but it didn't come from either Divita. Ursula was standing in the doorway all of a sudden. Her tux was completed with a black top hat and tails.

The Divitas were aroused by her laugh. There was no ironic menace in Ursula's laugh, just pure happiness. The vampire glowed as she took each of their hands.

"Are you both alright?"

"Yes. I feel like a kid again," Dominic firmly answered. Lucia agreed.

"Who here is up for a little evil?"

It was still early in the evening, but Via Veneto was already crowded with a colorful array of actors, artists, and onlookers.

A film had just finished production that afternoon. Nearly everyone in the cast and crew had hit the street to celebrate. They were not alone. Countless members of the paparazzi were out in full force. Anyone who appeared rich or famous was hit with a barrage of camera flashes as they made their way into the restaurants and nightclubs.

Ursula's large, black car pulled up in front of a nightclub called The Cave. The onlookers and paparazzi gathered around the car, hoping to catch a glimpse of the rich and beautiful.

Ursula sat between the Divitas. She was still holding Dominic's hand, when she noticed Lucia's leg revealing itself out of the slit of her dress. She carefully wrapped her hand around Lucia's knee. Ursula didn't acknowledge Lucia's body tensing up. She went on to explain her ground rules for the night.

"Now, tonight will be your first kill. Some vampires stumble because they believe themselves to still be human. I want you both to remember that you are now above them. They are cattle, nothing more," Ursula instructed.

"I have a question."

"Yes, Lucia, my sweet?"

"I noticed that I could see myself in the mirror. Are we still partly human?"

Ursula smiled at her young disciple.

Dominic listened closely. He had noticed this well. As usual, his more direct wife brought up the topic.

"Do not despair, you are both vampires. The myth that we cannot be seen in a mirror is only half right. You see, we control our own image."

"How is that?" Lucia asked.

"By sheer will."

Lucia and Dominic continued to listen. Ursula believed the young couple understood, but she was getting bored explaining it. She preferred to teach by example rather than talk.

"Come. I will show you."

The paparazzi had grown inpatient. The crowd was convinced that someone famous was in the car. The longer it took for the door to open, the more it seemed to prove their suspicions right. They pushed each other closer to the curb and the photographers held their cameras above their heads in anticipation.

Lane exited out the front driver's side. This caused a couple of cameras to snap prematurely.

Ursula stepped out of the car first. A series of flashes lit up the front of the nightclub. Men yelled for her autograph, even though they had no idea who she was. She looked over the small gathering. The rush of other people's blood was flowing through Ursula's veins. Any one of these onlookers could be dinner and they were all eager to deliver themselves to her.

She didn't wave to the crowd, she merely pulled Lucia out of the backseat by the hand and didn't let go. Dominic had Lucia's other hand as he followed. Ursula leaned over to them and whispered in their ears.

"Simply wish not to be photographed and it will happen."

The three walked into the club, arm in arm. Lucia was disgusted by the group of men and women begging for their attention. These were the same people that would have called her a "Gypsy whore" just a few days earlier. Lucia had always considered them to be worthless, little people that believed hanging out with the rich would rub off on them. Ursula had changed all of that; from that moment on they were food.

"Who do we eat?" Lucia asked.

"I'll show you inside."

The three vampires walked past the line in front of the club. The appalled murmurings of the people waiting to get in only served to make Dominic and Lucia snicker. There wasn't any communication aside from an exchange of knowing smiles between Ursula and the bouncer.

The paparazzi halted because they were not allowed into any of the nightclubs along Via Veneto. When the photographers developed their film hours later, they wondered why they had taken so many pictures of nothing but an excited crowd.

The Cave was less a place of business than it was an ongoing party. The nightclub had been designed to look like an old cave, complete with plastered walls meant to resemble rock. The room was packed with people drinking, dancing, and even some couples slipping off to neck in the hidden corners of the building. A live band was doing its hardest to impersonate Buddy Holly.

Dominic's and Lucia's new senses were assaulted by all of the sounds and smells. Lucia broke away to shout at a young man from across the room for saying obscene things about her. He was taken by surprise, considering he'd only whispered them to his friend seated next to him.

Meanwhile, something about the drummer froze Dominic in his tracks. It was his hands. He had been playing so hard that his hands were bloody.

A woman brushed by him. She smiled at him. She found his dark, roguish features tempting. Dominic was overwhelmed by a scent that was stronger than her perfume. It was blood; the woman must have been menstruating.

Suddenly, he could smell them everywhere. There were women bleeding all around him. He had never understood until that moment how intoxicating blood smelled.

He was yanked out of this self-induced trance by Ursula. She had already dragged Lucia away from almost starting a fight and she wasn't about to let them ruin their first night so soon. She showed the couple to a booth that the owner had reserved for her.

A waiter appeared moments after they'd seated themselves. Ursula ordered three glasses of champagne and he quickly went on his way. Lucia and Dominic were confused.

"We can still eat?" Lucia asked.

"Why not? We can eat. We can drink. It's just not what keeps us alive," Ursula was pleased to report. The waiter returned and was eager to please the exotic blonde.

"Will that be all, madam?" He had to shout, due to all of the music and noise.

"Yes. Thank you!" Ursula was so casual that it hardly seemed like yelling at all.

"Will you be dining tonight?"

Questions like that always brought a grin to Ursula's face. She never grew tired of the irony.

"We'll let you know." She looked the young lad up and down. He darted away, unsure if he was aroused or frightened.

"Are you going to eat him?" Dominic asked Ursula.

She giggled and playfully brushed up against him. This didn't make Lucia jealous in the slightest. It was odd how quickly she had become a part of them, like family.

Lucia thought of her family all of a sudden. She wondered if the children were still safe with Rosa.

"I think I've had my fill of waiters right now. Tonight is about the two of you. When was the last time you enjoyed being alive?"

Dominic looked past Ursula hoping to find an answer in Lucia's eyes, but she didn't remember either.

"The fact that you both need to think about it is very telling. You need to step out on the dance floor. You're Italians! You should start acting like it!"

"But what about finding--" Dominic didn't get to finish his question.

"Your prey will find you! Go! Go!" Ursula pushed them off their seats.

The band had begun playing a slow song called "Donna." Dominic held Lucia close. Her rose scented perfume engulfed his senses. They danced in a small circle together. Ursula was right. It had been far too long since they had taken time to appreciate each other. Lucia whispered something in his ear.

"This is a stupid song."

"Of course it is," he chuckled.

"It's true! Most songs are shit. All this music that comes from America is just fake sentiment. It doesn't make you feel."

"What is it supposed to do?"

"Music should grab you by the heart. It should make you want to dance and forget about how awful life is for a little while. I should be able to feel that singer's joy or pain. I want to fucking hear it in the way they play their instruments."

Dominic always took great delight in discussing the arts with her. This often gave him the opportunity to play devil's advocate.

"What about all those people who love that fake music? They seem to find something in it."

"It's lifeless music for lifeless people. They deserve each other," Lucia said quite plainly.

A serious silence overtook the moment. They both realized that being vampires seemed to fit their world view. For the rest of their lives, Dominic and Lucia would be able to act on their philosophies.

The band finished the song and changed to an upbeat tune. It wasn't any song that Dominic or Lucia was familiar with. They thought it was perhaps some original piece. It featured heavy guitars and, thankfully, no vocals.

Dominic stepped back, away from his wife. He was no dancer and he wasn't about to try to keep up with her. He decided to make his way to the bar and watch her on the dance floor.

Lucia took over the room with her moves. Her adopted mother had taught her oriental dancing, otherwise known as belly dancing. Her style was an awkward fit for the song that the band was churning out. Once she'd made eye contact with the lead guitarists, they attempted to alter the tune to suit her moves. Lucia wasn't sure if she had pushed them or if they'd done it on their own.

Dominic drank his beer on the sideline. From here he could observe how the men and women reacted to Lucia's dance.

Most of the men nearby cheered, some merely stared. Some of the women were jealous that their men were paying more attention to her than themselves. A few of the females were just as excited as the men.

Dominic's attention was pulled away by a voice in his ear. It was Ursula.

"She wants you."

He turned around only to find the young bartender nervously preparing someone's drink. It was probably his first night.

Then, he heard her voice again. It felt like a whisper in his ear. He could feel her hot breath on the back of his neck.

"The young girl at the end of the bar."

There were a few girls at each end of the bar, but he knew just who she was talking about. She was a tall, thin woman that looked to be Dominic's age. She wore her long blonde hair to the right of her face. The woman looked local, but was hoping to fit in with the crowd by showing off in her only fancy red dress. Dominic instantly met with her eyes. She must have been staring at him for the last five minutes.

"Take her."

Dominic slowly got to his feet and walked over to her. Ursula was right. He could smell the sweat building in her palms. Her heart skipped a beat when he headed in her direction. He could feel her body quiver as he drew closer. She tried to cover her fears with a smile that only revealed her overbite.

"Hello." He sounded so confident that he barely recognized his own voice.

"Hi. Are you with the movie people?" She lit a cigarette, hoping that he would be impressed with how cool she was.

Lucia hadn't broken a sweat despite dancing for a half hour straight. She felt as if she could go all night.

The men on the dance floor labored to be her main partner, but she ignored one after another. This only seemed to make them want her more.

She halted during one of her undulations when she sensed a small hand caressing up her back. When it reached the base of Lucia's neck, she could hear a voice.

"He is undressing you with his eyes."

Lucia twirled around to discover that Ursula was still at her table, but it sounded as if she was right behind her.

"The man by the door. Do you see him?"

She continued to dance as if there was nothing unusual going on. She scanned the people at the door only to locate an average man of average weight and height. His black hair had been slicked back. He sported a pencil thin mustache, which he nervously smoothed out from time to time.

Lucia focused her gaze on him as she performed a sensuous snake hips move. She gestured to him with her eyes that she wanted him to come over. He quickly made his way through the crowded dance floor. Lucia could sense his heart racing and his erection swelling as he drew closer.

Dominic and the woman had exited the building and found a quiet place in the back alley to be alone. The woman, named Anna, believed that Dominic was a friend of Federico Fellini, and even that he co-wrote the film, Nights of Cabiria.

Dominic had never lied to her. It was her unfounded notions of him that would be her demise.

"My mother always said I should be in the movies. People ask me all the time if I'm an actress. I like to smile and just let them think what they want."

"Is that so?" He sounded interested.

"I know! Aren't people stupid? I knew you had to be in the movie business, but I had you pegged as an actor."

"Why do you say that?" Dominic almost laughed.

"Well, aren't writers supposed to be fat little mamma's boys? You're too good looking for that."

"Thank you. Didn't you say that you wanted to act?"

Lucia followed the man outside. His large, off-white car smelled of beer, cigarettes, and body odor. In other words, the car smelled like him.

His hands sparkled with the many rings he wore, with the exception of his wedding ring finger. All that was left there was a mark around his finger where it was usually worn. He opened the door to the backseat.

"Come into my office." He emphasized the word "come" hoping it would make Lucia laugh. It didn't.

Her silence made him nervous. He desperately wanted her to like him, but that was the one surefire way to get on Lucia's bad side. She hated it when people tried to force her to enjoy their company. The man didn't want to give up until she thought he was wonderful.

"My name is Angelo and you are...?"

He was surprised when she took hold of his jacket and tossed him into the car. This excited Angelo more than it frightened him. This woman was aggressive and dangerous, unlike his wife.

Anna braced herself, her back to the wall of the nightclub. She was done with the "getting to know you" chit-chat. She dug her thumbs under the straps of her dress and tugged them off her shoulders.

Anna thought that Dominic would not just be her lover, but maybe her way into the movie business. He took a deep breath. Dominic could hear her heart race, pumping all that intoxicating blood throughout her system.

Angelo waited for Lucia to join him in the backseat of his car. He spoke of how well she danced and how lovely she looked.

All Lucia could hear was the beating of his heart. Ursula had warned them that the first time might be difficult. Some young vampires still held on to their humanity and considered what they do to be murder.

Lucia thought of this as she studied Angelo. She concluded that he was beneath her. She decided that Angelo was a typical example of what it meant to be human. He was a selfish, unoriginal, and stupid creature that was under the belief that he was the most unique being in the world. People just like him killed each other every day for little to no reason -- and she is supposed to be a monster.

Lucia decided she wanted nothing to do with being human.

Dominic noticed something that he never had before that evening. He had never realized how frail people look.

Anna was leaning up against the wall. She appeared so thin he wondered how she got by in life without breaking. She seemed aroused, but there was some deeper emotion hidden behind her eyes.

She was afraid, but not of him. He sensed a greater fear lying within her -- it was a fear of living. Anna was worried that she would never make a name for herself in the movies. She feared growing old without a husband or a family to care for her.

To live in that weak shell of flesh and bone for fifty plus years seemed unnatural to him all of a sudden. His front teeth enlarged to the point that they cut into his bottom lip.

"Oh, baby! Come here. I got something for you!" Angelo pleaded.

Lucia could only reply with action. She shut the car door with her foot and pushed his head to the side. Her new fangs dug into his neck and she tore an opening to drink. It felt like biting into a tomato.

She was a little surprised that he didn't scream or even try to escape. The rush of blood exiting his veins and the repeated sensation of Lucia's tongue quickly digging into him was too much for him to react.

Anna sounded as if she was about to orgasm as Dominic began to lap the blood from her neck. She held on to his wide shoulders as well as she could. Her body stiffened and finally gave out. Dominic felt Anna's hands lose their grip before she fell to the ground.

He met with her eyes one last time before she grew still and, to his surprise, he saw a look of ecstasy rather than horror.

Lucia rose up once she had sucked every last drop she could get from Angelo. She found a handkerchief in his front jacket pocket, relived his body of it, and began to clean her chin of the blood.

Then she noticed the smile frozen on his face, his eyes still displayed a confused gratification. Prior to her experience with Ursula, such a sight would have unnerved her. It was obvious to Lucia that it was worth risking one's own life for the release a vampire offered.

"Very good," Ursula's whisper called to them. "Meet me in front of the nightclub."

Dominic only had to walk around the building while Lucia had to exit the parking garage and walk back down the street. She decided to choose her next victim based on where they were parked.

When she reached the nightclub, she found Dominic waiting. Without words they held each other tightly. After a moment Lucia discovered his shirt was covered in blood.

"Look at you! You got blood everywhere!" She pushed him away.

"I'm sorry. I'm not sure how to do it without getting covered yet."

"You always were a sloppy eater," Lucia giggled.

Dominic pretended to laugh along with her, but there was no fooling his wife. Lucia could tell what he was feeling. She'd always considered him to have the most honest eyes of anyone she had ever met.

"What? It's funny. You know it's true!"

"No!" he chuckled. "It's not that...it's just..."

"It's just what? Use your words. I can't help you if you don't use your words."

"I miss the kids," he confessed.

"I do, too."

Dominic and Lucia stood in silence for a few seconds. Even though it had been such a life altering 48 hours, they'd still had the children in the back of their minds the whole time. Lucia made the pronouncement.

"It's almost dawn now. We'll go back for them tomorrow night."

"What about Ursula?" he asked.

"If she loves us, then she will love our children."

"And if she doesn't?" Dominic always considered the worst case scenario.

The lights of Ursula's car engulfed them.

There was a conviction in Lucia's eyes that told him everything he needed to know on the subject. There would be no compromise on this issue. Lucia answered simply.

"She will."

CHAPTER FIVE

U rsula's mansion was only a two mile drive down the street, but to the three vampires in the backseat it was an eternity.

Ursula, Dominic, and Lucia stared out the front window hoping to see the house as they held each other's increasingly sweaty hands tightly and labored to chat about the nightclub.

Once the Mercedes pulled into the driveway, the trio burst out before Lane had even had a chance to put the car in park. The Divitas followed Ursula, shaking with anticipation.

The older vampire discovered something about herself during these brief seconds on her way to the bedroom. She was nervous. She could have sex at any moment with anyone, but this was different -- this was love and love could go wrong. An anxious smile forced itself onto her face as she looked back at the couple.

"Would you like some coffee sent up?" Ursula rested her jacket on a leather chair in the corner of the room. She attempted to sound casually in command, but to Dominic and Lucia she came across as jumpy.

"Ursula," Dominic spoke urgently.

"What is it?"

Dominic and Lucia stood close together, their shoes had already been kicked off. Their warm eyes and smiles drew the cold hearted vampire closer.

"Come here," Lucia added.

Ursula was a few inches shorter than the Divitas, whose embrace seemed to envelop her whole body.

Suddenly, everything was happening in slow motion and all outside noises fell away. All that she could hear was her own breathing, which sounded as loud as a jet engine.

Dominic and Lucia kissed behind her ears and made their way down her neck in unison. Ursula's hands unhurriedly caressed their chests.

Ursula found herself being pushed back toward the bed. She fell onto her back once her legs struck the foot of the mattress.

This wasn't what she'd had in mind. She had always been in control. For hundreds of years Ursula had seduced countless men and women. It never mattered if they were simple peasants or world leaders, they always knew who was the master. Maybe it was time, but all that Ursula knew was that she wasn't in charge.

Dominic peeled off her socks, pants, and undergarments. Lucia worked her own underwear down her to her ankles and positioned herself above Ursula's head. Lucia's robust thighs rested on either side of her face.

Ursula gazed at Dominic removing his shirt. She placed her feet firmly on his chest, feeling his heart beat faster and faster. Ursula was so aroused by this that she barely noticed that Lucia was undoing her tuxedo top and bra.

She felt her feet slip up to his chest and past his shoulders. Lucia flipped her skirt over Ursula's face. The scent of Lucia sent a ripple throughout her body, but it was nothing compared to the sensation of Dominic entering her. Instantly, Ursula found herself mimicking his motions to Lucia with her tongue.

Ursula's breathing picked up momentum as she released an energy that surged throughout the house. Nearing dawn, much of the staff was fast asleep.

The chef, Katherine, woke with a sweet taste in her mouth. The blonde dressmaker felt a sturdy muscle enter her body. She reached down to help push it in farther.

This phenomenon kept repeating itself as each of Ursula's employees found themselves unable to sleep or continue their work. Two maids and a young butler on the night shift fell to their knees, quivering from head to toe.

Lane stood outside, smoking and watching the sunrise. He listened to the moans that could be heard all over the house. The groundskeeper, asleep in his tiny bed, was unaffected.

Lucia reached her orgasm first, sending a chain reaction that went from Ursula to Dominic and finally to the rest of the house. Many of the personnel openly wept from the overwhelming sensation that had invaded their bodies.

Lucia managed to pull her sweat covered dress up and over her head, dumping it on the floor. Her eyes met with Dominic across the bed, she had never seen such unapologetic passion. They found themselves holding hands over Ursula's still shaking frame.

"I love you," he whispered.

"I hope so!" Lucia laughed to herself.

The blonde dressmaker quietly began to giggle, which seemed to spill over to the other employees of the house. Everyone under that roof felt a sense of belonging, a sense of security.

Dominic and Lucia lay down on the bed with Ursula sandwiched in between them. The smaller vampire reveled in feeling Lucia's breasts pressed against her back.

The three of them couldn't lie there motionless for long. The sensation of moist skin rubbing together was too much for the trio.

Ursula murmured something in-between moans. Dominic asked her to repeat herself.

"Don't stop, both of you...don't stop. Please...don't stop..."

CHAPTER SIX

T he little girl was terrified. The lights were out in her house, the air raid sirens stabbed her eardrums, and each bomb shook her home with fury.

She didn't understand what was going on outside. She imagined God himself pounding the street with his fists in anger. She hid under a table, crying for her mother to return, holding on to the lantern she had left for her, fearing that the next bomb would cause it to go out. A voice shouted for her.

"Lucia!"

It was her father. He was curled up in the corner with a topless young woman that she didn't recognize. He was a huge man, more than twice the woman's size. Their dark hair was covered in dust. The woman was so frightened that she appeared to be in a trance. He held his gigantic hand out for his daughter.

"Lucia! Where's your mother?"

The three-year-old was confused. She wasn't sure how to answer him and the explosions didn't help matters much. She reached out for her father to save her.

"She's looking for you!" she cried.

Something suddenly dawned on her. Lucia wasn't looking at her father any longer. It was Dominic in his place with Ursula underneath him.

She was strangely aroused, no longer noticing the bombs going off around them. Dominic was as frightened as her father had been.

"Lucia! Where is Isabella?" he screamed.

Lucia closed her eyes. A slight tickle at her ribs caused her to open them once more. The dream was over. There were no more bombs, no more horror. She was lying safe in bed with her two vampire lovers.

The sun had set on a long day of passionate lovemaking. Dominic was still fast asleep on the other side of Ursula's petite body. The older vampire had been awake for some time.

"Good evening," whispered Ursula, who was buried under a network of Dominic and Lucia's arms and legs. She had patiently watched the Divitas sleep for hours.

"Hello." Lucia never said "good morning" -- or, in this case, "good evening" -- because if it was truly good, she would still be sleeping. "What time is it?"

She blinked repeatedly, hoping to break away the crust that had formed in the corners of her eyes during the day. The taste of blood remained in her mouth.

"It's a quarter after ten. The sun set an hour ago. You two slept like bloodthirsty babies. Would you like some espresso?"

"Of course," Lucia answered.

Ursula called to the maid to bring in the espresso. Lia had been a maid for under a year. She was cleaning the kitchen when she heard Ursula call to her. She looked forward to feeling her mistress's voice tickle her ears. It was an experience that everyone in the house could encounter at any given moment.

"Yes, mistress."

She stopped setting the table to pour three cups of espresso. She placed them on a small silver tray and swiftly took them upstairs. The door opened by itself allowing her to enter without risk of dropping the tray.

Heavy, black drapes covered the bedroom windows to keep the sun out. Ursula asked her to open them to allow some moonlight into the bedroom. Lia did this without losing sight of her beautiful mistress. The maid was like everyone else who worked in the house; she adored Ursula Orlock.

The aroma of the beverages was enough to wake Dominic. For a moment he was reminded of when he was a young boy living at home above the family restaurant. However, Dominic felt that waking up with two exquisite women and being served espresso was not a bad trade off. He labored to a sitting position as Lia handed him his cup.

Ursula took a sip. It was excellent, but something seemed to be missing. She waved for Lia to come closer. The maid sheepishly stepped over to the bed.

"Yes, mistress?"

"Could you be a dear and prick your finger with one of your safety pins?"

Lia removed a pin from her apron and pricked her right index finger. Lia grew excited as a bead of blood formed on her fingertip. Ursula held out her cup to the young maid.

"Drop some in here, would you?"

Lia placed her finger over her mistress's cup and bled into her espresso. She rubbed her finger slowly in order to get the blood out quicker. Dominic and Lucia marveled at how excited she became with each drop. Ursula slid her hand over her cup.

"That's enough. Maybe the Divitas would enjoy some."

Dominic and Lucia both felt it was worth a try. They held up their cups and Lia bled into them. Dominic politely smiled at her to indicate that they had enough. Lia's blood gave the caramel espresso a rich aftertaste.

"Very good. Thank you," he told the maid.

Lia had hoped to stay, but her mistress snapped her fingers and pointed toward the door. She didn't dare to show her disappointment, so she cheerfully left the three of them alone.

Ursula turned to face the Divitas.

"Tell me. How was it?"

"Why did you have to push me toward that thin mustached man?" Lucia cried out.

This prompted Dominic and Ursula to laugh almost to the point of falling off the bed. Lucia fretted that they weren't taking her seriously.

"It's true! He was disgusting! Men with thin mustaches are always perverts!"

Ursula answered while trying to hold back her laughter.

"We know it's true. If there is anything I've learned over the last century, it's that. I was thinking more in the line of the overall experience. Was it what you expected?"

"No. It was better. I've never felt so much control in my life," Dominic answered plainly and honestly. He had come to terms with what he had become.

"I think I prefer this life," added Lucia.

Dominic held up his cup in order to toast. Lucia raised her cup as well, but he didn't say anything. Instead they both looked to Ursula to complete the triangle. The elder vampire was caught off guard by such a gesture. They had accepted her. She gladly connected cups with the Divitas.

"To a new life." Once those words left Dominic's lips, he and Lucia realized that they needed something from their old lives. The feeling was communicated between the two without words. Dominic set his cup down on the night table and kicked his feet out of bed.

"We need to get going," he said.

Ursula was taken aback. She had expected to make love with them once again and enjoy an evening meal. She glanced over to Lucia to see if they were both really leaving.

"What? Where are you going?"

Lucia looked her in the eyes. She had always believed in directness.

"We need to see the children. We left them with a friend two nights ago."

"To say goodbye?" Ursula hoped that their children would become part of the past that they had talked about moments earlier. She wanted to be careful not to appear desperate in her question.

If she did, the Divitas didn't acknowledge it. Dominic took Ursula's hand. He pleaded to her with his honest, brown eyes and asked her a vital question.

"Ursula, we need to bring our children here. Is that okay with you?"

Lucia was surprised by his frankness. He didn't beat around the bush for twenty minutes, he just came out with it.

Babies. They wanted to bring human babies into her home. The fingers on Ursula's right hand tingled with anger. She could feel the nails grow sharp as she visualized ripping Dominic's heart out from his chest.

The blood of the young was the most pure, the most intoxicating, of the human race. The first thing she sought out on a hunt was a lost or runaway child. Sometimes, she got lucky with a neglectful mother leaving her child's bedroom window open. The last thing she wanted was to allow three of them to have the run of her house. Ursula attempted the best smile she could muster.

"Only if you promise that they will not call me 'Aunt Ursula!'"

It was a grin that had fooled kings and popes alike, but Lucia wasn't so convinced. The young mother decided it was better to trust her for the moment. Ursula sensed no hesitation with Dominic as she hugged him.

"I love you both very much. I would be happy to have your

children here."

"Thank you, Ursula," they jointly answered.

"Should I come with you?"

Dominic released her from their hug, Lucia moved in closer to them.

"I think this is something we need to do on our own," he told her.

"Very well, I'll have dinner waiting for all of you. Before you go, you need to understand that you're both too young to walk during the day. Don't get caught in the sunlight. Also, you must stay away from anyone or anything Catholic."

"Thank you. We'll be careful," Dominic reassured her. He and Lucia each kissed her goodbye and headed off toward their dressing rooms from the previous night.

Ursula didn't move. She closed her eyes and let her mind wander through the house. She searched the hallways, the staff's quarters, and the other bedrooms until she found Lane in the downstairs office handling some paperwork. He halted once he felt her presence.

"Lane, could you start my bath please?" Ursula politely asked.

Dominic and Lucia found Caesar Ginsberg's Fiat sitting in the garage next to one of Ursula's Mercedes. The keys sat in the ignition as though no one cared who took the modest little coupe.

Lucia decided that she should drive since she was the one who had borrowed the car in the first place. In less than two minutes of being on the road she was screaming out her window at the other motorists. Two years earlier they'd had to sell their car to make ends meet. Lucia was somewhat grateful for that, because Romans were notoriously bad drivers.

Via Veneto was nearly a parking lot. People cruised by to a snail's pace to catch a glimpse of the rich and famous entering the cafes and nightclubs. Tourists rode their brakes so they wouldn't miss one building of historical interest. A trip that should have been twenty minutes became an hour long journey.

"We're never going to get there," Lucia huffed.

"We'll get there. Just relax."

Dominic always had a way of easing her nerves. He had a calm nature about how he handled situations. She had often wondered if her husband was confident or simply indifferent about life.

Lucia's mood changed when they entered Jewish Rome. The neighborhood they had lived in for the last few years suddenly appeared broken, lifeless, and without hope. Were they really going to raise their three children here?

Dominic laid his hand on Lucia's leg for reassurance. Both were even more thankful that Ursula had given them a chance at a new start, if not for them, then for their babies.

The light was on in their apartment window, which hopefully meant it wasn't too late. Leaving the tiny Fiat in front of the building, Dominic took note of how alien the hallway felt. He wondered if they really did live there.

Roberto hadn't stayed awake long enough to hear the end of *The Lion, the Witch, and The Wardrobe*. Rosa held on to him as he slept on her shoulder. Vincenzo and Isabella were too excited by the story to worry about their bedtime. They were not only dazzled by the book, but by Rosa's voices for the characters.

After reading to her own children for so many years, Rosa had developed quite a flair for the dramatic. Isabella sat in her lap holding on tight, worried over what would happen next. Vincenzo was seated on the small brown rug that took up the middle of the living room. He rocked back and forth, imagining that he and his siblings were taking part in the great adventure.

Their story was interrupted by the sound of keys entering the front door lock. Even Roberto was woken by the noise. The twins looked at each other with anticipation. Lucia was first into the apartment followed by her husband. Rosa was relieved to see them together and seemingly happy.

"We're home everyone!" Lucia howled.

All three children raced from the middle of the room. Isabella leapt into Lucia's arms, Vincenzo wrapped around her waist, and Roberto hugged his father with all of the strength he could muster. He was not only delighted to see them, but to see them together again.

It was very obvious to everyone in the room that something about them had changed, other than Lucia's new black pants and red blouse. Rosa could tell that a weight had been lifted from their souls. The Divitas were not only content, but they seemed more vibrant. Rosa had a million and a half questions, but those questions were going have to wait.

"All right. We don't have much time to explain, but we need to start packing our bags," Dominic explained.

"Why?" Isabella spouted.

Lucia picked Vincenzo up and held him and Isabella as if they weighed nothing. She embraced the pair tightly, never wanting to let go of them again.

"Because we found a new job that requires us to leave this apartment," Lucia explained to the twins.

Roberto looked to his father to verify this news. He smiled and nodded at the boy, who couldn't be happier that things were going to work out.

"I love you, Poppa!" Roberto said.

"I love you, too. Now follow your mother and the twins into the other room. They could use your help."

"Yes, Poppa!" The boy darted into the bedroom, leaving Dominic and Rosa alone in the living room.

She guessed that his pinstriped suit and the new job were the result of two very eventful days. Her initial deduction was the mafia, but that didn't explain the blonde German woman. Rosa had her doubts, but she decided it was healthier for everyone if she assumed the best.

"Is everything all right now?"

"Yes. Thank you, Rosa. And thank you for looking after the children this whole time. Oh, and thanks for the car." He handed her the keys to the Fiat.

"Of course. Caesar and I would do anything for you young people." She paused, a worried look crossing her face.

"What is it, Rosa?"

"Are you two leaving the restaurant?" The words didn't come easy for her. She wiped away the tears as if they were a minor annoyance.

"Yes. I'm afraid so. Tell Caesar that Lucia and I have enjoyed working for you both and we'll miss you."

"Can't you tell Caesar that yourself? He would like a chance to say goodbye. He'll be so happy for you!"

"I hate goodbyes, Rosa."

"I'll tell him." The laugh lines formed by her smile were flooded with tears.

Dominic allowed her to fall into his arms. The Ginsbergs had been like surrogate parents to him over the past few years, and letting go was harder than he thought it would be.

As they held on to each other, she inadvertently kicked over a long-forgotten cup of tea that sitting in front of the couch. Rosa was embarrassed and without thinking she grabbed a towel from the kitchen. Dominic kneeled down to pick up the cup.

"Rosa, you don't have to do that."

"No! It's my mess, I'll clean it up." When she bent over to wipe up the cold tea, her crucifix fell out from her blouse. The gold plated cross connected with Dominic's hand, burning it on contact. He jumped backwards, startled from the unexpected pain. Rosa almost fell over herself at Dominic's outburst.

"Oh, my God! Are you all right?"

"I'm fine!" His only instinct was to lie. Rosa was as confused as she was concerned for him.

"Did you cut yourself? The tea wasn't hot. I can't--" Rosa never finished her question. A stunned silence overtook her. All that she could do was focus on the cross shaped burn on Dominic's left hand.

As an experiment, she removed the cross from around her neck and held it in Dominic's direction. He recoiled in severe pain from the small piece of metal.

Rosa had never been a devout Catholic, marrying a Jewish man was proof of that, but at that moment she saw how religion could protect one from the darkness.

Dominic had been reduced to a fetal position. His skin burned as if he was on fire. His insides felt like he had swallowed a handful of needles that circulated throughout his body. To even look at the crucifix would be like rubbing sandpaper across his eyes. He had to get away.

Lucia stepped into the room, the children behind her.

"What is happening out here?" Lucia shouted.

She had her answer once she caught sight of the scene playing out between Rosa and Dominic. Before she could say or do anything, Lucia felt a stinging sensation in her eyes. Her body started to cramp all over. Though it hurt terribly, she wasn't experiencing the same kind of pain her husband appeared to feeling.

Roberto ran to his father, while the twins hide behind their mother.

"Poppa!" Roberto cried.

"Roberto, no! Stay away from him! He's not your father anymore!" Rosa's words confused the children, but they didn't budge from their parents' side.

"Vincenzo, Isabella! Please come over here! They aren't your parents anymore! They're vampires!" It was no use. Vincenzo and Isabella clung tighter to Lucia. They were more afraid of Rosa than their mother.

Roberto wanted to help his father, but he had no idea what to do. He wondered if Dominic was having heart pains like the man next door, who had died from them last month.

"Please, Rosa, we just want to take our children," Lucia pleaded, unable to look directly at her.

"And do what with them?"

The words tore at Lucia. The suggestion that she would hurt her own children was too much for her to bear. She looked Rosa in the eye and took a step closer. The twins didn't leave her side. The pain from the cross remained steady, but it wasn't increasing.

"Do you honestly think that I would harm my babies?"

"No! But you're different!"

Dominic noticed Lucia's effort and staggered to his feet. His body was being ripped apart by the cross, but he couldn't lose the children. Roberto did his best to help his father brace himself.

Lucia responded to Rosa.

"No. We're not different. We're the same people you've known for the last few years. You know us. You know that I would die before I let anything happen to my babies."

Rosa observed Dominic, fighting to stay on his feet, despite the torment he was going through. Her mother, the movies, and the legends had all warned her that vampires were evil creatures.

However, Rosa knew Dominic and Lucia and she knew they loved their children. Everything she had been taught didn't seem to add up anymore. For reasons that she could never put into words, she tucked the cross back under her blouse.

Dominic's pain instantly subsided. Roberto held on to his father, not understanding what had just happened. The sting left Lucia as well, but she wondered why it hurt her husband more.

There was little to say at that point. Dominic went into the other room to fetch their things, which included his only suitcase and a bed sheet tied up around the children's belongings. The suitcase was the same one Dominic had used when he'd walked out of his parents' house years ago. This scene with Rosa reminded him of that day.

Dominic stopped to say goodbye to Rosa. Since his arms were full, she gave him a farewell hug. He could feel the crucifix burn through their clothes, but pretended not to notice it.

"Goodbye, Rosa." He exited the apartment before Rosa answered him. Roberto followed him out.

Lucia held Vincenzo and Isabella by their hands as she neared Rosa. The two women embraced for a few moments.

"I'll miss you!" Rosa cried.

"I'll miss you, too. Thank you for everything."

Rosa leaned down to kiss the twins goodbye, but they recoiled from her. They didn't understand how she was hurting their parents with the magic cross. They hid their faces against their mother's thighs. Lucia's first instinct was to scold them for being rude, but Rosa knew better.

"Vincenzo. Isabella. I'm sorry I yelled at your mamma and poppa."

The twins each carefully poked an eye out in her direction. This gave Rosa a reason to smile.

"You are?" Vincenzo meekly asked.

"Yes, honey, I'm sorry. I just didn't understand, but I'm better now. Your mamma and poppa are the best people I know and you'll always be safe with them." Rosa stood up and grabbed the book she'd been reading to them earlier. She handed it to Isabella.

"Your mamma and poppa will be able to finish this for you."

CHAPTER SEVEN

Karla was the daughter of a well-known blues guitarist from America. One day while she was touring with him through London, Karla had met an exotic, petite, white woman with an accent she had only heard in the movies. After spending a few minutes with the strange woman, Karla had left the hotel, not even leaving a note for her father.

It hadn't worked out. Ursula came to realize that she had too much attitude to be one of her servants. On the other hand, her blood made the perfect bathwater. One body isn't enough to fill a tub, so Lane had to spend the day selecting two prostitutes to help complete his mistress's bath.

Ursula loved to soak for hours in a crimson pool. She sat back and poked her feet out from the surface. She enjoyed how the blood squirted between her toes.

The vampire lost track of time in the tub, longing for Lucia and Dominic. Ursula ached for his muscular frame and her soft round curves. The blood had grown cold, so it was time to rinse off and check if the Divitas had returned. Once she stepped out of her bedroom, wrapped up only in her white robe and slippers, she detected tiny voices from downstairs.

"Are those children I hear?" Ursula playfully shouted from the top of the stairs.

Vincenzo and Isabella froze in their tracks the moment they set eyes on this mysterious new woman. The twins' mouths dropped open as though they were gawking at a store's candy display. Roberto took cover behind his father.

Lane had assembled a small group of staffers, forming a line to greet the family in the lobby. The twins were so impressed that their new home contained maids and butlers that they began to hop up and down.

Ursula slowly began to creep down the stairs. Lane was a step behind her, as always.

"Welcome home, children. My name is Ursula Orlock."

A maid came forth from the row. The five-foot-tall woman wore a brightly colored robe native to her home country of India.

"This is Sachi. She will be the children's nanny when we are away. Say hello to the children, Sachi."

"Hello." Sachi had a soothing voice.

"My mistress has told me so much about the three of you, but she neglected to inform me of how beautiful you all are."

Vincenzo and Isabella blushed, each taking a step closer to Sachi. Isabella gave her a hug. Vincenzo took her hand and kissed it. The boy had seen a man doing it in a movie a few weeks prior and he wanted to try it out.

Roberto came out from behind his father, put at ease by her words. He wondered if he had overreacted when he'd met Ursula for the first time. After all, his parents seemed to be very friendly with this strange woman.

He observed his mother and father kiss Ursula with an affection he had only seen them display within the family, but he couldn't get Rosa's words out of his head. "They're not your parents anymore! They're vampires!" It was something that he couldn't just brush off.

Ursula gave the children a smile that hid many secrets.

"Would you like to see your new rooms?"

"Rooms?" shouted Vincenzo and Isabella.

"Yes, rooms! I couldn't help but notice how cramped your old home looked, so I thought you might enjoy your own separate bedrooms."

Even Roberto became excited over the prospect of having some space from the twins. Ursula led the five of them up the stairs to the second floor bedrooms. The four-story house was bigger than their entire apartment building. The servants stood at attention when Ursula and the others passed by them.

"You're pretty," Isabella told one maid, who in turn looked to Ursula on how to respond. Her mistress merely nodded.

"Why, thank you, Miss Divita," the maid beamed.

Isabella had never been referred to as "miss" before. She suddenly felt like an adult. She attempted to stroll down the hallway, swaying her hips left and right. Vincenzo laughed at this change in body language.

"You're stupid!"

"She is not stupid. She's a woman now, don't tell her who she is," Lucia corrected.

"Don't tell me who I am!" Isabella repeated the motto, much to Lucia's joy. Mother and daughter giggled at the boy's frustration.

As Ursula did her best to ignore them, she loudly announced the first bedroom to the family.

"This will be Roberto's room!" She swung open the door with a powerful zeal.

The first born son couldn't believe his eyes. The beige bedroom was easily as large as their entire apartment. The young boy marveled at the mammoth bed sitting in the middle of the space, and the balcony that overlooked the street below.

But there was one item that overshadowed everything else. Roberto discovered the television. It was a colossal wooden structure that stood four feet tall. Its dials alone were nearly the size of Roberto's palms.

"I have the TV?" Roberto was as puzzled as he was excited.

"No, you have *one* of the televisions. There are four in the house." Ursula laughed at the seven-year-old's question.

"Four TVs! You're rich!" screamed Vincenzo.

"Do we have one? Do we have one?" Isabella kept repeating.

"Follow me and find out." The twins were right behind Ursula, with Dominic and Lucia lugging Roberto along.

The next room was at the other end of the hallway. This bedroom was adorned in whites and pinks, obviously decorated for a girl. Isabella's room not only had a television, but it also sported a gigantic record player. The wooden machine was nearly the length of a couch.

Isabella opened the record cabinet on the bottom of the console. She quickly thumbed through the vast collection of blues, jazz, and rock albums. Many of the artists' names were unknown to her, but she couldn't wait to hear what they sounded like.

"What's this door to?" Lucia asked.

It was a door that Isabella hadn't noticed due to her fascination with the record player. She asked Ursula if she could open it herself. Ursula nodded "yes" to the young girl. It was a long bathroom that connected to another bedroom.

Vincenzo raced into the new room, just knowing that it was his domain. Ursula didn't disappoint with the third room, which was decked out in red. Vincenzo screamed at the sight of the next television.

Lucia was quite impressed with the three rooms. She stepped out onto the balcony to see the groundskeeper repairing the grave that she and Dominic had dug themselves out of two nights earlier.

"I take it you three like your new rooms?" Ursula inquired.

The children unanimously agreed that they did indeed love their new surroundings.

"The children like it. What do you think?" Ursula embraced Dominic from behind as she directed her question toward him and Lucia. Dominic twirled her around as if they were performing a waltz.

"I think it's wonderful! Thank you!" He set her back on her feet. She stood up on her toes to whisper in his ear.

"Maybe now that the babies are settled, we three can get back to my bedroom?" Ursula cooed.

"Oh, I don't know. Lucia and I wanted to spend some time with the kids." It was difficult to turn down sex. He suddenly felt like a newlywed.

Ursula took a step back from Dominic, her eyes widened with disbelief. As he sensed her intensity, his lighthearted smile disappeared and he wondered if she was about to start screaming at him.

Lucia joined in the exchange, playfully tickling Ursula's sides. The older vampire giggled and jumped away, demanding her to stop.

"Listen to me. Dominic and I just need to tuck the babies in and we can join you later. How does that sound?" Lucia teasingly suggested.

"That sounds acceptable." Ursula found it easy to give in to Lucia. She smiled and kissed each of them on the cheek. She addressed the children, who were trying in vain to find something good on the television.

"Have a good night, children."

"Goodnight!" all three said together without looking away from the TV.

She threw the Divitas a suggestive grin and exited. Both Dominic and Lucia felt relief take hold of them.

"Well, that was almost something," Dominic stated. Lucia agreed, but felt no need to worry about it right then.

"She's just going to have to get over it," she answered.

"True. I -- shit! I left the kids' things downstairs. I'll be--"

"Poppa!"

"Yes, Roberto?"

"Are you all right?"

Dominic was unprepared for his son's query. He was a bad liar when caught off guard. Roberto understood this from listening in to his parents' conversations.

"Oh, of course. Why would you ask?"

"It's just..." Roberto wasn't sure how to push this subject any further. He suddenly felt stupid for bringing it up. "...nothing."

Lucia understood that these two men were never going to get anywhere on this matter, so it would be up to her to level with the children about herself and Dominic.

"Isabella, Vincenzo, Roberto. Your father and I need to tell you all something."

Dominic and Lucia sat down on the huge, soft bed with the children.

"Does anyone here remember what Rosa was saying before we left?" Lucia asked.

"She said you were vampires!" Vincenzo piped up.

"Oh! Is this true? Are you really?" Isabella hopped into her mother's lap. She grew excited over this possibility.

Dominic was curious if they truly understood what they were trying to say.

"Now, wait a minute. Where did you two hear about vampires?"

"At the movies," Vincenzo responded.

"We sneak in." Isabella whispered in her mother's ear, but it was loud enough for everyone to ear.

Lucia and Dominic gave each other a look, hoping the other would know what to say next. This discussion wasn't turning out the way they thought it would. After a few awkward seconds, Dominic found the words to continue.

"Look, your mother and I have become vampires. Do you three

understand what they are?"

"Oh, yeah! They live forever and they bite people and they turn into bats and fly around!" Vincenzo hopped to his feet which sunk deep into the soft mattress. He flapped his arms as if they were bat wings. He hissed at his twin sister, who returned the hiss in kind.

"Well, we can't turn into bats, but --"

"Is Ursula a vampire?" Isabella interrupted her mother.

"Yes, honey. She's the one who made us into vampires."

Dominic noticed that Roberto hadn't said anything for the past minute. The boy was as pale as a ghost. He put his arm around the young man and pulled him closer. Dominic kissed him on the forehead.

"Why? Why did you do it? Why?" He began to cry. Dominic slipped off the bed so that he could kneel down to the trembling boy's level and wipe away Roberto's tears.

"Hey. It's gonna be all right. Would you like to know why?"

The boy nodded.

"Your mamma and I were tired. We were tired of being poor. We were tired of being bitter."

"What's bitter mean?" Roberto didn't want to interrupt, but he needed to make sure he understood their reasons.

Dominic chuckled to himself. He had forgotten that he was speaking to a child.

"I, um. It means that...it's when you feel like the world has cheated you somehow. You're mad, but it's a cold, quiet kind of mad." Dominic tried to read the boy's face. It seemed like he understood, so he moved on with his explanation.

"Anyway, we needed a second chance and not just for us, but for the three of you. Now we can put you in the best schools, the best clothes, the best of everything."

"Is it fun to be a vampire?" Isabella asked her mother.

Lucia always tried to tell the children the truth. She leaned down to the girl and smiled.

"Yes it is. We'll never die and we promise to always be there for you."

She held out her hand for Roberto, who was eased by his parents' words. He held his mother's hand as he leaned on his father's shoulder.

"Could we be vampires?" Isabella sounded so innocent, asking such a volatile question.

Lucia and Dominic were at a loss for words. Vincenzo became thrilled at this idea. He resumed his vampire impression.

"What a great idea! We can all be vampires! I want a black cape."

"Oh, I don't know," was all that their father could answer. He looked to his wife for something better.

"Do you really want to be vampires?" She addressed the question to all three children, but only the twins replied.

"Yes, Mamma!" the twins cheered. Roberto remained silent.

"All right, but believe me, you won't want to be in a five-year-old body twenty years from now. However, when you're older and if you still want to be vampires, we'll make you."

Vincenzo and Isabella shouted for joy, but Roberto wasn't so enthusiastic. His parents were monsters, his siblings longed to join them, and he had moved in to a house populated by unholy killers. He did his best to put on a happy face.

CHAPTER EIGHT

Isabella stared at the sewing needle she'd found downstairs. She was trying to find the courage to stick herself with it. Her brother, Vincenzo, gave her the necessary push.

"Give it if you're not gonna!"

"I'm doing it!" she snapped. The twins sat in their shiny new tub in the connecting bathroom. All three children had had a long day of shopping for clothes with Sachi and enrolling in a private school with Ursula. Isabella and Vincenzo were still fascinated with the idea of becoming vampires. She pricked herself with the needle.

"Oww!" A bright red bead dripped from the tip of her index finger.

"Does it hurt?"

"A little."

"My turn." He put his hand out for the needle. Now that his sister had found the nerve, there was no turning back. Vincenzo stabbed his own finger until it drew blood. Isabella studied her drop and decided to see what it tasted like. She licked it from her finger.

"Ew! Ewww! What's it taste like?"

"See for yourself." She giggled knowing full well he wouldn't be able to resist. He placed his finger in his mouth and sucked on the tiny wound.

"It's sweet!" They were both delighted by this discovery and giggled between themselves.

"What kind of vampire do you want to be?" Isabella asked. Her brother didn't need any time to think about his answer.

"Like Dracula! I want a black cape and a suit."

"I want to be like Mamma." Isabella gave her response without even needing to be asked. The twins continued to squeeze their fingers in an attempt to suck more blood when Sachi knocked on the door.

"Children? What you doing in there?" Their nanny was somewhat concerned. She wasn't only worried over their safety, but her own if anything was to harm the Divita children.

"Nothing," Isabella and Vincenzo answered with droll reassurance.

"Your parents have awakened for the evening and they would like to see you."

On the first floor of Ursula's mansion was a spacious library built in an oval shape. Dominic sat on a ruby red couch in the middle of the room. Roberto took a seat beside his father and handed him a copy of *The Lion, the Witch, and the Wardrobe.*

"This is one of our old books. Are you sure you don't want me to read one of the others here?"

"I'm sure." Roberto then showed his father where had Rosa left off.

Lucia listened to Dominic read as she investigated the room. The small library was stocked with hundreds of books, mainly occult, history, and some fiction. She expected to find books on vampire folklore, but was impressed with the eclectic array of different subjects. Lucia discovered a book on Jewish magic and another one dealing with Gypsy legends.

One very old book, entitled *The Holy Book of Striga,* piqued her interest. She was almost afraid to open it, fearing that the dry, yellow pages would break apart in her hands.

Once the book was opened, Lucia felt assaulted by a number of scents -- it was a mixture of rotting corpses and sexual fluids. This book had a history -- Ursula's history. The more she read, the more the book felt like a bible.

"That's quite a book you're reading." Ursula's voice came from behind her.

"Oh, Ursula! I didn't hear you come in."

"Heh! That's because I'm the best. Are you two ready for tonight's hunt?"

"Soon. We're just waiting for Vincenzo and Isabella to come down before we go."

"Of course." Ursula was a skilled actress. Lucia was too involved with the book to notice her irritation.

"What sort of book is this?" Lucia asked.

Ursula politely took the book from her and started to glance through its pages. The book created a feeling of nostalgia within her. She shut it suddenly and handed it back to her. Lucia wondered if Ursula wasn't up to sharing those emotions with her new lover at that point.

"It's a bible, a bible for the one true religion." Whatever emotions the bible had stirred up had abruptly grown cold. Lucia hadn't expected Ursula to be a religious woman. She was filled with questions.

"What would that be?"

"Striga is the religion of the vampires. We...heh...there I go again! Strigori follow the teachings of the father of all vampires, Jesus Christ."

At that moment, Dominic stopped reading to his son and turned around to make sure he'd heard that last sentence correctly. Lucia studied Ursula for a second to be sure that she wasn't simply joking.

"Vampires worship Jesus?"

"Not all of them. Some don't believe."

"What exactly do they believe?"

"The same as the Christians; Christ was the son of God, here to deliver a message to the world. The difference being, it wasn't the humans that were the chosen ones, it was us. When the humans heard what he had to say, they staked him to a cross in the sunlight. Does that sound familiar? That action has left a curse on all of us. Why do you think the sight of a cross hurts us so?"

"Are you a Strigori?" Lucia slowly chewed on the word as it crawled out of her mouth.

"They saved me, as I saved the both of you. However, the Striga leaders and I don't agree on certain matters."

"And that matter being?" Lucia hated when her husband spoke in generalities, and she wasn't going to let Ursula get away with it as well.

"They believe Jesus will return as soon as everyone on earth is saved. Think of it, an entire world of bloodsuckers out in the open! Who will fear us when that day comes?"

Dominic wandered over to the two women in order to place himself into the conversation. Roberto watched in silence, hoping to learn more about this new situation they were all in. Once Ursula caught him listening, he felt it was best to turn around and pretend to read.

"You know, of course, that I was raised a Catholic." He was careful on how to phrase his words. "If you had told me this a few years ago, I probably would have been offended."

Ursula waited a moment to see if he was finished before she began to snicker. This caused him to feel a bit uncomfortable. He hoped that he hadn't insulted her.

"Well, Dominic, I'd say that you're slightly less Catholic these days."

He shrugged his shoulders, feeling stupid for bringing it up. Ursula understood and moved over to him. She wrapped her fingertips around his belt and tugged him closer to her. She gave him a knowing smile, the kind that a parent gives their child when he misinterprets some simple fact of life. He returned the smile and she tenderly kissed him on the neck.

"I'm sorry. I didn't mean to laugh at you, my love. It's just that I know becoming a vampire was harder for you than it was for Lucia, due to your Catholic upbringing. I was hoping that knowing this might help in some way."

"I know. It does. It's just a little hard to take in all at once." Dominic's hands found themselves on Ursula's waist. He had struggled with his faith since his family had disowned him. In the years following, he had learned from Lucia that there were many beliefs and maybe there wasn't one answer. At this moment, he wondered if maybe it wasn't the message, but the messenger, that was wrong.

"You see, Dominic, we're not the children of the night. We are the children of God."

Lucia felt like an outsider for the first time since she had become a vampire. She didn't mind sharing her love, but Ursula and Dominic had found a connection that she could not be a part of. She was an outcast once again in her life because of Jesus.

Lucia was thankful to see Isabella and Vincenzo race around the corner into the library. Sachi was doing her best to keep up with the two. Their presence changed the climate of the room, refocusing the attention on them.

Dominic released his hold of Ursula and joined Lucia in welcoming the kids into the room. The children had much to share with their parents about their day with Ursula and Sachi. Vincenzo and Isabella were very impressed with the large school they'd visited. They also wanted to show them the clothes Sachi had picked out for them.

"I'm sorry we couldn't be there with you today," Lucia told them.

"How come Ursula can be out in the day and you can't?" Vincenzo asked his mother.

"Well, Ursula is older than your Mamma and Poppa. She can handle the sunlight," she answered.

Ursula had quietly removed herself from the family circle, standing a few feet away. She was caught off guard when Isabella walked over to her direction.

"How old are you?"

Ursula stiffened up trying not to notice the small cut on the tip of her finger. She yearned to suck the girl dry. It took all of her willpower to fight these urges.

"Old."

Lucia thought that was a rather cold response to her daughter's question. It was then that she sensed the cut as well. Her mother's instinct kicked in and she politely called Isabella back over to her. She knew how much Ursula loved her and Dominic, but she wondered if she was a threat to her children.

"Isabella, why don't you show us your new outfits?" Lucia took her by the hand and motioned to Roberto to follow them. Dominic, Vincenzo, and Sachi tagged along.

"Ursula, we'll just be a few minutes. We can go as soon as we're back downstairs." Lucia smiled at her, trying to cover up her doubts about their threesome.

"'How old are you?' 'Old,'" Vincenzo mocked the vampire. The other two children laughed at his impersonation.

Lane entered the room seconds after they were gone to see if they would be leaving soon for their night out. He could tell by Ursula's expression that it was going to be a little while longer.

"The laughter of children is vastly overrated," she grumbled.

CHAPTER NINE

The children were tucked in their beds. They each soaked in the clean, cool, silk sheets as they drifted off to sleep. School uniforms, dresses, and American blue jeans hung neatly in their closets. Lucia turned out the lights and took Sachi aside to chat. Dominic went downstairs to tell Ursula that they were ready to leave.

Lucia hadn't had the opportunity to get to know the nanny. She felt uneasy about leaving them in the house now that she had witnessed some tension between Isabella and Ursula.

"Thank you for taking care of the children."

"You're welcome, mistress." Sachi was grateful for the kind words. She spoke to Lucia in a pleasant manner. Her voice sounded like a well-tuned instrument.

"I love my babies very much. I want your word that no harm will come to them from anything or anyone."

"Of course. Ms. Orlock and I have already discussed this matter. She informed me that if the children were hurt in any way, that I would suffer a most painful death."

Lucia had always had a talent for reading people and becoming a vampire had sharpened those skills. The nanny was telling her the truth. It was odd to hear someone explain death threats made to them in such a congenial fashion, but that seemed to be how things worked in this house.

"Good. I just want you to know that if anything does happen to them, you'll find that I won't be as merciful."

"I understand. Have a good evening, mistress."

It was a bumpy ride as usual. The streets of Rome were narrow and in desperate need of repair. Ursula clutched the Divitas by the arms. Dominic thought there was something needy about the way she was holding on to both of them. He started a conversation, hoping to ease her nerves.

"There is something about being a vampire that I didn't expect. Do you know what that is?" Neither woman answered, but they were listening.

"It's the red urine. I suppose it's only natural, but it still came as a shock to see blood coming from down there."

"That's only because you're a man," Lucia deadpanned. Ursula cackled over this exchange and kissed her behind the ear.

The silver Mercedes parked by the Fountain of the Four Tiaras. Water shot past King Neptune blowing into his conch shell, surrounded by his subjects.

"We are going to split up. Once we have fed for the night, we will meet here. Make sure the two of you are back before sunrise. If either one of you find someone worth sharing, please bring him or her along. Any questions?"

They didn't have any. Ursula kissed them and they went off in opposite directions. Ursula just sat there. Lane adjusted the mirror so that he could better see his boss without turning around. There was no reflection.

"No, Lane. This is important. I want you to face me."

"This is about the Divita children, isn't it?"

Ursula dug a silver cigarette case from her jacket. After selecting one, she held it in a position to indicate that she wanted him to light it. Lane snapped his fingers and it lit.

"Why did you choose Sachi to be the children's nanny?" The backseat's leather creaked as she leaned back.

"She once had three children of her own."

"Oh, yes! I had forgotten them."

Ursula closed her eyes and licked her lips as she remembered their taste. Her mind drifted out of the car and down the road. She could see her home. In it, she peaked into Isabella's bedroom. The little girl was asleep and holding a brown teddy bear that Sachi had bought for her during their shopping spree. Sachi quietly picked up dirty clothes.

"I could kill them so easily. All I have to do is will it."

The nanny heard an alluring voice in her head. She did as it commanded and grabbed a pillow off a chair. She drew closer to the sleeping girl with the intention of placing the pillow over her face. Sachi only thought of how it would please her mistress if she suffocated Isabella to death.

"Lucia and Dominic would know it was you if one of your employees did it. They're smart enough to realize that the staff have no will of their own."

"I know, I know. It's just so tempting." Ursula sat back up. It was enough of a gesture to break her connection to the maid. Sachi edged away from the little girl. She dropped the pillow back on the chair before leaving the room.

"Children disappear all of the time. Perhaps I could turn them into rats and set them loose in the streets. I could even drop them off in their old neighborhood, so they won't be homesick." Lane's British wit was showing again. He felt it was his duty to keep his boss's spirits up. This time he wasn't having much luck. She remained silent. Lane turned around to watch the night sky.

"Lane, did the papers report on the people the Divitas killed at The

Cave?"

"No. Apparently, the Church has kept it from the public eye. Do you have an idea?"

"Just look into it."

CHAPTER TEN

I t had been over a week since Angelo Calvino had been found dead in the backseat of his car. Camilla had always tried to be a good wife. She knew where her husband went when he had to "work late." She kept her mouth shut and raised a fine son, Dante, who had recently turned fifteen. Both wife and son put on a brave face for the family and friends in attendance.

The rain held out that day and the sun managed to poke through the clouds on more than one occasion. It was a lovely sendoff.

Camilla was already a skinny woman, but this week had drained her of a few more pounds. Her long, black hair had been tucked back under her veil. The wake afterward was at her house. Camilla's mother and best friend, Martina, cooked a pleasing feast. She watched as Angelo's co-workers and acquaintances sat around the house and chatted about the food and how much they would miss her husband.

Camilla sat in Angelo's old chair, trying to catch a whiff of his scent. Father Puzo noticed the tiny woman sinking into the chair and made his way over to her. He wasn't alone. At his side was another priest who was slightly taller and reminded Camilla of an American because of his bushy mustache and cowboy boots. She didn't know that priests were allowed to wear such things, but right then wasn't the time to ponder the issue.

"Thank you, Father. That was a beautiful service."

"He was a fine man, Camilla. I thought he earned it." Father Puzo stepped back to introduce the priest to his left.

"This is Brother Dick Walker. He is studying here for the time being."

The young American didn't speak. He only communicated through the sorrowful look in his eyes. He shook her hand with the strongest handshake she had ever encountered. Camilla found him attractive, which in turn caused her to feel shame. She had buried her husband only hours earlier. She wondered if she should even confess this next week.

The simple act of sitting on the couch beside her chair revealed the differences between the two men. Father Puzo was an older man in his late fifties. His slightly out of shape body seem totally at ease, whereas Brother Dick still appeared tense.

"How are you holding up?" The elder priest took her hand. There was concern in his voice, but she could feel Dick's eyes studying her. Camilla was almost too nervous to answer.

"Luckily Angelo's life insurance is going to help us out, but I'm afraid we'll have to move anyway." She quickly glanced around the room as if it were the last time she would have a chance to do so.

"Dante has been very strong. I don't know what I would have done without him." Camilla stopped for a moment so that she wouldn't burst into tears.

Brother Dick leaned over to Father Puzo and whispered something to him. When he felt she was ready, he asked another question.

"Did the police discover anything yet?"

"No. They said it looked like a robbery."

"Did you notice anything strange before his passing?"

"Strange? What do you mean strange?"

Brother Dick tilted over again to Father Puzo and murmured something else. It was obvious that these were his questions. The elder priest contemplated his query for a moment.

"Strange, as in any odd people visiting your home or your husband acting distant days before his death."

"No, nothing like that." She didn't want to be questioned again over her husband's murder. All she wanted to do was escape these two men. Camilla got her chance when she heard her name being called from across the room.

Father Puzo and Brother Dick were disappointed when she excused herself. At first she thought it was her son that had called on her, but he was chatting with a pretty teenage girl. She inspected the living room in hopes of catching the attention of whoever was talking to her.

"Camilla."

It was a male voice.

"Camilla. Out here."

The gentle voice was coming from the backyard. It sounded familiar, but she couldn't place who it was. She unlocked the wooden patio door and stepped outside. Camilla didn't realize until then that the sun had already set. The lights from the house lit the otherwise dark yard.

"Who is out here?"

A shadow emerged from the night, taking the shape of her husband.

"It's me, Camilla. It's Angelo."

Camilla's skin quivered. She wanted to believe that there was some mistake. Perhaps it was someone else in her husband's coffin, but she had seen him at the funeral with her own eyes. She had identified him at the morgue. Angelo was dead. She wanted to hug him. She wanted to run away. She couldn't do either. Camilla was frozen where she stood.

"Angel...Angelo!"

"Camilla. I have missed you." Angelo seemed oddly at peace.

"Angelo! Darling, what happened to you?"

"I was taken from you."

"By who?"

"A vampire whore killed me."

"Angelo, I don't understand."

"Only you can avenge me."

"Mamma?" The voice came from behind her. It was Dante. He had heard his mother outside and decided to check on her to see if she was well. He found her alone in the dark, crying. Camilla nearly jumped when she noticed him there.

"Mamma, you all right?"

His mother was sweating and out of breath. Camilla looked like she had been running. He put his arms around her and she collapsed into his chest. He let her lean on his shoulder as they walked back into the house. He told her that he loved her and promised her that everything would be better soon. Camilla looked back at the empty backyard.

"I love you, Angelo."

Ursula sat alone in her library. She'd been relaxing in a red leather chair. She opened her eyes and smiled. She laughed quietly to herself over the foolish human's belief in her husband's ghost.

"I love you, too."

Soon, the vampire would have Dominic and Lucia all to herself.

CHAPTER ELEVEN

Lucia had been in the library for hours when she felt the presence of someone watching over her. No one had entered through the door, the only way in was the window that was cracked open to allow a little night mist into the room. There was no scent. Lucia quickly became irritated with this game and looked up to see Ursula sitting with her legs crossed on the ceiling.

"I'm sorry." Ursula was mournfully quiet. Her white nightgown hung as if she wasn't upside down. She stood up and flipped down to the floor. Her perfect landing would have made any circus performer jealous. Lucia wanted to ask how she could walk on the ceiling, but Ursula's sorrow took precedent.

"Sorry about what?"

"My behavior over the past few days. I was rude to your daughter. I'm not very good with children. I hope I didn't frighten her."

"No. She likes you. I was worried."

"Don't be, darling! I love your children. Isabella favors you most of all of them. I can imagine what you may have looked like at her age."

Lucia didn't respond. She only thought of how little she wanted to talk about her childhood. Ursula sensed this feeling and gently lifted Lucia's feet so that she could sit next to her on the couch, letting them rest in her lap.

"Lucia?"

"I'm sorry. It just hit me. Were you just on the ceiling?"

"That's all right! It's been quite a week. I didn't want to bore you and Dominic with every detail of my life. I thought we would discuss them as they came up." She began to massage Lucia's left foot. The kneading created such a relaxed sensation that she nearly dropped her book.

"Like your religion. How long were you going to keep that from us?"

Ursula stopped rubbing her foot, fearing that an argument was about start.

"No, no. You can keep doing that," Lucia laughed. Ursula chuckled to herself, feeling a little silly, and resumed the massage.

"I'm sorry as well for that. I know you felt pushed aside when Dominic and I were discussing my beliefs. I take it that you're not moved by such an idea."

"Not really. I don't believe in regular Jesus or vampire Jesus." Lucia held up the book on Jewish mysticism that she had been reading. "What I find surprising is all the different books about religion and magic. Are these yours?"

"Some. Most of these are Lane's. He's a wizard. Or is it warlock? I can never remember the difference."

"A warlock is a male witch. They're humans who use magic and a wizard is a magical person, born with powers."

"Oh?" Ursula was startled by Lucia's knowledge of magic.

"Well, then he is a warlock." She already knew the distinction between the two. What the older vampire wanted to discover was how well versed the Italian Gypsy was in the magical arts.

"I found him during the English witch hunts at the beginning of the seventeenth century."

"Seventeenth century? He looks good."

"He does, doesn't he? Lane was a judge with a very dark secret. He was a student of witchcraft. He personally sent many innocent women and men to their deaths with the hope of driving suspicion away from himself. That horrible life was changed the day he met me."

"What did you do?" The muscles in Lucia's body tensed up as she learned of Lane's past life. She hated persecutors and wasn't happy to be living under the same roof as one.

"I helped him with a spell that granted him immortality. It's funny how he can't seem to do anything about his white hair. Maybe he likes it." Ursula could feel Lucia's revulsion of her right hand man. She found this hatred intoxicating.

"What does he do for you in exchange?"

Ursula sat back and relaxed to feel out where Lane was in the house. After a moment, she resumed rubbing Lucia's right foot.

"He and the groundskeeper are currently disposing of the chef's body. She made a dreadful breakfast today. You would have been sickened."

The conversation had run its course. Ursula had grown weary of chatting and Lucia couldn't care less about the gruesome fate of her staff. The two vampires sat in silence. Lucia found it satisfactory just to sit and read while Ursula massaged her. Ursula was bored with sitting around, so she peeled off her nightgown. Her small white frame seemed to glow in the darkness.

She picked up Lucia's right foot and bit into the bottom of it. Ursula's bite caused every nerve in Lucia to catch on fire. She held the foot over her, allowing it to bleed down her bare chest. She then sunk her teeth into her own wrist. The blood spurted until her breasts were covered with their blood.

"Come here."

The expression in Ursula's eyes reached a spot in Lucia's soul that even Dominic had never found. She knew how powerful this vampire was, but she could see the vulnerable girl hiding just underneath the arrogant persona. The two women never discussed it, but they understood that each had a very personal hardship that bonded them.

The book fell to the floor next to the white nightgown. It was soon covered by Lucia's own white dress.

There was something going on in the garden. For the past hour Roberto had been on his brother's balcony, spying on the groundskeeper who was hard at work burying a brown sack. Lane stood behind the giant, talking. They were too far away for his orders to be heard by anyone in the house.

The young boy had been observing the two men for the past week. Whenever the colossal, gray man disposed of a bag, a staff member turned up missing and no one seemed to care. He watched these scenes play out with a cold distance, almost like he was watching a movie.

Every night he locked his bedroom door and placed a chair under the doorknob. Roberto would lie wide awake in his bed for hours, listening for any sound. During these periods he'd had a lot to think about. He wondered why his parents had brought him into this nightmare. Did Ursula cast a spell over them? Why couldn't his brother and sister see the danger? Roberto prayed to God to protect him and to help his parents see the light.

When following the groundskeeper, Roberto was becoming more brazen. He barely tried to hide from him anymore, because it seemed like he didn't care if the boy witnessed his actions.

The groundskeeper emerged from the hole in the garden with the empty sack over his shoulder. He began to shovel dirt back into the grave without taking a moment to rest. Lane checked his watch and exited the scene. He and the groundskeeper didn't seem to have much of a friendship. The white haired man gave commands, but the large groundskeeper never spoke in return.

The boy strained to see who had been placed in the grave. He pressed his face as close to the bars on the balcony as he could. He thought of simply standing up and gazing over, but he didn't want to be too obvious.

Suddenly, the groundskeeper stopped shoveling and looked directly at him. Roberto froze, fearing that he had finally pushed his luck too far. However, the gray giant seemed to be staring past the child. Someone was behind him.

Before he was able to turn, Roberto was tackled and forced to the cement floor of the balcony. His high pitched screams were not enough to elicit any emotion from the groundskeeper. He went back to work filling the hole. Roberto was too afraid to look at his attacker until he recognized the little bodies on top of him.

"We got you!" Vincenzo shouted.

"You're dead!" Isabella giggled.

Roberto knocked them both away from him. He was angry with his siblings, but more so with himself for letting them get the best of him.

Vincenzo had his hair greased back and wore a blue towel pinned around his neck. He would have preferred to use a black one, but this was the closest he could find.

Isabella chose to wear her black party dress. She had ransacked her mother's makeup case, applying too much eye shadow. Her lipstick was so thick that it stained her teeth red. Isabella had also drawn the lipstick down the sides of her mouth to simulate blood running down her powdered, white face. The young girl looked like an elderly, former child star that had lost her mind.

"Get away!" Roberto had felt even more like a third wheel since his sister and brother had decided to embrace their parents' new lifestyle. The twins didn't acknowledge his anger. No one understood the danger that was around the corner, except him.

"Do you want to play vampire with us?" Vincenzo asked. Roberto turned back around toward the garden to continue his stakeout.

"We got you a cape!" Isabella's words had no effect on him.

The twins stared at his back for a few moments until the sounds of digging grabbed their attention. They sat on either side of their older brother to watch the groundskeeper at work. The three of them dangled their skinny legs through the bars of the balcony. Roberto speculated over how the groundskeeper could rapidly shovel the dirt without seeming tired or taking a break. Isabella was becoming bored by the scene below. She began to kick her feet in an effort to entertain herself.

"Why are you watching the dirt man?" She had grown frustrated by the lack of action.

"Ursula killed somebody."

This revelation changed the whole situation for the twins. Vincenzo and Isabella didn't act in the slightest bit horrified over the possible murder. They simply pondered who could be in the grave. The twins came to the conclusion that it must be the chef.

"Breakfast was awful!" Isabella pretended to throw up over the side.

"Go away!" Roberto found their lack of fear or compassion disgusting. He stood up to separate himself from the two of them.

"Just leave me alone! Go bother Mamma or Poppa!"

"Poppa is out hunting and he wouldn't take us!" Vincenzo protested.

"Where's Mamma?"

"She and Ursula are kissing," Isabella spat out.

The two younger Divita children sat there giggling. Roberto felt a sickness in his stomach. He couldn't believe that his parents would let that monster touch them.

"We looked through the keyhole and they were doing what

Mamma and Poppa do." Vincenzo thought for a moment about what he had said then turned to his sister.

"Do we have two Mammas now?"

"Oh, I hope so!" Isabella thought of all the presents they would get on their birthdays. She looked at her brother, unsure of what he was so upset about.

"What's wrong?"

"Nothing! Go away! I just wanna spy on the man!"

"Why don't you ask him?" Vincenzo didn't face his older brother. He just pushed his face into the bars.

"Ask him what?"

"You know, who's dead."

"Dirt man can't talk back," Isabella interrupted. This confused the boy. There was something she knew that she hadn't shared with him. He wondered why she kept calling him "dirt man."

"Why can't he talk?"

Isabella looked to Vincenzo, worried if it was okay for her to tell him about what she had seen. It hadn't occurred to him that she couldn't share her secrets with Roberto. He gave her a nod. Isabella pulled her legs out from between the bars of the balcony and spun around to face him.

"He's made of dirt."

Roberto didn't understand. It certainly wasn't what he expected to hear.

"What?"

"He's made of dirt!" She hated to repeat herself. It was so simple to her, why didn't he get it?

"He's made of dirt?"

"Yes!" she whispered in a mock scream.

"Is he a dirt monster? How do you know?" Roberto needed more of an explanation. He was beginning to regret asking his sister anything.

"I went into his house when he was sleeping and I thought he was dead so I touched his face. It's dirt. He's dirt. There's a word on his head."

"Where?"

She pointed to her forehead.

"What word?"

"I don't know."

Roberto tried to piece it together in his mind. How could dirt walk around like a man? He examined every idea he could muster until it hit him -- magic.

He was raised in a non-religious family, but growing up in Rome made it hard not to know something about the Church. He had learned how to pray from his friends, and now seemed like the perfect time to ask for God's guidance.

He fell to his knees. There, he silently asked God to forgive his parents and to forgive his brother and sister. They had all been seduced by evil, but they were not bad people.

He had only asked for God's help every once in while in the past. Whenever his parents were fighting or when it seemed that they were going to be thrown out of their apartment for not making the rent, he had secretly begged for God's assistance. This was different. This was about good versus evil and he knew that only God could save them.

Vincenzo and Isabella were unsettled by their brother's sudden action. They had noticed him behaving oddly ever since they'd first arrived at their new home. But they really didn't care too much, and their interests quickly changed.

"Let's see what Sachi is doing!" Vincenzo cried out.

The two would-be vampires ran off to find their nanny. Roberto could no longer hear the groundskeeper filling the grave. He had finished his work and stomped back to his quarters.

Lucia lay flat on the floor of the library, Ursula's head resting on her belly. Both women stared at the plain white ceiling as if it was a starry night sky. They were still covered in each other's blood. Neither had troubled to clean up or to dress. Lucia didn't move, with the exception of her index finger that twisted a bit of her own long, black hair continuously.

"You were raised a Gypsy, but you weren't born as one," Ursula declared. Lucia was surprised by her bringing up the topic.

"What makes you say that?"

"You don't taste Romanian." The two women enjoyed a good laugh at Ursula's observation. She took Lucia's laughter as a confirmation and continued.

"It's true. I am centuries old and in that time I have tasted everything humanity has to offer. My favorite is the Spanish followed by the Italians, both of them have this wonderful, rich texture to their blood."

"Who is your least favorite?" Lucia found herself smiling in anticipation of her answer. Ursula thought to herself for a moment, mainly due to the fact that there weren't any countrymen that she truly hated.

"The English. They're very dry. The French are very enjoyable, but there is a bitter aftertaste. The Russians! Oh, the Russians are so tragic! They were once one of my favorite people to drink. It's as if the cold weather kept the blood fresh inside their bodies. They had such strength to their blood. After drinking from one Russian, I felt as if I could single handily massacre a whole village! Since the revolution, their taste has become stale. Like I said, it's so tragic. I used to adore eating them. The only people I can find similar to that flavor are the Americans."

"The Americans? Ugh! I don't want to eat a stupid American!" Lucia protested.

"Oh, but you must have an American someday! There is quite a kick to their blood and there is so much race mixing among its people it has developed a nice, eclectic flavor!"

"No! I hate the Americans! They're such stupid idiots running around in their cowboy hats, bragging about freedom as if they invented it. If they love freedom so much then how come they don't let the black people eat in the same restaurants as everyone else?"

On hearing this, Ursula decided not to mention that while living in pre-Civil War America, she had owned hundreds of slaves. The notion of being able to own people, and no one caring about what you did to them, was what had brought her to the United States. A slave revolt drove her out of the country, which she had only visited twice since then. It was better that Lucia didn't know this part of her history. Ursula simply listened to her talk.

"Now these fucking cowboys have the bomb! My fate could be decided by assholes from some other country! It's disgusting!"

"Lucia? Whatever became of your real family?"

"What?"

"We started this conversation about you being raised by Gypsies, but we got off the subject."

Lucia didn't answer her.

"Do you know what happened to them?"

"They died."

"How did they die? Was it during the war?"

"Yes. I'd rather not talk about this."

"Why not?"

"Because it won't help anything! They'll still be dead! I won't feel any better about it!"

"I'm sorry. I just thought that maybe you wanted to share."

Lucia stood up, forcing Ursula to roll off of her and quickly slipped her dress back on over her bloodstained body.

Ursula's attempt to connect with Lucia about their common hardships had failed. The conversation stopped dead in its tracks, leaving only the slapping sound of Lucia's feet walking across the tile floor of the library.

"I'll see you upstairs," was all Lucia had to say.

It had become apparent to Ursula that Lucia could not be manipulated like the others. She was just too strong. She would have to devise some other means to bring them closer. Before she could take more time to ponder such thoughts, she was interrupted by the sounds of the Divita children directly outside of the door.

Ursula carefully poked her head out to see what they were screaming about. It was Dominic. He had finally returned home from the night's hunt. But she wasn't the first that he greeted with open arms, it was his children. Isabella and Vincenzo leapt into his arms like dogs welcoming their master home.

Isabella bit her Poppa on the neck in order to show him what a good vampire she could be. He laughed and asked her not to leave any lipstick marks so he wouldn't get in trouble with Lucia.

Ursula became sickened by the look of love in Dominic's eyes for his children. It was a love that equaled, or perhaps even excelled, his love for her. She feared that she was losing both Dominic and Lucia.

Ursula decided to step up her plans. In five days' time, the children would be dead.

CHAPTER TWELVE

MONDAY

Camilla hadn't seen Angelo since his funeral. She began to wonder if she had simply imagined having the conversation with her recently deceased husband in the backyard. But it was what he had said -- "A vampire whore killed me!" -- that troubled her. She waited in the backyard for hours after the sun set, but no Angelo. Maybe she was crazy.

Dante had decided to spend the night with his best friend, so she was all alone. The two-story house had never been so dark and quiet. Camilla realized that the ghostly image of her husband wasn't going to appear.

It was getting late and she had a job interview the next morning. Angelo's life insurance was enough to pay off the house, but to pay for the remaining bills, Camilla had settled on finding work. A friend had suggested a position as a secretary at the law firm where she worked.

She took a shower and picked out the suit she was going to wear the next day. It was the same black outfit she'd worn to Angelo's funeral. She set her brass alarm clock for 8 a.m. and turned the light out. Camilla was wide awake. She tried to ignore the sounds of the house settling and of the clock ticking. Every noise seemed to be magnified a thousand fold.

An hour passed, and her eyes had adjusted to the darkness. She created a little game for herself out of boredom. Camilla tried to make out faces in the swirls of plaster in the ceiling, one face looked like a long-haired woman, and another appeared to be a fat man. A third face seemed to come out of nowhere. She hadn't noticed the shape before, which was odd considering how much detail seemed to be in the face. She wondered if maybe she was getting better at this game.

The face was that of a young man, a teenager. Camilla laughed at herself for thinking how much it resembled a young Angelo. He'd been a handsome man back then, with a full head of hair and a bright smile. She'd fallen in love at the first sight of him in his army uniform. The day the Americans released him as a prisoner of war, he had proposed to her. Now she was seeing his face in the ceiling plaster. She was beginning to feel silly, until the face winked at her.

Camilla ducked her head under the covers. She felt a numbing sensation overcome her. She waited for a few minutes before she found the nerve to poke her head out from under the sheets. The face was gone. Camilla wasn't sure if that should comfort her. Before she had time to decide, something made itself known under the sheets.

A small lump had appeared between her knees. It felt like a burst of warm air that grew in two directions, past her ankles and up her torso. Camilla's fear evolved into a sense of calm. If this was Angelo, or death itself, she was prepared for whatever they had in mind. A face kissed her stomach and pushed its way up her chest.

Angelo's head emerged from the under the sheets. He looked like he had on the day he married her. His smile eased her anxiety. She no longer cared if he was a ghost or a delusion. She was just happy to see him. He held her tightly so that his erection was pressed firmly against her body.

"Oh, Angelo! Please take me! I've missed you so much!"

"I've missed you too, but we can't be together just yet."

Camilla never took her eyes off of his, she pulled up the skirt of her nightgown so that her bare legs could wrap around his naked body. She couldn't remember the last time that sex had made her feel alive.

"Why? Why?" Camilla kissed him on his neck while her hands explored his back. He ceased moving at that point and hung over her like dead weight. His mood changed from passionate to sorrowful. He grabbed her suddenly by the shoulders with great force.

"Because the vampire has my soul!"

The young Angelo sunk into the sheets once more. Camilla yanked them off of her, but he was no longer there. She switched on the light and stared at her bed, hoping to find some proof that he'd been there. Nothing. She fell to her knees and wept. Angelo had not gone off to a better place, he was a prisoner. She would do anything to free his soul.

TUESDAY

Camilla hadn't slept at all the rest of the night after her encounter with Angelo. She needed to be awake for her job interview, so a cup of espresso seemed like just the thing to breathe some life into her. It worked.

The interview couldn't have gone better for her. The young man in charge of hiring the staff, Mr. Filippo, was different than what she had expected. He barely looked thirty in his pin-striped suit. He was sympathetic toward her situation. She could start the following Monday.

Camilla was so delighted at this turn of events that she decided to walk to the market near her home. She planned to cook a victory dinner for herself and Dante. Before stepping inside of the bakery, the sight of her church froze her in her tracks. She had skipped service the past week. She didn't want to tell anyone about seeing her husband at the funeral.

The massive stone building loomed over her like God himself. She couldn't keep what she had seen or done from God. She needed to talk to Father Puzo.

Camilla had been going to this place all her life and she was still struck by the atmosphere. The bricks and the wood that make up the church seemed as old as Christ. The church was fairly empty, even for a Tuesday afternoon. An old man was praying in the front row. The large, golden depiction of Jesus on the cross seemed to be listening to the old man's troubles.

Father Puzo wasn't in his office. His assistant told Camilla that he was taking confession. She waited at least twenty minutes until her turn came up. She rapidly sat down inside the cramped booth, gave the sign of the cross, and began to confess as if she had never met Father Puzo before.

"Forgive me Father, for I have sinned."

"How long has it been since your last confession?"

"Three weeks. Father, I have given in to temptation." Camilla had no other way of describing her plight.

"I understand child. With whom?" He tried to cover his disappointment in her.

"Angelo..." Camilla whispered. It sounded stupid to her coming of her mouth.

"Now, I don't understand. What are you saying?"

Camilla couldn't hold back the tears any longer. She sounded like she was hyperventilating. She had tried so hard to act as if everything was normal, but the truth was now spilling out of her.

"Camilla? Camilla?"

He decided to sit in silence until she composed herself. It was a long five minutes. Once she had quieted down, he spoke again.

"Camilla?" She didn't answer, but he could see that she was listening. "What do you mean?"

"I've seen him. Angelo! I've seen him twice now. Once at the funeral and the second…"

"Yes?"

"He visited me in bed." She felt so ashamed.

"What did he tell you?" He had no idea why he asked that question. But, given what he knew about Angelo's death, it was the only thing he wanted to ask. Camilla was silent again, but this time was different. He sensed her fear.

"Please. What did he tell you?"

"Father Puzo?"

"Camilla?"

"Are there vampires?" she asked as quietly as a frightened child.

It was Father Puzo's turn to be silent. He had sworn an oath to God and the Catholic Church that he wouldn't share his knowledge of the supernatural with the world. It must remain a secret, but she needed to know what forces were at work. He wished that Brother Dick Walker was near, these matters were his mission. He often felt lost in the politics of the Church.

"I can only tell you that there are creatures that walk this earth that have no place among the righteous. Are you sure this is Angelo you're talking to?"

"Yes, Father! It's him! I think he's suffering! He says a vampire killed him and has his soul! Can vampires do that?"

"Vampires have been known to use magic. Perhaps this is a succubus?"

"What are those?"

"They're vampires that lure victims with pleasures of the flesh, only to feed on their souls. Awful, awful monsters."

"Father what can I do?"

"If you see Angelo again, contact me without haste and I'll notify the proper authorities."

"You mean the American? Who is he? Is he with the Church?"

"Camilla, we cannot speak of him. I've already said too much. Please do what you must to protect Dante and yourself."

"I will. Thank you, Father."

WEDNESDAY

Tuesday night passed without a sighting of Angelo. There was a moment Wednesday night when Camilla thought she had caught a glimpse of him.

After Dante went to sleep, she checked on him to see that he was safe. That was when she spotted Angelo in the corner of the room. In the blink of an eye he was gone. Camilla spent the night sitting at her son's bedside.

THURSDAY

Dante was startled to wake up to his mother staring at him. The dazed expression in her eyes gave him cause to think that she hadn't slept. It reminded him of the nights she'd waited for his father to return home from work. He wondered what she was waiting for this time.

"Mamma? You okay?"

Camilla blinked as if coming out of trance. She smiled at him like nothing was out of the ordinary.

"Oh, yes! I'm fine. It's just that I couldn't sleep is all. Now come on, I'll make you some breakfast."

Camilla fixed the teenager a simple plate of bacon and eggs while he dressed for the day. Once he was sitting at the table, she positioned herself in Angelo's old chair in the living room. Camilla didn't bother to change her clothes, she just sat there in her nightgown and robe. Dante slowly approached his mother after finishing his meal. The young man was growing concerned over his mother's sanity.

"Mamma?"

"Yes, dear? Was breakfast all right? Do you want more?"

"No. No, it's just...are you all right?"

"Yes, I'm fine. Now you go run along and do whatever you had planned today, I'm just going to sit here and rest."

Dante wanted to believe her, but he knew that she was having difficulties with his father's death. He thought it was best to do as she asked. He kissed her on the cheek and left to meet with his friends to watch a local football game. Camilla sat there.

She stayed in Angelo's old chair for hours. The phone rang a few times during the day, but she didn't get up to answer it. When the time came to go to the bathroom, she simply went where she sat.

The time she spent waiting for her husband to show himself again gave her an opportunity to reflect on her marriage. She looked back on the parties and carnivals they had attended together, the perverted sex they'd had in the back of his car. Angelo had loved the danger of getting caught fucking in the car.

Dusk set in and darkness began to creep into the house like a cloud. Camilla caught herself nodding off to sleep. She pinched her own arm to keep awake. She wondered if she needed some coffee or maybe she was going crazy. If she was right about her mental health, then she would need more than coffee.

As Camilla labored to get up, she found Angelo lying on the floor in front of her. He was the same age he was at the time of his death. He was in a fetal position. Blood covered his suit. The blood was running down from his neck.

She was now fully awake as a cold blast of air engulfed her. She reached down to hold Angelo. He looked at her with pitiful eyes. The pain of his neck wound caused him to shake all over.

"This...this is what she di...did to me!"

Camilla couldn't speak, she just held him tightly and listened.

"That vampire slut seduced me and tore my throat out! You know I would never have been unfaithful to you!"

"No! I know now you wouldn't have! I love you." Tears ran down her face and dripped onto his.

"You must stop her! She'll do this to others! She might do this to Dante! Please protect him!"

"I will! I will! Does she still have your soul?"

"Yes! Her children feed on my soul by day! You must free me!"

"Her children?"

"Yes! Yes! They look like children, but they're the spawn of a vampire and the Devil himself! They are going to spread evil all over the world! Only you can free me!"

"What can I do?"

"Kill them!"

The lights suddenly switched on. It was Dante, very unnerved by the sight of his mother on the floor, crying by herself. He quickly came to her side to help her up when the smell of urine and shit hit him. He offered to call Father Puzo for help, but she only pushed him aside. She screamed at him to leave her alone. He didn't pay any attention to those commands and held her. He wanted to hold her until she wasn't crazy anymore.

After a few minutes, it seemed to be working. Camilla stopped crying and shouting. The young man was pleased that he was able to help in this moment of weakness. He was unaware that she had quieted down so she could hear Angelo talking to her from across the room.

"I have to leave. Tomorrow night I'll show you where you can find her and her Hell-spawn. Can I count on you?"

"Yes! Yes!" She repeated as she cried on her son's shoulder.

CHAPTER THIRTEEN

FRIDAY NIGHT

Camilla waited patiently for the ghost of her husband to appear. She spent the day cleaning up the house, preparing dinner for her son, and having her hair cut so that it wouldn't hinder her ability to kill the demons that had been feeding on his soul. She sat at the kitchen table, dressed in black capri pants, a black blouse, and flats. The table was bare, with the exception of her olive colored purse.

"Are you ready, my love?" Angelo's voice sounded like he was sitting across from her at the table, but he was nowhere to be seen. Camilla nodded yes, so that her son in the next room wouldn't think she was talking to herself again.

"Good. Go to the car." Camilla didn't hesitate and didn't stop as she said goodbye to Dante.

"I'm going out with Martina, there's food for you in the refrigerator. Goodnight." It was so casual she almost believed it herself.

"Goodnight, Mamma." He laughed at how she marched out the door. She was going out with friends and starting a new job on Monday. Dante finally felt like everything was going to be all right.

Lucia gazed out of the passenger window, watching the lights of the city go by. The Mercedes was quiet. Lane didn't speak, as usual, Dominic was reading the Striga Bible, and Ursula sat on the other side of him in her own little world. Lucia no longer felt like going to this high society party that Ursula had been talking up for the past few days. She just wanted to be home with her children. She poked Dominic in his side.

"I'm bored. Talk to me."

"About what?" He was annoyed that she had made him lose his place.

"I don't know. About anything!"

"Well, there are some interesting things in this Striga religion."

"Never mind," Lucia groaned.

"Oh, what's wrong?"

"You know how I feel about religion."

"But this is different."

"How is this different?"

"In other religions, there is no proof, but in Striga we are the proof." He stated it so clearly that Lucia figured that he was reading it straight from his bible or he was quoting Ursula.

"Why were you a Catholic?" she asked.

Dominic had never heard such a question before. He was uncertain of how to answer.

"I don't understand."

"What made being a catholic better than any other religion? Why weren't you a Christian or a Jew?"

Dominic thought about this for a few seconds. Only the sounds of the car running over bumps in the road could be heard. He looked Lucia square in the eye.

"I don't know. I suppose it had something to do with being raised in Rome by Catholics."

"That is exactly my point! If you were raised in Egypt, you'd be something else. Isn't it funny how every 'chosen people' just so happened to be born in the right place. The Greeks lived under Mount Olympus, which was home to their gods, and the Hindus were luckily to be from India, otherwise they may never have heard of their god. The list goes on and vampires are no different. They're more powerful than humans so they must be the 'chosen ones.'"

Dominic let Lucia's ideas sink in for a few seconds before responding. This new religion allowed him to feel even closer to Jesus than before.

"I don't know. If religion is meaningless, then why does the cross hurt us?"

Lucia folded her arms. Dominic had struck on something that had been bothering her since the cross incident with their friend Rosa.

"I've been wondering about that. The cross hurt you more than it did me." Lucia hated to admit it, but she had no clever answer for him.

"Perhaps you were christened as a baby?" he asked.

"I don't know." She had no idea if she had been or not. She knew very little of her natural parents. If they had baptized or christened her, would this give credence to Catholic or Strigori beliefs? She hoped not.

Dominic turned to Ursula, curious on her thoughts regarding the effects of the cross on non-believer vampires.

"Ursula? What do you think of all this?"

Ursula didn't answer him. Her eyes were open, staring out at nothing. Her mind was elsewhere, a few miles to the east to be exact.

She quietly watched Camilla driving the very same car her husband had been killed in. The smell of cleaning products was such a strong presence that she kept the windows open. The woman was by herself, talking to the disembodied voice that she thought was her husband. She nervously rambled on about how much she missed him. Camilla only stopped talking when Angelo would interject with a "turn left here," and a "stay in this lane."

Ursula knew that she would momentarily lose her hold on Camilla once she and the Divitas reached the party.

"Camilla, do you know where Via Veneto is?" Angelo interrupted a story about their son's birth.

"I think so. That's where all the cafes are."

"Good. I must return for a moment so that the demons think I'm still their prisoner. I'll rejoin you once you are there."

Angelo was gone once again. The empty feeling that spread through the car was difficult for her to take, but she wasn't going to cry this time. He needed her to be strong on this night and she wasn't about to let him down.

Lane parked the Mercedes directly in front of a house that was all glass and curves, a very modern looking structure, surrounded by a vast forest. The party had already been going on for a few hours. The front yard had been transformed into a parking lot. A chorus of laughter and cheers came from inside the newly built mansion.

The host of the affair was the home's owner, a man known only as Carmine, although anyone could easily look up his last name if they really cared. He operated one of Italy's foremost fashion magazines.

When his three newest party guests entered the room, Carmine eagerly made his way to greet them. Ursula, dressed in white top hat and tails, entered the party as if she owned the house and everyone in it.

Carmine had known that she was a vampire for years, but these two new companions of hers were to die for. He was easily impressed with Lucia's red, sequined dress, belted at the waist, with a slit running down her right leg. He guessed that it was sheer willpower that kept her breasts from spilling out of the top. Dominic's black suit was missing its tie and his open shirt gave him a feral masculinity. It was Carmine's notion that loving a single gender was too closed minded. He would give anything to be in Ursula's position.

The first thing Lucia noticed about their eclectic host was that his walk, which had an almost tango-like movement to it. His hair was as black as his silk shirt and tight slacks, much too dark for a man of his age.

Ursula peeled the little white glove off her right hand so that he could kiss it. Her skin was so soft. He could tell why so many had sacrificed themselves just to touch it.

"Welcome to the party, Ursula. You're still a goddess among men." He glowed at her very presence.

"Thank you, you're looking fine as usual. Allow me to introduce my guests."

Carmine interrupted, turning his attention on Lucia. Dominic was surprised to see someone interrupt Ursula and live. Carmine kissed Lucia's hand as well. Normally, she hated it when strangers touched her; however she couldn't help but be amused by his campy charm.

"There's no need to introduce such a beautiful lady! Ms. Orlock informed me of your dancing talents. I look forward to catching you perform somewhere."

"Thank you!" The idea of performing again delighted the young vampire.

Carmine then took Dominic's hand and was quite impressed with his strong grip.

"And you, sir. I cannot wait until I can be seated at the very best table at your restaurant. Do you have a name yet?" Dominic had no idea what he meant. He looked to Ursula for help. She smiled and nodded, hoping he would play along.

"We're still talking it over."

"I assume that red wine will be on the menu?" Carmine winked in Ursula's direction.

"Only for the proprietors." Ursula and Carmine laughed in unison as if they'd been waiting all night to make that joke. It was obvious the pair had some history together. The Divitas decided to not make mention of it until later. Carmine leaned over to whisper to Ursula, but was still within earshot of Dominic and Lucia.

"I have to go now darling, but please enjoy yourselves. I made sure to invite people I didn't care much for anyway." And off he went. Such a comment surprised them. Carmine didn't act like he was a vampire, or as if he was under Ursula's control. Lucia asked if Carmine knew they were vampires.

"Lucia! You know by now that any woman can control men using the powers she was born with. Carmine thinks it's rather continental that I'm a vampire."

Lucia couldn't believe that someone would allow vampires into their home just because he thought it was cool. She felt that she was right about humans; they really *are* stupid creatures. Lucia quietly excused herself from her husband and lover to feel out the party goers.

The house was ripe with worthless people. Ursula and Dominic marveled at the manner in which Lucia tempted the others around her. Wherever she went in the house, a small crowd soon surrounded her.

"Which one will she take?" Dominic found himself getting caught up in the moment just watching. Ursula closed her eyes and breathed in the room. She took his hand, prompting him to do the same.

"Can't you feel it, Dominic? Listen closely and you can hear their hearts beat faster as she nears them. If you pay attention, you can sense the blood rushing into their groins."

He could feel it. For him, becoming a vampire was taking a step back from humanity. Dominic could suddenly see everything he had been missing until then. There was almost a red glow in the men and women that gathered around Lucia.

There was a man among the admirers that stood out among all the others. His gray sport coat with huge shoulder pads resembled a concrete suit. His ego was visible from across the room. He wanted Lucia. He couldn't wait to impress her with stories of his important job, or woo her in his Ferrari. He would be dead within the hour. Dominic and Ursula shared a laugh over his impending fate.

"She is breathtaking! I truly do love her," Ursula marveled.

"Yes, I know. You remind me of myself back when I first met her," Dominic snickered.

"Do you remember when you first saw her?" she inquired.

"No, I don't."

Dominic's answer surprised her. Ursula observed him as he watched his wife court her potential victims.

He was reminded of how she would dance on the street corners of Rome as a teenager. He had passed by Lucia and a smaller, blonde girl dancing near his father's restaurant for weeks before he'd found the nerve to talk to her. That day came when an English tourist started to harass the smaller girl. At first, he shouted rude comments at her, but then he grabbed her by the shoulders and demanded that she come with him. Lucia had pushed him away from her friend before he knew what had hit him. This drunken man was more than twice Lucia's age, but she had at least an inch on him in height.

"Pushing around girls is one thing, until you meet one that can push back." The man found himself stepping back, away from the fifteen-year-old girl. He looked down at his shoes as he claimed that he wasn't about to fight her because her dress had cleavage and if they fought, her breasts would fall out in front of the gathering crowd.

"Now you want to be a gentleman? I don't care if everyone here sees my tits!"

A man passing by cheered.

"Come on! Be a man! Hit me! Show these people how tough you are!"

Dominic had watched in stunned silence, along with the rest of the onlookers, as the man quietly walked away out of embarrassment. He felt like jumping in the middle, but something inside had held him in place. He'd often wondered if it was fear that had kept him put.

Dominic had had a crush on this Gypsy dancer for some time, but at that moment he knew why he wanted her. She was brave. Lucia would stand up to anybody the way that he wanted to stand up to his father. The young girl's icy stare followed the drunken man until he disappeared around the corner. Then she turned and looked directly at him. She seemed caught off guard at the sight of him for a second. Her anger subsided and she smiled at him. It was an expression mixed with love and fear. He had to have her.

"No, but I remember when Lucia first saw me," Dominic told Ursula. He faced away from her, hoping she wouldn't see him choke up over the memory. Self-doubt abruptly replaced Dominic's mood as he thought about how he had felt that afternoon. He had always hoped that he could stand up to someone in that same manner. After he'd married Lucia, he never went back home. He hadn't fought with his parents for her; he'd choose not to face them again.

"Self-loathing is not sexy." Ursula playfully nudged him.

"What?"

"You know I can sense emotion. What's troubling you? Are you jealous at the sight of our beloved tempting other men and women? I can assure you that she only means to kill them."

"No. It isn't that. I just...um...sometimes I feel as if I let Lucia down somewhere along the line. I feel like I let my family down. The only reason we have a future is because of you. Some days I feel helpless and I don't know what to do about it."

Ursula stood on her toes so that she could run her fingers through his hair. The gentle action forced a smile on his face. This woman had killed and tortured countless beings, but she could cheer a person up just as easily. Manipulating others was second nature to her.

"You shouldn't feel helpless. Did you know that you will be able to turn people into familiars someday?"

"How do you do that by the way?"

"It's easy!" she giggled. "All you have to do is force the person of your choosing to swallow a tiny, little drop of your blood. Vampire blood is too addictive for mere humans to handle. The blood takes control of the human and they become an extension of you. Once that's done, they will become yours and that is that! That person will be yours until they die."

"Why?"

"It's the power in your blood. Do you know how the Strigori found me?"

Dominic looked back at her blankly. She knew that he didn't know. Only vampire historians were familiar with the tale. She had kept this from him for as long as she could, hoping to discuss it at length once the children were dead and buried, but Ursula was getting eager to share that part of her life with him. She didn't see any harm in letting a little slip out.

"The Strigori found me shortly after a band of Visigoths destroyed my village."

"Visigoths?"

"They were these barbarians that were trying to bring down the Roman Empire. Somehow, raping and killing everyone in my village fit into their plans." Ursula took a deep breath. She had not expected to relive that day -- nearly fifteen-hundred years ago -- at that moment.

Dominic could see that it was still a painful memory for her. He caressed her cheek and told her that she didn't have to discuss it if she didn't want to. She loved him for that, although it did cause her to wonder if he was too gentle to be a vampire. She pushed down her emotions, and continued without appearing upset by the events.

"I was the only one left alive. Once they had each had their way with my lifeless body, they moved on. I don't remember how long I laid there in the snow before I was saved by the Strigori. They took me to their leader. She saved my soul as well as my life that night."

"The head Strigori is a woman?"

"Does that truly surprise you? She was so beautiful. She took me into her arms and released my pain. As I drank from her wrist I felt life for the first time, how it was supposed to be. You see, she was made a vampire by Christ himself. I tasted not only her blood, but our savor's as well. It is his blood that runs through you and Lucia."

Dominic couldn't breathe for a few seconds afterward. Was it true? All his life he had pretended to drink the blood of Christ at Mass, and now that blood might actually be a part of him. He tried to concentrate hard enough to feel it. He wondered if, after all this time, his savior truly was with him in body as well as spirit.

Ursula placed her tiny hand firmly over his heart. She could feel it becoming stronger with each beat, so much so that it was nearly making her fingers numb. When he looked down into her deep blue eyes he knew that all was right with the world.

"All the strength you need is right here. Why do you think they want to stake us in the heart? You should never feel powerless."

Her words made sense to him. He was sure that everything was going to be okay. If only that were true. Ursula could feel Camilla's impatience. It was time to act.

She suggested that Dominic begin to look for his prey for the evening. He agreed. Dominic picked her up off her feet and kissed her. She thought she would melt out of her white tux, but there was much work to be done.

"When we kiss again, I want to taste blood on your lips," she said with a smile. Dominic left her to find his next meal, with more certainty than ever before.

Ursula found a nearby window with a view of nothing but the party guest's cars.

"Camilla," she whispered.

"Yes, Angelo?" She had nearly nodded off when the voice of her husband snapped her to attention.

"It's time." The voice told her to pass all the cafes and nightclubs and look for the large, white house on the corner.

"Pull up in the driveway."

The man in the huge gray sports coat asked Lucia if they could find someplace away from the others. She smiled and pulled him upstairs by his tie. He was going to be under her spell for the rest of his life.

Inside Ursula's home, Isabella, Vincenzo, and Roberto watched *King Kong* with Sachi in Vincenzo's bedroom. The boys loved the film, but Isabella thought that Fay Wray screamed a little too much. Sachi wondered why Kong's fur moved in such a strange manner.

Dominic discovered a curvy Greek woman standing alone on a balcony, staring at the stars. She seemed to be studying every star in the clear night sky.

"Are you finding the party boring?"

The woman didn't seem startled at all. She slowly turned around to face her visitor. She looked him from head to toe with a quick glance.

"Not anymore," she beamed with delight over her new friend.

There weren't any lights on in the house as far as Camilla could see. The thin, dark woman slowly made her way to the front steps. She was surprised by how unafraid she was feeling. It was all adrenaline at that point. She reached into her purse.

"Go in," the voice said.

CHAPTER FOURTEEN

Roberto had to pee, but he dreaded having to get up off of Vincenzo's cozy bed and miss part of the movie. Once the commercial finally came on, he darted into the bathroom that connected the twins' rooms. The moment after he began to use the toilet, he noticed that the door to the other bedroom was cracked open. The bathroom light made the darkness from Isabella's room seem even blacker.

He tried not to think about what could be on the other side of the door. He did his best to ignore the feeling that someone was watching him. He attempted to reach the door as he urinated, but he couldn't without wetting the entire floor. Roberto's fingertips were just inches away as he heard a cracking noise outside the bathroom. Thankfully at that moment he finished up and swiftly shut the door.

Roberto jumped back onto the bed as the three children watched in stunned silence as Kong climbed up New York's Empire State Building.

"We're going to live there!" Isabella blurted out suddenly. Sachi and the two boys were confused by her random statement.

"What do you mean?" Vincenzo asked without taking his eyes off the screen.

"I don't know. I just know."

The two boys tried to make sense of Isabella's prediction. Vincenzo asked what they would be doing in New York. She didn't know.

Roberto asked her when they would be going. She didn't know that either.

During the questions and answers, Sachi heard Ursula speaking to her. Everything in the room fell away. All that mattered was her mistress's voice calling to her.

"Do not speak, my dear Sachi, just listen. I need a favor of you. A woman will come to you and ask if you are Lucia Divita. You are to say yes. Do this and I promise I will love you forever." Sachi didn't speak, she just did as Ursula had requested. She smiled and nodded to no one and tears formed in her eyes.

The children failed to notice Sachi's emotional state. They were too busy talking about New York. Isabella had no idea how to handle their questions. She couldn't see anything; it was just something that she knew. The boys didn't understand why their sister had made such a prediction. The moment was interrupted by three solid knocks at the bedroom door.

All three children fell silent. Normally, a member of the staff would knock, quickly followed by "may I come in?" That wasn't the case this time. There was no cheerful greeting, just three more knocks slowly delivered on the door. Sachi didn't hesitate when getting up to answer the door. Roberto wanted to stop her, but the words wouldn't form in his mouth. He knew that this was it. Someone or something had come for them. He moved back a few inches pulling the confused Vincenzo and Isabella by the hands.

Sachi cracked open the door. The children couldn't see the face of the person through their nanny's back. The hallway light had been turned off. It must have been dark all over the mansion. Roberto switched off the TV to hear their conversation better.

"Are you Lucia Divita?" the woman at the door asked.

"Why, yes. I am," the nanny smiled.

The bedroom door swung open with enough force that it the

doorknob wedged in the wall. Camilla flashed a large kitchen knife over her head. She brought it down with all her might into Sachi's chest. The scream Camilla emitted was high pitched and nearly inhuman. She was able to stab Sachi three more times before the nanny's knees buckled, bringing her down to the floor. Camilla's primal screams turned into words as she jumped on top of her target.

"Die! Die, you vampire whore! This is for my husband! Whore!" She went on to stab Sachi six more times, screaming "Whore!" each time she ripped into her chest.

Roberto, Vincenzo, and Isabella were unable to make a sound during this attack. They were too frightened to react. This was the first time that any of them had seen such violence before. They hoped that she would just go away afterwards.

Isabella was the only one in the room to notice that Sachi was smiling. Sachi had done what her mistress had asked of her and soon they would be together forever. Her eyes glowed with joy until all life left them.

Once Camilla was sure that the vampire was not getting back up, she focused her attention on the three demons disguised as children. They disgusted her. They had fed off of her husband for weeks, and now looked at her with fear.

"Where is my husband's soul?" Camilla's throat was strained from screaming. Her voice sounded like rusty springs being dragged across a sidewalk.

She leapt toward the three children. Roberto took his brother and sister and dragged them by the hands into the bathroom. He was able to lock the door before Camilla reached them. The angry woman pounded against the door with all her weight. The door cracked on the second try.

"Mamma!"

Lucia's head shot up from her intended victim's neck. She could have sworn that she heard her children screaming. She wondered if it might be someone the next room, but why would they shout "Mamma?" Lucia took stock of the man underneath her. He was in a daze from lust. She slapped him to clear his head.

"You! Did you hear something?" The man seemed unsure of where he was, as if he was just waking up from a dream. He didn't answer, so she struck him again.

"Did you hear something?"

"What?"

Lucia pulled herself off of him in a fit of frustration. He heard her mutter something about him being useless. She didn't bother to grab her shoes as she stormed out of the bedroom. The man begged for her to stay, but she wasn't listening. This man would live for another fifty years and each day he would miss her.

She cut her way through the crowded hallway toward the stairs. Lucia needed to find where that scream came had from. She hoped that it was someone yelling in the other room. She just wanted to find her husband and go home to the children.

"Mamma!"

This time Lucia had clearly heard Isabella's voice. She ran down the stairs, pushing over a number of drunken party guests. Everyone's attention began to shift over to her. Ursula felt Lucia's panic and headed off to intercept her.

"Lucia, is something wrong?" Ursula knew what was wrong, but she didn't let it show.

Lucia didn't answer, she just kept looking around the house for her husband. Dominic connected with Lucia from across the room. Without a word between them, they raced from the party.

"I'm sure there isn't..." Ursula tried to calm their nerves, but Dominic and Lucia weren't even paying attention to her. Ursula couldn't hold back the anger rising from her gut. Her hair stood up on end and her fangs were showing.

"You will stay here!"

Lucia and Dominic ran out the front door. They took big, leaping steps across the gravel driveway of Carmine's home. Lane had been leaning up against the car, enjoying a smoke, when he saw them approaching. He had felt the change in Ursula's mood and wasn't too surprised to find the Divitas leaving the party so soon.

"I'm sorry, but the car seems to be--" Dominic slammed him against the side of the car. His fingers wrapped around Lane's throat, holding him still as Lucia fished through his pockets for the keys. When she yanked them out, the edge of one the keys ripped Lane's pants slightly.

"I have them! I'll drive!" she cried out. Dominic agreed and tossed Lane to the ground as if he were a wet towel. They got into the Mercedes and sped off, hitting a few of the other parked cars on the way.

Isabella and Vincenzo were too busy crying to notice that the banging on the bathroom door had stopped. Roberto did his best to listen over their wailing. There was some noise going on outside, but he couldn't make it out. He shushed the twins long enough to hear what sounded like metal tapping against metal. Camilla was trying to pick the lock. The only other sound that the children heard was strained laughter, or possibly crying.

Roberto had grown impatient waiting for one of Ursula's staff to come to their rescue. They were going to have to make a run for it. He gave his brother and sister a washcloth to dry their tears, hoping he could pull them together. His plan was simple -- They were going to run out the other door through Isabella's bedroom and find someone on the house staff to help them.

Just when his hand was about to touch the doorknob, the noise at the other door ceased. There was no more picking at the lock, no more giggling. Isabella and Vincenzo didn't understand his hesitation. Roberto feared that Camilla had decided to wait for them in Isabella's room. He didn't want to see her there the moment he opened the door.

He did the only thing he could think of. He slowly moved to the door to Vincenzo's room, carefully wrapping his fingers around the doorknob, so as not to make a noise. He had a plan to find out which room Camilla was in and run out through the other, empty room. Roberto pointed to the door, hoping that his siblings would understand. They just stared at him. Undaunted, the boy jiggled the knob as though he were about to open it. A loud crash nearly brought down the door from Isabella's room.

Roberto quickly opened the door. The twins followed him out of Vincenzo's room and into the hallway as fast as they could run. Camilla was close behind them. The three children could feel her slash the knife in the air just inches away from their backs. They knew that if they slowed down, or stopped to look back, she would get them. The lights were out all over the house and no staff member could be found.

"Help! Help!" the children screamed. Camilla continued laughing.

No one came out of their rooms to aid them. Ursula had given direct orders to all thirty members of her staff not to leave their rooms. They sat on their beds waiting for the screaming to stop, after which the cleanup could begin. The children would have to keep running down the stairs.

Camilla was not as familiar with the house so she tripped over one of the steps and rolled head over feet down the stairs. She knocked into the children on her way down to the first floor. Roberto, Isabella, and Vincenzo picked themselves up. They could see Camilla's lifeless body lying on the floor.

Lucia had the pedal placed flat on the floor of the Mercedes. She didn't bother to turn on the headlights since they could both see in the dark. The car became an invisible bullet that raced down the country roads back into Rome.

The couple didn't speak so they might hear their babies shouting for them. Every second that the children were silent, Dominic and Lucia grew more and more scared. They had to get home.

Isabella was the first to notice the cut on Vincenzo's right arm. Camilla's knife had connected with him as she'd fallen past the children. The young boy's heart was pumping so fast that he didn't feel anything. The wound almost looked fake to him. Before he could inspect it any further, Roberto nudged the twins to show them that Camilla was not getting up.

"What do we do?" whispered Vincenzo.

"I...I don't know..." Roberto had felt like he was the leader since arriving at Ursula's house, but now he was a child again. He just wanted his mamma and poppa to burst in the room and take them away from this monster.

Roberto didn't know what to do. He wondered if they should try to snake past her; but what if she wasn't dead? He thought of hiding until help arrived; but what if the woman woke up and found them first? Finally, he figured that maybe they could just yell for someone; but what if the shouting woke her up?

As Roberto pondered all of these ideas, Isabella started down the stairs with Vincenzo in tow. He wanted to scream for her to stop, but it was too late. He knew that the die had been cast and the only thing to do was to go along with them.

Lucia and Dominic had finally reached the city, which made their struggle even more difficult. Lucia was careful not to hit the other cars or bystanders that got in their way, only so they wouldn't slow them down.

Their babies' screams had been replaced with something else, something that worried them even more. They could smell their children's blood. Dominic felt Roberto's heart pounding with fear.

"Drive faster!" he shouted. It was the only thing he could do.

"Shut the fuck up!" was Lucia's only response. She took the car off the street and cut through a park. It bounced up and down over the ground without losing any speed. They narrowly missed a young couple, having sex in the bushes, by just a few feet. Via Vento was just minutes away.

Isabella and Vincenzo stood on the final step. They looked for clues as to weather or not the crazy woman would be getting back up. Roberto was behind his siblings. He watched them take each other's hands and slowly take a step onto the floor. Blood ran down Vincenzo's arm, filling up the space between his and his sister's hands. Camilla hadn't moved. The children couldn't tell if she was breathing or not, but they weren't about to get close enough to check.

Roberto didn't take his eyes off of the body as the three children tiptoed around her. He knew that as long as he was watching her, she wouldn't make any moves. They hoped to find a staff member for help.

"Maybe dirt man can help?" Isabella whispered to her brothers. Roberto quickly leaned in toward her ear.

"He won't help us, he--" Roberto was pulled away from his sister by something powerful.

It was Camilla. Her grip dug into his little arm. A smile tore across her suddenly pale, white face. She had her knife above her head, ready to bring it down into Roberto's chest. The other two children were frozen in place. Camilla looked as if she was laughing, but she wasn't making a sound.

CHAPTER FIFTEEN

Lucia slammed on the brakes and the Mercedes' tires did their best to bring the car to a halt before crashing into Camilla's car. She and Dominic flew out of the sedan. He was first through the front doors of the house. They found Camilla lying on one of their children. Roberto lay crying underneath her still body. Lucia then noticed Vincenzo and Isabella hiding under a table just a few feet off to the side.

"Come here, babies. Mamma is here now." The two grabbed their mother and held on to her with all their might. Lucia stood up, holding her children tightly against her chest. She could feel their tears roll off their small faces onto her skin. She was almost too frightened to turn and check on her oldest son.

Dominic didn't recognize the woman on top of his boy. All he could tell was that she was dead. He pulled her body off of Roberto, who slowly picked himself up and wrapped his arms around his father's waist. Dominic held tightly to his son. He looked into Roberto's eyes and could see that the experience hadn't broken him. He kissed the boy's forehead and told him that he loved him.

After a few more moments, Dominic leaned forward to inspect the corpse. Roberto quickly positioned himself behind his father. The skin was unnaturally white. He wasn't a doctor, but as a vampire he could sense that one of her arteries must have burst. She had bled out of her mouth, ears, nose, and eyes -- every orifice. Her belly had swelled due to the blood rushing down.

Dominic wondered who this woman was and why she had wanted to kill their children. Lucia had another question, one that turned her fear into anger.

"Where the fuck is everyone? Where is Sachi?" She shouted the open question throughout the room. Vincenzo and Isabella became upset again. They cried that the crazy woman had killed Sachi. Roberto broke his silence. He spoke with a sense of calm his parents had never seen a child display before.

"We were watching TV with Sachi and she came in. She killed her and came after us. Then she just died."

"It doesn't matter now." Ursula's voice came from the front doors and had a grim, matter of fact quality to it. The entire twenty-eight person staff that cleaned, cooked, and dressed the Divita family walked into the front hall and surrounded them. Lane and the groundskeeper stood behind their mistress.

"How did you get here so fast?" demanded Lucia.

"We flew." The vampire stated matter-of-factly. She casually stepped over to Camilla's body. Ursula could see that Dominic and Lucia knew that this attack was her doing. Her pawn suddenly dying before completing her task had ruined everything. The staff was supposed to catch Camilla after she murdered the children, and Ursula would have been there to comfort her lovers over their loss.

"You had to fight my control, you pathetic bitch! Your son will suffer for this!" She kicked a hole in Camilla's gut, blood spilling all over the floor. The smell overwhelmed Roberto so much that he almost fainted.

Dominic didn't want to believe that it was over. He looked to Ursula, hoping that he was jumping to conclusions. Her expression told the whole story in one sharp, hateful glance.

"Please! Please, say you didn't do this!"

Ursula didn't answer him.

"Why? How could you do this to us?" Dominic was barely able to get the words out. Lucia didn't speak. She just stood there and stared at them. She was waiting for the right moment to strike.

"Don't pretend that you're upset over this." Ursula was disgusted by Dominic's hurt. "These 'little treasures' took everything from you. They cost you money, they forced you to stay together long after it was over between you. They only gave you grief in return and, believe me, they will spit in your faces after everything you've ever done for them.

"I, on the over hand, have given you your lives back. I could have made you both gods, and how have you thanked me? You choose to love these little bags of shit over me!"

"What the fuck are you talking about? We didn't choose anyone over you!" Dominic didn't want to fight with Ursula. He loved her. He tried to make sense of what had happened, but he knew it was too late. He hoped that he and his family could leave in peace.

Lucia focused her attention on Lane and the groundskeeper. She could see by Lane's body language that they were going to make the first move.

"Yes, you did, when you brought your children into this house. Your love is for me and me only! I will not share it!" Ursula's eyes looked like those of a wild animal. She suddenly seemed unfamiliar to Dominic. He knew that it was over among the three of them.

"We're going. We're taking our children with us," he stated.

Ursula closed her eyes and took a long, deep breath, savoring every second. Lane didn't wait for a signal from his boss. He looked over to the groundskeeper and told him to kill Dominic and Lucia. The huge, gray man pulled a stake from underneath his dirty coat. His first target was Dominic. Roberto ran to his mother for cover.

The groundskeeper took Dominic by surprise with the speed with which he wrapped his giant fingers around his neck. He lifted the young vampire off his feet. Before he could plunge the stake into his heart, Lucia jumped on top of him. She knocked away his dusty, old hat to get a better look at the word carved across his forehead. It read EMET, the Yiddish the word for "truth." She rubbed off the E, leaving MET, meaning "death."

The golem let go of her husband and melted into his own clothes. The spell was broken and he became nothing more than mound of dirt once again.

Dominic fell to his knees, gasping for air. Roberto, Vincenzo, and Isabella rushed to his side. Lucia took great joy in smiling in Lane's direction.

"Be still," Lane commanded. The warlock shot his hand out at her. Lucia found herself unable to move. Lane stepped in front of Ursula as he chanted his spell.

"Gone. Gone are the flesh and bone. Now this vampire has turned to--" Lane was unable to speak the next word. He was suddenly facing Ursula. A second later he realized that his head was turned around.

Dominic didn't understand magic as well as Lucia, but he knew it would be a good idea to interrupt Lane's chant. He had simply gotten up and broken Lane's neck. The warlock was dead the instant his knees touched the floor. Once Lucia could move again, she kissed Dominic for saving her life.

"Take the babies," she whispered to him. Before he had a chance to protest, Lucia stepped toward Ursula. She hoped that her long skirt would cover up the fact that her knees were shaking. The children watched her from behind their father.

"Come here, bitch." Ursula came at her quicker than she had anticipated. Before Lucia could utter another word, she had grabbed her around the throat and pulled her close.

"I seem to remember this is how we first met. Let me tell you something, you were always my favorite. As a matter of fact, I can't even bear to kill you myself."

Ursula leaned in to give her lover a goodbye kiss, but Lucia snapped at her. The older vampire laughed at her own stupidity and threw her into the library. Lucia's body crashed through the doors and slammed into the bookshelves, which came tumbling down on top of her. As she tried to dig herself out from under the mountain of books and wood, she saw the entire house staff crowding into the room after her. They were all there -- the three dress makers, the young man that had escorted her from the grave, and Lia, the young maid that prepared their espressos every evening -- armed with stakes, crosses, and bottles of holy water.

"Why don't you go save her? Are you afraid to act?" taunted Ursula as she took off her jacket and rolled up her shelves.

Dominic wanted to leap into the library and rip her attackers apart, but he couldn't. He knew that meant leaving Roberto, Isabella, and Vincenzo behind with Ursula. The most important thing in the world to him at that moment was getting the children out of the house.

"Ursula, please let us go. If you loved us at all, please--" Dominic wasn't able to utter another word because Ursula had her hand around his neck. Her thumb stabbed into his throat just under his Adam's apple. The children screamed, but were frozen in fear. The blood ran down Ursula's arm into her shirt. It was satisfying to her.

"Love? I did everything out of love for you and your wife. That's over now." Ursula then threw Dominic over her shoulder and onto the floor as if he weighed nothing. She turned her attention to the three Divita children.

Roberto, Isabella, and Vincenzo pushed themselves into a corner as the vampire came closer. The thumb shaped wound in Dominic's throat had healed once he picked himself up off the floor. He leapt toward Ursula's back without a moment's thought, but his hands went through a cloud of mist instead. The momentum of his strike took him face down in front of Roberto. His eyes met his son's for a brief second. The helplessness expression on Roberto's face quickly turned to horror as he looked behind his father.

A tiny hand ripped into Dominic's right shoulder and flipped him over. Ursula wrapped her short legs around him, pinning his arms to his sides. She was vastly stronger and was able to keep him still. She hit him in the face with enough force to push the cartilage in his nose back to his brain. A human would have died. A vampire would recover in seconds, but still felt the pain. What Ursula cherished about killing other vampires was that she could torture them for hours, even days, before bringing the final blow.

"Ursula--"

"No! Don't even think you can tell me that you and Lucia don't love the children more than me. Don't give me that 'we love them differently than you' bullshit! You and Lucia heard those little shits calling out to you at the party! You've only been vampires for a few weeks! You shouldn't have any powers of the mind, and yet you heard their screams!"

His face had reformed. There was still blood in his eyes and in his mouth. Roberto and the twins sat a few feet away, unable to stop her as she continued to pummel their father. She punched him repeatedly until the hitting became clawing. Her razor sharp nails tore into his chest. Ursula splattered blood and flesh each time she pulled up her arms.

The more it hurt, the more he wanted to die, but Dominic knew that his babies would be next. With every bit of his strength, he used his legs to roll over on top of Ursula and bit into her neck. He wasn't trying to drink, he just needed to do as much damage as he could. He dug deep. The pain was enough that she unwrapped her legs from around him in order to back away.

Dominic hit her in the chest with enough force that she went sliding her across the room. Somehow, he got to his feet and took his children in his arms. He ran deeper into the house, only because that was the way he was facing. He hoped they could escape out the back way. He didn't turn to look, but he could hear Ursula's footsteps right behind them.

He felt his children tense up at the same time that he heard the sound of Ursula's two feet change into the sound of four feet. Ursula had become a white wolf as large as a bull. Before he knew it, she had caught up to them, slamming her front paws into his back. The children fell to the floor of the hallway.

They looked up to find their father in Ursula's jaws. She thrashed him back and forth like a chew toy. She plowed him into the wall, knocking several paintings down off their hooks. Finally, she tossed him through the glass doors leading out to the backyard garden. Dominic's body did it's best to recover from the bite marks and cuts. The bits of glass hurt even more as they were pushed out of his skin.

He got to his feet again, waiting for Ursula to leap out, but she wasn't there. A chill ran up his spine as he realized that the children were still in the house with her.

Before he had a chance to act, he heard the sound of wings flapping. Ursula flew out of the house in the form of a white, six-foot bat with a ten-foot wingspan. The only part of her body that didn't resemble a bat was her face. Dominic noticed this just before she grabbed him with her talons and carried him high into the air.

The children ran out into the garden just in time to see Ursula take their father above the clouds. They waited, each afraid that they would never see their parents ever again. Isabella wiped the tears from her eyes as her brothers stared blankly at the sky.

Suddenly, a tiny black dot shot out from the clouds. It was Dominic. He plummeted down to earth at breakneck speed. He hit the side of the house, crashing through the wall. The children ran past the smoke and the falling debris to find him in a small crater in the floor of the front hallway.

"Poppa?" whispered Roberto. He was in shock at the sight of his father. Dominic's arms and legs were mangled and broken. He could barely move his head in the children's direction as he heard their voices.

"Ggg...go! Run..." was all he could muster.

Instead, the children tried to help him up. They weren't going to leave him.

Roberto hoped that Dominic would be able to walk within a minute. However, his hopes ended once he saw Ursula at the broken doors. She stood there, still dressed in her white outfit, as if she hadn't transformed at all.

"You really should listen to your father. After all, he has sacrificed so much for you." Ursula pushed the three aside and sat on Dominic's chest. She could feel his broken bones underneath her body. She wiggled her butt around on top of him and the pain nearly drove Dominic unconscious. Ursula snickered.

"There is something even I don't understand about vampires. Do we need to breath or not? A vampire can lie in a coffin for years without any problem. However, if I put my hands around your neck," and she did, "and strangle you, will you die?"

Ursula's grip tightened. Dominic tried to twist around to knock her off, but he was too weak for it to do any good. His body still hadn't recovered from the fall.

The children stood there, dumbfounded, unsure of what to do. They knew that Ursula could kill them without any effort. Vincenzo spotted a table leg that had broken off when Dominic crashed through the wall. He took a small step toward it.

Dominic's vision became cloudy with blood. He could no longer see, except for Ursula's silhouette moving around in a dark field of red.

Vincenzo had picked up the table leg, but stopped when Ursula stopped choking his father. Then she did something that none of the children had expected her to do. She leaned over his face and kissed his eyes. Dominic screamed in anguish. She kissed his other eye and he screamed again.

"Stop it!" Isabella yelled.

Ursula slowly turned to face the young girl. At first Isabella thought that she was sucking on some large grapes, until she and her brothers got a closer look.

The vampire was sucking on their father's eyes. Ursula gave them a muffled laugh that told them that they would be next. It was then that Vincenzo hit her in the back of the head with the table leg. Dominic's eyes shot out of her mouth and landed at Isabella's feet. The girl jumped out of fear, almost stomping on them.

Vincenzo took another swing, but it didn't come close. The look that she gave him prevented him from taking another shot.

Ursula decided that it was time to finish things. She reached down and dug her fingers into Dominic's chest around his heart. She broke past his rib cage and lungs and could feel his heart beat on her fingertips.

"I meant what I said about the power of Jesus in your heart," she whispered. "That's why I'm taking it."

Ursula was startled when Dominic's hand snatched her wrist. He used every last drop of life he had to pull her fingers out of his chest. Once the initial shock wore off, she took his hand and crushed it. Dominic's arm fell to the floor. Ursula was ready to dig a new hole in his chest when a dark figure appeared in the corner of her eye.

It was Lucia, drenched in blood and standing in front of the doors to the library. The top of her dress was torn and it didn't seem to bother her that her breasts were exposed. Her right arm was behind her back, obviously trying to conceal a weapon.

Ursula quickly focused on the library behind her. She sensed that every member of her staff was dead. The room was covered in blood and body parts. Ursula was as aroused as she was angry. She licked her lips in anticipation.

CHAPTER SIXTEEN

Lucia said nothing. Ursula waited for her to make some sort of bitter comment or scream about trying to kill her children. Lucia didn't do anything except give her a hateful, angry stare with no room for forgiveness. It started to make Ursula a little nervous.

While Ursula was distracted, Isabella was quick witted enough to pick up her father's eyeballs and carry them back over to him. To Roberto's amazement, she didn't act horrified about what she was doing at all. Dominic sat up when he felt his daughter at his side. She handed him the eyes.

"Here, Poppa," Isabella whispered. She kissed him on the cheek.

His wife had bought him enough time for his body to heal itself. He carefully inserted his eyes back into his sockets, not knowing which one was which. He felt the nerves reconnect and when he was finally able to see again, he saw the two women in a standoff.

"Say something!" Ursula demanded, but Lucia didn't answer. Ursula couldn't hold back any longer.

"Don't look at me like that. You knew who I was. You knew that there was a chance that I would kill your babies, but you didn't care, so long as I kept giving to you!"

Lucia just stared at her.

"I saved your lives! Without me, you and that weak husband of yours would have withered up and died! You said yourself that humans are beneath you! They're stupid, short-sighted dogs that kill one another for less than we do! Do you really think that these three are any different?"

Ursula began to cry like a hurt child. Her tears failed to move Lucia, who remained silent. She wiped the tears from her face, embarrassed that she had shown weakness. Her remorse for their relationship was getting the best of her.

"I loved you," was the last thing Ursula said before something snapped deep inside her. Her hair stood up on end, her teeth became fangs, and her nails turned into claws. Her eyes glowed yellow and looked more like those of a wild beast than of a human. She leapt toward Lucia as she let out a deep, guttural howl that could be heard a mile away.

Lucia stood her ground. She pulled a wooden cross out from behind her back, putting it up to her face. Ursula came to a complete halt. Fear overtook her, causing her to trip and fall backwards.

It was a sight that she thought she would never see. A vampire with fangs exposed, holding a cross, but without feeling any pain. The bottom of the cross bad been sharpened into a point. Ursula's eyes burned, her knees were weak, and she became nauseous. Dominic looked away since the cross still tore at him as well.

"How...could you do this?" Ursula stuttered.

"I've been thinking about it ever since our friend came at Dominic and myself with a cross. Why doesn't it hurt me as much as it did him? After wondering for weeks, it came to me just before I ripped apart your familiars. I don't believe."

This confused both Dominic and Ursula. The words swam through their heads, trying to make sense. Lucia could tell that they didn't understand, so she continued.

"I wasn't raised to believe in this. The cross isn't a symbol of good or evil, to me it's just two sticks put together. Even vampires who aren't religious are affected because everyone says it's going to hurt them.

"Look at you now, this is killing you. I bet that even if you tried not believing right now, it wouldn't work. That would mean everything you believe is wrong, and you'd rather die than have that happen."

Ursula threw up what seemed like an endless amount of red. After a minute she attempted to get to her feet, but once she looked at the cross again she vomited a second time. She fell back down, cowering at Lucia's feet, covered in her own sick.

"You disgust me," Lucia spat. She looked over to Dominic, who was shielding his eyes from the cross. She was disappointed that he hadn't learned anything from this experience.

"Dominic! I want you to take the children outside. I don't want them to see this."

"Right. We wouldn't want them to see anything that might upset them," he joked.

"Shut up! When you come back, bring some gasoline."

"Where would I find gasoline?" he asked.

"I don't fucking know! Try the garage or the groundskeeper's shack!"

No words passed between Lucia and Ursula as Dominic rummaged around the grounds for a gas can. The three children followed him around. They wouldn't leave their parent's side that night. Soon, he found a can behind a tire in the garage. He ordered the children to stay outside by the front door and wait for them to return.

Vincenzo, Isabella, and Roberto watched from a narrow window next to the door as their father pour gas all over the floor and furniture. Dominic searched his pockets, but he was out of matches. He found a silver lighter inside Lane's jacket. He flipped the top open, but hesitated because of Ursula's sobbing. He knew that doing this meant that it was truly over.

"Pl...please! Please don't do this! I'm sorry...I love you both. I...just didn't want to lose you. I'm sorry! I love you so much, Lucia! Please!" Ursula's pleas failed to move Lucia. She looked down at her former lover with an icy cold stare of disgust and disappointment. She wondered how she could have been so wrong about a person. Ursula's tears just fueled her anger.

"I love you, don't do this--" Lucia shushed her and bent down on one knee. She reached behind Ursula's head forcing her to look her square in the eye. Dominic eased his grip on the lighter.

Lucia stabbed Ursula in the heart with the sharpened end of the cross. Ursula's screams could be heard from down the street. The windows on the first floor shattered, nearly cutting the children up. Dominic couldn't look at Lucia and Ursula as he tossed the lighter into the gasoline puddle in the middle of the room. Lucia pulled the cross out of Ursula and gripped it with both hands.

"No! Please, Lucia! No!" Blood spurted out of Ursula's mouth, still surprised that she'd actually gone through with stabbing her.

She pierced Ursula's chest with all her might. The cross punched through her heart and out of her of back, nailing her to the floor.

Ursula's screams sounded like the wails of a dying animal. The fire spread quickly up the walls and into the library. Soon, it reached the second floor. Dominic took off his jacket and covered Lucia with it as he pulled her out of the house.

Dominic picked up Isabella, and Vincenzo jumped into his mother's arms. Each parent took one of Roberto's hands. The Divita family walked away feeling the heat from the burning mansion on their backs. No one said a word. Isabella and Vincenzo gave each other a knowing smile. They knew at that moment that their mamma and poppa were the best vampires ever.

INTERLUDE

1943 was hard on everyone. France and Poland were under German occupation and England was in near ruins. The Americans had been in the war for a year and a half, increasing the pressure on the Germans, who in turn were pushing their Jewish population into death camps as fast as they could. In the middle of all of this was a young Gypsy woman named Nadia.

She was a short, frail girl with large eyes and beautiful black hair. Nadia was around twenty years old, although she wasn't sure since she didn't have proof of her birth. For years, Nadia's family had traveled from town to town, and country to country, without too much trouble. Her father would read palms and her mother would dance for anyone curious enough. Her family had been torn apart when the Nazis took power in Germany. Her parents were carted off to a concentration camp and she was left with a small band of Gypsies, doing their best to escape from under Hitler's boot.

Nadia's new family consisted of the group leader, Bela; his wife, Olga; and their sons, Boris, Emil, and Ferdinand. Bela was an old man who had taught Nadia's father how to read palms. Olga's specialty was a snake dance, which she hoped to pass on to Nadia since she had no daughters of her own. The six of them had been able to sneak out of Germany and into Italy, only to find themselves in the middle of gunfire.

They would have all been killed if they hadn't convinced a man to give them a ride in the back of his delivery truck. The driver, Alfonso, had found them trying to sneak into his truck just as he had finished bringing food and supplies for the troops protecting the borders. He waved them out of the back.

"I'm sorry. No riders," he said.

Bela took off his hat, leaving his hair wildly standing up. He got down on his knees and begged for the driver to take them wherever he was going. His tears disappeared into his big, bushy mustache.

Alfonso looked at Bela's striking wife, his young sons, and Nadia. They were all dressed in dusty old clothes and no shoes. None of them looked like they'd had a bath in weeks.

The driver had lost two sons to this war and his daughter couldn't wed the man she loved because of Italy's racial laws banning Aryans from marrying Jews. He was no friend of Mussolini. However, he knew if they were caught he would be arrested, or possibly killed. He needed something in return.

Alfonso would take them back to Rome and in return he asked to have sex with Nadia. Bela refused. He turned to walk away, but Nadia grabbed his shirt.

"Bela, I'll do it!" she pleaded.

"No! I can't let you!" Bela protested.

"Bela, either I do this or we die. I'm doing it." She had become an adult since her parents were murdered by Germany and this was her decision to make.

The trip was long. The family hid in the back of the truck, riding along some of the bumpiest dirt roads in Europe. The vehicle was bare, with the exception of a large, wooden crate that they would hide in whenever they were stopped by soldiers. Every time they stopped for gas and food, Alfonso and Nadia would slip off behind some bushes.

The older, slender man smelled of dough, but he seemed to care for her. They didn't have sex at every stop. One time he simply held her, weeping, and another he just spoke of his late wife. She felt that it was a small price to pay for her family's survival.

They reached Rome just before dawn. Alfonso backed the truck up to a bakery and opened the door. He walked off without saying goodbye to anyone, including Nadia.

"Now what do we do?" asked Olga.

"I don't know." It had suddenly hit Bela that he hadn't planned on what to do after arriving in Rome.

"We should find some clothes and try to blend in here until the war is over," he decided.

The six Gypsies made their way out of the truck and looked around the back alley that they had been dropped off in. There was a line of clothing hanging from a second story balcony. Their plan was simple; The three sons would climb onto each other's shoulders and pick off the garments from the line. Boris had gotten on top of Emil easily enough, but Ferdinand had grown too big over the past year to be on top.

That job went to Nadia. She tied her long, dark hair into a knot and pulled her skirt up so it wouldn't get in the way. Both men were in their late teens and the excitement of a young woman climbing on top of them was not overlooked in their minds. She kept her balance well as she picked some pants off of the line and dropped them down into Olga's waiting arms.

"What are you doing?" A huge, baritone voice shouted at them from behind. It was a man, well over six feet tall, coming out of the back of the building next to the bakery. He was younger than Bela, but older than the sons. His voice shook all three young people off their footing, causing them to crash down on top of each other. The man's tone changed from anger to concern as he raced to their side with Bela and Olga.

The man helped the three to their feet. Nadia blushed when her eyes met the stranger's gaze. He gave her a quick smile of reassurance to show that everything was going to be all right. Nadia stood up without making a sound. Her large, brown eyes didn't blink in his presence. He tried not to notice her stare, instead he asked the boys if they were well.

He asked Bela if they had a place to stay. The old Gypsy just shook his head. The man wrapped his mammoth hand around Bela's shoulder.

"Can any of you sew?"

"Yes! Bela and I can sew! We make our clothes from nothing!" Olga proudly stated, as if they were performing again. It may not have been very wise to brag, since their clothes were torn and filthy from their journey. They had not worn shoes for months and their feet were blackened. The man didn't know how they'd made it this far.

"I need help, but I can't afford to pay you due the war. However, the room over my tailor shop has been abandoned since my family and I moved to a larger home. You can lie low there for a time, in exchange for helping out -- if you promise not to take anything that is." The Gypsies agreed and thanked him for his kindness. Bela asked for his name.

"Why, I'm Roberto Mazzini," he seemed to have said that right to Nadia.

"Thank you!" Her smile lit up her grimy face.

Rome was a tense city. The war was not going well, and the citizens' belief that Mussolini was always right was in decline. Inflation had hurt many businesses across the city. Roberto could no longer afford to keep the hired help he had brought on over the past few years. Bela and Olga worked for room and board for themselves and the others.

Roberto told his customers that he had family from the north visiting to help while times were hard. People were too caught up in their own worries to concentrate on their bigotry.

Roberto worked alongside of Bela, Olga, and Nadia during the day. He labored as best as he could to not stare at the young woman. Her laugh was carefree and infectious. The first time that he'd heard it, he felt weak in the knees. When they spoke, it seemed like there was something left unsaid between the two of them. Roberto passed the girl a pair of scissors and when their hands touched a current of energy was felt by both. The two looked each other in the eye to see if the other felt the same, and quickly went back to work as if nothing had occurred.

At dusk he returned home to his wife, Nicola, and their three-year-old daughter, Lucia. It had been years since his wife had smiled at him the way that Nadia did. The tall, voluptuous woman, with long hair that was as dark as night, barely spoke to him anymore. Sex was rare and often cold. The two spent hours together in their large, brick house without exchanging words. They had become strangers. The only thing that made noise was Lucia.

The little girl was oblivious to her parents' marital troubles and the war outside of their neighborhood. On the day that Sicily was invaded, Roberto came home to find his daughter dancing on the coffee table. Lucia's long black curls came down over her pink party dress. She wore her mother's black shoes that looked ten sizes too big. She sang a song that she had made up about flowers and boys. Her mother clapped along, the only audience for the performance. The show ended once she saw her father come through the door.

"Poppa!" she shouted. Lucia hopped off the table, the shoes flew from her little feet as she ran for her father. Instead of a kiss, she licked his cheek.

"Oh! What was that for?" Roberto wiped the saliva from face.

"That's a dog kiss!" Lucia giggled.

"Well, maybe then I should put you out in the backyard like a dog!" He joked as he carried her to the back door.

"No! No!" She screamed and kicked through her laughter. Nicola stood up and marched into the kitchen. She didn't bother to look at the two of them.

"All right. Dinner will be ready in a few minutes," Nicola said. There was coldness in her voice whenever she spoke to her husband. He could only hear the way she used to sound when she talked to Lucia.

Their twelve year marriage had ended long before the little girl's birth. She had been Roberto and Nicola's last hope to bring them together once more. It wasn't working.

He let Lucia go, the child ran into the kitchen. The sunset was beaming a blinding light into the living room. Roberto closed the curtains, blocking Nadia's view. She had followed him that night, as she did most nights.

Above Roberto's tailor shop, Nadia and Olga toiled over several pairs of pants that needed alteration. It wasn't difficult work, but this particular customer had one leg shorter than the other and he needed every new pair he bought fixed to fit. The three boys were in the back alley, practicing their juggling. They had even drawn a small crowd of children. Nadia and Olga could hear the laughter and cheering from where they sat.

The room above the shop was barren, with no furniture at all, just a small number of blankets acting as beds and tables. The family slept on the floor at night, went downstairs in the morning to work, and returned upstairs at dusk. It was still better than anything that they had dealt with in a long time.

"Olga! Come here," Bela called from downstairs. Olga smiled to her adopted daughter and politely excused herself. Bela stood at the bottom of the stairs. His tense body language suggested that he wanted speak to her in private. She only came halfway down the steps.

"What is it? Can't you see that we're busy?" Olga knew what he was going to tell from the look in his eyes. Bela was a nomad and staying in one place too long was going to kill him.

"We should go soon. Sicily was invaded! Rome will be next, I tell you! Don't you feel it? This city is doomed to fall again." Bela was shaking as he spoke. The old man no longer cared about himself. He just wanted his wife, sons, and Nadia to survive this war. Olga knew that he was speaking the truth. She didn't argue with him.

"When should we leave?" Olga took his hand, but didn't look at him.

"I don't know. Roberto pays us in food, so we'll have to store some up. I'll see if I can find a ride out of town. This time without making Nadia pay the price."

Nadia sat at the top of the stairs weeping silently to herself. She was not only going to leave the man she loved, but she might be leaving him to die, like her parents. She pretended that she hadn't been listening when Olga and Bela made their way back upstairs.

That night, after everyone else had gone to sleep, Nadia broke into a nearby flower shop and took two red candles and a single red rose. Nadia placed a candle on each side of the rose and waited until sunrise before taking the rose outside by a window facing east, or least she thought it was east anyway. Nadia held the rose in front of her and inhaled its fragrance.

"This red rose is for true love. True love, come to me," she said aloud.

Nadia took the rose back to its original position. She lit the candles and imagined the love that must be burning in Roberto's heart for her.

"That love charm won't do you any good," Olga's voice said from behind her. Nadia was startled, but Olga wasn't angry. Instead she felt sorry for her. She had seen the way that the girl looked at Roberto during the day and she knew what was to come.

"Here. We have some time before he gets to the shop. Do you want me to show you the snake dance?"

Roberto arrived that morning to find the two women dancing in the middle of the shop. Nadia had some rolled up cloth, substituting it for the snake. Olga had sadly had to release her own pet snake into the woods before they escaped Germany.

Nadia had her top tied up so that one could see her stomach. The cloth snake had been wrapped around her neck and waist. There wasn't any music, just Olga clapping in time. Roberto couldn't take his eyes off of her.

"Remember! You must use your hips to make the snake look like it's moving on its own!" Olga knew what she was doing. She was well aware that Gypsy magic was no match for a man's lust. Roberto did his best not to stare at the girl's hips as they slowly moved in time to Olga's clapping. He pretended not to look as he went into the back to count the money for the register.

He was hers from that point on. They worked together all that day without saying a word to each other.

He couldn't let himself give in to these temptations, no matter how bad his marriage had become. He wondered how his daughter would react if she knew that her poppa had left town with a Gypsy girl. He was able to distract himself by talking to Olga about whatever random subject he could think of. His hatred of Mussolini was often the topic.

Roberto would escape to the bathroom in the back of the shop whenever felt too threatened by Nadia's presence. On one such trip, he found Nadia waiting by the bathroom door as he exited. Roberto's massive form took up a great deal of space in the tiny hallway, pushing the girl's back to the wall. The two found themselves dumbstruck.

"Oh! Hello," he said.

"Hello," she smiled back.

Silence.

Olga must have been out of the shop, because the only thing that could be heard was the clock ticking on the wall. Roberto and Nadia couldn't look away from each other.

"I want to thank you and your family. I really needed the help around here."

"No, no! It is us that should be thanking you. We might have been killed somewhere in the street if not for you. Thank you."

"It was my pleasure."

More silence.

Roberto felt her breathing increase and her body tense up. He couldn't hold back any longer. He leaned in and kissed her. Nadia wasn't tall enough to reach around his shoulders, so she placed her palms on his chest. They kissed until the bell at the door rang as someone entered the store. They quickly broke away to attend to the customer. They did not speak of this for the rest of the day.

That night Roberto lay in bed, thinking of kissing Nadia. He nudged Nicola's leg with his foot hoping that it would stir something lustful inside of her. She jerked her leg away.

Nadia couldn't sleep. She got up from her blanket to check on her rose. It was dying.

The next afternoon, Bela stormed into the shop with great news. He took Olga by the shoulders and gave her a quick joyful kiss. Nadia and Roberto were also in the room. Roberto had been dealing with a customer. It was the man with one leg shorter than the other. The man was pleased with the work they had done. Roberto couldn't hear him. He was too busy listening in on Bela telling his wife that he had found a way out of Rome. There was a small band of traveling musicians that had agreed to take the whole family down the coast. The group was leaving the following morning to perform at a rich man's wedding.

Upstairs, the rose had died and the candles were burnt out.

That night, Nadia's adopted family went to sleep early so they could be ready for the long trip ahead of them. One by one they all drifted off, except for Nadia. She had to see Roberto one last time before they left. She put on her white top and brown skirt and carefully sneaked out.

Once she was standing in front of his house, it struck her that she had no idea how to get his attention. She couldn't simply knock on his door, or call, or even throw stones to his window since he shared his bedroom with his wife. So she sat there in the yard and cried. To her surprise, the front door cracked open. Nadia wiped away her tears and ran to the door.

Roberto stood there in his light blue pajamas; the shirt had a pocket for some unknown reason. The sight of such a powerful man dressed in what she thought was a domesticated outfit caused her to laugh.

"What's so funny?" He felt less nervous and smiled.

"Nothing! Nothing. It's just...your clothes are very nice." She struggled to form the words.

"What are you doing here?" Roberto sounded a little more serious.

"I had to see you. How did you know I was out here?"

"I just knew. Isn't that strange?"

"No. No, it's not."

"Come inside. We should talk."

But they didn't talk. Roberto escorted her to the basement. They held each other's shaking hands. He pulled a cord dangling from the ceiling. It switched on a single bulb that lit the cramped room. As Roberto and Nadia went down the wooden stairs they feared that each creak would wake Nicola. They walked down slowly, but that only made it sound worse.

The basement was filled with clothing and materials to make more dresses and suits. It looked like his extra workshop. They stopped in the middle of the room and kissed. He was much taller than her, so he leaned down as she stood on her toes. They let go of all of their fear, sadness, and loneliness in that kiss. Each of them wanted to forget their lives, if just for a few minutes. It lasted longer than that.

Nicola was wakened by a noise. It wasn't a creak or a moan -- it was an explosion, strong enough to shake her out of bed. A bright yellow light came through the windows of her bedroom. The American invasion of Rome had begun. Planes blanketed the night sky, raining bombs on the ancient city. The Allies were coming for Mussolini.

Nicola could hear screams and shouts that sounded like they were coming from everywhere at once. Lucia came running into the room in tears. The three-year-old screamed that the world was coming to an end. Nicola knew that she needed to ground herself in order to take care of her daughter. In those moments, she noticed that Roberto was missing.

"Lucia, was your father in your room?" Nicola hid her fears in her motherly voice.

"No!"

"Let's find him."

The house shook again. A series of bombs began to fall, bringing the mother and daughter to the floor. Lucia screamed for her poppa. She had started to think that he wasn't coming back. Nicola couldn't wait for Roberto, she needed to get Lucia somewhere safe -- the basement.

The electricity had been knocked out. Nicola lit a lantern that was hanging by the door, she held Lucia close to her as they carefully walked down the stairs into the dark basement. Another explosion nearly pushed them down the steps. Clouds of dust rained down on the two. Nicola sat Lucia underneath a table normally used to cut material. She gave Lucia the lantern and kissed her on the forehead.

"I'll be back, honey! I'm going to find your father!" Nicola leaned in close to speak in the little girl's ear, due to the explosions outside.

"No! Mamma! Don't go!"

"I need to, baby! I'll be right back!" She stood and ran up the stairs to find her husband. Lucia cried as she hugged the lantern as tightly as one could.

It suddenly became quiet. Lucia only heard her own breathing, until a voice startled her from behind. Lucia turned around to see her father and Nadia. He was wearing his pants with no shirt and Nadia was just in a skirt. She didn't care who the young woman was or why she was there, she was just happy to see her father.

"Poppa!" She jumped onto him.

"Lucia! Where did your mother go?"

She didn't know how to answer him, she simply held him tighter. The little girl gave Nadia a quick glance that seemed spiteful to her. She wondered if Lucia understood what was happening. The Gypsy girl reached for her top, no longer able to look the child in the eye.

Roberto's eyes watered with guilt. He knew why Nicola was out there, she was looking for him. It was the first act of love that she had displayed for him in years. Roberto kissed his daughter on the cheek. He smiled at her to calm his nerves.

"Don't worry, Lucia. I'll save her."

He handed the child to Nadia and kissed Lucia once more. He did not kiss Nadia. He simply looked at her with fear and nodded. He made his way out of the basement without looking back. Lucia screamed for her father. Nadia held on to her as well as she could. It wasn't easy. The child bit and clawed at the woman's arms, hoping to break free.

Lucia's screaming stopped abruptly when a chorus of whistles filled the air. Explosions deafened the two as one bomb after another hit the ground. The house couldn't take much more punishment and shook as if it was about to cave in on them. The lantern went out and Lucia held on to Nadia. Both of them screamed and cried as the bombs kept landing faster, until one shell nearly brought the whole house down.

Nadia and Lucia sat there, covered in sweat and dust, for hours. Neither of the young women spoke. They simply listened to the screams outside of the rubble.

Nadia pulled herself up with Lucia's arms still wrapped around her waist. They climbed through the fallen beams and knocked over tables. The wooden staircase was still intact, creaking worse than it did before the attack. The basement door was gone. The entire front of the home had caved in due to a massive explosion that had occurred in the yard. If the bomb had landed a few feet closer, it would have taken down the whole house.

Nadia's attention was quickly grabbed by all of the people running about. There were men attempting to put out fires across the street. People were carrying loved ones' bodies from destroyed homes. The smell of burnt concrete was everywhere. She looked like a woman stepping out from a dream. She was so busy with watching all the commotion that she lost track of where Lucia had run off to.

Once Nadia had regained herself she found Lucia standing in the middle of a small crater. The little girl wasn't moving. Once Nadia reached her, she understood what she was looking at. Roberto and Nicola's blackened bodies were mixed up among the debris of the house, their faces frozen with a wide-eyed expression of fear. They were there for each other at the end.

"Lucia, look away!" Nadia couldn't pull the girl from seeing their bodies. The girl stared like a soulless doll at her parents, as if she had chosen not to accept what had happened. Nadia picked up the girl and ran. Lucia's limbs dangled helplessly in her arms as the Gypsy girl made her way to the tailor shop.

The streets were covered in glass, bricks, and bodies. Men were shooting looters all over the neighborhood. She just needed to reach the shop to see if the others were all right. Bela and Olga could help her find the girl a home and finally leave Rome. She knew that was simply a pipe dream once she turned the street corner. The tailor shop had been reduced to a burnt out pile of rubble. Bela, Olga, Ferdinand, Boris, and Emil had all been asleep when the bomb hit the small building.

Nadia fell to her knees and wept until she felt like she was going to pass out. What kept her from blacking out were the little fingers running through her hair. She glanced into the toddler's face only to see an adult soul looking back at her. Nadia understood her expression to say "pull yourself together. I need you." She held the child close. Lucia's tiny arms tightened their hold around her, as if to comfort her somehow. From that point on, they were all alone as mother and daughter.

PART TWO

CHAPTER ONE

NEW YORK

1977

Frank Crocetti's head was killing him. He'd had a bit too much to drink the night before, only to wake up with a kid screaming in the next room and someone banging at the door. He pushed Nancy off the bed, hoping that would prompt her to shut her child up and get the door. The young dancer picked herself off the floor and grabbed one of Frank's shirts to cover herself. Her dyed blonde hair still smelled like the club she had been working at for the past year.

Nancy did her best to step over the toys and beer cans that littered the small, two bedroom apartment. She could barely see with the bright light coming in from the half open blinds. She wasn't ready to face the day. Nancy poked her head into her five-year-old son's room.

"Jason! Shut up! If you want breakfast, you'll shut up while Mommy has company over!"

The boy's huge, green eyes widened under his long, brown bangs. He decided to calm down instead of getting another beating. He would have to tell his mother about the cut on his finger some other time.

Nancy unlocked all five locks on her door and let the two large gentlemen inside. Both were heavyset, Italian men in their thirties, with large, meaty faces, and short, dark hair. The only way to tell them apart was their clothes; one wore a blue suit and the other sported a gray suit. They hated to wear suits on a such a hot June day, but they had business to do.

Nancy kissed the man in the blue suit.

"Hey there, Ricky! How's your boy?"

"Still stupid. Is Frank in there?"

"Oh, yeah. Do you and Tommy want some coffee? I'm gonna make some."

Ricky waved his hand to say "no thanks" and the two men stepped into the bedroom. Frank was sound asleep, face down, draped fully naked across the bed. Tommy picked up what he hoped were Frank's pants and threw them onto his head. He was aiming for his butt.

"Hey! Frank! Get up. We got work to do," Ricky shouted.

"Work? God, damn it! What time is it?" Frank mumbled under his pillow.

"We're so sorry to wake you up at the crack of noon! We got some places to go today. Come on, we're late as it is already!" Ricky said.

Frank rolled over onto his back. Tommy looked away so that he wouldn't see his penis. He lay there for another minute before attempting to move off the bed. He suddenly realized that he was nude in front of his men and reached for his briefs that lay nearby.

"Smoke," he mumbled to Ricky, who tossed him a cigarette. Tommy handed him his lighter. He took a few puffs and was ready to face the day. Frank took his shirt back from Nancy, who didn't mind being naked in front of the other men, since they saw her at the strip club almost every night anyway. Frank grabbed her by the hair as he kissed her and wrapped his meaty hand around her bare buttocks.

"See me at the club tonight, baby? I work from eight to four."

"Yeah, that is if I can get away from that fucking bitch for two minutes."

The three men had a lot of work to do that day and they were getting off to a late start. They worked out their plan at a dark and smoky cafe on Mulberry Street. Frank always sat at the same table; in the back, facing the door. This would mainly be a collection day. There were four businesses that were due for a visit, two that were overdue, and one new contact -- a disco, of all things.

New York had devolved over the years. The town was touched on every level by crime. Drug pushers and prostitutes were clearly visible on every other block. Gangs ran wild like packs of wolves. A killer known only as the "Son of Sam" made just walking outside at night a risky venture. Graffiti watched over the entire city. The art covered walls, even the inside of subway trains, making many people feel like the hands of others were closing their grip on them.

Frank, Ricky, and Tommy walked without fear through all of it. They were all associates of Joey Paparazzo. Joey was a Mafia boss. He owned most of the prostitutes that walked up and down Broadway and the surrounding streets. He also owned a good deal of the porno theaters, nightclubs, and strip clubs, as well as the drug pushers. He owned it all and Frank was responsible for making sure that the smaller businesses kept in line.

The first two shops paid, so it was mainly a light day. There was a proprietor of a liquor store that wouldn't have the money for another three days, so Tommy and Ricky broke three fingers on his teenage son's right hand. Frank told him that there better not be a fourth day. This got them pumped up for their last visit.

They had attempted to make contact with the disco on West 28th Street twice before, but were unable to find the owners. They would have to be more aggressive this time.

The disco was a four-story building that had once been a movie theater, called The Mystery Theater. The Mystery had gone bust in the sixties, and had been a porno house for a few years, until it was bought out in the summer of '76. The Inferno had opened in early March of

1977 as the largest new disco in New York and had become second only to Studio 54 in popularity. Joey Paparazzo had been paid for protection of the porno house and he thought it was only fair that this new business kept up the deal.

No one answered when Frank knocked on the glass doors. He knocked again, almost hard enough to break the glass. Tommy and Ricky got a look at the outside of the disco as they waited. The building still looked much like it had during the thirties. Its name was boldly displayed on a giant sign surrounded by lights. There was even a spotlight sitting by the door to let people all around the city know that they were open.

Finally, a young woman noticed Frank and the others standing out front and came to the door to greet them. The average looking girl had red hair that ended just below her ears. Her pale white skin and black framed glasses gave him reason think that she would be a nerdy pushover. She unlocked the door. She was wearing the company uniform of black pants and a bright red shirt.

"Umm...hello? Can I help you?" The young hostess's voice sounded rather meek to Frank.

"What's your name, sweetheart?"

"Zoe."

"Zoe what?" She didn't respond. Frank asked the question again, this time he raised his voice. "Zoe what?"

"Zoe Strickland!" the young girl squeaked.

"Well, Zoe Strickland, we're here to see the owner. Can you bring him out please?"

"Oh! Well, I'm sorry, but he and his wife aren't here right now. Maybe you could leave a message? They could call you back--"

"Look, sweetheart, that's what the other hostess told us yesterday. We want to see the owners now!" Frank gripped his meaty fingers around the edge of the door. This made her even more nervous than she'd already been.

"Now, you get your fat ass back there and bring the owner out. Do you hear me, you little bitch?" Zoe was frozen in fear. She didn't understand why he was being so awful to her.

Frank's patience had run out. He pushed the hostess backwards onto the lobby floor, then he and the other men walked in like an invading force. He squatted down next to the young woman, grasping her by the jaw.

"I thought I could just ask nicely, but you had to give me some bullshit! You little bitch! Now get him out here!"

A tall Italian man stepped out from behind the red satin curtains that draped the lobby. Frank stopped what he was doing once he caught sight of him. He stood up and readjusted himself to address the newcomer.

"Are you Mr. Divita?"

"I'm a 'Mr. Divita,' but I don't think I'm the one you're looking for." He helped the young woman to her feet. She scurried off to the ladies' room.

"Oh, right!" It suddenly dawned on him that the man was too young to own a nightclub. "You're his son. Is your father here? I have some business to discuss with him?"

"Yeah, no kidding! My parents run a disco. They work all night and they sleep all day. They won't be here until after 9pm. Why don't you come back then?"

Frank gave him a cold, dead stare. He didn't want to leave and come back. He wanted to see Nancy at the club later. But, he guessed that there wasn't any other way to see Divita except at night. He took a quick half step in order to startle the young man. He didn't budge, since he had seen much scarier things than a middle aged mobster.

"All right, but they better fucking be here."

"They will."

The three men slowly exited the building, hoping not to look like they were forced out in any way. The young man didn't take his eyes off of them until they had disappeared into the city. He exhaled once they were gone. He thought for a moment about what he was going to tell his parents, until he remembered the hostess. He made his way to the door of the women's bathroom and politely knocked.

"Umm...you okay?"

The hostess carefully stepped out. Her eyes and nose were red from crying. The man put his arm around her and asked if she was going to be okay.

"I'll be fine. Thank you, Mr. Divita."

"Mr. Divita is my father, call me Roberto."

CHAPTER TWO

S tacy couldn't believe she had gotten in. The Inferno was the biggest disco she had ever been to. Her friends had been talking it up for the past few weeks and it was finally her turn to check it out. Her friend Leta had made friends with the bouncer earlier that night, so he let them in. This club was similar to Studio 54, but without the "cooler than thou" attitude that she hated so much.

Stacy and Leta had spent hours preparing for this night. They had bought tight new dresses and worked on their hair. Leta struggled to get her Afro into a perfect, round shape while Stacy thought that her cornrows gave her face a stronger African look. They were two young women in search of getting drunk, or laid, or both. Stacy almost forgot this once they stepped into middle of the club. The four-story building was remodeled after the epic poem, The Inferno, by Dante.

Scaffolding had been built in circled layers. The top circle was a small peep show, where patrons could talk with a pretty girl behind a glass. The circle under that was a small bar which overlooked the areas below. The third circle down was a little strip club, three women at a time on a runway. The mini porno theater on the forth circle was closed off from the rest of the nightclub. The VIP room on the fifth circle was a little party room for those who paid for the space. The shouts from the S&M room on the second circle could almost be heard over the music. All this was built around the first circle at the center of it all, the disco floor, complete with a stage in the middle.

Stacy and Leta were awestruck by the scale of the whole operation. The sea of people moved in time with the music. The place was lit by the flashing red lights that seemed to come from everywhere at once. The girls danced together and with any random stranger that caught their attention. Stacy noticed one man above the others. He was tall, thin, and moved effortlessly through the crowd of dancers.

"Hello! I'm Leo!" He put his fingers through his flawless blond hair and smiled at her. Stacy fell instantly in love with the stranger in the red snakeskin jacket. They danced to the fast songs and to the slow songs. He held her close.

"Let's go somewhere. Just you and me!" He nibbled on her ear. It took a moment for Stacy to get a hold of herself to answer.

"But...but what about Leta?"

"We'll come back for her."

Stacy chose to believe her new boyfriend. The two ditched Leta and headed to the back exit, holding each other close. Leo considered himself lucky to find such a lovely meal so early in the evening. The vampire was unaware that he was being followed by two other predators. A pair of wiry, eighteen-year-old twins had had their eyes on him for the past hour.

Vincenzo puffed on his cigarette as his sister, Isabella, nursed what appeared to be a bottle of whiskey. Leo popped open the exit door and peaked outside to see if anyone was out there. The back alley was empty. He smiled again at Stacy.

"This is going to be cool. I gotta' show you this--"

Just as Leo took a step outside, he felt Stacy being jerked away from his grasp. Isabella told her that Leo had been seen assaulting women at the club in the past. She apologized for the trouble and said that drinks were on the house. After a few seconds away from Leo, Stacy felt as if she had just snapped out of a trance. She wondered what she had seen in him in the first place and ran off to find Leta.

"What the fuck was that about?" Leo shouted. Isabella stood next to her brother, giving the vampire only one way out. Now that he'd had a moment to regain his composure, he got a look at his attackers.

The pair seemed to be just teenage, human punks. Vincenzo was dressed in ripped jeans and a dirty white t-shirt. His hair was greasy, black, and spiked, but his earrings looked like a good weak spot to exploit. Isabella's olive skin jumped out in contrast with the short black dress and army boots she was wearing. Her face was much like her brother's, framed by her sharp eyebrows and strong jaw.

"Oh, wait. I know who you are. You're the owner's kids, right? I almost tore you both apart. Look, it's okay. I'm not here to cause any trouble. I'm just here to eat someone."

"That's great. Now leave." Vincenzo's reply was cold and to the point. Leo snickered, waiting for one of them to laugh as well. The twins just stared at him until his laughter dissipated.

"You're kidding right? Every night stalker in town knows the Divitas are vampires!"

"That is a rumor. However, if our parents were vampires, I'm sure they would not allow any feeding on or around the premises," Isabella said.

"This is bullshit!" Leo took a step toward the twins. His fangs emerged and he was ready to kill. To his surprise the twins smirked at each other, as if they were in on some private joke.

Vincenzo ripped his shirt off, revealing a small cross tattoo over his heart. Leo felt his body collapse out from under him. The sight of Vincenzo's tattoo burned his eyes. The twins pushed him with ease out of the club and into the alleyway.

"What do you think I have in this bottle? Booze? How about something more holy?" Isabella took a sip from her bottle as Leo nervously watched. Vincenzo took the opportunity to kick Leo in the groin. The vampire fell to his knees, still trying to look up at them.

"I think he's learned his lesson." Vincenzo already looked bored. Isabella agreed that they were finished, so she broke the bottle on his head. Leo's skin bubbled and popped as the holy water burned him like acid. The water began to burn on the inside as it seeped into the cuts from the glass.

"You're crazy!" Leo screamed at a high pitch.

"Don't tell me who we are!" Isabella kicked him over into the puddles of the ally. He got up and ran as fast as his legs could carry him.

"What a big fucking pussy." Vincenzo laughed.

"That's for sure! We're going to be much better vampires than that jerk." Isabella and Vincenzo returned to the club through the front doors, since they had locked themselves out of the back.

On their way in, the twins noticed three older men who had "mob" written all over them. Roberto had told them about the scene with Zoe earlier. Vincenzo and Isabella quickly fought their way through the dance floor to inform Dominic of their visitors.

Frank was not in good spirits because it was 9 o'clock and he wanted to see Nancy, but instead he had to work. He hoped that Divita would turn his offer down. He was in the mood to break someone's arm. Tommy and Ricky were not men of the 70's. They were more of the era of Sinatra, rather than Donna Summer. The three men were surrounded by young people who were all dancing up a sweat in tight, colorful outfits.

"Jesus Christ! Would you look at all these fucking faggots jumping around!" was Tommy's reaction to his first disco. The two other men could barely hear him. Frank and Ricky were too busy looking for the hostess from their earlier visit.

Their search was interrupted when the lights went out. The crowd on the dance floor halted and then applauded wildly. Tommy thought he was going to go deaf from the high pitched screaming. Spotlights fell onto a white piano sitting on the stage in the middle of the dance hall, a band playing in the background, and finally a trio of the most lovely backup singers Frank had ever seen. The black gentleman at the piano, wearing a white suit, began a song that the audience seemed to recognize.

The whole building erupted when Lucia Divita floated down from the rafters by a wire. She was a goddess in a white dress, complete with gold glitter makeup across her face. If one could get close enough, they would be able to see her fangs twinkle in the burning disco lights. Lucia belted out the song -- Never Can Say Goodbye -- on top of the piano. The song, by Gloria Gaynor, was about a woman unable to give up on love even when it caused her heartache.

This world belonged to Lucia. The crowd jumped in sync perfectly to the beat. Every man and woman in the room fantasized about making love to her voluptuous body. Once she had finished the song, Lucia dropped the microphone and leapt back up to the rafters. The lights quickly pulled away from the performers.

The Inferno exploded with the screams and cheers of the audience. Frank and his boys knew that their ears would be ringing long after this evening. The darkness lifted as the music returned and everyone began to dance again. Frank caught sight of Roberto waving the three men over to an elevator.

"About fucking time!" Frank shouted at Roberto, not out of anger, but only so that he might hear him. The younger Divita didn't speak to them on the ride up, so they talked among themselves.

"You see the tits on that singer?" Frank smirked at Tommy and Ricky, who laughed in agreement.

"I was hoping that they would jump out of her dress." Tommy

mimed large breasts with his hands.

"Yeah! I don't normally like 'em that fat, but holy shit! Can you picture those big fucking tits bouncing around while she's on top of you? I'd fuck that bitch until her arms fell off." Frank started to get into the idea when Ricky interrupted with his own thoughts, so Frank just let speak.

"Oh man! The great thing about fatties is that you can fuck them in their fat rolls and in between their big fat tits. And they love it because they got dick all over them. It's like they got three pussies or something." Frank took the floor back from him.

"You're forgetting that they give the best blow jobs. I mean they're used to stuffing their faces already, so they forget it's you after a minute and they're thinking you're some hotdog!"

Roberto hoped that staring at the floor lights would make the elevator go faster. The elevator slid past the top circle to a floor unseen by any of the club goers. The doors opened to an unimpressive hallway with plain, wood paneling walls. There were a number of doors, but Roberto led them to the door at the end. He waved his hand at the Mafia men, asking them to wait. He knocked on the door.

"Let them in," the voice from inside spoke in a very business-like manner. Roberto opened the door and walked back toward the elevator.

The office was a great deal more interesting than the hallway outside. The walls and the tile floor were burgundy. Pictures of the Divita family covered every wall. The photos seemed to be taken all around Italy and New York. The beat from the music downstairs reverberated through every inch of the room. A long window overlooked the entire night club, from which all levels of the club could be seen.

The thing that struck Frank as the most interesting was Dominic Divita himself. The man sitting behind the simple, wooden desk did not appear old enough to get into a disco, much less own one.

"So you've been waiting to talk to me?" Dominic sat forward in his chair. Tommy and Ricky stood behind Frank on either side of the room. Frank just stared at him, hoping to find some sign of age in his face.

"Hello?" Dominic smiled.

"You really Dominic Divita?"

"I am." Dominic's Italian accent was slightly stronger than his son's.

"No shit? You don't look any older than your son!"

"I take care of myself and I have really good genes. My whole family looks a lot younger than they actually are. So, you want to talk some business?"

"Yeah. No fucking shit, I want to talk some business. You never responded to our initial note, so we came in person."

Dominic acted confused for a brief second. He muttered "note" over and over again as he quickly glanced at the papers on his desk. He found it. The note was acting as a coaster for his espresso. He picked it up and reread it.

"Oh, I see. You're asking for money."

"We're not asking. We're telling you--" Frank stopped short of grabbing Dominic by the neck when he heard the door click open behind him. Lucia walked in, dressed in a black bath robe and munching on a box of animal crackers. She hopped up on a table at the other end of the room.

"I'm sorry I'm late. I just got finished with my first number." Lucia's voice was as smooth and thick as her long legs that emerged out from under the robe once she crossed them. Tommy and Ricky both got a better view of the glitter makeup that ran down her chest and her legs.

"Who the fuck is this?" Frank asked Dominic as if she wasn't even there.

"This is my wife, Lucia."

Frank leaned in close to Dominic.

"Well, that's great, but things may get a little heated, so you may not want your wife to see this."

"Lucia co-owns The Inferno with me. So I think this meeting concerns her as well," Dominic whispered back.

"Yes. Once Roberto told me that you were here, I knew I couldn't miss this. I'm happy that you enjoyed my performance," she said as if she had heard the two men from across the room.

All three men were suddenly uncomfortable because they realized at that moment that Roberto was her son. Lucia smiled at Frank as she broke an animal cracker shaped like a pig between her teeth.

"Look, I'm sure we can all come to an agreement without getting crazy." Dominic walked out from behind his desk. Frank hadn't expected him to make that forward of a move, so he grabbed Dominic by the collar of his jacket.

"Listen to me, you pussy whipped bastard! There is no discussion about anything. You are going to fork over ten percent of the profits of this fag joint. If you don't, or if you call the cops, we are going to come down on you like the hand of God. Maybe we'll break your son's legs, maybe we'll show your wife a good time, or maybe, just maybe, this place gets burned to the fucking ground!" Frank had done this act hundreds of times and this was when the victim would normally cave in. Dominic was the first one to smile back.

"You're not giving me much to work with here, Frank. How about we just let you and the members of your family in for free? Even the drinks will be on us."

"You're not listening to me. This isn't some sort of deal that we can negotiate."

"May I say something?" There was a level of impatience in Lucia's voice. Frank turned to her without missing a beat.

"Why don't you shut your mouth, you fat bitch?"

Tommy and Ricky's laughter quickly drifted off into silence. Only the muffled music from the dance floor could be heard. Once Frank turned his back on Lucia, he heard the sound of ripping flesh and two thuds. He felt the release of energy one feels when a person is freshly killed, it was a sense he knew all too well. Dominic did his best to keep a straight face.

Frank didn't want to see what was behind him. He slowly peeked in Lucia's direction. Tommy and Ricky were lying face down in a pool of blood. Lucia stood, literally red handed, over their bodies.

"I'm sorry. What did you say to me?" she asked him like an angry mother. The mobster reached for the gun tucked in his pants. Dominic slammed him on the desk before he had the chance to shoot her, instead shot Dominic in the chest. Frank kept firing until the gun clicked. Dominic didn't fall and die like a normal person would. He spat blood in the gangster's face as he chuckled.

"You should have gone for a shot to the head. It hurts more." Dominic licked the blood from his fangs. He took the useless gun from his prey's shaking hand.

"What? What the fuck?"

"Shhhhhhh! You're going to listen to me now. We tried to be nice. I attempted to talk it over with you like adults, but you just had to have your way. You had to play tough guy. Do you still feel like a tough guy?"

Frank muttered something along the lines of "Please don't kill me!" through his tears. Dominic was having a hard time making out what he was saying due to the hyperventilating.

Lucia took the opportunity to fetch her box of animal crackers. She walked back over to Ricky's body and turned him face up. She dug out a cookie in the shape of a puma and dipped it into the slit in his neck.

The bloody cookie wasn't as good as she had hoped.

"I take it that your answer is 'no.' Well, I have good news for you. You're going to live through this little horror movie. You're going back to your boss and you're going to tell him about every gory detail that occurred during our meeting. What's your boss's name?" Dominic's question hung in the air without any kind of response from Frank.

"What's your boss's name?" Dominic shook him violently.

"Joe...Joey Paparazzo!" Frank was so frightened that he would have given up his own mother at that point.

"You can tell Joey Paparazzo that we gave his offer some serious thought and our answer is 'fuck you, we're vampires.'"

Frank could hear something going on behind Dominic that sounded like cracking and spurting. He realized what it was once Dominic pulled him to his feet and Lucia put the heads of his friends in his hands.

"Here. Tell your boss that they tasted terrible," she said. Frank began to hyperventilate again as the blood from their heads ran down his legs and into his socks. He had seen and done some horrible things in his life, but this was more than he was prepared for.

"Shouldn't you put those in a bag?" Dominic deadpanned.

"I thought it would be more dramatic this way." She smiled and nuzzled against her husband. Dominic reached out to take Frank by the shoulder, causing him to jump in fear.

"Look. There is a freight elevator at the other end of the hall. It leads right out into the alleyway. After that, I hope for your sake that you parked close by. Now get out of here."

Frank nearly slipped on all of the blood as he struggled to open the door while holding his friend's heads. He ran so fast toward the elevator that he failed to notice a broom closet that was cracked open. Zoe Strickland had spied on this scene from the hallway and quickly ducked into the closet just before Frank ran out. She waited until Frank was in the elevator and Dominic had shut the office door before she made a break for it.

Zoe tip toed as quietly as she could past Dominic's office. She heard them argue over how they had handled the situation with the mobsters.

"Why weren't they fucking dead by the time I got here?" Lucia's voice was sharpened by her annoyance.

"I thought I could reason with them first!"

"They're fucking Mafia! There was no reasoning with them!"

Zoe wasn't calm until she got on the elevator and headed back to the disco. Once she had reached the ground floor, she found Roberto near the front lobby. He noticed that something had shaken her up just by the look of her.

"Zoe? Are you all right?"

"I guess I'm still a little upset over what happened earlier today. Can I go home?"

"Sure, I'll call a cab. It's not safe out there with Son of Sam running around."

"That's fine. I'll be okay." Zoe didn't want to wait for a ride so she thanked him and hurried out. Soon, the music and the noise of the crowd began to fade, leaving her with her thoughts. She had been so startled by the scene outside of Dominic's office that she'd forgotten how dangerous it was for a young woman to be walking around New York after hours. Zoe regretted not taking Roberto's offer for a ride. The city was the Son of Sam killer's hunting ground at night. Every slight echo in the shadows between the buildings caused her heart to skip a beat.

A block away from her apartment she noticed heavy footsteps keeping pace with her. She didn't dare look back, focusing entirely on every tap of the stranger's footsteps. She tried not to think of how he could be just a few feet behind her. A crazy man with a gun could kill her just easily as any monster.

Zoe was actually relieved to see the old homeless bum, Reggie, lying across the entrance to her building. The frail, dark skinned man with dirty, white hair gave her a toothless smile. His yellow eyes lit up at the sight of her.

"You shouldn't be out by yourself like this, pretty girl. It ain't safe," Reggie moaned. Zoe fished out a dollar from her pants and handed it to him.

"Thank you!"

Zoe kept looking over her shoulder as she unlocked the security door to her building. The stranger who'd been walking behind her was a young, black teenager who seemed worried about getting home safe himself.

Finally, she was safe inside her fifth story apartment. By the window was a small, raven haired woman tending to her plants and flowerpots.

"Zoe? What's wrong?"

"I...I found our vampires!" Zoe couldn't hold back her excitement.

CHAPTER THREE

A massive pair of red lips that stood twenty feet tall began to sing a song about every sci-fi movie that ever existed. There were men and women dressed in fishnets and wigs sitting in the audience. People shouted lines back at the film and were throwing rice, of all things, during a wedding scene. This was Vincenzo and Isabella's birthday present to Roberto, a trip to the Waverly Theater to see The Rocky Horror Picture Show.

Once the film was over, the three found themselves caught in a sea of leather clad fans. The mass hit the sidewalk and split off in a hundred different directions. Roberto, Vincenzo, and Isabella were only a few streets away from home so they walked. Roberto was quietly hoping that they would not ask him about the movie, but he should have known better.

"Well?" his siblings asked jointly.

"I don't know. I mean...what the hell was that anyway?"

"Oh, come on! You didn't like it?" Vincenzo hit him in the shoulder, knocking him into Isabella, who pushed him back toward her twin. Roberto's brother and sister each went into why Rocky Horror was the greatest film of all time. They told him that the movie was about life and enjoying every second. The two were preaching to deaf ears.

Freddie the mugger was having a lucrative night. Central Park was ideal for men with money hoping to find young, male prostitutes. Some men even walked right up to him asking for a good time. The best part was that many of them would never report the incident, fearing that their secret would be uncovered.

He was about to call it a night when he came across a sight that was too good to pass up. A couple was cuddling on top of a small hill, looking up at the night sky. He drew his gun and crept up behind them. Before he was able to get a word out, five tiny spikes pierced the top of his skull and twisted his head around until his neck cracked. Freddie quickly lost all feeling as his body crumbled into the soft grass. Dominic sat up from the dead woman and discovered Lucia walking toward him. She was counting a fat roll of twenties.

"Lucia! I heard him coming."

"I know. I just wanted his money. So tell me, why are you cuddling with your prey?"

"She asked me if she could watch the stars as I drank from her neck. She wanted that to be the last thing she saw."

"That's sweet. I left mine in a dumpster."

The moonlight fell on Lucia in such a perfect way, it almost seemed planned. Dominic felt the sudden urge to kiss her on the spot. It was a passionate kiss without any fear or boredom. Lucia could taste the woman's blood on Dominic's lips.

"She was Spanish. Very nice," she moaned.

"I love you."

"Of course you do."

"I want to take you right here." He nibbled lightly on her left ear. Lucia tensed up, wanting to do just that.

"That sounds like fun, but we need to get back before the children do."

Dominic smiled and attempted to convince her by rubbing his

pelvis against her. Lucia could feel his erection, prompting her to wonder how hurt the children would be if they were a few minutes late.

"How about a quick one?" His guttural whisper excited her, but her babies came first.

"Well you can just jerk off because I am not going to be late." They made their way home, leaving someone else to attend to the bodies left behind.

Dominic and Lucia returned home to #10 St. Luke's Place to find that the kids had beaten them back. Their Italian style brownstone hadn't changed much since its construction in the 1850's, with the exception of the many murals painted by Vincenzo and Isabella. Each room of the house was decorated with depictions of the city. The living room featured a scene of The Inferno disco, complete with Lucia singing on stage in the middle of all the action. She would often look at herself in the painting and marvel at how happy she seemed.

Roberto, Vincenzo, and Isabella were drinking beer and smoking pot on the roof as they enjoyed a little people watching. Vincenzo made a mad dash to hide the marijuana at the bottom of a plastic cooler when he spotted his parents turn the corner up the street. He pushed the bag under as much ice as he could. Roberto and Isabella flicked their joints into the street below.

The three pretended they were in mid-conversation when their mother and father stepped onto the roof. Dominic carried a white frosted cake, lit with twenty one candles, as he and Lucia sang "Happy Birthday." The twins joined in, hoping that they wouldn't notice the lingering pot smell.

Roberto seemed a bit embarrassed as his father held the cake out for him to blow out the candles. His eyes met his parents' and they all shared a warm laugh together. After all that had happened over the past fourteen years, his mother and father were still there for him. He closed his eyes and thought of a wish that only he and God would know before blowing out twenty of the twenty one candles. Lucia blew out the last one.

"Mamma!"

"I'm sorry, baby! I couldn't help it!" His mother winked at him.

Lucia then handed out paper plates and forks. After they had enjoyed the moist, chocolate cake, Dominic dug an envelope out from his jacket pocket.

"Roberto, this is from your mother and me. We worked very hard for this over the years"

It was a check for twenty-five thousand dollars. Dominic took him by the shoulder and pulled him into a hug. Lucia kissed his cheek and wiped away some cake that had stuck in the corner of his mouth.

"But...what?" is all the young man could muster.

"It's money to find a place of your own. Your mother and I know that you've been restless lately and we just want to help get you started."

"Oh, Pop! I...thank you!"

"We also have another surprise. This one is for all of you." Lucia sat her unfinished piece of cake down in order to make the announcement. Vincenzo and Isabella got very quiet and seated themselves in front of their mother.

"Since it's Roberto's birthday, and Vincenzo and Isabella have one coming next month, and we've been talking about this for some time now. We have decided that if you all still want to be vampires, we'll make you."

Isabella jumped up and kissed each of her parents. Vincenzo took that moment to see how his brother was reacting to the news. Roberto's fake smile didn't convince him completely. He chose to not worry about Roberto and stood up to hug his father.

"So? Do you still want to?" Lucia asked.

"Oh, yes, Mamma!" the twins cried out. This was the happiest day in their lives. Roberto, on the other hand, quietly smiled.

"Okay! Now let's break out the pot and celebrate!" Dominic announced. Their children tried to act like he wasn't making any sense.

"Pot? What are you talking about?" Isabella was normally the best liar out of the three siblings, but she didn't have a chance against her parents. Lucia caressed her cheek and looked at her as if she was being silly.

"Honey, we could smell that shit from up the block. Now get it out of the cooler and share it with us!"

Their little party went on into the night. The family danced to records, smoked, and finished the cake. Dominic broke away once he realized that Roberto had been gone for a while. He found his son sitting on his bed in his room, reading. His sister had painted his bedroom to resemble space. There were planets and stars all over the walls. She even used glow in the dark paint for the stars on his ceiling. The door had been left cracked and Dominic's knocking pushed it open a bit more.

"So this is where you disappeared to."

"Oh, yeah. I was getting tired. I didn't think anyone would notice."

"I did. What are you reading?"

"Your vampire bible. It's hard to read."

"Interesting choice for someone who is tired."

"Yeah." Roberto was quiet for a few seconds, prompting his father to feel like leaving him alone. As he took a step out of the room, Roberto spoke.

"Do you really believe in this?"

"Some days. I've read that book off and on ever since we left, you know, *her*. I even met a Strigori three years ago. He seemed really at peace. Nice fellow."

"Nice fellow? He's a vampire! He kills people!" Roberto realized it was the wrong choice of words, but they had already been said. "Sorry."

"It's all right. It's all right. Roberto, I know this may sound strange, I know it sounds strange to your mother, but I feel closer to Jesus as a vampire than I ever did as a human.

"You see, I was raised in a very strict Catholic family where everything was evil and everyone was going to Hell. I was a good Catholic boy until the day I met your mother. My parents told me that if I married 'that no-good Gypsy,' then I would not be welcomed back. My family turned their backs on me for falling in love with someone different than themselves. After walking away from that life, I realized that I only believed in Jesus because I was afraid of what would happen to me if I didn't.

"Once we became vampires I felt as if I was connected to something larger than myself. I didn't understand until Ursula told me--"

"Ursula?"

"I know! I know Ursula was crazy, but she told me that the blood of Christ runs through my veins, that he was the source of my power. I still find that hard to swallow, but it feels right. I'm sorry, I don't know if that makes any sense."

"It does, Pop."

"Look, um, what I'm trying to get at is that I want to give you something that my father never gave me, and that's a choice. If you don't want to become a vampire, then we'll support you. It will be hard watching you grow old and..." Dominic didn't wish to finish that thought. "It'll be hard."

For the first time, he truly thought about what it would be like to lose his son due to old age. The idea of watching him weaken with each passing year was painful. However, he knew that this wasn't his decision to make.

Roberto looked at Dominic and saw something new. He wasn't

just his poppa, or even a vampire. He was a man, and a good one at that, underneath it all. It was the first time that Roberto felt he could save his father's soul.

CHAPTER FOUR

Cardinal George McGinnis loved his job. It had been ten years since the Pope himself had selected him to be Archbishop for the New York Diocese. He felt that St. Patrick's Cathedral was more of a home to him than any place he'd ever known. Every day gave him hope that the world was becoming a better place, until the day that he met Joey Paparazzo.

He knew that something was amiss when he failed to see his secretary, Betty, at her desk. There were four gentlemen in his office. Two of the large men in suits stood by the door, and the other two were seated in front of his desk.

"I take it you're my one o'clock. Where is my secretary?" Cardinal McGinnis already regretted making an appointment with the mobster.

"She had to powder her nose." Joey stood up when he caught sight of the archbishop and shook the man's hand. He made sure that the archbishop felt a firm grip to know that he meant business.

"We are honored that you agreed to meet with us, Your Eminence." Joey Paparazzo was a tall, thin man with a comb over and a pointy face. His perfectly tailored black suit, topped off with a red tie, gave Cardinal McGinnis the feeling that the devil himself had just slipped in.

The large man sitting in the other chair fell to the floor and bowed down before the archbishop. He kept muttering about protecting him from evil.

"Do you mind explaining all this?" McGinnis put a gentle hand on the mobster's head as he waited for Joey to answer. Joey helped his friend to a chair and let the man pull himself together.

"My name is Frank Crocetti, Your Eminence. I work for Mr. Paparazzo here. On a day when I was--"

Before the man could finish his sentence, two tall figures, dressed in black cloaks, wearing silver crosses that dangled from long chains, entered the office. They looked more like long shadows than men. Frank jumped behind his seat at the sight of them, causing Joey to be more than a little embarrassed by his behavior.

The two figures pulled the hoods off from their heads. One was a man in his fifties. His gray crew cut seemed sharp enough to draw blood. The other man pulled a cowboy hat from under his cloak and sat it atop his wavy, salt-and-pepper hair. His bushy mustache hung down on both sides of his mouth.

The man with the crew cut spoke with a deep, graveled voice that Joey could feel on his skin.

"I am Brother Amadeus. This is Brother Dick Walker. The archbishop informed us that we were needed here."

These men were killers. Joey could sense it. He looked over to the archbishop and the man just smiled back at him. Joey was unsure if it was meant to instill calm or menace.

"I called these men after we talked on the phone."

"Who are they?" Joey asked the archbishop, but it was Amadeus that answered him.

"Someone that can help you. I understand that you had an encounter with something unholy."

Joey's words stuck in his throat for a brief moment. He was finally able to speak once the initial jolt had worn off.

"Yeah...um...my associate here, Frank Crocetti, paid a visit to a disco called The Inferno to discuss some business."

"What sort of business?" Amadeus grumbled.

"I don't think that's important here."

"We need to know any details that you can give us. I know you can't go to the police about this and whatever Mr. Crocetti tells us will not leave this room," he assured them.

Joey noticed a silver, five foot long broad sword sticking out from under his cloak. He took that as his cue to step aside and let Frank tell his story. He sat down and grabbed some mints out of a candy bowl on the archbishop's desk. Frank looked to Joey to see if it was all right to speak freely about what their business was. Joey gave him a nod.

"Ricky, Tommy, and me, we went to The Inferno in order to get a piece of the action. At first, I sent them a note and they didn't respond and so we stopped by to talk. However, every time we went during the day they weren't there."

Dick Walker decided to roll a cigarette for himself as he listened. The archbishop gave him a disgusted look because, time and time again, he had been asked not to smoke in his office. Dick smirked and stuck it behind his ear for later.

"The last time, we met one of their kids. Young guy, like twenty I think. So, um, he tells us to come back after they open, around nine. Now I'm not happy about this 'cause I wanna be with my family at that time, but I had to meet them at night." Amadeus didn't buy his reasons, but he let the man continue.

"Anyway, we walk into this huge disco. People are dancing and drinking everywhere, but in the middle of all this is this beautiful woman singing some song. She's, like, a big girl; maybe six feet tall; long, dark hair. After she's done, one of the sons takes us...ah...up to meet the boss. That's when I met Dominic Divita."

"What does he look like?"

"Young. That was the first thing I noticed about him. He looked as young as his kids almost. I tell him that he needs to pay us, um, protection for the place. Just then, the singer walks right in." Frank froze there in his story. Amadeus could see the change in his body language. The mobster had become stiff with fear over the memory. Amadeus grabbed him by the shoulders and shook him back to the present.

"What happened next?"

"The singer, she was Divita's wife. She...she...killed Ricky and Tommy, like it was nothing. She acted like it was no big deal. Then... then...she ripped their heads off...and she gave me them!" Frank fell to his knees and attempted to pray. Amadeus lost his patience with him and pulled him to his feet with one hand.

"What else happened? Of all the things you have seen and done, you can't possibly be this weak with fear! Now talk! The lives of others are depending on this!"

Frank used his new found fear of Amadeus to get a hold of himself. He wiped the tears and sweat from his face.

"You're right. You're absolutely right. I've done some things that I'm not proud of, but what I saw in that office was pure evil, straight from Hell itself. After she handed me my friends' heads, the other one, Dominic, he told me..."

"Yes?" Amadeus was confused by his hesitation.

"Well, Dominic said 'eff you, we're vampires,' and they tossed me out. I was covered in blood. It was the worst thing I ever saw. I had to make up some story to tell their wives. Oh! It was awful. Just awful!"

"He said that? He said they were vampires?"

"Yes."

"Are their children vampires?"

"I don't think so. One isn't. I've seen him during the day."

Amadeus pulled his hood back over his head and slipped out of the office. His mind was too filled with the possibilities of what was to come next. Brother Dick yanked the cigarette from behind his ear and smiled at the two mobsters.

"Thank you, fellas. We'll be in touch," Dick said.

"Hey! Where the fuck do you think you're going!" Joey leapt from his seat to chase after the two men, but once he reached the door, they were already gone. He darted up and down the hallway, but there wasn't a sign that they had even been in the building. He stood there, wondering if he had truly met a couple of holy ghosts.

The truth was that the huge, wooden confessional next to the Archbishop's office featured a false back that opened up into a long passageway. The hallway was carpeted and well lit, hiding the fact that it was as old as the cathedral itself. The two men stepped onto an elevator. Amadeus stood in silence with his arms folded. Brother Dick watched him for a full minute before he spoke.

"Now, you've never been all that talkative, but I can see something is bugging you."

"You can see that, huh? It's nothing special, I just hate dealing with Mafia. Those stupid, immoral thugs always come crying to us whenever they encounter something unnatural. They're every bit as bad as the monsters we face. I wish I could walk right back up there and chop his head clean off."

"Well, I don't think you'll be doing that," Brother Dick snickered at the thought.

"No, of course not. He is human after all." The word "human" left a bad taste in Amadeus' mouth.

The lift finally reached a large, gray room filled with desks where a number of men in black cloaks were busily working. At one desk was a brown haired young man typing away on a report concerning a fox spirit located in Central Park.

"Brother Jack," Amadeus announced. Brother Jack spun around in his chair and jumped to his feet. The two men had to take a step backwards due to his immense size. The six-foot-three man was handsome, still untouched by the hardships of life that awaited him.

"Brother Dick, this is Jack Cain. He is my new apprentice. He'll be joining us on this mission."

"Dick Walker? Is it true you single-handedly dispatched Ursula Orlock?" The young man wouldn't admit to anyone, but this meeting with Brother Dick Walker was more exciting than his meeting with the pope nine days earlier.

"I wouldn't say single-handedly, kid. I had God right there backing me up." Brother Dick took a puff of his cigarette. Amadeus took his young pupil by the shoulder, taking him away from his paper. When Jack looked back to his desk, Amadeus sensed a little fear in the lad.

"It is time, young Jack, to step out into the night to face evil head on."

"What is the mission, sir?"

"We just got word of some vampires operating a den of sin on West 28th Street. I want you to find out everything you can about the Divita family. I want everything. Who are the vampires? How long have they been in New York? Who are their friends? Everything."

"And then?"

"And then we're going to stab them in their hearts and cut their heads off. After that, may God have mercy on their souls."

CHAPTER FIVE

Z oe practiced what she needed to say to Roberto in the mirror of the ladies' room. Whenever someone stepped into the room, she pretended to be checking her hair. At this rate she wasn't going to be ready, so she pulled herself together and went to find the younger Mr. Divita. She had meant to confront the Divita family the night before, but it was July 4th and had been much too busy to get a minute with any of them.

Zoe felt herself batted around by the number of bodies that filled the disco. The crowd seemed to want to dictate where she was going, but she fought back as well as she could. She spotted Roberto near the front doors. He was rushing to the elevator with a dress in a plastic cleaner's bag over his shoulder. She struggled to reach him before the elevator doors closed, but a waitress prevented her from moving any farther.

"Zoe? Do you know where the janitor is? Some asshole dropped his cocaine all over the men's room."

"Ummm...I think I saw him at the peepshow?" Zoe's sentences often sounded like questions. The waitress seemed satisfied with her answer and darted away.

"I don't know why I bother. It's all going to be snorted up by the time I get him," the waitress muttered.

Zoe had to wait for the next elevator up. As she stood inside the slow moving lift up to the top floor, she did her best not to think about the all of the blood coming from the severed heads of the mobsters. After a minute, she realized that it was all she was thinking about. She began is sing the theme to The Addams Family to calm her nerves.

The scene that she stepped into was less than easy going. Roberto stomped out of his mother's dressing room. The white dress he had picked up from the cleaners came flying out of the room like a ghost.

"You said to get the dress from the cleaners and that's what I did!"

"I said to get the *red* dress, not this white one!" Lucia followed him, dressed only in her black robe, her stage make up completely done. Zoe could only think of how gorgeous she looked.

"That's the dress he gave me! If you want, I'll go right now and get it!"

"Don't bother! I'll just perform 'Fever' in a white dress!"

"No! There is still time! I'll just run back over there. They're open for another half hour, so you'll get your dress!" He stepped into the elevator with Zoe, who edged back so she wouldn't seem intrusive.

Lucia slapped her hand on the door so it wouldn't close, an action that had Zoe's back to the wall. Lucia was too used to people being frightened of her to acknowledge the hostess's fear.

"What is happening to you?" Her question surprised him.

"What? Nothing! Nothing, Mamma!"

"You've been gone a lot lately. You haven't been helping very much and when you do, you fuck it up! Is this about what we talked about on your birthday?"

"No!" Lucia could hear his heart skip a beat, but she didn't need vampire-sharp senses to know that he was lying.

"I'm just tried! You have me run around town all day, every day, to take care of your business and to clean up --" It suddenly occurred to Roberto that Zoe was standing right there. "-- to clean up your messes! I've been doing this since I was seven and I'm a little tried!"

His comment took the wind out of Lucia's sails. She took a step back while still holding the doors open. She looked at him with apologetic eyes. He calmed down a bit, knowing that he had gotten through to her. A lot was said between the two without letting Zoe in on their history.

"Go. Go get the red dress. I have enough time before I go on." Lucia ran her fingers through his short, wavy hair. She had not gotten used to how quickly he had grown into this beautiful young man, especially while she had not aged in fourteen years. He was, and would always be, her little boy.

"Okay," Roberto reassured her.

"I'm sorry. I just worry about you so much. I…" Lucia gave Zoe a quick glance. "I just want you to be happy." She let go of the doors.

"I know," was all he was able to say before the doors closed shut.

Roberto and Zoe rode in silence all the way down to the first floor. This was her golden opportunity to speak with him, but it just didn't feel like the right moment. She stood there, hoping that he would initiate a conversation, but it wasn't happening. He didn't even seem curious as to why she had come up to the top floor in the first place.

It did strike him as odd, after they had reached the disco, that she was still walking by his side. He wondered to himself if she had a crush on him, since she always dealt with him more than the others in the family. He stopped and turned to her. His smile caused her to feel more comfortable.

"Zoe, what is it? I have to go, but if you want to ask me something…"

"Oh! Um…I…"

"Zoe? Speak up! I can't hear you over the music!"

Zoe laughed at herself for being so stupid. She was about to shout what she needed to say to him when she spotted a man a few feet away. He was in his mid-twenties, but he didn't look like he fit in with the rest of the crowd. His dark hair was too perfectly combed and his tan leisure suit appeared too ironed. The man's white shirt was buttoned down, revealing a large silver cross. It was a design that she recognized.

The man had been staring at them ever since they'd stepped off the elevator. She excused herself from Roberto. She began to call home on one of the pay phones, when she realized that they might be listening. Zoe knew that they had to act fast before it was too late.

Dick cracked open the door to Amadeus's office. It was a bare room that looked more like a cell, with unpainted cinder block walls that matched its owner's demeanor. Towering over an old, wooden desk was a seven-foot-tall silver cross. Amadeus was kneeling under it.

"This better be good. I'm seeking guidance."

"Brother Jacob has just reported in. The oldest son rushed out of the club after meeting with the mother. He wants to know if he should follow him."

"Negative." Amadeus stood and brushed off his knees. He gestured to Dick to switch the lights on. After doing so, the cowboy leaned up against Amadeus's desk.

"So, what next, boss?"

"Assemble a team for tomorrow."

CHAPTER SIX

Dominic was dreaming that he was a child again, watching his parents cook in the family restaurant, when he realized that the smell of burning flesh was his own. He woke to the sight of his arm on fire. Six men in black cloaks stood around their bed. One of the intruders had removed the heavy brown tarp that protected them during the day. Lucia's back ignited in the light.

Both jumped from the bed into a darker corner of the room, just like the men had planned. Four of the six drew shiny swords and guns, with one red headed young man holding out a cross in order to keep them in position. The young man's green eyes never broke away from the couple. Amadeus, a tall, black, faceless ghost, stood just a few steps behind the others.

Dominic and Lucia's burns were slowly beginning to heal, but they were already weakened by the mere touch of the sun's rays. Dominic felt his energy drop as soon as the gleaming cross was flashed in his face.

The man in charge spoke.

"Judas was paid thirty pieces of silver for turning in our Lord and Savior, Jesus Christ. He chose personal gain over what was right. I often wonder what he was intending to use that money for. Food? Goats? Maybe he wanted to impress that special girl," he laughed at the thought. "Now, may I ask you, why did you turn your back on him? Money? Power?"

"You forgot sex," Lucia smiled. She wanted to show him that he didn't scare her.

"I'm sorry you think this is funny. I am Amadeus, Grand Master of the Knights of the Silver Cross. The time has come for you, Dominic and Lucia Divita, to pay for your sins in silver."

"Where are our children?" Lucia demanded.

Amadeus didn't answer her, but he knew that Brother Dick had led a group of Knights into their children's rooms minutes earlier. Vincenzo and Isabella were still drunk and wearing their clothes from a party last night. They had just returned an hour before dawn, so they didn't put up much of a fight. Roberto didn't resist in the least as he was yanked out of bed in only his underwear. All three had been taken downstairs in handcuffs into a waiting black van. Dominic and Lucia couldn't tell where they were, but both felt their children's fear as if it were their own. A call had been placed to the chief of police to ignore any calls within two blocks of St. Luke's Place that morning.

"They're safe now. That's all you need to know." There was a finality to Amadeus's words that hardly surprised them. Dominic and Lucia had heard stories of the Knights, but they had never spoken to a vampire that had faced them and survived.

Amadeus stepped in closer, just behind his men. The young Knight holding the cross kept it focused on the two naked vampires. Dominic wondered if it was a good thing that the cross didn't hurt as much as it once did. He still couldn't look directly at it. The shiny piece of metal kept him on the floor.

"We are here before God to deliver these poor damned souls from evil's grasp. Please have mercy on them as they make their way to your judgment." Amadeus wasn't able to get to his next line. Lucia looked up at the men.

"Fuck you!" Lucia leapt for the arm of the Knight that was holding the cross. It came off from his torso easier than she thought it would.

The hand was still clutching the cross. The Knight didn't have time to scream because, in one quick move, she swung it around and hit him with his own arm. Blood exploded across the room and all over his fellow Knights. Two Knights fired on Lucia as the one-armed man fell to the carpet.

Lucia had been shot enough times in the past to know how to ignore the sharp pain of the bullets ripping through her flesh. But these weapons were different. The initial shots hit Lucia in the legs and exploded the second they broke the skin. Thousands of tiny wooden splinters tore through various points of her body. Each shard stabbed her insides. She fell, just inches away from her attackers.

The Knights held Lucia down as she twisted in pain under their boot heels. A hefty Knight casually walked up and kicked her face. He pulled his sword and raised his weapon for the killing blow, but the bedroom wasn't tall enough for his five foot board sword. The blade stuck in the plaster ceiling. Before he'd had a moment to correct his blunder, something tore him from groin to collarbone.

Dominic had gotten to his feet. The sight of Lucia being taken down so easily was more than he could handle. The pain from his attackers' crosses was slowing him down, but he had needed to act in order to save himself and his wife.

The two gunmen knew that they wouldn't have enough time to reload. Instead, they reached for their swords. This kept their arms too busy to defend themselves. Dominic gave one Knight a right cross that sent his lower jaw flying across the room, landing under Lucia's dresser. The second gunman had enough time to throw a punch in Dominic's direction, but he partly missed and the glancing blow didn't make an impact. This let Dominic get close enough to snap his neck. That left only one more swordsman.

"Search them for markings," Brother Dick ordered. Two other Knights held Vincenzo down and studied every inch of his neck and wrists. They found nothing.

Isabella was crying and screaming for her parents. Just when they had turned their attention on her, the rear doors of the van flew open. Brother Dick and the other Knights felt a strong force pulling at them.

Dominic was in a standoff with the swordsman, who was standing in the light by the window. He hoped that he could draw the Knight out. He'd noticed that his own strength was building, despite all of the crosses they wore, and wondered if he could briefly handle the sunlight for just a minute.

While Dominic was planning his next move, five feet of silver sliced through his torso. He had forgotten about Amadeus. The blade had pierced the small of his back and come out the middle of his chest. He had missed Dominic's heart, but it was close enough to hurt.

Amadeus didn't bother saying anything. He swung Dominic around by the sword with enough might to hurl him out the window. He watched Dominic crash onto the pavement before turning his attention on Lucia, who still hadn't healed from her gunshot wounds. He picked her up by a fist full of hair and dragged her over to the broken window. The daylight was already burning her.

"Follow your husband. Follow him into Hell!" Amadeus' voice was a chainsaw in her ears. He let her go and kicked her out the window.

Lucia fell three floors down, breaking her neck against the sidewalk. She landed facing Dominic, who was trying to crawl over to her. His legs were useless and his body was in flames by the time she landed beside him. Dominic wanted to tell her that it would be all right, but he saw fear in Lucia's eyes and he knew it was over. Her motionless body slowly caught fire. They each wondered to themselves if their children would be all right as they kissed one last time.

That was when everything went gray. Clouds came out of nowhere and nearly blackened the sky before an ocean of rain came pouring down. The sudden storm not only put out the flames, but protected them from the sunlight. Dominic and Lucia were confused over this development. They looked as if they had woken from a night of heavy drinking.

The black Ford van that the Knights had been using quickly pulled up next to them. However, it was Vincenzo and Isabella that popped out of the side. They wrapped their mother and father in the same black cloaks that their attackers were wearing and carried them into the vehicle. Their skin was still heavily brunt from the sun's rays, to the point that they could barely move. Roberto slammed the door shut and the van rocketed away.

It took a little time before Lucia and Dominic could tell what was going on. They only knew that their children had saved them, but they had no idea who was driving. It was a small woman with long, dark hair. Beside her in the passenger seat was the familiar face of Zoe Strickland. The strange woman behind the wheel spoke with a faint Irish accent.

"Are you all right Mr. And Mrs. Divita?"

"No! What the fuck do you think?" Dominic heard himself shout. The next questions came from Lucia.

"What is this, Zoe? Who are you, really?"

Zoe shrunk back into her seat.

The grand master inspected the damage in the Divita's bedroom. Blood was splattered all over the walls, covering the murals painted to resemble the city of Rome. Three of his men were dead. The other remaining Knight was on his knees praying for safe passage into

Heaven for his fallen brothers.

Amadeus peered out of the broken window to see Brother Dick and the others picking themselves off the ground. The storm had disappeared as rapidly as it had rolled in. This was supposed to have been an easy hunt. The answer suddenly gutted him like a Bowie knife.

"Witches."

CHAPTER SEVEN

The strong smell of cats and marijuana hit the vampires even before they set foot in Zoe's apartment. Dominic and Lucia moved slowly due to the burns they had received on their feet as they'd run from the van to the building. The cloaks taken off of the fallen Knights only provided so much protection from the sun's deadly rays.

It was a tiny, one bedroom place with a kitchen that resembled a closet. Dark, heavy blankets covered all of the windows, suggesting to the Divita family that they had been expected. Inside, there were plants whose vines wrapped all over the room; posters of sci-fi and horror movies adorning the walls; and dolls, that varied from old baby dolls to modern action figures based on super heroes and Star Trek, covered shelves and tables. The thirteen cats that called this apartment home seemed to have no trouble navigating around all of these objects.

The family was greeted by a chorus of meows. Dominic leaned over to Lucia and asked, "Lucia, how many cats does it take to make someone a crazy cat lady?" His wife studied the room for a moment before giving him an answer.

"One," she muttered.

Vincenzo checked the windows to make sure they were truly keeping out the sun. He gave his parents a nod to indicate that everything seemed okay. The small woman with the Irish accent guided Isabella and Roberto as they helped their parents into the bedroom.

"Here, they can rest on our bed." Lucia could feel Roberto tense up on the word "our." She knew at that moment that he had a crush on the dark haired woman and it could never go any further. In any case, she would have no time to dwell on her son's heartbreak, as both she and Dominic fell fast asleep once they lay down on the bed. One second, they were listening to the others making plans to ditch the van, and the next it was dark. The couple was left alone in the strange bed, except for the cats.

Lucia woke up first, but she didn't dare disrupt the moment. She feared that this might be the only peace that she and her family would have for some time.

"Can we come in?" Isabella's soft voice helped bring her father back to the land of the living, so to speak. She motioned to the others that they could follow her inside. Vincenzo and Roberto kneelt by their parents' sides. Zoe's friend was right behind them. Zoe herself paced back and forth in the hall, trying to find the nerve to join everyone else. She peeked around the doorway.

The new woman's slender frame was covered by a white poncho and jeans. Lucia hoped that this person wasn't a hippie, because she hated them. The woman stood at the foot of the bed and addressed Dominic and Lucia.

"How are you feeling, Mrs. Divita? The bullets that hit you were specially made for vampires. It took some magic to heal those wounds." Lucia gave her a nod to indicate that she was fine. The stranger continued.

"My name is Morgan. Zoe and I live here." None of the Divitas responded. The silence made her feel rather awkward. "Would you like something to drink? I'm afraid we don't have anything human."

Morgan's question gave Lucia her only reason to snicker that entire day. Dominic asked if they had any coffee, which sounded good to Lucia and the twins as well. Zoe agreed to go make a pot, mostly so she would have something to do.

The aroma of fresh coffee soon filled the apartment, relaxing everyone. Zoe entered the bedroom with an old, yellow cafeteria tray that held a coffee pot, which sat on a homemade doily, and five mugs, along with little bowls of cream and sugar. She couldn't bring herself to look any of the Divitas in the eye as she passed around the tray.

"Morgan, right?" The young woman politely waited for Lucia to take another sip of coffee before continuing. "Who the fuck are you? I'm guessing that you've had Zoe spying on us for months. Is this about those butt fuckers that tried to kill us in our own home?"

Morgan was hardly surprised by Lucia's bluntness. Zoe had described the entire family to her in great detail. She carefully sat down on the foot of the bed. Zoe came up behind her and put her arms around her shoulders. Morgan caressed Zoe's forearms absentmindedly.

"Zoe and I were planning on making you an offer, but I'm afraid that the Knights of the Silver Cross came for you at an awkward time."

"Well, you have our attention." Dominic sat forward on the bed almost spilling his coffee as Morgan continued.

"Zoe and I have been searching for two years for a Daystalker vampire in order to complete a very important spell. An immortality spell."

"A Daystalker?" asked Isabella.

"Well, I suppose there are many names for them, Master Vampire, Elders, and some even call them Originals. I think the Israeli Government is calling them Level One Vampires. In other words, vampires that are at least five-hundred years old are the more powerful ones. Just a few drops of their blood can grant a witch immortality."

"Then we're done here, because Dominic and I have only been vampires for fourteen years." Lucia threw her arms in the air, feeling as if they had been wasting their time.

"We know." Morgan's stare hit a nerve with Lucia, mostly because people often feared her gaze.

"Five-hundred year old vampires are pretty difficult to come by thanks to the Knights. I don't think there are any recorded numbers, but vampires are definitely on the endangered list. That's why we wanted to offer you both a deal in exchange for your help. The older vampires have all the best powers. A normal vampire has the strength of a hundred men, while a Master has the strength of a hundred vampires. They can transform into wolves, bats, or even mist. Their mental abilities are far greater. They can crawl on walls and, most importantly, they can walk in the daylight without getting burned."

Isabella suddenly felt a cold chill run down her spine as she realized how close she came to losing her parents that morning. She climbed up on the bed and put her arms around her mother. Morgan knew that she had the entire family's attention.

"There is a very obscure spell that allows a young vampire to skip ahead years of growth and evolution to become a Daystalker."

"How?" Isabella's head didn't budge from Lucia's shoulder.

"A vampire must drink the blood of a werewolf, a fairy, an elf, and a succubus in order to reach their full potential, without any human blood in between.

"I must warn you, it's not a simple task. Many vampires have given up on the spell due to their dehydration. We have done our research. We know where to find all of the creatures necessary for the quest."

The news of this spell drew silence from everyone in the room. Dominic looked at Lucia to gauge her reaction. She seemed as interested as he was. Vincenzo and Isabella appeared hopeful that they would do it. Roberto sat there, unconvinced, arms crossed.

"So, let me get this straight. If you turn us into Masters or Daywalkers or whatever, we'll grant you two immortality?" Dominic always had to clarify matters. It was a minor annoyance to Lucia. She thought that he was just wasting words when it was obvious to all.

"No. Just Zoe here."

"Why?" Lucia was now confused.

"Because I don't need to." Morgan took a deep breath as she ran her fingers through her hair and pulled it behind her pointy, elven ears.

An energy was felt in that room that caused a small chuckle that spread to everyone sitting there. Zoe almost came to tears as Morgan held her hand as hard as she could. Morgan looked Dominic and Lucia square in the eye. They knew what she was about to say, as far as her motives, but she said it anyway.

"You see, I have lived nearly a hundred and fifty years. I'm a young elf, but I have already lost more loved ones from natural causes than I care to remember. One year they're happy and everything is good, until they just fade away. Humans are such grand souls in these fragile, little shells. They die. Over and over again. It's almost been five years since I met Zoe here. She is such a wonderful person. She has so much life in her and I just...don't want to lose her like the others."

"Okay." Lucia said.

"Okay?" Dominic was startled by her flat out response to this offer. "What do you mean 'Okay?' We need to talk about this!"

"Talk about what? What else can we do? Do you want to move again? Leave in the middle of the night because the townsfolk are on to us? Bullshit! I'm tired of running! I'm sick of being afraid of the humans! I hate feeling that my life is dictated by some lower life forms. Even as a vampire, I don't feel like I'm in control. I'm doing this with or without you!"

No one dared to continue the discussion from there. Lucia's outburst had settled the issue and set the path of fate of everyone in the room.

CHAPTER EIGHT

The three dice bounced across the table. When they rolled to a stop, the numbers facing up read 6-6-6. Isabella cheered her brother over his cool trick and dared him to do it a second time, but Vincenzo was too distracted by the other objects on the table to appreciate her applause. There were lead figures of all sorts of creatures spread about; notepads with attack plans jotted down; and a hand drawn map of some sort of elaborate building, which sat in the middle of everything.

"Oh man..." Vincenzo suddenly worried that they may have walked into a trap. He casually pointed to the battle plans, hoping that Isabella would have an answer. She was just as confused. He called over to Roberto, who was finishing his sandwich in front of the cheap, black and white TV. He walked up behind Isabella and studied the drawings as he took one last bite of his peanut butter and jelly.

"Roberto, what are these?" he asked.

"I don't know. Let's ask Zoe."

"What? No!" It was too late for Vincenzo to change his brother's mind. He had already stuck his head out onto the fire escape where Zoe had been meditating. Roberto politely, albeit firmly, asked if she could explain something for him. He sounded so serious that it made the young witch nervous, even so, she put on a smile as she cautiously followed him back inside. Zoe was worried that something had come up to upset the family. To her relief, it was just about her Dungeons and Dragons game. Her laughter only confused the three Divitas even further.

"I'm sorry! I thought...I thought you were upset about something! Oh! This is a game!"

"A game?" Vincenzo leaned forward wanting to hear more.

"I get together with some friends every week and each of us takes on a fantasy character and then we go on a quest."

"What type of characters?" Isabella asked.

"Well, I play Eve, who is a beautiful dwarf princess. She beats people up with a mace. Jeff, the bartender from work, is Cadmus, the wizard. Another girl I know is an elf, and this other friend is just a human warrior. Kinda' boring, and humans aren't that powerful, but he won't change to another kind of creature. I keep telling him over and over again he'd be more successful if he was an elf or a troll and all he says is 'I don't want to be some blanking troll!' So here we are, stuck in some mud pit surrounded by bog-men and we don't know how to get out of it because it's his roll and he's going to have to roll a high number in order to get us out of there."

"Does Morgan play with you?" Isabella inquired.

"No," Zoe replied disappointedly. "I keep asking her, but she says that she lived that life already."

Morgan had been too busy over the past two days to play games. She had spent that time making arrangements for the journey to come. She'd shopped around for new clothes for Dominic and Lucia, and bought a car in cash, under one of her assumed names. The elf was careful not to bring any attention to her actions. She knew that the Knights were searching the city and its surrounding areas for the vampires and any accomplices.

An agent of the Knights had broken into Dominic's office the night that the Divitas had escaped them. The young man brought back a list of as many employees of the disco as he could find. The next morning, Knights went knocking on the doors of every name they had dug up, disguised as salesman or Mormons -- that was Amadeus's little joke.

It was around seven o'clock when Morgan returned with a bag filled with groceries. She was determined to start the process that night. She was too busy contemplating what was to come to say hello to Zoe or the others. Roberto attempted to help with the last remaining groceries, but all he got was a package of toilet paper. He took it to the bathroom as if it was some great gesture on his part. Morgan folded up the empty bag and put in a box of other paper bags.

"Okay. Done. We can begin. We just need to wait until your parents rise."

"They're already up, Morgan," Isabella's words were emotionless. Morgan heard the hair dryer in the bathroom click on.

Dominic and Lucia hadn't spoken much since they had struck the deal about the spell. The vampires blamed each other for the situation that they were in. The night before, Dominic had even slept in the living room with everyone else.

Morgan was worried that their plan was already coming undone. She eased over to the bedroom door and gently knocked. Nothing. She knocked once more.

The door shot open. Dominic stood there, wearing only the pair of jeans she had bought him the day before. His eyes were hurt and weary, Morgan almost cried when she looked into them. She turned away, pretending that she was embarrassed over his lack of dress. The sound of Lucia's hair dryer invaded the rest of the apartment, loudly mimicking her anger.

"What is it?" Dominic asked.

"We'll be ready when the sun sets. Are you and Lucia ready?"

Dominic looked to Lucia, still fixing her hair in the bathroom. He was going to ask, but he was not in the mood to speak with his wife at that moment.

"We'll be ready!" He promptly shut the door. Zoe quietly came up behind Morgan and put her arms around her. The elf could feel the anxiety in her lover's arms.

"Let's prepare the room, my little Gypsy Moon," Morgan whispered to the scared young witch.

Isabella, Vincenzo, and Roberto helped clear the middle of the room. Zoe dug out some chalk from a dusty cabinet and drew a pentagram on the wooden floor. The twins, wanting to feel helpful, assisted Morgan in lighting every candle in the apartment.

Roberto simply watched. He didn't want to lose his parents, nor did he want to take part in making them into even worse monsters. There was a part of him that wished that the Knights of the Silver Cross would burst through the door and take the decision out of his hands.

When Dominic and Lucia finally stepped out the bedroom, Morgan was sitting on a cushion, which had been pulled from the couch and placed in the center of the pentagram. Zoe stood behind her. Roberto leaned up against the refrigerator chewing on his thumb nail, while the twins sat on the old couch, sharing a beer as they tightly held hands.

Zoe flipped open a beaten up notepad with Wonder Woman on the cover. She found the spell that she had carefully researched in preparation for this moment. At the top of the page was the address to the Star Trek Fan Club and a doodle of Morgan and herself holding hands on a hilltop.

"To these vampires, I present this elf. She has come to share herself."

"Do spells always have to rhyme?" Vincenzo whispered to his sister.

"Shut up." Isabella found the whole thing fascinating. To her, Zoe sounded like she was presiding over a wedding. Roberto was doubtful, to say the least. The last time a stranger had presented his parents with a chance to improve themselves, it had turned them into monsters and his life into a nightmare.

"Her knowledge, her power, her beauty; It is all for these vampires."

Morgan raised her wrists. They did not tremble. Dominic and Lucia each took hold of one of the elf's slender arms. The vampires waited for Zoe to give the word.

"Drink. Drink the elf's blood, my vampires," the words quivered out of the Zoe's mouth.

Lucia and Dominic's fangs carefully cut into Morgan's flesh. At first the blood was smooth and rich, though the two soon discovered that they couldn't stop drinking. A rhythm of pulses overtook their systems. They swallowed the blood so fast that it burned going down. It had been a long time since devouring blood had had this effect on the two of them. Both suddenly missed Ursula, if only for a few brief seconds.

Roberto looked away. He couldn't stand the sight of his parents drinking blood. Vincenzo and Isabella grew increasingly excited as they watched Dominic and Lucia grow stronger as they drank. There was a feeling in the room that could only be described as an electrical charge. The spell was working.

"Enough!" It was the first time any of the Divita family had heard Zoe shout. Lucia and Dominic were addicted; it was actually painful to step away from Morgan's wrists. Once they were settled, Zoe rubbed her thumb in the blood that still dripped from the elf's wounds. She wiped a spot of blood on Lucia's forehead and then on Dominic's.

"She has shared her gifts with you," Zoe read from her notepad.

The vampires felt the room shake as they struggled to stand. The magical high caused both to fall to their knees. The children stepped toward their parents, concerned that something had gone wrong, but they halted when Zoe held out her hand. Suddenly, the world stopped quaking for Dominic and Lucia. They looked up at the nerdy witch, her smile warm and loving.

"Now enjoy them." Those were Zoe's own words.

Amadeus had only slept a few hours during the last couple of days. He had given the pope a call to report about the fox spirit that his men had destroyed earlier that day. Once business was finished on the phone, Amadeus went looking for Jack. He spotted the young Knight at a desk, writing passionately.

"What are you working on?" Amadeus asked in an almost friendly manner.

"I'm taking stock of who we've talked to from the disco. It hasn't been easy, a lot of people work at that place and some were asleep because of the hours they keep."

"I just got off the phone with His Holiness. He was concerned about the Divitas. Have you found out anything that can help?"

"Well, one name is unaccounted for. Her address didn't check out." Jack fished under some paperwork and yanked out a list with one name circled. "She has an address, but when our people went there it was a White Castle burger place."

"What's the name?"

"Zoe Strickland."

"She's the one!" Both men said in unison, as if a voice spoke through them with the answer.

"I'll check city records and see what I can dig up about her." Jack seemed to find a new rush of energy for his search.

"I have faith in you," Amadeus said.

"What are you doing? The sun will be up soon." There was a noticeable level of concern in Roberto's voice. While the Church's vampire hunters were ripping apart the city in search of his parents, they were sitting on the fire escape with Vincenzo and Isabella, watching the New York sky. He was worried that the spell hadn't worked and they were about to commit suicide.

"That's what we're waiting for," Isabella answered. She was too comfortable in between her mother and father to look back. Vincenzo was leaning against the wall behind them. He smiled at his older brother as if he knew something he didn't.

"Having trouble sleeping?" Vincenzo knew full well that Roberto had only been pretending to sleep as he watched over Morgan the whole night. The elf and her girlfriend had been sharing a sleeping bag only three feet from him. He guessed that his brother couldn't take seeing them together any longer. Before Roberto could reply, his mother jumped in, as usual.

"Vincenzo! Stop tormenting your brother! This may be the last time we'll be together as a family, so don't fuck it up!" Lucia's stern words wiped away Vincenzo's smirk and reminded everyone how serious the situation had become. Roberto sat behind his parents and Isabella.

"Mamma? Why are you waiting for the sun?" He took her hand in his.

"Morgan told us that this was one of the gifts from the elf blood. We can now walk in the daylight." The young man looked to his father, who nodded to reassure him that everything was okay. Roberto looked to the small crack of light piercing the edge of the city. Once he realized that this was actually going to happen, he found it difficult to contain his emotion.

"Awww! Don't cry, Roberto! Everything is going to be all right," Lucia said as she wiped the tears from his cheek.

"It'll be just like before," Dominic told him, but he knew his son wasn't fully convinced. He decided not to continue any further. The sun was starting to rise. The light washed over the city like a slow wave. All three children grew tense as the sunlight approached them. Isabella's hold on her parents became tighter. She decided that if her mother and father burst into flames, she would join them.

Dominic and Lucia didn't explode as the rays warmed their skin. They felt as if they were reconnecting with something they had lost within themselves. They had become so accustomed to the night that they had forgotten what it was like to be alive. Although neither one expressed it, both were reminded of their long lost parents.

"I love you, Lucia," Dominic said. Lucia gave him back a smile that was twice as warm as the sunlight they were enjoying.

CHAPTER NINE

Zoe held on to Morgan for most of the morning. When she wasn't clasping her hand, she had her arms around her waist. This made it rather difficult for her to pack. Morgan was still a little weak from the bloodletting. She did her best to avoid losing her patience. She politely released Zoe's arms from her whenever it was getting too awkward.

"Zoe, please. You have to finish packing."

"I know, I'm just...I'm just going to miss you." Zoe had the soulful expression of a misbehaved child. She had hoped that Morgan would be coming along with her and the Divitas. She didn't want to admit it, but she was afraid to journey off with the two vampires. Zoe hadn't given it much thought until she had started getting ready. She wanted to tell Morgan how much she loved her, except the words wouldn't find their way to her mouth.

Dominic and Lucia strolled in with their bags stuffed with clothes. They were dressed casually in jeans, t-shirts, and sneakers . Roberto and Isabella were following a step behind them. Once his parents entered the room, Vincenzo got off of the couch to join them by the door. Morgan zipped up Zoe's backpack and held it out to her.

"I guess that's it. Ready?"

Zoe stared at the backpack and then looked straight over to Lucia and Dominic. Lucia knew that her eye contact caused her legs to wobble a bit and she relished it.

"Well, are you ready Zoe?" Lucia snapped her jaws and smiled. Zoe shrank about an inch. Dominic instantly recognized Zoe's fear and playfully grabbed Lucia by the arm.

"Lucia! We have a long trip ahead of us! Let's not eat her the first day." Dominic turned to Zoe and winked. The young woman wasn't sure if she should relax or run. When Dominic opened the door, a silence overcame his children. Isabella stepped in front of her parents.

"Mamma! Poppa! I..."

Lucia firmly took her by the shoulders. Her smile always had a calming effect on her daughter.

"This isn't goodbye. We're coming back, and when we do we're going return everything to normal. We'll even make you and Vincenzo vampires if you want."

"You mean that?" Isabella's eyes widened. For just a second, she forgot all about the Knights and the mob and thought of the long nights ahead of her. She was reminded again of their troubles when her brothers began their farewells.

"Good luck, Mamma. I hope you find what you need," Roberto whispered as he gave his mother an extra-long hug.

Vincenzo had wanted to ask his father something ever since they had decided to go on this quest. He couldn't get himself to bring it up until this last moment.

"So, Poppa, do you think you can get me a werewolf tooth?"

"I'll see what I can do!" Dominic laughed as he, Lucia, and Zoe carefully made their way down the stairs and out into the hectic street.

This was the first time that they had seen New York in the daylight. They weren't pleased. The city was dirtier than it looked at night. Trash was everywhere. People in loudly colored clothes pushed each other aside to get to their jobs.

"I forgot how ugly people were during the day." Lucia sneered.

A tall man in a blue, three piece suit rudely brushed through in between Lucia and her husband. Dominic worried that his wife was going to rip the businessman in half. Their home was only few streets away and the Knights were still in the neighborhood looking for them. Thankfully, Lucia wasn't about to make any stupid moves. No one spoke until Lucia spotted the brand new Pontiac Firebird Trans Am that was waiting for them. Its Firebird emblem jumped off the jet black hood.

"Ah! Perfect! Just like I asked!" Lucia cried out.

Zoe gawked at the chrome and steel monster in disbelief. When Dominic opened the trunk and placed their bags inside, she realized that they weren't kidding.

"But...but this isn't the Pacer! I thought Morgan was going get a Pacer." Zoe's disappointment nearly put the poor girl into a trance. Lucia, slamming the trunk shut, woke her out of it.

"I know. Morgan let it slip about getting a Pacer the other night. I told her Tran Am or no deal," Lucia explained.

"What? Why would you risk everything on...?"

"Come and I'll show you why." Lucia dug the keys from her pocket. She got goose bumps just seeing the Firebird emblem on the leather keychain.

Zoe felt glued to the pavement. She was more afraid of the muscle car than the vampires. She looked over to Dominic for some sort of help.

"This is going be fun!" he chuckled as he politely opened the door and pulled up the front seat for Zoe. She awkwardly climbed into the backseat. Once everyone was settled in, Lucia turned the key and the Firebird gave an angry roar. Lucia growled at the sound and rumble of the motor. Dominic had only heard his wife make that noise when she drinking blood or climaxing. They slowly pulled out into the congested New York traffic.

"All right, where are we going again?" Lucia demanded. Dominic turned back to look at their silent passenger. Zoe was unsure if she had the directions on her. She wore a panicked expression as she ripped through her purse, which she had made from an old pair of jeans. Lucia impatiently eyed her in the rear view mirror. Zoe snapped the map out of her bag, holding it up in victory.

"Sorry, I couldn't remember if it was in the trunk or not."

"That's okay," Dominic took the map from her shaky hands. He opened it up and carefully studied the directions.

"So, what's the name of this town again?" Lucia did her best to sneak a peek at the map without taking her eyes off the road.

"Normal. Normal, New Jersey," Dominic stated rather plainly.

"It's the town with the biggest number of werewolf sighting over the past thirty years!" Zoe proclaimed.

"Wait a minute, wait a minute! It's in New Jersey?" Lucia interrupted.

"Yeah, everything we're looking for is in New Jersey," Dominic answered.

"Shit!"

Joey Paparazzo leaned in carefully to make the shot. He knew he only had one chance at his target. He closed his eyes and made his move.

The eight ball bounced off the side, failing to go into the corner pocket. Ever since he put in the pool table, Joey's three-story home had become the regular meeting place for him and his men. Today's conference hadn't started yet because Frank was an hour late. This was already their third game. Paul picked up his cue stick and chalked it up. It had been so long since his turn was up, he had nearly forgotten if he was playing solid balls or striped. Lou, Joey's underboss, sat back and watched the game as he glanced at his newspaper.

"You think that Son of Sam guy is a vampire?" Paul didn't even take his eyes off the table as he spoke.

"What?" Lou looked up from counting slips. He couldn't believe what his own capo was asking. Joey nearly spit out his beer laughing.

"Get the fuck outta' here with that shit!" Joey choked on the words.

"No, listen! Think about it!" Paul stood up from taking his shot to defend his statement. Joey gestured at him to get back to his move. He sunk a five ball and turned back around to continue his point.

"Think about it. He stalks the streets at night; He's satanic or something; No one ever sees him until it's too late. Maybe he's connected to these vampires Frank saw." Paul missed his next ball. Joey stood up to get the layout of the table, but instead he was contemplating his friend's theory. Lou wasn't as convinced.

"Bullshit! Since when do vampires fucking shoot people?" Lou shouted. He was now completely distracted from his work, and into the conversation. Joey chuckled at the question. Paul gave it some serious thought.

"What if...what if it's a cover up?" Paul waited for the two men to answer, but neither had anything to offer. Paul felt confident enough to continue. "What if it's a cover up? Think about it! What if they make it look like gunshots? You know, maybe they muck with the bodies and get fake witnesses. You know, like we do!"

"Who? Who is 'they?'" Lou sighed.

"I don't fucking know! Maybe the government or..." Paul stood back and threw his hands in the air as if he came across an incredible discovery. Joey and Lou were waiting patiently. "...or what if it's those creepy church guys you and Frank met?"

"Why would the Church do that?" Lou's guard was down and Paul's rant was starting to make sense to him. Joey forgot all about the game and thought about those priests. He knew they were more than what they claimed to be. He knew they were killers.

"I don't know! Maybe they don't want people to panic, like they did during those witch trials. Think about it, how many of those things are out there on the streets right now. We'd kill each other looking for them!" Paul's words hung heavy in the room. Joey and Lou wondered about every abnormal person they had met and every strange moment that they'd passed off as nothing.

The phone rang, which caused all three men to jump and grab their chests at the same time. Joey threw his pool cue at Paul, but his aim was way off.

"You trying to give me a heart attack?" Joey took a second to gain his composure before picking up the phone. "Yeah?"

Joey's posture tensed up. Lou and Paul could tell that it was bad news without hearing the other end.

"Frank?... What?... What the fuck?... Where are you now?... You wait there! I'll be there in twenty minutes! You stay right there!" Joey slammed the phone down in aggravation. Lou and Paul were afraid to ask him anything.

"Joey? What's wrong?" Paul hoped that it wasn't cops. It was worse. Joey took one last belt of his beer.

"Paul, get your shit. We got a body to bury."

Lucia sang along to the radio for nearly the entire two-hour trip to Normal. Dominic attempted to join in, but often didn't know the words. Zoe sat in the back and stared at the roadside speeding by.

They made only one pit stop, so that Lucia could purchase a Donna Summer 8-track and to allow Zoe to use the little girl's room. Lucia took the opportunity to purchase her first pair of sunglasses, although she wouldn't need them once they entered Wharton State Forest.

It was late in the afternoon and the sun had ducked out of sight behind the vast green towers on either side of the highway. Dominic got the sense that they had wandered into the den of another predator. The Trans Am rolled into a clearing in the forest. That's where Dominic spotted a wooden sign, painted white with dark letters reading:

WELCOME TO NORMAL
WEREWOLF CAPITAL OF THE WORLD
POPULATION: 225

"I guess this is the place," Lucia laughed.

On the way to the town square they passed through miles of nothing, interrupted by the occasional billboard. One sign advertised a diner called The Mystery Meat Café -- Home of the Wereburger.

The town itself looked no different than any other. The colonial style houses each had a white picket fence. An elderly couple walked around the town square as children played in the front yards of a number of homes. Lucia stopped at Normal's one and only gas station. The tiny station had only two pumps and would be closing at dusk.

The thing that was curious about Normal was the abundance of werewolf merchandise. It was available all over town. There were little shops selling t-shirts, toys, and all sorts of cheap items that had werewolves on them. There were even signs warning tourists not to enter the forest at night. Dominic couldn't shake the feeling that every single man, woman, and child was staring at them as they drove through town.

"Jesus! What a tourist trap!" Lucia spouted. She seemed to be doing more sightseeing than driving. To both of the Divitas' surprise, Zoe jumped forward in her seat to point straight ahead at a charming, brown building up the street.

"That's it! That's it! That's the inn!" Zoe shouted. Lucia motioned her hand to suggest that Zoe sit. After she carefully sat back down, Lucia turned the car into the brick driveway. The wooden sign hanging above the front doors read Wolfsbane Inn. It was a simple, brown, three-story building sitting atop a small hill. The window panes had an old European style.

Zoe exited the back of the Firebird in a weakened condition. Lucia had had the widows open during the entire trip from New York City. Zoe's brown mini skirt was okay, but her green, long-sleeved blouse just wasn't handling the summer heat very well. Lucia was stunned that she'd even attempted to wear such a thing in July. While Dominic fished their bags from the trunk, Lucia took Zoe aside.

"Zoe, why are you wearing that hot thing?" Lucia asked.

"I don't know."

"Yes, you fucking know why! Now tell me."

"I...I'm just..." Zoe's sentence trailed off into an unintelligible whisper. She realized that this only aggravated Lucia more, so she answered again. "I'm embarrassed."

"Of what?" Lucia knew what the answer was at this point. Zoe didn't speak. She took a deep breath and peeled off her sweater. Even Lucia was surprised by her buxom chest that stretched her plain white t-shirt to it limits.

"Honey! Big breasts are never wrong," Lucia suddenly felt like the girl's mother, teaching her a basic fact of life. Zoe just shrugged her shoulders.

"It's true! Who needs magic when you're born with these! They have the power to reduce men to their basic instincts for just a moment. Just watch. Dominic! Come look at Zoe's huge breasts!" she called out to her husband. Dominic dug his head out from the car's trunk to see what she was talking about. Once he saw Zoe fully revealed, it took him a second to come up with something appropriate to say.

"Ahh...you look nice, Zoe." He did his best to sound respectful to the girl. Lucia smiled at her as if she was sharing the secrets of the universe.

"See, honey! In the time it took for him to react, you could have killed him. Don't be afraid of this power."

Zoe giggled, feeling that Lucia and Dominic had finally welcomed her into their fold. The three of them hauled their luggage into the lobby of the inn. The old man behind the front desk greeted them. He had white, wavy hair that exploded in all different directions.

"Hello! You must be the New York people?" the old man said.

"Yes. Two rooms for...um...Strickland," Zoe piped up. As the old man turned to grab the keys and the registration book, Lucia tapped Zoe's thigh. She gestured with a head nod in the direction of a bell boy who was standing and staring at Zoe.

"See," Lucia whispered.

Zoe blushed, but all she could think about was the milky-white face of the woman she loved. She appreciated Lucia's effort to be nice, but she wanted to be seen as more than her bust. Zoe also wondered if this power over others was worth the backache and discomfort.

Their two rooms were next to each other on the second floor at the end of the hallway. They were small, but cozy. The accommodations reminded Lucia of their old apartment in Rome, except these rooms were more cheerful. Wood paneling covered the walls, along with paintings of wolves and forest scenery. Dominic threw himself onto the bed. Lucia picked up the bag he had dropped and took it to the bathroom. She had to pull out the bathroom items, and place all of her things in order, before getting comfortable.

"So, who's the werewolf we have to see?" Lucia asked from the little bathroom. Zoe replied with a blank stare. Dominic noticed the silence and sat up on the bed. Lucia stepped out of the bathroom in a huff. She was in no mood to play twenty questions.

"Zoe?" Dominic asked so that his impatient wife wouldn't have to inquire again.

"I don't know." Lucia exhaled in disgust, which prompted Zoe to expand on her answer. "But wait! There is at least one in town. There's a full moon tonight, so we just need to wait until dark. We're bound to find one!" She almost sounded like she was pleading for her life.

Both of the Divitas seemed satisfied. Lucia stepped back into the bathroom to finish putting her things away. Dominic stood up and took a look out the window. The view from their room was of the dense, dark forest that surrounded the town. Whatever they were searching for would be waiting for them out there.

Joey knocked as lightly as he could. There was no answer, so this time he spoke up.

"Frank, open up! It's me!" Joey decided that if he heard "Me who?" he was going to kick in the door and start blasting. Instead, he heard someone doing their best to unlock the door. He could tell how nervous they were from the trembling, rattling sounds of the locks.

The door swung open. Frank was in his dress slacks and a sleeveless undershirt. The smell in the room told Joey half the story. Since this was Frank's mistress's apartment, he knew who he was going to find dead. Frank was talking a mile a minute, only a third of which made any sense. Joey pushed him down onto the couch. He stopped talking the second he sat down.

"Frank! Where is she? Is Nancy dead?"

Frank pointed to the master bedroom. Joey crept slowly toward the door and nudged it open.

There was a woman's body lying under the dirty, white sheet. He pulled it off of her. Nancy's face was frozen in a look of disbelief. Joey carefully closed her eyes and covered her back up. He gave the sign of the cross, even though he didn't know if she had believed in anything.

Joey took his time stepping back into the living room. Frank sat on the couch, hiding his face in his hands. The crime boss settled beside him and gave him a reassuring pat on the back.

"Don't worry. I asked Paul to bring a couple of guys over. We'll get her to the junkyard and get rid of her there."

Frank lifted his face out of hands. His eyes were dead to the world.

"What about the kid?" Frank asked. Joey's heart sank. He fell back into the couch.

"What kid?"

"Nancy's kid. He...he heard and he came into...into the room. He saw. What are we going to do?" Frank sounded far away, lost in his own memories. Joey sat back up and took the lead, as he always did.

"We'll bury them together. We're just going have to wait until the sun sets, that's all."

The two men barely spoke over the next few hours. They played cards, ate what was left in the refrigerator, and watched TV. Just after dusk, Paul knocked on the door. He, and two other darkly dressed men, stepped inside. Their eyes surveyed the room. Joey took Paul to one side.

"We're going to go. When you take the bodies, make sure to take some clothes, some money, and whatever, to make it look like they left or something. Make sure that nothing is left to cause anybody to wonder."

The two men traveled back to Joey's home in the suburbs of Newark. He knew that Frank was in no shape to face his wife at that point. Joey's own wife was a bit startled over the sight of her husband's friend. She had seen the man countless times, but she had never seen him so withdrawn.

"Oh, my God! Is Frank all right?"

"He's fine, Babs. He's just had a day, that's all. We're gonna go into the poolroom."

Frank took a stool at the custom-made bar. Joey disappeared behind the counter and came up with two beers. Frank gestured that he didn't want a beer, but his boss insisted. He took hold of the bottle and swallowed half of it.

"Jesus! My wife is gonna leave me!"

"Your wife is going nowhere. The boys are cleaning everything up right now. Look, if it makes you feel better, I'll call your wife and tell her that I have you tied up in some meeting or job."

"Thanks, Joe."

"So, what happened?"

"Aw, Joe! I don't really want to say, really. I--"

"Bullshit! I'm taking a huge fucking risk covering up your crime of passion. You also cost me one of my best dancers. People are going to be pissed when I tell them she quit. You can at least tell me what set you off like that."

"She made fun of me." Frank was squirming in his seat. He wasn't used to admitting to an act of violence.

"What did she say?"

"I...I don't wanna say exactly, but it was in bed."

Joey acted like he'd had the wind knocked out of him. He quickly took another sip of his beer before Frank continued.

"Look, that shit with the vampires, I can't think of anything else. I close my eyes and I see that evil bitch. I carried Tommy and Ricky's heads for almost a whole block! Their blood was all over me. I...I just can't let it go."

"You did the kid cause he heard, right?"

Frank wouldn't look at him. It was the first time that he had actually felt shame over a murder. He was able to raise his head again once Joey patted him on the back.

"Look, you haven't been focused since that night you came back from the club. What if we do something about those vampires?"

"But what about those priests we talked to?"

"I've had a guy watching that club for a week now. He says he hasn't seen any of the family. The place is just run by their staff or something."

"What are you saying, Joe?"

"I'm saying let's go finish the job."

CHAPTER TEN

The Mystery Meat Café was a charming little diner. The spacious eatery had a red and white checkered cloth covering each table and posters of werewolf movies on the walls. Dominic sat back in his wooden chair to get a better view of the autographed photo of Wolfman Jack that hung over Luica's head. It read, "To Mayor Bert, the scariest cat I know! - Wolfman Jack."

"This is so exciting! I can't believe we're really here! Do you think that one of the townsfolk is the werewolf?" Zoe had been talking more since they had reached the town hours earlier. Lucia let the final piece of her very rare steak roll around under her tongue before answering.

"I've had my eye on that boy over there," she said. Zoe turned to look, thinking that she was talking about a child that was leaving with his parents.

"No, no, no. That one. The one with the football jersey that says 'Butch' on the back. His overbite gives him away." Lucia pointed to a sandy-blond teenager that was working behind the counter.

Zoe looked for any signs of werewolf in the young man, until he noticed her staring and gave her a toothy smile. Startled and embarrassed at getting caught, she quickly turned back around to a giggling Lucia. Zoe's face was as red as the meat. She feared that she had ruined everything, but the boy had gone back to work as though nothing had happened. She tried to return to the conversation by bringing in Dominic.

"So, Mr. Divita, who do you think it is?"

"Zoe, you saved our lives. I think you can call us by our first names." Lucia gave the witch a little wink in agreement.

"If you ask me, I think it's the mayor." The two women peered up at the signed publicity photo on the wall.

"What? Just because he knows the fucking Fonz?" Lucia laughed.

"Actually, Wolfman Jack is the greatest radio DJ of all time. Oh, and if you could watch your language in here, darling, this is a family establishment." The forcefully polite voice behind them was that of their waitress, Norma Jean. The three were caught off guard by the lanky woman, since it seemed she had been across the room just a second before.

"Oh! I apologize," Lucia smiled, not wanting to cause trouble. The women went on to discuss how long the car trip had been from the city. Dominic's attention went from them to a man dressed in a jean jacket, sitting at the booth in the back of the diner. He was in his early fifties and his long, gray hair fell freely around his shoulders. The man was simply enjoying a cup of coffee and a slice of apple pie while reading his newspaper, but Dominic sensed an aggressive power radiating from him.

"That's Mayor Bert, by the way. He's been the mayor here forever." Norma Jean snapped Dominic out of his fixation on the strange man.

"Aren't there elections here?" Lucia asked.

"Oh, he's been challenged from time to time, but nobody can beat old Bert! If you like, I could ask if he'd mind introducing you folks to the town."

"That would be nice, thank you," Dominic answered.

"Sure thing. I'll also grab your check. The sun is almost down and we're about to close." Norma Jean buzzed over to Mayor's Bert's booth. She whispered in his ear about the three tourists from New York. Zoe felt herself jump in her seat when Bert's eyes locked on to them. Bert wiped his chin and made his way over to them. Zoe became move nervous with each step of his cowboy boots against the wooden floor.

"Hello, folks. I'm Mayor Bert and I hope you're enjoying your stay in Normal." Zoe could feel Bert's voice vibrate her glasses. The mayor shook Dominic's hand. The men were like two animals sizing each other up.

"Hello, Mayor. I'm Dominic, this is my wife, Lucia, and this is our friend, Zoe." Bert took Lucia's hand and gently kissed it. He tried the same with Zoe, but she opted to just wave. Lucia tugged at Bert's arm.

"Thank you, Mayor, but we haven't seen any werewolves yet. Why is your town called 'the werewolf capital of the world?'"

"Well, there are stories about the spirits, who the Indian tribes followed, that had nowhere to go after the Indians were pushed out of these areas. These were beasts that could take the shape of men during the day, but at night they were free to hunt in their true forms. They're out there. You have my word on that."

"And what is the safest way to see these beasts?" Dominic asked.

"I suggest the Full Moon Hay Ride. It's a little something we put together every month on the full moon. People come from all over the east coast to ride. If you're lucky, you may see one. Now I need to get going, I have mayor stuff to attend to. You have a good night." Bert gave the three visitors a quick wink and excused himself. He shouted to Norma Jean that the pie was as good as usual before he headed out the door.

Once Mayor Bert walked out of sight, Zoe began to breathe again. There was no need for discussion. The hay ride was where they were going next. Dominic got up and flagged down Norma Jean as he dug out his wallet. She yanked out one of the four pencils that were tangled in her short, curly, brown hair and waved him over to the register.

Lucia was about to excuse herself for the ladies' room when she smelled blood. She noticed it gushing out of Zoe's right nostril. It took a few moments for Zoe to realize that not only was she having a nosebleed, but a vampire was staring at her. She quickly stuffed a napkin into her nostril and leaned her head back. She shifted away from Lucia, as if to hide what she was doing.

"Zoe, are you all right?"

"Yeah! I...I get nosebleeds when I get nervous. Are...are you okay?"

"Me? I'm fine. Why?"

"It's 'cause...I'm bleeding and you're..."

"Oh, honey! Don't worry, I don't eat friends. Anyway, we can't drink human blood until this spell is finished. Right?"

"Yeah. That's right. I'm sorry."

"Besides, I'm not going to suck blood out of your fucking nose." When Dominic returned to the table, he was pleased to see the women laughing about something. He only hoped that it wasn't about him.

Dominic, Lucia, and Zoe stepped out into the clean night air. It was easy to find the Full Moon Hay Ride, since there were signs posted all over town to point the way. Norma Jean said that the rides ran every half hour.

A family of five was heading in the same direction. Lucia watched the mother with her five-year-old daughter hop along a few paces in front of them. She closed her eyes and thought of Isabella and her sons. She could feel their hearts beating as strongly as her own. Lucia's favorite part of being a vampire was that she never felt alone. She could feel them now, much like she could when they were in her womb.

"Feeling better?" Dominic whispered.

"Hmmm?" Lucia didn't completely hear him.

"Are you feeling any better?"

"Why?"

"You're holding my hand."

Lucia peered down at their hands as if she was waking from a dream. Once she had her footing in this world, she attempted to worm her hand out of his, but he wasn't releasing her.

"Well, fine. You can just let go if you don't like it!" he offered.

"No! I like it," she stated in an attempt to sound emotionless. Her husband wasn't fooled.

Zoe wasn't fooled, either. She had observed the Divitas very closely during this trip. Dominic was much more open about his love for his wife than she was with him. It was as if he was incapable of hiding his feelings. Lucia, on the other hand, would look lovingly at her husband, but only when she thought he wasn't paying attention. Zoe wondered why anyone would be afraid to be seen being affectionate with their soul mate.

Watching them reminded her of the night that Morgan had walked her home from work. Their bodies getting close to brushing against each other, pretending that their conversation had nothing to do with their excitement. Everything changed when the soft skin on the backs of their hands connected. Morgan stopped walking to take her in her arms. Zoe had never kissed another woman in public before. She was frightened of taking such a bold step, but she couldn't hold back. It began to rain the moment their lips touched. It rained the entire night, as they went back to Morgan's apartment and made love for countless hours. Time seemed to slip away when they were together. Zoe needed this plan to work, to hold back time as long as possible.

They continued to follow the modest pathway that led to a small barn. In front of the barn, on an old dirt road, was a horse and wagon, which was laid out with hay bales for seats. There were already half a dozen people waiting by the time they showed up, and more coming along the path behind them.

Wolf howls were coming from the rusty loud speakers at the top of the barn. There were three men and two women working the show. One man stepped onto a tiny wooden platform. The barker was a young, long-haired man, dressed simply in jeans and a t-shirt, but he spoke like a politician.

"Thank you for coming out here tonight. In these woods are the deadliest of beasts. They hunt by night. They embrace the dark side that haunts and torments every one of us. I'm talking about the werewolf! I don't care if the outside world believes if it's true or not. I've seen them. I've even lost friends and family to these damned monsters.

"Now! Now you have the chance to learn about these creatures from the safety of our wagon. Those of you who are weak-hearted may want to turn back. Those of you who stay, rest assured that there will be two men at all times riding in the wagon, armed with shotguns. These shotguns are loaded with silver bullets. No harm will come to you if you stay in the wagon.

"Who will be first?"

Each person in line paid their five dollars and climbed into the hay wagon. Dominic, Lucia, and Zoe were able to make the first ride. Their fellow passengers were the family of five that had passed them outside of the diner and two teenage couples on a double date. Joining the barker was a driver, who was a simple woman that didn't look at the tourists; and a tall, board shouldered man in plaid. The tall man was armed with a double barreled shotgun. He kept looking in different directions, as if he was expecting something to attack at any moment. The barker began his act the moment he stepped foot on the wagon.

"And now, ladies and gentlemen, I must tell you that--"

"Stop!" An unseen voice halted the horses without any help from the driver. Though startled, the barker acted like he recognized the voice. He stepped up to the front of the wagon to find a priest standing in the wagon's path.

Lucia could feel Dominic tense up. She put her hand on his knee to suggest that they wait and see what happened next. Zoe's nose began to bleed again. She quickly put a napkin from the diner to her nose. The barker let out a sigh of relief and turned to address the tourists.

"Sorry, folks. This is the town priest, Father Zachery Wood. What is it, Father?"

"I apologize for the disturbance, but I had a terrible feeling about tonight's ride. Is there anything I could do to persuade you to turn back?"

"Well, Father Wood, we've done this hundreds of times and no one has ever gotten hurt."

"If you won't turn back, I'd like to say a prayer for good measure."

"I don't see why not."

"Oh, Holy Father, please protect these travelers. Tonight, they step briefly away from your loving arms to view the depths of what lurks within the dark nature of what man could be without you. Please see that none of them step off the path into evil."

Dominic had an odd notion that the priest was looking at him during that last line. He worried that he was talking about the three of them instead of a possible werewolf. Father Wood then stepped out of the way of the hay wagon and the driver gave the horses the sign to move. Dominic couldn't look at the priest as they slowly rode past. He didn't want to know whether or not it would hurt to look at him.

The others traveling with them were the picture of a perfect middle class family. The father held his ten-year-old daughter's hand as his teenage son looked everywhere he could, hoping to spot a werewolf. The mother held the youngest daughter in her lap.

The two teenage couples chatted endlessly about horror movies that this trip reminded them of. Zoe temporarily forgot her unease, distracted by the amount of times they got movie scenes wrong. She wondered if any of them had ever actually seen a horror movie.

Once they got some distance from the barn, the host tapped the driver on the shoulder and began his speech again.

"Stop here, Debbie. Our tour begins over here. This tree is where the most recent victim was found. She was a tourist, just like you folks, from Delaware. She and her boyfriend had a fight--"

"About what?" asked one of the teenage boys in a mock sincere tone. The host recognized this, but he answered anyway.

"Whatever couples fight about. Some fight about money or children. In the case of you and your girl, I imagine it's about size." A few of the riders had a good laugh over this and the host went on with the story.

"She thought it would be safe to walk alone along the outskirts. She thought wrong! The following morning, her boyfriend had begun to worry. He wondered if she'd gone home without him, or maybe, just maybe, the stories were true.

"I remember that day. He ran all over town asking everybody if they had seen her. We knew. Nobody had to see what happened to her to know. He finally found her under that tree. Her body was turned inside out by some creature that she came across during the night. Whatever beast did this left only scraps, barely even resembling a human body."

A silence fell over the tourists. Even Dominic and Lucia didn't say a word. They were too busy trying to decide if his story was true. The riders all stared out into the woods, hoping to spot something moving. The host tapped Debbie's shoulder so that they could resume the tour. The horse's hoof steps were the only sound within miles.

"The boy was distraught. He blamed himself for the girl's death. He did the only thing he could do. He waited for the next full moon. Once it came, he drove here and marched straight into the forest, armed with a gun loaded with a single silver bullet. That was the last anyone ever saw of the young man. All that was left of him were his clothes, torn to pieces just a few yards into the woods. Many of us now believe that he stalks these very woods at night. A lone wolf indeed. Any questions so far?"

"How do you know he brought a gun?" one of the teenage girls piped up.

"We found it near his torn pants." The host then called on the ten-year-old girl, who had her hand raised like she was at school.

"How can you become a werewolf?" the girl asked.

"A single bite from a werewolf is all it takes. Once that happens, the dark spirit takes over your body and soul. It forces the victim to give in to the evil that men try so hard to fight within themselves every day. When the full moon comes, the poor soul transforms into a mindless beast in search of blood. The only way out for them is death. Death is the only cure for their soul."

"How do you kill a werewolf?" The girl held on to her father a little tighter.

"Silver. Anything silver will kill a werewolf. Silver bullets, silver knives...anything."

"Why silver?" Lucia joined in to the conversation. The host took a moment to answer, trying to choose his words carefully.

"No one knows exactly. Some believe it's Gypsy magic."

"Is that so?" Lucia raised her eyebrows in mock amazement. She knew he wasn't telling the truth. He knew the real answer.

The host almost broke character in a sudden case of nervousness. Much to his relief, the rifleman started to eye something in the woods. The show was about to begin for real.

"Quiet everyone!" the rifleman called out.

Debbie halted the wagon. The children raced to their parents' side and the two couples held each other close. Dominic and Zoe grew excited. They hoped that they were about to find what they were looking for, but Lucia wondered why the horses seemed so calm. There was a rustling in the nearby bushes.

"There!" the rifleman shouted and pointed over to a group of bushes on the right of the wagon. A pair of furry ears popped up into the moonlight. The creature gave a blood curdling howl that caused the teenage girls to scream and the children to duck for cover.

Lucia jumped off the wagon and leapt into the woods, with Dominic only a step behind. Zoe was so excited that she almost forgot to follow them. She attempted to climb out, but fell to the ground. The host was caught off guard by their actions.

"What? Wait! Wait! Don't go into the woods! Stop!" There was a panicked quality in the host's voice that suggested he was more frightened for himself than he was for the three crazy tourists running off to certain doom.

One of the teenage boys suddenly wasn't afraid of the big bad wolf any longer, and he certainly wasn't going to be shown up in front of his girlfriend.

"Hey, let's go too! I've always wanted to see a--" The host grabbed the young man by the shoulder with enough strength to cause his knees to wobble from under him.

"You will stay," the host ordered with the conviction of a god. The young man sat back down like a good boy.

Dominic and Lucia saw the wolf man the second they entered the forest. The beast had the head of wolf, but he was still dressed in a long shelved, blue shirt and brown slacks. He thought that he could use the cover of night to elude them, but it wasn't working on the vampires. Dominic tackled him from behind, bringing him down into the dirt. Lucia stood back and wondered why the werewolf's head seemed to be twisted around.

"Dominic! Dominic, wait! Look at him!"

Dominic pulled him to his feet to get a better look. Zoe was already covered in sweat once she had caught up with the others. She could barely keep her breath.

"Is...is...he...?" Zoe tried to get out, but there wasn't any further point to ask. They had gambled on this spell. Zoe and Morgan had spent two years researching the details. Lucia and Dominic had put their lives on the line to find this man so they could keep their children safe.

The monster was nothing more than a man in a mask. Lucia reached under his chin and yanked it off his face.

"Who the fuck are you?! What the fuck are you doing?!" Lucia screamed.

"I'm trying to make a living! Who the fuck are you?" The skinny, pale man was just as upset as his captors.

Dominic released the man, since there was no need to hold him. The spell was finished, even before it had really begun. He had trouble holding back his frustration, kicking dirt up in the air.

Zoe turned away. She didn't want the others to watch her cry. She felt so stupid, like she had ruined everything. She feared that Lucia and Dominic would kill her, or at the very least not speak to her on the way home. Zoe would have chosen either at that moment. She hoped that the yelling from Lucia and the fake werewolf would drown out the sound of her weeping. She took off her glasses so she could wipe away her tears.

Putting her glasses back on, Zoe noticed something moving about thirty feet from where she stood. It was a lean, hairy looking silhouette gently stepping out from behind a tree on all fours. There was intelligence in its yellow eyes, and it was watching them.

Zoe slowly stepped back until she bumped into Dominic. Before he could shout at Zoe, his attention instantly moved from the witch to what she was staring at. The animal moved its head up and down as if it was studying him.

"Lucia." He didn't want to yell, fearing that he might scare off the wolf, but Lucia and the impostor's shouting didn't seem to have an effect on it.

She didn't ask what he wanted. She knew by his expression to simply turn around. Both vampires could feel the wolf's strong heartbeat. It was more than what it appeared.

Before any of them could think of what to say, the wolf took off into the woods, leaving behind a cloud of dirt and grass. Dominic and Lucia didn't react; they just went after their target. In a flash, Zoe was by herself with the actor in the wolf mask. The actor began to snicker.

"What are you waiting for, little girl?" He chewed on those words, rather than speaking them. His eyes narrowed on her. His voice became calm, suggesting he knew much more than she did about the situation they were in. He seemed like a different person, as though the actor he had been a moment ago was just another mask.

"I thought you three were hunting werewolves. You'd better hurry before you lose them." He hunched his shoulders up and took a step toward her. He looked ready to jump her. Zoe decided that she might be safer chasing after the wolf. She didn't look back as she clumsily stepped off in pursuit of the others.

The wolf was racing through the darkness. It gracefully leapt over rocks and dodged low hanging branches without slowing down. Dominic and Lucia had managed to keep up fairly easily. They ran along, side by side, through the dense forest.

Something was intensifying inside each of them. Their hearts raced with every step. Their clothes were getting soaked with sweat and torn by tree branches. The idea of just catching their prey caused Dominic and Lucia to run faster. The excitement overtook any fear they may have had seconds prior, and they began to laugh.

Zoe was barely able to tag along. She was not a runner. She kept a sluggish pace with her arms up to protect her face and she tripped about every ten yards. The witch did her best to follow the sounds of the others.

Dominic and Lucia divided, hoping that one of them could cut in front of the beast. Lucia disappeared into the dark woods as he stayed on its tail. He was almost close enough to reach out and grab it. Dominic grew impatient and leapt, but the creature slipped through his arms as he smashed into the ground. He quickly bounded back to his feet, but the wolf was gone. Lucia was nowhere to be seen. He was suddenly alone among the trees and crickets.

Zoe couldn't run any longer. She was nearly out of breath when she came to a small clearing in the woods. She would have to wait until the others caught the wolf and brought it to her. A nauseous punch in her gut brought her to her knees and finally rolled her onto her back. She stared up at the stars until they'd stopped spinning.

She looked at those stars and wondered if Morgan was gazing out at them as well. She remembered a story that Morgan had told her, about how elves and humans came from stardust. She often studied the night sky to see any resemblance to her lover's face. Thinking about this eased her nerves and made her feel less alone, but she wasn't alone.

Zoe instantly sat up when she heard something breathing near her. It was the wolf again. She tried to run, but her legs failed her. She flopped around in the dirt, doing her best to keep away.

"You were watching me," the wolf said. Zoe couldn't speak, but the wolf knew she understood him. He continued. "In the diner. You were watching me in the diner. Somehow you knew what I was. Didn't you?"

"You...you...were following," is all Zoe could muster. She did her best to crawl away from him. The wolf tensed up for an attack.

"I was just picking the weak from the herd." The wolf grounded himself where he stood before he charged, bounding for the panicked girl. He as only inches away when something grabbed him from behind by the mane and threw him back. He flipped over in midair until he collided with a tree. Bark exploded everywhere as he fell to the ground. Zoe was too frightened to move, until Lucia calmly approached her and wiped off the wolf's saliva that had spattered on her face.

"Zoe? It's okay. I'm here." Lucia's smoothing tone gave her the nerve to open her eyes again.

When she did she saw Dominic enter the clearing from the woods. He hastily studied the scene and asked if the women were all right. Everybody had their body parts intact. The two vampires then turned their attention to the beast a few feet in front of them. Zoe didn't move from her spot.

"Hello?" Dominic called out to the shaggy creature.

The wolf didn't answer, instead he stood up on two legs. His torso rolled upright into human form and his snout flattened against his face. His naked, human-like form was offset by his wild, yellow eyes, which still came off as very angry. He was growling through his overbite.

"Hello, Butch." Lucia was pleased that she had guessed right and hoped that, maybe, she could calm him down a bit. It didn't work.

"Goodbye!" Butch snarled as he sprang at the vampires. He split Dominic's stomach open on his way to attack Lucia. He grabbed her by the throat and slammed her against a tree. His sharp craws dug into her neck.

"Rip...your...head...off!" Butch tried to be quick, but Lucia kicked his leg out from under him, forcing the werewolf to release her.

Dominic had recovered by this point. He twisted the wolf around, punching him back over to Lucia. She tried to grab him, but he was ready. Butch jumped out of her reach and suddenly he was behind her. He rapidly picked her up and threw her into Dominic.

He took that moment to strike the fallen couple. He ripped into both of the vampires, but didn't count on how much punishment the two could take. Dominic and Lucia each took him by an arm and found their way to their feet. Dominic worked his way behind Butch and held his arms down. The wolf-man kicked and thrashed, but he wasn't getting free. Lucia poised herself in front the two of them.

She spoke directly to the werewolf. She repeated "Butch? Can you hear me? We're not here to hurt you." over and over again. He could understand her, but he didn't seem to care. All he wanted was to be out of her husband's hold.

Dominic felt something shift within the young creature's body. His hands were losing touch with each other as the wolf's chest began to expand. Butch's hair grew thicker once again.

"Dominic? Do you have him?" Lucia asked with growing concern.

Zoe kept her distance from the scene. Dominic's fingers were unlocking.

"I have him!"

"He's getting bigger!" Lucia said.

Butch's snout was growing long and his legs reshaped into a wolf's, making him less human by the second. He stood three feet taller, lifting Dominic slightly off his feet. Breaking his hold was easy for Butch. He flung his arms up, snapping Dominic's limbs. When the vampire fell, the werewolf picked him up by the ankle and pounded him into the ground, breaking his back. The hairy beast climbed over Dominic with every intention of eating his face off.

Lucia felt a deep, burning passion building in her gut. She had held it back while chasing the werewolf, but it was something she could not deny any longer. Zoe jumped away from her when she saw her fangs and claws develop in an instant. Lucia leapt onto the werewolf, punching, biting, and ripping without a second thought. Her rational mind slipped away as instinct took over her body.

The two rolled off together in the dirt. Butch howled in pain when Lucia dug her claws into his chest. The second that Dominic felt his bones reconnect he joined his wife in combat with the monster. The more they beat the werewolf, the less they cared about the spell.

Zoe cupped her hands over her mouth in shock. She thought that they were going to kill him, momentarily forgetting that the creature was too powerful to die so easily.

Butch halted their attack when he grabbed them by their necks and tossed them off of him. Lucia and Dominic made dirt tracks where they landed on either side of Zoe. Instead of going back on the offensive, Butch tensed up and shook the blood out of his fur. He paused to sniff the air around him and let out an ear-pricing howl.

Lucia and Dominic watched him from where they had landed. Zoe hadn't moved from her spot. She looked down at the vampires, hoping they knew what to do.

"Dominic, do you feel it?" Lucia was worried.

"The heartbeats? Yes."

"Heartbeats? What?" Zoe felt panic stir in her belly.

"The heartbeats of the other wolves." Lucia didn't sugarcoat it. There were others coming to answer his call. The three of them could hear howls in the distance, drowning out all other animal sounds. There was a commotion in the trees and bushes all around them. Lucia and Dominic pulled themselves to their feet in time to see fifty pairs of eyes blink on, all at once, from the darkness. They were surrounded.

Zoe couldn't hold it in any longer and fell to her knees to throw up. The pack was repulsed by the funk of the girl's vomit and became worked up to strike. Lucia and Dominic stood their ground when the werewolves jumped out, each in one of the three different forms they had seen Butch take; wolf, wolf-man, and full werewolf.

Zoe crawled away from the fight, as the pack ran past her to destroy the main aggressors. Werewolves grabbed Lucia and Dominic by their limbs and held them down as others ripped into the bellies, pulling out their undigested meal from the diner. The pack grew into a wild frenzy as the vampires healed and kept fighting back. For every werewolf they knocked away, two more would pile on top.

The Divitas managed to stand with the werewolves still picking the flesh from their bodies. Lucia took one of the wolves from around the neck when she noticed all of the pencils tangled in her fur. She removed one of the pencils and jabbed it in Norma Jean's neck. She wailed as Lucia dropped her and moved on. Dominic and Lucia had finally knocked the werewolves off of themselves, but they were still in the middle of the circling pack.

The werewolves changed tactics and began to jump them one at a time. Dominic caught one werewolf by the jaws, forcing them open until they snapped. He threw the beast down and went for the next attacker. Three wolf-men attempted to hold Lucia down. Instead, she broke two of their arms and kicked the third across the clearing. Dominic punched one werewolf, cutting its eye and knocking its teeth out. The creature blindly lashed out, missing Dominic and tearing open the face of another werewolf.

Norma Jean remained where Lucia had dumped her. She transformed into a more human-like werewolf so that she could take the pencil out of her neck with her own hands. A quick shot of pain raced through her body as she yanked it out. Norma Jean was about to rejoin the others when she noticed Zoe, on her knees, just a few feet away from her. She was amazed that everyone had overlooked the girl. She was soft, round, and tasty. Zoe's back was to her and she was too busy digging a pentagram in the dirt to notice her.

The pack overtook the vampires once again, due to their sheer numbers. Lucia and Dominic fell underneath the small mountain of beasts. They weren't letting go of their prey.

"Rip them apart!" Butch howled. The other wolves shouted to tear off their arms and to turn them inside out.

Zoe found the spell in time and hastily it read out loud as Norma Jean was inches away from the kill.

"The light will shield us at this sight," she repeated over and over again until a dome of light exploded from her body. The light hurled Norma Jean into the air and expanded over the fight, blowing all of the werewolves off of the Divitas. The confused wolves bounced off the nearby rocks and trees.

"What was that?" Dominic marveled at the sudden end to the fight. Lucia looked back to see their young friend falling from the recoil of the energy she had shot forth.

"I think Zoe did something." Lucia would have laughed out loud if she was sure the danger had passed. The vampires went to Zoe's aid, unsure what was next. The protection spell had briefly knocked the witch unconscious. It reminded Dominic of his mother's dizzy spells that she would fall victim to during the summers.

"Zoe? Zoe? Are you there?" Lucia's motherly concern showed itself once again. While Lucia helped Zoe up, Dominic remembered the werewolves. He carefully scanned the area, but didn't see one within the clearing. He could hear them whispering to each other as they tended to their wounds. They were regrouping.

"Lucia? Zoe? I think we should get moving," Dominic suggested calmly.

"But you drove all the way out here from New York, why turn back now." quipped a familiar voice that froze them to the spot. The werewolves stepped back out from the woods. Even more of them surrounded the clearing. They were holding back.

Lucia could see the pack in all sorts of forms. Some of them were fully wolves and others were more human-like in shape. One figure was wearing the werewolf mask that the actor had been sporting. He pulled it off to reveal a face that was all fangs and fur. Norman Jean staggered to the front of the crowd. She almost tripped, only to be caught by another werewolf with a metal cross hanging from his neck. The image of the cross only stung Dominic's eyes slightly. He had no time to wonder if his faith, in either religion, had melted away.

Mayor Bert walked out of the darkness. He was the only human looking member of the group. His mood seemed unchanged from their meeting in the diner.

"You picked a bad night to hunt werewolves. You see, the myths about our kind are a little off. We can take the form of a wolf anytime we please. It's just that during a full moon, we're at our most powerful. Do you know what a full moon is?"

"The sun's light reflecting off of the moon," Lucia answered without hesitation. The mayor was impressed with the vampire.

"That's right. A vampire is weakest during a full moon, so this was a poor night for you to pick a fight with us," Mayor Bert said. There was an uproar in the pack as something charged him. It was Butch. He transformed into human form when he reached the mayor.

"We gotta' kill 'em Dad! They were hunting us! One even broke my jaw!" Butch shouted to his father. Mayor Bert slowly faced his naked son and studied his face.

"Butch, your overbite is gone." Mayor Bert hardly seemed surprised. Butch quickly put his hands on his own face to check. His jaw had indeed healed evenly. The young wolf-man was dumbfounded.

"If we don't eat them, I want you to thank them," his father said.

Dominic and Lucia began to feel a little more at ease after watching that exchange. It was obvious to Dominic and Lucia that none of the pack would challenge their leader and wouldn't attack without his say so. He casually walked up to the Divitas and Zoe, who was hidden carefully behind Lucia.

"All right. I'm going to ask this just once. Why were you chasing my son?" Mayor Bert's tone was straight forward. He didn't have time to play nice. Lucia respected the hell out of him.

"We weren't hunting anybody. We need help," Dominic answered without pause.

"Go on." The werewolf's interest was piqued.

"We're on the run from the Knights of the Silver Cross." His mention of the Knights drew much anxiety among the pack. Lucia and Zoe watched the wolves cringe together at the very name. Mayor Bert was unsettled by his answer. He took Dominic and Lucia by their arms and walked them a few yards away from Zoe and the pack to talk in private.

Lucia and Dominic told him, as briefly as they could, about how the mob mistakenly brought in the vampire hunters. They told him that they preferred not to run, but to fight. They explained the spell that Zoe was going to perform to give them the power to defend themselves.

"Wait a minute! If we let you drink werewolf blood, you'll have the power to kill all the Knights in the tri-state area?" Mayor Bert could hardly believe his ears.

Dominic looked to Lucia, unsure of how to answer. He hadn't thought that far in the plan. He knew they would have to kill them all, but hearing it said out loud made it real.

"That's right. We're going to kill every last one of them," Lucia put it bluntly.

"You can have my blood." Mayor Bert's smile was an array of fangs.

"Really?" Dominic was encouraged by his reaction.

"Really. I run a small town of good people who only want to live their lives, raise their children, and hunt at night. We have to operate this sideshow in order to hide in plain sight. The thing is, I know it won't last forever. Someday they'll get wise to us." The mayor took a deep breath because his own words created some ugly imagery in his mind. He needed a moment to erase it out of his head.

"It would be worth all my blood to protect these people."

In a matter of minutes, Zoe was preparing for the ritual by drawing a pentagram in the dirt. Many of the pack had stayed to watch. They felt that this was going to affect their lives, hopefully in a positive way. Some of the townspeople even changed back into human form to sit down more comfortably. Lucia took off what was left of her bra and tied the remains of her torn up t-shirt into a makeshift top. She almost went topless, since no one else in town seemed to care about public nudity, but she could sense some of the male werewolves sniffing too close to her for her liking. In this case, Lucia thought it might be better to cover up.

Mayor Bert was busy getting instructions on the ceremony from Zoe, leaving Dominic with nothing to do. He stared at the huge full moon watching over the scene. He heard someone coming up behind him. It was Father Wood, still in a wolf-man form. He had swung his cross over to his back, hoping it wouldn't harm the vampire.

"Hello, Father...?"

"Actually, it's Father Wood, but you can call me Michael if you like." The priest seemed a bit sheepish to Dominic. It was a bit awkward, since he was very used to a more stern attitude from members of the church.

"So, are you really a priest?"

"I'm afraid so. I wanted to apologize if I hurt you and your wife earlier."

"It's fine. Our wounds heal pretty fast." Dominic touched his own stomach where it had been ripped open during the fight.

"Oh, good. It's just...I meant about the cross. I didn't know."

"It's fine. The cross doesn't affect Lucia and it hurts me a lot less these days." His answer confused the priest. He had never seen a vampire that wasn't affected by the cross before. These visitors were proving more interesting the more he found out about them.

"I don't understand."

"It seems that the myths about vampires are a little off as well. My wife wasn't raised Catholic and a few years ago she discovered that the cross doesn't affect vampires that don't believe."

"Is that so? You mentioned that the cross hurts you less these days. Are you having a crisis of faith?"

Dominic wasn't sure if he wanted to get into this conversation. He looked over to the others to see if they were ready. They weren't. He decided that if there was any priest he could talk to, it would be this one.

"It's more like a crisis of *faiths*." Dominic's voice came off a little less guarded.

"Faiths?" Michael asked.

"Catholic and Strigori. After becoming a vampire, I discovered that religion. Have you heard of it?"

"Yes." Michael stiffened. Dominic could tell that he found the Strigori offensive. He decided not to linger on the subject.

"I was brought up in a strict Catholic home, but I don't know what to believe anymore. I've seen so much horror and I've done my share of horror. I just don't feel the same as I used to when I was a child."

"I know how it feels to have your faith conflict with who you are."

"The church would kill you if they knew who you were. Why do you stay with it?"

"I often wonder why God made me the way he did. Maybe he is testing us."

"I don't know. If God truly is our 'Father in Heaven,' then why does he abuse us so much? To see how much we love him? I would never treat my kids like that. The church kills whatever doesn't fall in line with God's word. How can he allow that?" Dominic asked.

"They used to burn Protestants as they kill werewolves today. Someday, they'll come around. Please, you mustn't blame God for what his follows do."

"Why not? These are the same people who tell us what to believe. If we're not to have faith in them, then why believe in anything they say?" Dominic's question created a moment of silence between the two.

Michael understood that they were only talking in circles. He hoped that the young vampire would find the answers on his own. Dominic could see Lucia wave them back to the others. Michael would have to wait until later to finish their conversation.

Zoe and Mayor Bert waited in the middle of the clearing. The pack had gathered around the area in a half circle. The bright full moon watched over them in the starry night sky. The whole setting struck Dominic as a bit more romantic than the last time, with Morgan. Lucia was already in place, she winked at her husband as he found his mark beside her. The mayor had removed his clothes and sat down on his knees between the couple and Zoe. He was displaying a sense of calm that was almost alien to the vampires. Zoe began to read the spell.

"To these vampires, I present this wolf. He has come to share himself; His knowledge, his power, his beauty." That line caused Mayor Bert to quickly snort. The humor wasn't lost among the pack, who tried not to laugh too hard. Zoe lost her place out of nervousness. She looked to Lucia for help.

"Just keep going," Lucia grunted through a phony smile. The witch placed her hands on the mayor's shoulders, giving him the sign to raise his arms for the vampires. Lucia and Dominic each took hold of a wrist.

"Drink. Drink the wolf's blood my vampires," Zoe read out loud from her notepad. Dominic and Lucia sunk their fangs into Mayor Bert's veins. The werewolf grunted, with what could be called a sexual joy, that seemed to challenge the two on how much they could drink. His blood sent a primal surge through them that brought them to their knees.

"Yes! Take it! Do you feel it?" Mayor Bert screamed. Zoe was frightened of the pack leader once more. She wanted to ask if the Divitas were okay, but their eyes were glazed over. Dominic and Lucia were no longer aware of the world around them. They could see memories of hunting under the moon, tearing warm flesh apart with their fangs and claws. It was, all of a sudden, broken down into its rawest form. In a flash, they tasted every beast that walked the Earth. Every death gave them life.

Dominic and Lucia fell back, letting go of his wrists. When the world had stopped spinning, Mayor Bert stood above with his hands extended out for them to take.

"Now, come hunt with us," he smiled as he had helped the vampires to their feet. Fur spread over his body and by the time his front paws were touching the ground, Mayor Bert had transformed into a large, gray wolf. The remaining members of the pack that were still in human form transformed into what they called their "real forms." Lucia and Dominic ran along with the pack as they all followed the mayor into the woods. All of them left Zoe behind in a cloud of dust.

Lucia and Dominic had no idea when it happened, but they discovered that they were now running on four legs. It didn't take long for each to realize who the black wolf they were running beside was. Their clothing seemed to have melt away. The cool grass felt moist under the pads of their paws. They raced through the forest without fear. Lucia and Dominic could see, smell, and hear every living being in the woods.

The trees gave way to an open field. When the vampires caught sight of the beautiful night sky above, they only wished to reach out for it. Lucia and Dominic found themselves floating over the others wolves. The wind still blew through their fur, but it also carried them on wings of leather.

Dominic and Lucia had transformed into two black, seven-foot-tall bats. They spread out their fifteen-foot wingspans and climbed higher in the air. Neither vampire was at all clumsy, almost as if they had been training for this from the day they were born.

The pack stopped to take in the view of what they had helped create. Zoe finally made her way out of the forest. At first, she was confused as to why the werewolves were parked in an open field looking up, until she saw them.

Zoe was entranced as she watched the vampire bats dance across the moon and stars. Dominic could see into the still human face of his wife. The thrill of flying paled in comparison to the pure joy he saw in her eyes. She was the most beautiful woman he had ever seen. He could see the wind caress the curves of her body as he followed her down, descending through the clouds. He couldn't contain his passion any longer.

Dominic held his wings tight to his torso to speed up his fall. He collided with her, wrapping his wings around her body. It took only seconds for Lucia to realize what he wanted.

"Let go! I don't want bat-people sex!" she protested.

"Yes! You do!" Dominic heard himself shout. He had never been this forceful with her in the past. They had always met on equal footing as partners, as lovers, and as friends. He had never taken control in such a way before. It was so primal. It was so sexy. Dominic was right. Lucia let him enter her, right there, hundreds of feet above the ground. Their wings wrapped into a massive furry ball, heading to earth like a sex fueled metro.

Zoe was unable to make out what was happening. She feared that the two were having some sort of trouble and couldn't pull out of their dive. She ran to the spot where she believed that they were heading. She dug out the notepad from her back pocket, hoping to find a spell for catching someone, but nothing looked right.

When she looked up, she found that they were directly above her, thirty feet in the air. Zoe fell to her knees, covering her head in a desperate attempt to stay safe. Dominic and Lucia pushed away from each other and split off twenty feet from the ground. When Zoe looked again, Dominic and Lucia had swooped over her and back into the sky, missing her by mere inches. Zoe sat where she had fallen as she watched them climb higher into the sky with wide-eyed excitement. She had practiced witchcraft for half of her life, but this was the first time she had actually felt true magic.

"Wow!" Zoe marveled.

CHAPTER ELEVEN

Roberto was becoming restless. There wasn't anything on TV and he didn't feel like reading or playing Dungeons and Dragons with his brother and sister. The twins were engaged in a campaign that took them across the sea on a quest to locate a magical sword. They had started playing game out of pure mockery, but had quickly become hotly involved with the life and death struggles of the characters they had made up.

The oldest Divita son envied the many cats that called this apartment home. They seemed to come and go at will, while he was stuck here, watching the active streets below from the window. Morgan nudged him out of his train of thought. Her smile was as warm as summer, but without the humidity.

"I'm making some tea, care for a cup?" Morgan asked.

"I'd love one." Roberto tried not to seem too interested. Morgan wasn't fooled. She poured two cups and waved Roberto out of the apartment. He didn't move.

"Where are you going?" he muttered.

"I'm going to the roof to enjoy the view with my tea. You can join me if you like."

"But what about the Knights?"

"The whole building is charmed. The Knights won't be able to see us as long as we stay in or on the dwelling. So, care to get some air?"

Morgan was giving him one last chance to escape the apartment, after which she was just going to turn and go alone.

He accepted the invitation and when they had climbed the stairs to the roof, there were two green-striped, folding lawn chairs waiting for them. They drank their tea as they watched the city below and the full moon above. Roberto spoke to Morgan about astronomy. She did her best not to interrupt with what she thought of the moon and the stars. It didn't take very long for the topic to run out of steam and the two sat there staring into space.

"So, who is in charge of the Inferno while all of you are gone?" Morgan inquired.

"Eddie. My parents have an agreement with him that he's the boss if they're missing for a few days."

"He knows what to do?"

"It's pretty easy. He only needs to keep out the other vampires and Andy Warhol. So, how long have you and Zoe been...?"

"Together? Five years." She sat there quietly without continuing on the subject. Roberto watched her stiffen a bit, it was the most uncomfortable that he had seen her. He pressed on with the topic.

"Where did you two meet?"

"At this bookstore she used to work at. I was always in there looking for whatever I could find about nature and magic. She was more than willing to help me. I knew how she felt about me. She was always beet red whenever I was around. I found her charming. I saw someone that I could tell all my strange little secrets to."

"You two must be very happy together."

"Yes. We are." Morgan's response was forced and detached. Roberto wasn't sure if she was trying to convince him, or herself.

"Are you sure?"

She sipped her tea in silence, using both hands so that Roberto wouldn't see them quiver. He didn't. He was too busy wondering if he had made a misstep in the conversation.

"Listen, I want to ask you something and I hope you'll be frank with me," Morgan looked him in the eye as she spoke. Roberto edged up in his lawn chair. A smile was ripping through at the corners of his mouth.

"Why don't you tell your parents you go to church?"

Roberto's heart sank. He fell back. The loud, crackling sound from the plastic chair filled the air in place of actual conversation. He could only stall for so long.

"How did you--oh, right! You and Zoe were spying on us. That's creepy!"

"Coming from the man with vampire parents, that's a bold statement. We were studying your family." Morgan was slightly offended at his accusation. "It's a good thing we did! Your parents would be dead and you and your siblings would probably be off to Rome right now!"

"I'm sorry! I'm sorry! This whole thing...I'm just...I'm sorry."

She decided not to take the matter any further. Both of them had topics they wished to avoid, and she just wanted to enjoy this moment. She closed her eyes and took in the city until a comforting sound eased her nerves.

"What?" Roberto noticed her delight, but was puzzled over what had changed her mood so suddenly.

Morgan quickly shushed the young human. It was obvious that he couldn't hear the out of tune guitarist playing on a nearby rooftop. Most likely, the person was doing some much needed practice.

"Just listen, you'll hear it." She took his hand in hers. The touch of her skin sent a rush of ecstasy up his arm and throughout his body. He could only hear the sound of his heart banging deep inside of his chest. He guessed that she was able to see how her touch was affecting him.

"Oh! I'm so embarrassed. This must be how an elf's touch affects people, right?"

"Actually, no. Elfish skin doesn't have strange effects on humans." It was difficult for her not to giggle.

His wide shoulders sank once he realized that he had given everything away in one stupid comment. Morgan pretended to forget what he'd said. She motioned him to stand up with her. She placed his left hand on her hip and the two began to slowly dance to the pitiful musician from the next building.

"Can you hear it now, Roberto?"

To his surprise, he did make out the music. The two swayed back and forth to what he swore was a Beatles song. She rested her head against his chest.

"You see, Roberto, this city isn't all hate and anger. There is beauty hiding all over. Nothing is truly evil or good. Once you dig deep enough, you can find both in anything or anyone."

Eddie sat alone behind Dominic's desk, counting the night's take. He hoped that the Divitas would return soon. The Inferno made less money when Lucia wasn't performing. He thought that tonight was the deadest he had ever seen the place. The footsteps growing closer to the office almost caused him to lose count. He reached the end of the stack of twenties just as Susan stuck her black, beehive hairdo into the room.

"Ready, Eddie?" Susan enjoyed saying that more than she should have. Eddie had heard the cute rhyme so often over the past week that he'd stopped complaining about it.

"Yes," he grunted as he finished putting the moneybag in the safe.

"You the last one left?" he bellowed.

"I sure am."

"You need me to walk you to the bus stop?"

"No! I want to be killed by some gun toting psycho!" she joked.

"Okay, okay, ha ha. I'll be down in a minute. Get your shit and I'll meet you at the door." He almost wished that it would happen to her. Susan was waiting for him by the elevator as the doors slid open. She had her purse over her shoulder and her work shirt untucked from her black slacks. The girl was dead tired, but the sight of Eddie coming to let her out gave her a new spring in her step. She loved working at the disco, the sea of bodies and smoke every night made the building seem alive. She hated the emptiness after closing; she could almost feel the ghosts of the dancers still parading around.

"Hey, I was just wondering. Why did you put all those crosses at all the entrances? Won't Mrs. Divita just take them down when she gets back?"

"Maybe. I'm just trying to give these people one last shot at religion before they enter this place. You see these freaks, they could use it."

"I guess. So, are you still trying to get Heather in the sack?" Susan cracked a knowing smile at her manager.

"Who says I'm trying?" He raised one eyebrow in the hope that he would look convincingly confused. Susan wasn't fooled. If there was one thing she knew about Eddie, it was that he was an awful lair.

"Everyone," she laughed.

"Oh yeah? Maybe *everyone* should shut the fuck up," he grumbled as he fished for the keys to the side exit door. He didn't bother to check the peephole. If he had, he would have seen the four men standing just outside, waiting for their chance to break in.

A thick arm shot through the doorway, knocking Eddie to the floor. The keys skidded across the room. When Eddie looked up he saw four men step confidently inside. One large man grabbed Susan by the throat and forced her against the wall. Eddie recognized two of the men as Joey Paparazzo and Frank Crocetti.

"What do you want?" He did his best to sound strong and

respectful without revealing how petrified he was. One of the other men, who Eddie didn't know, quietly shut the door and stood still in front of it. Joey gave Frank a nod. Frank kneeled down close to Eddie. His stare was without mercy.

"We're here to do God's work."

Roberto and Morgan didn't speak for the next few hours. They simply took pleasure in their own private concert. It hardly mattered if the guitarist was playing any more or not. When the musician took a bathroom break, they danced to the police sirens that passed every few minutes, the barking dogs, and even the neighbors fighting. Finally, they stepped back from one another without saying a word.

They only kissed once.

CHAPTER TWELVE

Isabella had fallen asleep with her head on the Dungeons and Dragons game board. She woke suddenly, her head snapping up. Her sleep had been disturbed by screams -- Eddie and Susan's cries of pain. She had no idea how she knew, but she knew. Vincenzo was nowhere to be seen.

"Vincenzo! Vincenzo!" The panic in Isabella's voice was so obvious that it brought Vincenzo running out of the bathroom. When he found his sister, she was emptying out the contents of the closet and throwing it out into the room. The cats were running for their lives, trying to dodge the flying debris.

"What are you doing?" Vincenzo asked in befuddlement.

"It's the disco! Something's wrong! I need a weapon!" she shouted without looking in his direction. He knew the consequences of leaving the building. He also knew to trust his sister's premonitions. She yanked out an old wooden staff that had clearly been used in a battle. It was only one weapon, but it was all they needed.

"Let's go!" Vincenzo commanded.

Morgan and Roberto were still on the roof, enjoying the aftertaste of their first kiss, when he noticed the elf's ears prick up.

"What? What do you hear?" He wasn't looking forward to her answer.

"It's your sister. She's going to do something stupid!" She was halfway down the stairs just seconds after she uttered those words. Roberto wasn't far behind. By the time they reached the apartment, the twins had already rushed off to the Inferno.

"Oh, shit!" Morgan knew how the scene was going to play out once she saw the disarray of the apartment. She quickly dove into the closet and pulled out three objects. Roberto watched her tie a small bag onto her belt and then unroll a cloth, which had been wrapped around an old, hand-crafted bow and a dozen arrows.

"Whoa! Whoa! What's this?" Roberto was realizing that things were starting to get out of control.

"It's my enchanted bow. Its arrows will find whatever their intended target is." She handed him a cigar box. He reluctantly opened it and pulled out the fully loaded 357 magnum.

"And this?" Roberto was aghast.

"It's New York, Roberto," Morgan smiled sheepishly.

Vincenzo and Isabella ran the few blocks to the nightclub, ignoring traffic, passersby, and a black car parked across the street from the disco. Inside the Ford LTD, two Knights of the Silver Cross called their superiors. They were told that a team would be there within minutes. Their stakeout had paid off.

Vincenzo fumbled with his keys and attempted to open the front doors as quickly as he could. Silence washed over them like a mist as they stepped carefully into the club. Then, the sound of a woman weeping echoed in the darkness. Vincenzo could make out two black shapes by the bar; The smaller one was shaking, in a fetal position on the floor; The larger one was motionless, on its knees. Vincenzo nearly slipped on the fresh blood that was still splattered across the floor. He realized that whatever had happened, it had been very recently.

He quickly stepped into the back room to switch on the lights, then froze in horror. There was Eddie, in the middle of the floor, a broomstick had been plunged so far up his anus that the handle poked out of his mouth. His wrists had been tied to his ankles with his own shirt and pants. The expression on Eddie's face suggested to Vincenzo that he had been alive during much of his torture. A note was attached to his chest with an ice pick. It read " *Vampires burn in Hell.*"

Isabella dropped the staff and carefully approached the quivering girl. When she placed her hand on Susan's shoulder, the waitress jumped away and cowered in a corner. Her eyes were swollen shut and her face was so badly beaten that Isabella could only tell who it was by her nametag. Susan swung at the air in a desperate attempt to protect herself.

"Susan! Susan, it's me! Isabella!"

Susan went silent with relief as her broken body fell happily into Isabella's arms. She passed out into a sleep that was almost peaceful, knowing that the Divitas were there to make everything better. Isabella held on to her tightly, she but didn't share her optimism.

Roberto and Morgan frantically bobbed and weaved through the traffic. Black cars furiously roared past them and halted in front of the Inferno. Men in black cloaks popped out of the sedans and took control of the situation outside of the disco. Some of the Knights ushered onlookers away. Three of them marched over to a black car that had already been parked there for some time. Morgan casually stepped into the doorway of a nearby pawnshop, pulling Roberto by the arm, however they had not gone unseen.

Amadeus pretended not to notice the duo up the street. He leaned in the driver's side window of the surveillance car as Dick and Jack looked on. The two young Knights inside the car were doing their best not to seem nervous in his presence.

"Situation?" he asked. Brother Paul, who was sitting behind the wheel, spoke first.

"Two of the Divita children just ran inside. The girl was carrying a staff. They haven't left yet."

"Anything else?"

The two didn't immediately answer his question. There was something they weren't sure how to explain. They knew Amadeus wasn't going to ask twice, it was plain by the expression on his face.

"Well, there were four other men that entered and then left the building. A few minutes after they left, the children entered the scene," Brother Brian piped up from the passenger seat. Dick struck a match on the side of the car and puffed on his cigarette.

"Did these fellas look like mafia?" Dick's question seemed to come out of nowhere, but after a second it made sense to all of them. Everyone suddenly knew what the situation had become. Amadeus decided not to shout out orders, in case supernatural ears were listening.

"All right. Follow me." He turned around and headed straight to the front doors of the club. Jack and Dick were a step behind him. Paul and Brian exited the car and followed them while Amadeus shouted to the four Knights at either side of the building.

"You four keep any bystanders away! Be ready for anything!" The five hooded Knights entered the building in a "V" formation with their leader in front. Their loud boot steps indicated that they wanted everyone inside to know they were coming. They soon found Vincenzo and Isabella with Susan and Eddie's body.

"In the name of God, I order you to step away from the bodies and surrender." Amadeus's booming voice shook the glasses at the bar.

Vincenzo wasn't about to give up. He was angry enough to fight God himself. In one rapid move, he pulled out the ice pick from Eddie's chest and threw it at the intruders. Dick caught it just inches away from his own face. Vincenzo leapt toward the Knights, hoping that it would be distracting enough to give him a fighting chance. It hardly made an impression on the men. Dick returned the ice pick by hurling it into Vincenzo's right thigh. The painful shot brought him to the floor before he had even reached his attackers. Dick stepped up to the young man and rolled him over with his foot. He delivered one kick to the face with his steel toed boot, causing Vincenzo to lose consciousness.

Isabella left Susan on the floor to save her brother. She picked up the staff and swung it at the Knights. It was obvious to Jack that she had never used such a weapon before. He easily avoided the attacks and finally, after three failed strikes, he snatched it from her hands. He used that moment of surprise to slip the staff under her right foot and flip her to the ground.

Jack held her face down as he quickly fitted her with handcuffs. The other four Knights inspected the scene as he did his best to hold her down as she kicked and screamed obscenities at them.

"Jack. I can trust you to handle her, can't I?" There was level of impatience in Amadeus's voice.

"Of course!" Jack picked Isabella up off her feet and squeezed around her neck until she fell limp. Dick leaned over Vincenzo to cuff his hands behind his back. He dragged the boy over beside his sister.

"I hope you didn't give her any brain damage. I've got some questions for her later on," Dick said as he smirked at the younger knight.

"She's fine!" Jack answered in frustration. Amadeus surveyed the bodies of the Divitas' employees. It was an ugly murder, as bad as anything he had witnessed in weeks. Paul checked on Susan. He was happy to discover that she was still breathing.

"Grand Master! This one is still alive!" he proclaimed.

"Good. I want her taken care of." Amadeus smiled at the good news as he bent down to pick up the note he found on the floor. The message told him all he needed to know about what had happened.

Brian became unsettled once he got a better look at Eddie. He couldn't believe how cruel some monsters could be.

"Did...did they do this?" Brian stuttered out of disbelief. Amadeus rose up and faced him. He flipped the hood away from his head. Brian felt his muscles tighten with fear over his own well-being.

"This happened because you and Paul did nothing when you watched the other men come in here. As far as I'm concerned, you helped create this horror."

Brian and Paul kneeled down before him in shame.

"Please. Please forgive us, Grand Master," Brian begged. Paul remained silent, letting his partner do the begging on his behalf. Amadeus motioned for them to stand. He put a firm grip on their shoulders so that they would understand his sincerity.

"I forgive you both. Tomorrow, I want the two of you to report to my office for your penance. Right now, we have other matters to attend to."

The scene outside was too calm for Morgan's liking. Her guess was that Vincenzo and Isabella had either been killed or captured by the Knights. It was time to act. She stepped out onto the sidewalk with two arrows drawn. Her targets were the two Knights standing closest to them.

"Wait! What are you doing?" Roberto was alarmed.

"What I have to do," Morgan answered coldly as she let her arrows fly. They instantly pieced the throats of the two Knights by the doors. The second pair caught wind of the attack and fired at the elf. Morgan ducked behind a parked Chevy Caprice as the gunfire tore the car and the storefront apart. Roberto hid best as he could from the bullets and flying glass. He was frozen in place. He had no intention of firing back at other human beings, but she needed his help.

The Knights inside jumped at the sound of the gunfire. Amadeus ordered them to hold their ground. He wanted the attackers to come to them.

Roberto soon realized that Morgan was better at handling herself than he had thought. She shot her next pair of arrows nearly straight up in the air. They then corrected themselves, almost as if they had minds of their own. The two Knights screamed as the arrows landed in their necks. They fell to the pavement in a bloody mess.

Morgan and Roberto rushed to front doors of the nightclub. She dropped her weapons to untie the small bag from her waist. Roberto stood at her side, watching the Knights gasp and flop around in pain. It tore at him that four more people were dying while he did nothing. He prayed to himself for God's guidance.

Amadeus and the Knights could finally see Morgan and Roberto. Morgan opened up the bag and dug out a handful of glittery dust. She held it up to her face and took a deep breath, inhaling the dust. Then something strange happened. A wind began to blow out of the building. The Knights found themselves fighting to stand as the wind grew stronger. The grand master wasn't all that surprised to see that the wind was only pulling the Knights and left everything else alone.

"Dick! Jack! Is this the same wind that sucked you out of the van on St. Luke's Place?" Amadeus shouted.

"It sure is!" Dick yelled back as he braced himself against the bar.

"Everyone! Hold on!" Amadeus ordered. He drew his broad sword and plunged it into the dance floor. He held on to it with all of his strength.

Morgan inhaled deeper, causing the wind to reach near tornado speeds, which was what Amadeus was waiting for. He let go of the sword, allowing himself to be blown toward her. He removed an iron pendant with a cross on the front from under his robe and held it out to her.

Once Morgan caught sight of the pendant, she felt the breath leave her chest. Amadeus landed on top of the elf, slamming her onto the sidewalk. He squeezed his legs around her to prevent her from escaping. He took the pendant from his neck and put it around hers.

"Like it? I've been carrying it since our encounter on St. Luke's Place." Amadeus then landed two solid punches to her jaw. The pendant was enough to contain her, but he was still angry for the loss of his men. Amadeus seemed satisfied that the situation was over when he heard a familiar clicking sound. Roberto stood just four feet away with his gun aimed at his head. The remaining Knights rushed toward them, ready to shoot or cut him down. Amadeus ordered them to put down their weapons.

"Let her go! Let her go or you're dead!" Roberto shouted. Amadeus knew that he meant it, but he wasn't letting any of them go. He looked Roberto in the eye.

"Would you really kill me, Roberto? I'm still a human being." His words cut deep into his heart. His gun began to shake a little.

"Just get off of her!"

"Why would you kill me, Roberto? I'm the only man who can save you."

"What?"

"I know you want to stop the killing. I know you want to be delivered from all this evil. It can happen, if you give me the gun."

"Will you hurt her?"

"I want to save all of you, Roberto. Just hand me the gun."

Roberto lowered his weapon. He was tired of running. He was tired of fighting. A sense of relief washed over him. He let go of the gun and fell to his knees. Dick quickly stepped in and took the weapon away. Jack pulled him to his feet and put him in the back of one of the sedans.

"I'm sorry! I'm so sorry!" Roberto sobbed, both to his parents and to God. He prayed that one of the parties would be able to forgive him.

CHAPTER THIRTEEN

"**M**ommy! Did the werewolves get them?" the ten-year-old girl asked in a casual tone. It took a few moments for the strange question to register with her mother. When she realized what was said, her head nearly snapped off as she turned to look in the direction her child was pointing. Dominic and Lucia were lying at the bottom of a small hill, splayed together in clothes that were torn with claw marks. She grabbed her daughter off her tiny feet. The woman's shrieking jarred the vampires awake.

"Jesus Christ! Turn off the alarm." Lucia cringed and turned over to avoid the sunlight. Dominic hoisted himself up to see the woman and her child running back to the inn.

"I think we scared someone." He was still half asleep, so this sounded like a series of mumbles to his wife. She responded in another series of mumbles. The world became less blurry to Dominic when he was able to stand on his own two feet.

The vampires stumbled into the Mystery Meat Café an hour later in fresh, new clothes. Lucia had bought the only pair of sunglasses in the gift shop that didn't have a wolf on them. She'd had a difficult time sleeping due to nightmares about the children. The more details she remembered, the more she wanted to call Morgan to see if they were still safe.

They found Zoe sitting across the table from Mayor Bert in his favorite booth. The events of the night before had eased her fears of him. He was helping her with directions to their next location when the Divitas joined them.

"Good afternoon, Mr. and Mrs. Divita. Sleep well?" Mayor Bert cheerfully welcomed the two latecomers.

"Like a rock!" Dominic said with a newfound sense of energy.

"No," Lucia grumbled. She turned to the mayor with a slightly more courteous tone in her voice. "Mayor, is there a payphone in here?"

"There sure is. It's back by the restrooms," the mayor pointed over his shoulder. Lucia jumped up while checking to see if she had a dime in her jeans pocket. She stopped to lean into Dominic's ear.

"If they're still making breakfast, I want a double stack of pancakes, bacon, eggs, and a pot of coffee," Lucia told him before marching back to the payphone. She pulled out a scrap of paper with the number for Zoe and Morgan's place. She dialed the number carefully and waited as it rang. It kept ringing. She let it go to thirty rings before she slammed the phone onto its hook. The bang turned some of the customer's heads.

Lucia dialed again. With each passing ring she could see a new, more horrible scene play out. Every one of these scenarios ended with her children being captured or killed. She wondered if they should turn back. She only had her gut feelings telling her that something was wrong. When she concentrated, she could still feel her children's hearts. She gently set the phone on its hook and inhaled silently. She told herself that she was just being a worrisome mother and that they were safe.

When she returned to the booth, Norma Jean was setting their orders down on the table. She took notice of Dominic beginning to dig into his plate of pancakes. He could feel the children as well as she could and he didn't seem to be suffering in the slightest. This calmed her nerves somewhat. As Norma Jean poured the coffee, Lucia spotted the neck wound she had given the werewolf, which had heeled rapidly into a bruise over the last few hours.

"Oh, I'm sorry about that."

"It's fine, darling." Norma Jean's assurance seemed forced to her. The waitress stomped off bitterly, but Lucia was too concerned about her own problems at the moment to worry. Lucia quietly ate her late breakfast as she and Zoe listened to Dominic and the mayor converse about matters that didn't really interest her.

The town seemed to have opened up to the three travelers that afternoon. Every face that they saw on the streets had a new meaning. Dominic thought they could now live and hunt and still be part of this world. The bellhop carried the bags to their Firebird without needing to say a word to them about the new bond that they shared. As Zoe was signing out at the front desk of the inn, Lucia noticed the mother and daughter that she and Dominic had frightened earlier that day. Lucia blew the two a kiss as they walked out.

Mayor Bert was waiting by the Firebird to see them off as the bellhop loaded the bags into the car's tiny trunk. He gave Dominic a firm handshake and kissed each of the ladies on the hand. Their parting was brief. Before stepping into the car, a cloud of confusion came over Dominic.

"Excuse me, mayor. I just realized, we were bit by so many werewolves last night. Are we --?" His question was cut short by Bert's chuckling. It was a question the old werewolf had been asked more often than he could remember.

"No, son, you and your lovely wife aren't werewolves. You need to be part of the bloodline for a bite to affect you." Mayor Bert gave him a reassuring pat on the shoulder. "Good luck to the three of you. I hope you find what you need out there. You're always welcome here."

"Thank you, mayor," Dominic warmly smiled in relief.

"It's Bert. You all can call me Bert."

Lucia left a tail of dust and leaves, never dipping below 80 miles per hour, as she whipped around the curving roads of Normal. Zoe realized that her fear of Lucia's driving had disappeared. Life in general was becoming less intimidating to the young witch.

"So, what were you and the mayor talking about?" These were the first words Lucia had spoken since they'd merged onto the highway. Dominic was startled by the break in the silence.

"What? Didn't you hear us?"

"Bits and pieces. I was somewhere else."

"I asked Bert about werewolves. He thinks they're a form of skin walkers. He believes that they walked the Earth long before man. 'The first race' is what he called them."

"What do you think?" Lucia sounded fascinated all of a sudden.

"I don't know. I asked him about how silver affects them. He didn't have an answer."

"I think I know!" Zoe shouted from the backseat. The Divitas waited for her to continue. She was more than happy to fill them in on the details.

"Metals tend to have some form of magic attached to them. Iron can depower a fairy or an elf. Silver seems to do the same for werewolves and other types of skin walkers!"

"Why?" Lucia demanded.

"Why? What do you mean, why?" Zoe was confused by the question.

"It's just metal. Why would it hurt anything by touching it? I don't get it. It's like how the cross makes other vampires shit their pants! It's just two sticks glued together! 'Oh! Oh! It's so painful!'" she mocked. Dominic remained quiet, hoping that the conversation wouldn't turn toward his beliefs. His silence was in vain.

"The cross doesn't affect you?" Zoe couldn't contain her amazement.

"Not a bit! It still hurts Dominic though." Lucia playfully giggled at Dominic's aggravation.

"It hurts you?"

"A little. Yes."

"I did notice last night you talking to that priest with no problem. Are you having doubts?" Lucia inquired.

"No! It's just that I'm still trying to figure things out."

"What's to figure out? You either believe or you don't! You know how you feel, you just don't want to admit it."

"Shut up, Lucia! Not everyone can make up their mind as quickly as you!"

"Don't tell me you're still buying that Strigori bullshit! Jesus wasn't a vampire!" Lucia didn't bother to hold back her disgust with her husband's indecision.

"Wow! Dominic, you're a Strigori?" Zoe interrupted.

"Maybe. It just makes a lot of sense. It makes being a vampire easier, knowing that there is some connection with him." Dominic defended his beliefs to not only the others, but to himself. Lucia's foot weighed down on the pedal as she listened to that line one more time.

"Connection? It's bullshit! Has it ever occurred to you that religion doesn't help. It gets in you, making you feel guilty about things that are only natural! It makes you powerless. Vampires aren't the chosen ones, any more than all the other 'chosen peoples.'"

"What do you think, Zoe?" Dominic turned to the backseat passenger.

"What?" Zoe wasn't prepared to be brought into the debate.

"Yes, Zoe! What do you, a witch, believe?"

"Well...I...Morgan says that all beings came into the world together. Humans, vampires, and the creatures of fairy like elves and stuff all have their roles in the world."

"No, Zoe. What do you believe? What does Zoe think?" Lucia's fangs were visible to the increasingly nervous girl. She understood at that moment that this topic had been a source of tension in their marriage for some time. Her mind raced through a short list of possible answers that could satisfy both parties.

"Um...um...I think vampires are magical creatures! Compare yourselves to the werewolves. When they transform, their clothes rip apart. When you turn into bats or wolves, your clothes just disappear and they reappear when you're human again. That's magic! I think they're here to keep a balance between the different worlds." Zoe's answer ended on a higher inflection, making it sound like a question. Despite that, it was good enough for her audience.

"Wait a minute. Zoe here believes in witchcraft. That's a religion!" Dominic snapped his fingers after the notion hit him. The two women waited for his follow up. "Witchcraft is a religion and it seems to empower her. We've seen witches and warlocks with our own eyes!"

"Well then, you practice witchcraft! You can prance around the house in some stupid wizard robes." Dominic didn't have a response for that. He just sat there fuming, but she knew what he would have said. -- "That's because you don't believe in magic! Even though you've seen it happen with your own eyes, you still don't buy it!"

"What do you believe, Lucia?" Zoe meekly asked. Lucia took a deep breath while she chose her next few words carefully.

"I was taught that magic is as real as this car. Over the years, I've come to realize that Gypsies and witches have stumbled on some unknown science that the world hasn't figured out yet. Magic can't be seen, but it has a power. It's no different than gravity."

"But, Lucia! Wouldn't you feel better knowing that something is there for you?" Dominic pleaded to his wife.

"I thought you were there for me!" Lucia snapped.

"That's not what I--" Dominic didn't get to continue his argument.

"I always hear that, over and over again, about religion. That people, vampires, or whatever, need some being to make them feel less lonely. That when times are rough, that everything will be all right in the end! I don't need that! I don't need anything! When times were hard, I had me! I refused to give up. I am there when you and the children need me!

"What if, in the end, there is nothing? That nothing was there for us all along? All this time we've made ourselves feel bad, made others feel bad, and all the people we've killed fighting over which god was right. What if we did all that for nothing? Maybe we should take care of our own damn selves!"

The only sound after Lucia spoke was the engine and the tires against the pavement. None of the three wished to carry the conversation any further. Zoe hated the sound of the Divitas yelling, Dominic wasn't in the mood to have his faith challenged any longer, and Lucia only wanted to reach the next gas station. It was in another ten miles and she had a phone call to make.

CHAPTER FOURTEEN

The bag tightly wrapped over Roberto's head was nearly suffocating him. A large pair of arms yanked him from the backseat of the car. His shoes scraped the pavement as he was brought into an elevator. He could feel a man standing on either side of him. No one spoke for the entire ride down. It was quite a long elevator ride. He wouldn't have been surprised if they were taking him directly to Hell.

"Where are my brother and--" Roberto got his answer in the form of an elbow to the midsection. It was enough to take him to the floor, but the other man held him up by the shoulders.

No one said another word as the doors slid open five levels later. The two men dragged him into a nearby room, leaving him alone and strapped to a heavy wooden chair. There was only the soft hum of silence to keep him company.

Over the next twelve hours, Knights, dressed in their simple priest's clothes, walked up and down the surrounding blocks in search of witnesses. They were hoping that someone had seen Roberto, Isabella, Vincenzo, or Morgan leaving a building. No one had seen a thing. Once all of the Knights had reported back, it was Jack and Dick's job to inform their superior.

They found Amadeus in the gym, pounding his bare fists into a misshapen weight bag. Dick didn't wait for his boss to notice that they were standing behind him before speaking.

"Grand Master, we got word back from our people in the field." Dick sounded too official for Amadeus's liking. When he spoke in this tone, it often meant bad news. He grabbed a white towel off a set of bar bells and cleaned the sweat from his brow and chest. Jack was distracted by the numerous scars that covered his body. He wondered if he was looking into a mirror at his future self.

"We talked to every hooker, bum, and bystander we could find and nobody saw a thing. It's as if those kids jumped from out of nowhere. We at least tidied up the disco. The girl is in a hospital bed under an assumed name and we have the fella's body in the morgue. I called an examiner, but we all know who did him in."

"An enchantment, " is all Amadeus answered.

"Yeah. That's what we figured, too. Now, these folks are up to something. They're not just running away. I was hoping you'd give me a crack at the elf and the Divita's children. I may be able to get something out of them." Dick waited for Amadeus, who used the time it took to put on a white t-shirt to decide what to do next.

"You can have them." There was no pleasure in the grand master's voice.

Roberto's body was weak, his arms and legs were numb. The restraints cut into his wrists and ankles, waking him every time he came close to nodding off.

He jolted when the door clanged open and a scuffle of people danced around the dirty concrete floor. Isabella's shouts of anger gave him some comfort, knowing who was coming inside. He guessed that Morgan and Vincenzo were the others being restrained in the three additional chairs.

One of the Knights snatched the bag off his head. Isabella was in the chair to his immediate left and Vincenzo was seated next to her. Morgan was at Roberto's right. The six Knights that had brought them in pulled the hoods off from their faces and briskly stepped outside. They didn't shut the metal door behind them, instead another Knight came inside.

Dick Walker entered the room with an ease that Roberto hadn't seen from the other Knights. He puffed on the cigarette that hung loosely from his mouth. His stride was casual and confident. The cowboy tipped his hat as a greeting to the four of them. Vincenzo replied by spitting in his direction. He missed by two feet.

"I see your spitting is as good as your throwing arm." Dick smirked at the boiling-mad young man, which only served to fuel his anger. One of the other Knights pushed a rusty metal cart into the room. He parked it at Dick's side and exited without a word. A black cloth was draped over the object that rested on top of the cart. Dick didn't make mention of it as he took off his robe and hat. He set the items on a lower shelf of the cart.

He studied the four carefully before speaking. He looked each one of them in the eye, feeling out their character. He liked his conclusions. He took his place exactly two steps in front of Morgan. Smoke shot out of his nostrils, like a dragon before its prey.

"That's a nice bow and arrow set you have there."

Morgan didn't respond.

"It doesn't look Elvish. It looks more like an Indian design. What tribe is it?"

Morgan continued to ignore him.

"She doesn't want to talk to you, Tex! Why don't you go rejoin the Village People?" Isabella shouted.

Dick slowly came around to face her. He took one long puff of his cigarette as he stood over her. He leaned in close to Isabella and put out his cigarette behind her left ear. The Knight was impressed that she didn't scream, even as it melted a tiny dot into her flesh. Vincenzo and Roberto yelled at the top of their lungs for him to stop, but he only looked into the hateful eyes of his captive.

"I was talking to the elf! Do not speak again! Is that clear?"

Isabella's careful nod didn't hide the look of pure hate for him on her face.

Dick fixed his attention back on Morgan. It was clear to him that she was furious over his attack on Isabella. She had nearly pulled her arms free from the chair. He laughed at himself for being so sloppy. Forgetting an elf's strength was a rookie mistake in his book. He took hold of one end of the cloth that sat on top of the cart.

"I'll get to the point, little lady. I am this diocese's chief interrogator. I'm gonna ask this nicely just once. What are the Divitas and Zoe Strickland planning?"

"I don't know." Morgan's voice didn't tremble. She was unafraid of him even though she knew what was to come. Dick wasn't able to keep a poker face like Amadeus. He couldn't keep from grinning from ear to ear.

"I'm glad you said that, because I really want to show you something. In interrogation, one sometimes relies on more than simple questions. You see, there are tools to my trade. It's uncanny what man has come up with in order to cause others pain. Sometimes, I think it's the only thing man does well. I've collected a good deal of these tools over the years, but since you're an elf, there was only one choice." Dick snapped the cloth away, making Morgan flinch. Underneath the cloth was an ordinary wrench.

"You elves are pretty impressive. Among your many powers is the ability to heal quickly. As a matter of fact, I'd say you're second only to the vampire in that field. Of course there are weaknesses. Everyone has a weakness. For your kind, it's iron." Dick picked up the wrench and brought it up close to her face. It was the first time that fear showed in Morgan's eyes.

"Stop it! What are you doing? She's not a vampire!" Roberto pleaded.

"Elves are not creatures of God. I can do whatever I want to her." Walker didn't take his gaze off her while addressing him.

"Help! Help! He's crazy! Help!" Roberto shouted. Dick snickered at his stupidity. The walls were soundproof. Even if someone could hear him, it didn't matter. All of the Knights knew what this room was for. Dick let him scream until his throat became sore. Roberto couldn't stop him from caressing Morgan's face with the wrench. Her breathing became more rapid as he slowly slid the tool down her right cheek, under her chin, and up her left cheek.

"Even simply touching your skin with it drains your strength. Doesn't it?" The terrified expression on her face was enough of an answer for him. Dick drew the wrench away for a brief moment before bringing it down across her face with all his muscle behind it. The others winced at the cracking sound that echoed off of the bare, concrete walls.

Three of Morgan's teeth squirmed around in her upper jaw until one of them rolled out onto her tongue. Dick took a step back to get a better view of his handiwork. The waif-like elf girl's head seemed misshapen due to the blow. The hate in her eyes was so palpable, it was almost tangible.

"Ready to talk?"

Morgan spit out her bloody tooth, pegging him directly in his left eye. Isabella and Vincenzo couldn't help laughing at him being shown up while he attempted to bully them. He quietly wiped the blood from his cheek as he gave his eye a couple of good blinks to see if it was fine. He noticed the twins enjoying his embarrassment. He quickly shut them up when he joined their laughter. There was a deep, dark anger in his laugh. He broke this laughter by giving Morgan a backhanded shot with the wrench. The strike had enough force behind it that it flipped her to the floor, chair and all.

Roberto, Vincenzo, and Isabella screamed Morgan's name in hopes that she was still alive. It wasn't obvious to them that she was breathing. Morgan had landed flat on her face while still strapped to the wooden chair. The violent explosion of screams from the Divitas only energized Dick further. He took hold of the legs of the chair and dragged Morgan's face five feet across the concrete floor. When he set her and the chair right once again, her face had a freshly bloody, rectangular scar that ran down from her forehead to her chin. Roberto couldn't see this from his vantage point, but Isabella's look of horror told him the story.

"Stop it! Can you please, in the name of God, stop it?" Roberto hoped that invoking God would move the Knight. He was sorely mistaken.

"Stop? Why, I've just started, kid." There was a hint of zeal in Dick's voice. He rotated the chair around to face Roberto, who nearly choked up at the sight of what he had done to Morgan.

"Here! I want you to see this." The Knight sounded like he was about to tell the funniest joke he had ever heard.

He braced her right hand down on the arm of the chair and carefully settled the teeth of the wrench around her index finger. He stared into Morgan's eyes, hoping to find a sign of vulnerability, as he turned the screw. The tips of the wrench pinched her finger just over the knuckle until she felt it crack the bone. Dick gave the wrench a quick jolt, breaking her finger.

Morgan didn't scream. The pain was obvious on her face, but she wasn't going to give in. She'd known what would happen if the Knights ever caught her. She just needed to hold out long enough for the Divitas and Zoe to finish their quest. He was only human, sooner or later he would have to rest.

Dick then repeated the process with the remaining fingers on her right hand. The twins shouted insults and begged for him to stop on every snap. He simply kept at his work by switching to her left hand. Once he was done with all of her fingers, he took in the moment. Morgan's fingers spread out in all different directions. She wasn't even close to talking. He knew full well that if she found her way out of that chair, she'd be on top of him in a second.

"You're not gonna tell me anything, are you?"

Morgan only stared at him.

"Maybe I should loosen up those teeth of yours."

Dick slapped his palm against her forehead, driving her head into the headrest of the chair. He set down the wrench as he fixed one restraint across her brow and another around her neck. After picking the tool back up, he forced open her mouth and positioned the wrench squarely on her front bottom teeth.

"I'm curious. How many teeth does an elf have? You spit a tooth at me, so you're down one," he said in a cold, conversational tone as he turned the screw of the wrench. Morgan felt the wrench lock around a tooth. She closed her eyes, preparing for the pain. She told herself that it was only pain and she could get through it. Dick gripped the handle tightly.

"I'll talk! You win!" screamed Roberto. Dick's head shot back at the young man.

"I'll tell you everything! What they're planning! Everything! Just stop!"

Vincenzo and Isabella were stunned by what they'd heard. They listened, hoping that they weren't really hearing what they were hearing.

"Well, go on. I'm all ears" Dick grinned in satisfaction.

CHAPTER FIFTEEN

The cell Vincenzo and Isabella had been thrown into had four cold, brick walls; two stained cots; and a toilet that was decorated with splattered brown spots that had long dried up. The twins had seen a lot of horror during their short lives, but the last few hours had eaten away at their insides. Isabella hadn't said a word since she'd watched Morgan brutalized and seen her own brother's betrayal.

She sat there and quietly caressed the wound behind her ear. The tiny bit of skin was still hot and soft from Dick Walker's cigarette. Vincenzo felt tears push their way out when he caught sight of her checking the burn. His felt like he was in mourning. He knew that Roberto had never approved of what the family was, but he'd always felt in his soul that he loved them. That was over. It was difficult for Isabella to comfort him at first, since Roberto was already dead in her mind and in her heart.

She held her brother close, hoping that it would make both of them feel a little safer. Every few minutes she said something encouraging to him, but with little effect. She wasn't even sure if he knew she was there. Each time she said "It's going to be all right!" it sounded less possible.

"Do you want to bite me?" she asked. It was the only thing she could think of to calm him down.

"What?" He was caught off guard.

"Would you feel better if you bit me?" She tilted her forehead down and braced it onto his. He gave it some thought, giving him a wonderful moment without thinking about Roberto.

"No."

"Would you like--"

"Our brother is gone!" Vincenzo's voice had finality to it. Isabella could no longer hold back her emotion. She did her best to ignore the tears rolling down her face. She lifted her head back up above his so that he couldn't see. She had to be strong for herself and for her only remaining brother.

"They're going to kill Mamma and Poppa!" Vincenzo cried out.

"No. They're not." She sounded so sure.

"Bullshit! They're going to stake them like animals and chop them up in little pieces and then we'll never see them again and then they're going to kill us! Fuck! Fuck! I don't want to lose them! I don't want to lose them! I just want to see them again! Fuck!"

Isabella had nothing clever to say to comfort him. She could only listen to him repeat what she was trying not to think herself. After his cries had slowly devolved into whispering moans, their silence was broken by the clang of a cell door from down the hall.

Vincenzo sensed every muscle in his sister's body tense up. They knew it was their brother, returning from his meeting with the grand master after ratting out his own mother and father.

Roberto stepped into the dank cell. The single thing that could possibly have lifted his spirits was shackled to the wall. Morgan had been given enough slack to sit on one of the rusted beds.

The elf looked up, fearful that more "questioning" was about to occur. All of that washed away once she caught sight of Roberto being escorted into the room. His hands were cuffed behind his back.

Neither of them spoke as one Knight brought him over to his bed while another blocked the doorway. He directed Roberto to face the wall as he unlocked his cuffs. Once they were taken off, the Knight joined his partner outside.

Morgan waited until the door's locked clicked and the Knights marched away. She tried to get his name out, but she could no longer choke back the emotions that had consumed her since he had been carted off to be questioned by the grand master. He rushed over to catch her as she crumpled. He marveled at how much she had healed since Brother Dick's torture. Her fingers had almost completely straightened out and the bruises were faded, as if they had been healing for days.

"Why? Why did you do it? It's not just your parents out there! It's Zoe! She's in danger now! I could have held out! I could take it. Why?" she demanded as he held her collapsed body. He cupped her small, wounded face in his hands. His strength reassured her enough that it halted her tears for the moment.

"I couldn't take it. I couldn't take seeing him hurt you. I'm sorry..." Roberto's voice trailed off. He was unsure of what else to say, fearing that she would become angrier if he continued.

Morgan couldn't believe it. This man would give up his own parents for her. She found it oddly romantic. It took her a moment to refocus before speaking again.

"What about Zoe?" Morgan's tone was quiet and serious. Roberto looked into her eyes. He was surprised that she didn't seem very upset with him. The feeling he was getting was concern.

"I told them that I would tell them what they wanted to know, if they promised not to hurt Zoe." Roberto suddenly remembered a detail from the conversation. The detail gave him hope.

"I asked them to swear to God...he gave me his word..."

"Who?"

"Amadeus. I told him everything I knew," he confessed. Morgan didn't trust the Knight's word as much as he did, but what was done was done. She ruffled her fingers through his thick black hair, amazed that he would risk so much for her. She could tell that this calmed him down a bit.

"It's okay. If their leader gave his word, then it's okay. Everything will be all right." Morgan had no idea if that was true or not.

Lucia and Dominic could feel their children's hopelessness from hundreds of miles away. Without knowing why exactly the children were feeling that way, it caused Dominic and Lucia to remain on edge. Each of them was afraid to bring up the subject, so they kept silent for most of the day as they waited for the Neverland Gentlemen's Club to open. A fairy was next on their list and everyone in the magical underground knew that this club was the place to find one.

They took interstate 287 through Crystal Lake and reached Franklin Lakes hours earlier than they needed to. Lucia decided to stop at a nearby strip mall to rest before their next encounter. Once she had parked and switched off the engine, she sat back without saying anything.

"Lucia? Are you all right?" It was the second time Dominic had asked that during the trip.

"Everything is fine!" Lucia answered in an annoyed tone as she stepped out of the car to find a restroom. Zoe was worried over Lucia's state of mind. Dominic, on the other hand, had seen his wife like this before, whenever she was under stress. He knew full well that she often internalized her concerns. He looked forward being finished with their quest.

Finally, midnight was close at hand and they were driving down the long, curvy road to the club. Gravity Road proved to be longer than they had expected. Lucia began to worry that they were going the wrong way. Dominic spotted someone walking on the side of the road and suggested they stop and ask him if he knew the way. Lucia grudgingly slowed down beside the dark figure.

As Dominic rolled down the window the shadowy man halted instantly. He was all black except for his long, gray hair that stuck up in all directions.

"Excuse me. Do you know where the Neverland Club is?" Dominic put on his most charming voice so not to alarm the stranger.

The man didn't answer. He turned around, as if he was trying to figure out what that curious sound was. When he stumbled closer to the car, Zoe gripped her hand tighter on the headrest of Dominic's seat. She could see that his eyes were all white, without of any sign of humanity. He made no noise as he crossed over the gravel to the car. Dominic almost got the sensation that he wasn't even there. The dark figure didn't speak. He simply looked around the insides of the car.

"Oh, Goddess! Do...do you know what he is?" Zoe nearly choked on the words.

"Yeah! He's useless!" Lucia grumbled as she put the Firebird in drive and peeled back out onto the open road, leaving the Midnight Walker to another lonely night. She decided to keep going forward since the landmarks at the sides of the road were getting more familiar.

They eventually reached the Neverland Gentlemen's Club. The unremarkable, one story building was surrounded by a hundred cars, from beat up trucks to brand new BMWs. The modest parking area was full, so they had to pull over in a field with another bunch of vehicles.

"Shit! This place is going to be packed," Lucia groaned.

"You don't mind the crowds at the Inferno," Dominic countered.

"That's because those crowds are there to worship me!" Lucia laughed. Dominic was comforted by her cocky laughter, but he knew that she was still troubled in her soul.

Despite all of the cars in the parking lot and nearby field, Dominic and Lucia wondered if the club was actually open due to the lack of noise coming from the building. There weren't any windows along the brick walls and the place didn't have any sense of life going on.

Zoe took the vampires' hands and yanked them toward the door. Just inside the rotten, oak door was a tiny room painted wall to wall in black. On the other side of the room was a rusty metal door and on their left was a glass booth. Sitting behind the glass was a diminutive, old man who must have been two feet tall, at the most. He was dressed in a blue velvet jacket with matching pants and a red velvet cap. His gold teeth sparkled through his furry, white beard. He acted like he knew what they wanted before they'd gotten the chance to ask.

"Well, well, well. It's been a long time since we've seen some vampires cross our doorstep. What can I do you for?"

"How could you tell?" Dominic asked with a little worry in his voice.

"The nose knows. This old gnome has been around. I've met my fair share of vampires and I've never seen anyone wear it as well as the two of you."

"Thank you. May we have a moment of your time, Mr...?" Dominic leaned in to the small opening in the glass.

"It's Papa. They all call me Papa. How can I help you?"

"We need to see one of your fairies."

"You're not eating one of my fairies! I take care of my girls!"

"No, no! That's not what we want!" Dominic protested. Lucia slid her way in front of him and gave the gnome a girly smile. She had his attention.

"Papa. My name is Lucia Divita. This is my husband, Dominic, and this cute little thing in the corner is our friend, Zoe. We mean no harm to you, your girls, or even your customers. What we need is your help. Our family is in trouble and all we want is a few minutes of one of your fairy's time. We own a nightclub ourselves. We know how valuable time can be. We'll gladly pay for however much that time is worth."

"I don't know…" A crack had appeared in his armor. Lucia's breath steamed up a tiny circle on the glass and she made a little heart with her finger before it disappeared. Papa was sold.

"Very well! You'll still need to pay cover. Ten bucks each!" Papa spoke to Dominic, but he was looking at Lucia. Dominic fished three tens out of his wallet.

"Of course, but isn't ten dollars a high cover?"

"Behind that door are the finest creatures from the other dimension. I think once you set eyes on them, you'll agree that ten bucks is very fair. Go to my office, I'll join you in a minute," Papa smirked. He waved his hand causing the metal door to creek open. Music and lights exploded out from beyond the heavy, black curtains that kept the full view from those waiting to enter.

"It's good to see you back," Dominic whispered to his wife.

"Getting in required charm, besides I'm fine," Lucia whispered back as she pushed open the curtains.

The building was larger on the inside. The three stepped into a stadium sized hall, only to lose their breaths. The fairies each stood from ten to fourteen feet tall, dancing over the heads of the entranced men and women seated at tables that ran up and down the great hall. They also danced on top of a wide, mile long runway. Lucia was so fixated on them that it took some time before she noticed that there weren't any lights to speak of; the dark room was illuminated by the dancers' very own bodies. The fairies were living illuminations that glowed yellow, red, blue, and green.

"They're…they're beautiful!" Zoe thought she was going to cry at the sight of them. Lucia and Dominic each tried to hold back their arousal long enough to meet with Papa.

Trays of drinks buzzed around the club, carried by small, bright green lights. They were pixies. One pixie flew up to the Divitas. She was a tiny, short haired, blonde girl dressed in a dark green mini dress. Her eyes were the same shade of green as her glowing skin.

"Hi! Can I get you something to drink?" The pixie winked at Dominic.

"Actually, that's what we're here to talk to Papa about. Where's his office?" Dominic asked. The pixie pointed to an ordinary looking door, twenty feet to their right. She quickly buzzed past Zoe.

"I like your glasses!" the pixie said.

"Oh! I...um...thank you!" Zoe blushed. She wanted to say more, but she noticed that the others were walking away without her. She stomped over to the office, pretending that she'd been following all long.

Dominic reasoned which door was his by the two doorknobs, one at normal height and the second at two feet. Papa was sitting behind his desk when they entered. His hands were folded together around the top of a diamond headed cane.

"So, how can we help you?" He waved his hand, closing the door behind them.

"Zoe, here, is a witch. She's helping us with a spell. Long story short, drinking some fairy blood will help us grow more powerful."

"I get it. You want to become "vampire lords," huh? I've met vampires who have tried that rare spell. They always failed because they couldn't find all the creatures before they nearly died of thirst. However, I like you two. I like your moxie so much that I'm not gonna charge for the use of one of my fairies."

"You're not?" Dominic was suspicious.

"No! Instead, you will owe me one favor."

"What's the favor?" Lucia spoke up.

"I don't know yet, but I'm sure that someday I will require the help of two very powerful vampires that remember who assisted them in their moment of need."

"Can we have a moment?" Dominic motioned toward the door. Zoe was right behind him, but Lucia hadn't budged, embarrassed that he wanted to step outside. She soon made her way out with the other two. Papa sat and waited patiently.

"What do you think?" Dominic whispered to the two women.

"What's your hold up?" Lucia barked out.

"It's just that every fairy tale I've read since I was a child warned against bargains like this. Maybe this is a bad idea."

"Dominic! We're already in the middle of a bad situation. Why don't we just go through with it?" Lucia felt that this conversation was a waste of time and she had no problem showing her impatience. Her husband looked to Zoe for a second opinion.

"Zoe?"

"Oh! Um...I don't know. I've never heard of gnomes making evil deals before. I think it's okay," she reasoned, shrugging her shoulders.

"Dominic, look. If he wants something unreasonable like Roberto's first born, we'll just kill him or something." Lucia wanted to get going. Her husband felt that if she and Zoe had no issues with the deal, then there was nothing to worry about. The three reentered the office and agreed to the pact. Dominic swore he saw a twinkle in the old gnome's eye as he shook his diminutive hand.

Papa asked them to follow him out onto the floor to find the right fairy to take part in the spell. There were too many excellent choices working that night. A blue fairy performing a table dance for a biker couple winked at them. A yellow fairy that flew into the air and landed on the stage in the splits tempted Lucia, but she resembled Ursula too closely for her liking. Papa tugged on Dominic's pants leg and pointed over to a red fairy who was pole dancing for a crowd of businessmen.

Her every movement was a work of art.

"Now, this is Jezebel, she is my best girl," the gnome boasted.

The fourteen foot tall fairy was nearly as tall as the pole. The second she swung onto her feet, she caught the Divitas watching her. Her naked body glowed bright enough to turn the whole corner of the club red. She excused herself from her disappointed customers when Papa called out to her. She didn't simply walk, she glided across the room. The vampires had never seen such a large being move so gracefully.

"Yes, Papa?" Jezebel's voice was almost musical. The willowy creature was over twice as tall as the vampires. She gave a warm, loving smile to them from her crooked mouth.

"This is Dominic and Lucia Divita. They're vampires who need some help. Would you mind stepping off the floor for a few minutes?"

"Not at all, Papa." Jezebel's wings fluttered in anticipation.

Papa asked all four to follow him into one of the back rooms, designed for group parties. There was a couch and folding chairs for additional guests. The room was large enough for the fairy to dance and even fly, if she wished to. Papa hopped up onto the couch to briefly explain what the Divitas wanted from her. He promised that it would only take a few minutes of her time.

"Are you going to do battle with those mighty Catholic boys?" Jezebel raised one sharp eyebrow as she leaned over to face Lucia a little better.

"Yes." The vampire was startled by the twinkle of her green eyes. Her thin, yet massive, hand caressed Lucia's silken cheek, causing her wings to flutter once again at the very touch. The fairy admired the vampire's strong, motherly soul and curvy torso. Lucia stood out among the slim bodies of the fairies that she saw night after night. She turned and studied Dominic's face. She saw a young, modern kind of man, but there was a spirit deep inside of him. It was something she hadn't felt for centuries. Both of them had it.

"In all of you, I can almost taste a great feast concocting. The pasta; the meat; the sauce. All of it is coming together, with a fine wine to wash it down. I'll do it, Papa. I'd be happy to help with this recipe."

Papa took great pleasure in this deal. He pulled out one of the folding chairs and hopped onto it for the show that was to come. His joy was interrupted when one of the pixie waitresses flew into the room.

"Papa! Papa! The Jersey Devil is causing a disturbance at the bar!" the pixie shouted.

"Ah, jeez! You didn't call him 'the Jersey Devil' to his face did you? It's 'Mr. Leeds!' Only call him 'Mr. Leeds!'"

"No! No! I'd never forget that!" she protested.

"Okay! Go on without me. I've got manager shit to do." Papa plopped back onto his feet and bolted out, barely even looking back. Zoe asked the vampires and Jezebel to take their places. The ceremony started out like the others. Zoe began to read the spell from her notebook.

"To these vampires, I give this fairy. She is filled with endless sex and life. Drink! Drink my vampires! Taste the fruit of life!"

Before Dominic and Lucia bit into her wrists, Jezebel gave them both a naughty little wink. Drinking the fairy's blood brought a sharp tingle to their lips. Following the pleasant taste of her blood, there was a blinding flash of light. Jezebel and Zoe disappeared from view as they began to fall into an endless, blue sky. Their clothes peeled away, transforming into flower pedals. The flowers multiplied and seemed to be raining down around them. Lucia and Dominic could see lovely fairies fly among the sea of pedals.

The fairies brushed against them. They tickled them. They kissed them. They loved them. They took them by the arms and legs and pulled them apart. The two vampires broke into a million tiny

Dominics and Lucias as they crashed into the ocean. They were suddenly part of the Earth, becoming the sea, the ground, the animals, and even the sky. The millions of themselves dried up and crumbled into the land and emerged out of the ground to be reborn. They grew into adulthood only to grow old and die once more. This happen over and over again. In one brief moment, they lived and died a thousand times. They were one with life, death, and the universe. They were happy.

It was then that Dominic and Lucia realized they were lying on the floor. Jezebel stood like a skyscraper above them. Zoe stepped into their view.

"Are you two okay?" Zoe's concern was mixed with confusion. Jezebel only smiled.

"What the fuck was in that blood?" Lucia said while doing her best to find her footing.

"I'm impressed. Fairy blood can be a spicy dish," Jezebel revealed.

"We've always been very good, um, fairy blood drinkers," Dominic tried to joke. Papa stepped in and to his dismay he was too late to watch the fun.

"I'm sorry I was kept away the entire night."

"Entire night?" Lucia was bewildered by the last sentence.

"Yeah, it's almost five! You kids have been in here a while," Papa explained. The gnome offered them one last beer before they went, but they claimed they needed to be off. Jezebel sat down on one knee and put her fingers through Dominic's hair.

"You're always trying to please everyone. Don't forget about yourself."

She kissed Lucia on the cheek and leaned in close to her ear. What she whispered to her was anybody's guess. It did give Lucia a feeling of hope. The vampire took hold of Jezebel's hand.

Lucia kissed her hand as she tried not to tear up in front of everyone. She didn't thank her, since she knew fairies hated to be thanked in words. Instead she handed Jezebel one of the silver rings, right off of her hand.

The fairy turned her attention to Zoe. She wrapped her long fingers around the witch's head and kissed her. It was passionate enough to literally lift Zoe off her feet. When she let her stand back on the floor once again, the fairy could see how affected she was by her touch. Zoe stood, eyes closed, not wanting to move. Jezebel softly touched her nose, waking her from her trance.

"My dear Zoe, you are my champion, my hero. You are so powerful, so wise, so beautiful, and it pains me that you have no idea of what you can do. Please, don't be afraid."

Zoe could only nod, still dazed from her touch and her words. She had never felt such confidence expressed in her. Dominic took her by the arm as they left the strange night club.

Papa waved goodbye and went to count the night's take when he noticed Jezebel tearing up. He pulled a handkerchief from his jacket and held it up for her to take. Once she grabbed the handkerchief and put it to her nose, it hit her how tiny it was and how stupid she was for forgetting. She let out a small laugh, which is what Papa had hoped would be her reaction.

"What's wrong, my princess? Did they hurt you?" Papa asked.

"No! No. I liked them, actually. It's just not fair. What I foresaw... There is so much pain in store for them."

CHAPTER SIXTEEN

"Stop!" shouted Father Wood. He stood in the path of the Full Moon Hay Ride's wagon of tourists. The driver gave the horse's reigns a tight pull, bringing them to a sudden halt. The two gunmen gripped their rifles, bringing a sense of apprehension to the tourists sitting in the wagon. The tour guide stood at the end of the wagon to find the priest in the middle of the dirt road.

"Why, it's Father Wood! Is there a problem, Father?" shouted the tour guide.

"I apologize for the disturbance. It's just that I have a terrible feeling about tonight! Is there any way I can convince you to turn back?"

"I don't know, Father. We've done this thousands of times before. Is there anything you can tell us about what you felt?"

"All I can tell you is that I feel that something evil awaits all of you in the forest."

"Evil? You got that right, Father," the heavy voice of Amadeus came from behind the priest. He stood in front of a cloud of shadows that marched out from the woods. A flash of silver in the corner of Father Wood's vision proved to be an arrow. Its silver tip pieced his chest, bringing him down instantly.

Three gunshots flashed from the crowd of a dozen Knights. The heads of the riflemen and the driver exploded. The tour guide leapt off the wagon, transforming into a wolf in midair, hoping to escape into the cover of night. He was shot before he landed on the grass. He attempted to regain his footing in his wolf man form, but was cut down with a series of gunshots. One Knight stood over his body to be sure he was finished, while another two hopped onto the wagon. The tourists jumped from their seats, fearful that they would be next.

Jack Cain gave a woman and her preteen son a comforting smile. He inspected the six riders. None were the vampires or the witch, and he was thankful that the two human, mid-twenties couples were unharmed. He waved to his grand master that the wagon was secure.

Amadeus had other werewolves on his mind. He walked over to Father Wood, who was still on the ground clutching the arrow wound in his chest. The pain from the silver tip ripped apart his torso so much that he didn't dare to move it.

"You are a priest?" The words sounded dirty when said by Amadeus. Father Wood didn't say anything. "Nauseating. Are you the reason why this whole town was able to remain hidden under our nose?"

Father Wood chuckled slightly in between gulps of air. Amadeus crouched lower to see him better. Father Wood went silent when the Knight reached toward the arrow.

"One of my investigators handed me a file before we left. Ten years ago, two Knights came here to see if there really were werewolves in Normal, New Jersey. It was you who convinced them that it was all for the tourists. How cute. Does that arrow hurt? After all these years of serving Christ, do you now feel his pain?" Amadeus plucked the end of the arrow. Wood felt as if his skin was peeling off. Brother Paul rushed over to Amadeus's side.

"Grand Master, we have yet to find the vampires or the witch." Paul looked at the ground as he spoke. Amadeus stood up, making Paul take a step back to avoid getting in his space.

"Keep looking. We have a lot of work to do tonight. I want to know if the Divitas are still here. I want the humans secured and I want the pack leader. We get the pack leader, we have the town!"

"How do we do that, Amadeus?"

"Don't worry. He'll come to us."

The inn was the first place that the Knights raided. Brother Paul led a team of five into the front lobby. The old man behind the desk didn't try to pretend; he vaulted over the desk to attack. Paul drew his guns before he finished transforming. The six shots to the chest threw him back into the wall. The room keys were knocked loose and rained down on the old man as he transformed, one last time, back to human form. Paul didn't have much time to inspect the desk clerk. The gunfire had alerted the bell boys, who both came barreling down the stairs in werewolf form.

The crowed lobby was no place for a werewolf to hunt. They were taken down by shots to their knees and heads. Paul went over to their bodies and put a bullet in each of the chests to be on the safe side.

A college student in his underwear sneaked his way down the staircase to see what all the noise was about. He discovered the bell boys, lying dead and naked, in front of the strange group of men dressed in black and armed to the teeth.

"Take him to the truck!" Paul ordered. One knight took the man by the arm and dragged him out to a large, black van waiting out front. A Knight in the back of the van covered the young man with one of their own black robes. He was told to remain quiet and sit still; He had no plans to do otherwise. The remaining guests of the inn and the Full Moon Hay Ride were soon ushered into the van.

Norma Jean's patience was growing short. The Mystery Meat Café should have closed nearly half an hour ago, but one last couple just wouldn't leave. Mr. and Mrs. Thompson didn't seem to care that she had put up the closed sign in the window, or even that she'd locked the doors.

They chatted about how delightful the town was and that they should suggest it to all their friends. Every time they looked ready to pay, they only asked for more coffee. Norma Jean wanted to kick them out, or at least gobble them up, but she was going to wait until they were done. She sat up on the counter and chatted with Vick, the cook, who had already stuffed his overweight torso into his street clothes.

"I'm thinking that they better tip well," Norma Jean grumbled quietly.

"Or what?" Vick chuckled.

"We don't have a special for tomorrow." The two laughed to themselves until they noticed Nadine, owner of the town gift shop, running in wolf woman form past the windows. Norma Jean and Vick stared in disbelief, wondering what had caused Nadine to risk the town's whole cover. Mr. Thompson noticed them and turned to get a look out the window.

"Tommy? Tommy? What is it?" Mrs. Thompson's question was laced with a thrill of discovery.

"There...there really are werewolves! They're running around everywhere!" he said with the wide eyed excitement of a child. A werewolf was then thrown backwards through the window, landing on top of him. Both were slammed into a nearby table.

Emily Thompson ran over to her husband. He was knocked out under the beast, which was rapidly reverting back to human shape. Norma Jean and Vick sat and watched in stunned silence. They could suddenly hear the gunshots and the howls all over the town. Normal was being invaded. Before either of them could take action, a team of four Knights entered the diner, armed with silver weapons.

The two werewolves jumped off the counter, doing their best to avoid the massive gunfire that exploded the wood, napkins, and glass around them. Mrs. Thompson held her husband tightly, hiding behind the dead, former wolf man for shelter. The Knights aimed high so as not to hit the humans. Norma Jean followed Vick out the back door.

Once Vick was outside, three bullets to the chest bought him down. Norma Jean had no time to mourn as Brother Brian, hiding behind a dumpster, had her in his sights. She flew over a fence, but not before taking a hit to the back of her right leg. Two Knights exited the rear after them where they found Vick's nude body at their feet. Brian hopped the fence in pursuit of the waitress.

Mayor Bert and his son, Butch, were enjoying a quiet night off, watching boxing on TV. The two went stiff when they heard the first gunshots drowning out the match. Butch leapt up and switched off the television as Mayor Bert sped to the door and listened. It was what he had feared would happen for years. The Knights were coming for them.

His people were dying and the town's years of peace had come to an end. The only choice he had was to save the pack. Places come and go, but what was important to him was the pack. Mayor Bert turned to his son. He was already beginning to change for battle when his father snatched him by the shoulders.

"No! You mustn't go with me!" Mayor Bert forcefully explained. Butch halted in mid-transformation out of confusion.

"What? Why?" Butch was dumbstruck.

"If I am to die tonight, then you are the pack leader! You need to stay out of this!"

"Bullshit! I can't run with--"

"I'm not asking you! You are the future of the pack. They are lost if we're both dead! Now--"

"Dad!"

"Dad, nothing! I need you to escape. Run. Run to your Uncle Benny's house. I can't worry about you while I fight them. If I turn them back, I'll come for you. I promise."

Butch knew that his father was right. He was always right. He could see the fear and impotence in Bert's face. He couldn't let his pride get in the way of his father's duty to defend the pack.

"All right. Dad...I..."

Mayor Bert took hold of his son for what he knew could be the final time. Each was more afraid for the other than for themselves. Father and son held each tight, trying to appreciate every second they could. Finally, Bert was able to push his son away.

"All right. You need to go. Now!"

Butch took one last look at his father, waiting for a sign that he would change his mind and ask him to follow him into battle. That sign never came. Butch ran out the door in human form as his father had instructed him. Bert didn't move a muscle until his son had faded safely from view.

Mayor Bert sniffed in the air. He could smell the gunfire and the blood. The noise was centered in the town square. That's where he would make his stand. He began to run, his clothes quickly torn from his body. He fully transformed into a wolf as he silently raced down the hill.

The wound in Norma Jean's leg wasn't getting any better. The pain prevented her from turning into anything other than her wolf woman shape. She wanted to fall over, but she knew that she had to keep moving. She could hear Brother Brian only yards behind her. It was easy to make out his clumsy steps gaining on her. He kicked her from behind and she rapidly rolled over in the dirt to face her attacker. Brian was paying too much attention to his prey as he drew his sword. He didn't notice the dark, furry shape that flashed in the corner of his eye until it was too late.

Amadeus stood still in the middle of the town square with Dick and Jack on either side of him. It was their job to shoot any attacking werewolf that came their way. At the grand master's feet was a brown, rectangular case that he was saving for the pack leader's appearance. A sudden stand down of the surrounding werewolves told him that he would soon have his chance.

A huge, dark shadow leapt onto the roof of the two story town hall. It threw something across the field, intending to strike Amadeus in the chest. Instead, Amadeus caught the wet, mushy ball just inches away from his torso. He deduced by the wavy, brown hair that the ball was Brian's head. He didn't wish to look at his face.

The shadow jumped from the roof, landing thirty feet from the trio of Knights. Mayor Bert, a seven foot tall beast, used that moment to assess his enemies. No one dared move, or even breath. The surrounding Knights and werewolves followed their lead.

Once Bert was satisfied with what he sensed, he transformed to his hairless form. Amadeus carefully handed Brian's head to Dick without taking his eyes off of the mayor.

"Here, Dick. Please recover Brother Brian's body," Amadeus gently spoke.

"You'll need a rake!" Mayor Bert growled. The werewolves laughed with a renewed sense of confidence. The Knights held their weapons tighter in apprehension. A feeling that the tide could turn washed over all of them.

The mayor's joke only increased Amadeus's drive. He removed his cloak, wearing only his simple black pants and priest's shirt. The vampire hunter removed his gun from his holster and gave it to Jack, then drew his sword and embedded it into the ground to his right. He reached inside the case at his feet and pulled out a pair of silver gauntlets. The armor reached up to his elbows and were decorated with crosses.

"I am Amadeus, Grand Master of the Knights of the Silver Cross! I challenge you to a fight to the death. No guns, no swords."

"What are those then?"

"These are my claws."

Mayor Bert considered his options. He knew that the Knights held all the cards.

"Accepted."

Amadeus leaned slightly toward Jack.

"Jack?" Amadeus almost sounded out of character for a brief moment.

"Yes?" Jack kept a brave face as they stared at the werewolf.

"If he wins, you're in change. You must lead these men out of town as fast as you can. They'll have the advantage and you'll be on the run. However, if I win the battle, but he still bites me, I want you to shot me."

"I--"

"Don't lose faith. I will want someone to save me from damnation. I can't think of anyone better than the man I want to someday succeed me."

"Thank you, sir."

Amadeus looked away from the mayor to give Jack a smile that seemed to come from nowhere. The young man wasn't aware that he could even make such an expression.

"It's Marvin. You can call me Marvin." There was a peaceful gleam in his face eye, as though he thought that what he was doing was uplifting in some way. Jack realized that there wasn't a monster alive that was as powerful as God.

Amadeus and Mayor Bert shot out of their positions to attack one another. They hit head on in the middle of the square. The mayor had fully transformed on his third step. He flung himself at Amadeus with his jaws aimed straight for his neck.

The old man was quicker than he looked. He swung his right arm to block the werewolf's bite. His teeth came down, but were unable to bend or break the silver gauntlet. He shook him around, doing his best to yank the armored glove off. When that failed to work, he decided to drag the grand master around the square. He smashed him into the white picket fence surrounding the courtyard and into several werewolves and Knights watching the duel from the sidelines.

The werewolf came to a stop when Amadeus braced his foot on the street curb. Bert was surprised when he grabbed a fistful of hair and swung him over his leg. The mayor tripped and landed on his back, letting go of his opponent. When he had regained his footing, Amadeus gave him a right cross to his snout. The townsfolk winced at the fangs and saliva splattering from their leader's jaws. The mayor did his best to recover, but silver wounds take much longer to heal. Amadeus didn't give him any chance to react as he bought both fists down on top of his head. The crack of the mayor's skull was heard by everyone within a few feet of the fight.

Mayor Bert couldn't see due to the amount of blood and matted hair that had fallen into his eyes. He felt himself becoming dizzy and he knew that lashing out blindly was not helping. He transformed to his weaker wolf man form and hoped that he was trading power for form.

Once he was strong enough, Bert went for his throat. He lifted Amadeus in the air and slammed him onto the ground. The Knight seemed to be fading with every squeeze and every struggle for breath.

Jack was becoming aware of the growing energy of the townspeople. He cocked his gun, just in case he had to fight his way out of town. He was tempted to aim the weapon at the wolf man to save his mentor, but knew he couldn't do it. He needed to keep his faith.

Mayor Bert squeezed harder, ready for the kill. He was going to end this Knight's life and rip his insides out to show the others that his town would not be invaded. He ignored the pain of the Knight's silver covered fists pounding his shoulders. There would be time to heal in the morning. He thought that maybe his foe had given up when he stopped hitting him.

Amadeus had other plans. He reached under Bert's claws, prying them from his throat and bending them backwards. Each snap of bone in the mayor's hands took its toll. He felt himself backing down. The Knight was able to push him away without letting go of the mangled fingers of his once powerful hands. He kicked Bert in the groin repeatedly until fell to his knees.

The grand master sat on his chest and hammered his silver armored fists into the mayor's face. He continued punching his fallen enemy, increasing the force with every blow. His blood sprayed all over the green grass. The townspeople trembled with every crack of bone they heard and felt. Amadeus wanted to stop after the mayor was dead. He couldn't stop himself. It just felt too good. He rarely felt so righteous.

The only thing that was capable of stopping Amadeus was his own aging body. His arms ached, his lungs couldn't get in enough oxygen. He halted himself before he fell beside the mayor's twitching, naked corpse. Jack ran to his side, fearful that he would be next to drop. He saw quickly that his support wasn't required. Amadeus didn't speak to the young man. Instead, he seemed suddenly remorseful over what had transpired.

"Sleep now. Your curse is over," Amadeus whispered. He reached up to Jack to help him to his feet. Once he was standing, he could get a better survey of the townspeople of Normal. They had almost all reverted back into their human forms. The fight had been taken out of the whole pack. Some of the werewolves looked angry, many more were broken in spirit.

"Your orders?" Jack asked.

"Kill them all." Amadeus was unflinching in his decree.

Twenty-five human tourists were huddled together in the rear of an enormous, black van. They had been pulled out of bed and off of the streets. Mrs. Thompson held onto her still unconscious husband as she listened to the echoes of gun blasts and the painful yelping of wolves. She almost swore that she could hear something human mixed with the howls.

CHAPTER SEVENTEEN

Brad and Beverly Jones had hoped to reach Newark before midnight, but they'd spent too much time at dinner. They felt that it was too late and their Ford Maverick was getting a bit cramped. His parents were going to have to wait one more day. The next town they came to was a farming village known as Stillwater.

Beverly spotted a billboard on the highway advertising a bed and breakfast called Under a Starry Night. As they drove through the town, everything appeared to be shut down for the night. The gas stations, the diners, and even the huge Presbyterian church that loomed over the center of town were all dark. What kept the couple going were the many signs that promised the bed and breakfast was just a few more streets away.

The way the light shone from the windows of the old house reminded both of them of a classic haunted house, like from every cartoon they had ever seen. As they drove up the winding, little road toward the inn, Brad pointed out to his wife the light from the moon bouncing off the nearby river. He put his hand on her leg. They both felt a little more comfortable spending the night in this charming setting.

As Mr. and Mrs. Jones climbed the creaky, wooden steps to the front doors, they could hear an old, scratchy record playing inside. The song sounded like it was from the 1930s or 1940s, with depressingly drunk horns backing a sad vocal. Brad wasn't sure if they should knock on the door.

"Wait a minute! What if these people are eighty-years-old or something?" Brady realized out loud.

"Well, where are we going to stay? Didn't you say that we're low on gas? And I don't know where the next motel is. Let's just try it. The sign here says 'Drop in anytime.'" Beverly was more nervous about getting stuck on the open road than she was of the creepy house.

An uncomfortable amount of time passed after Brad knocked on the door. Just before they decided to head back to their car, the door cracked open. A white, pointy face emerged from between the heavy doors. The thin woman was much younger than they had expected, probably in her thirties. Her hair was as black as her tight, Victorian dress and was tied into an impossibly tight bun. The woman was expressionless to the point of looking like she was half asleep. The Joneses felt a little guilty, they had the feeling that they were keeping her up.

"Hello. May I help you?" Her dry, English accent creaked almost as badly as the front steps.

"Hi! We were wondering if you had a room for the night." Brad used the most polite tone he could muster. Beverly stood behind him, looking around his arm. A crack appeared at the left corner of the woman's mouth. It was her smile, but it didn't seem to affect her dead eyes. Mrs. Jones ducked back behind her husband.

"Of course you can stay. What kind of monsters would we be if we turned away business? Enter, please."

The interior looked exactly how they had guessed it would. It was like walking into to the 19th century. There were working gas lights on the walls. A phonograph was still playing in the next room. There wasn't much to suggest anything modern. Even the front desk had an old fashioned cash register sitting on top.

"This place is really charming! Who designed it all?" Beverly was rather impressed with the authentic decor. The woman looked back at her as if she were stupid.

"Why, this is our home."

"Oh! Of course!" Beverly decided to keep quiet for the next few minutes.

The woman escorted them over to the guestbook on the desk. A slight creak came from the next room. It was a tall, thin man dressed in Victorian attire, carrying a candle. He was the perfect match for the woman. His hair was slicked back and his suit was so tight it could have been painted on his body. His white face practically glowed against his black hair and clothes.

"Eleanor? Do we have guests?" the man asked. His voice matched hers, only deeper.

"Yes, Mr. and Mrs.--Oh! I apologize. How rude of me. I didn't get either one of your names."

The woman's regret put to couple more at ease. Brad stepped up to the man and threw his hand out. The man studied the hand for a moment then gave Brad the most limp handshake he'd ever encountered.

"Hello. I am Phinnaeus March. I trust you have already met my wife, Eleanor. We are the proprietors of this establishment."

"Brad Jones! This is my wife, Beverly."

Phinnaeus kissed her hand. She thought it was pleasant, even though his touch was as cold as ice.

"Charmed, I'm sure."

"Why...yes," was all Beverly could utter.

"What brings you to our humble little village at this time of night?" Phinnaeus addressed his question to both of them. Brad had to speak for his wife.

"We're going to see my parents for their 50th wedding anniversary.

I guess we misjudged how long it would take to get there." Brad didn't want to tell them where they lived for some reason. Eleanor finished checking their guests in and came out from behind the desk. She seemed to glide, rather than walk, over to the others.

"How exquisite. There was a couple that owned the general store near the church that was married for fifty years. Cross was their name," Eleanor kept her arms folded as she spoke.

"Really? Oh, are they...passed away?" Beverly suddenly felt sorry for the people she just mentioned.

"Yes, I'm afraid. They were found together in their bed. The doctor said Mr. Cross died first, in the early evening. Mrs. Cross died hours later, close to morning. I presume that she woke up in the middle of the night only to discover that her husband had passed away. She must have noticed his body stiffen as it grew colder. His body surely evacuated the contents of his bowels. The smell must have been dreadful. This man she loved quickly became a shell of rotting meat. Was she afraid of a world without him? Did she just not have the will to continue with the daily routine of life, pretending to be strong when she was truly dead inside?"

If Brad and Beverly could have moved, they would have been running. Phinnaeus noticed their discomfort and decided to change the subject.

"You must forgive my wife. She is quite the romantic. Do you have any luggage?"

"What? Oh, yeah! I'll go get them." Brad went out to grab their bags from the car. Beverly silently watched her husband leave the room. She turned to throw the Marches an uncomfortable attempt at a polite smile. Eleanor gave an emotionless nod in return. After an uncomfortable moment, Mrs. Jones decided to help her husband with the bags. She was on his heels as he grabbed their stuff from the trunk. Brad stopped and turned around, suddenly standing nose to nose with his wife.

"What?" Brad's face was flushed red. Something had overtaken him.

"I was just...Don't they give you the creeps?" She was suddenly frightened by the man she had been married to for fifteen years.

"Sure, but do you know where else we could stay?" His voice had never sounded so masculine. "Look, if they try anything, I'll break those freaks in half!" he barked.

Beverly forgot about the creepy couple as she watched him throw their bag over his shoulder and march into the house.

Once inside, Eleanor showed them to a room on the second floor. She unlocked the door and stood aside so that Brad could dump the bags on the floor at the foot of the bed.

"What time is breakfast?" Beverly promptly asked.

"Whenever you wake up." Eleanor attempted another smile and exited down the stairs. Beverly replayed the sentence over again in her mind to be sure that Eleanor hadn't said "If you wake up."

The dark room was much like the rest of the house. It was all antique furniture, but well maintained. There wasn't a TV, or even a radio. It reminded the couple of their wedding night and the cheap little room they had spent their honeymoon in.

These memories inspired them make the best of their situation since, most likely, they would not be fooling around over the next few nights at his parents'. They quickly peeled off their clothes and yanked the sheets off the bed. They made love like teenagers, forgetting that either of their hosts could hear. Soon after Brad and Beverly had fallen asleep, the door slowly opened and two thin shadows entered the room.

The town of Normal, New Jersey had fallen to the Knights of the Silver

Cross. In spite of their victory, Amadeus was unhappy. He had overseen his Knights bravely dispatch the population within hours after arriving. The tourists were safe. Brother Michael had explained to them what danger they were in and that their silence was important to the fight. A number of them were Catholic and were willing to keep what they'd seen to themselves. The few that were not would have to be bought or threatened. The Church had enough in the budget for both.

What caused Amadeus concern was that Dominic and Lucia Divita were nowhere to be found. They had arrived too late. The information Brother Dick had received from Roberto was vague at best. He knew all about the spell to make his parents more powerful, but not about where they were going. Amadeus thought that maybe the son was holding back.

He sat on the hood of one of their sedans as he quietly watched his Knights. Some lined up the bodies of the townspeople of Normal as others prayed for their souls. He used a flashlight to study his map of the state, trying to find any clues to where the Divitas were going next. He was unaware of any fairy activity of late. He himself had taken part in the destruction of the last known fairy stronghold back in '69.

"The Divitas are gone." Jack sounded as worried as Amadeus felt. He pulled his face from the map, hoping that he and Dick had some news. It didn't matter to him if it was good or bad.

"They checked in at the inn the day before yesterday under 'Zoe Strickland.' They must be unaware that we're following them or they're getting overconfident."

"When did they leave?"

"This morning. We just missed them." Jack's news disheartened him.

"How many did we lose tonight?" He was not looking forward to hearing the answer.

"Only two casualties. You already know about Brother Brian. The second was Brother Elliot."

"Where is he?"

"He's just over here, in the town square." Amadeus pushed himself off of the car and walked over to where Dick had pointed. The two men followed him, passing the dozens of bodies that they would bury in a mass grave before the next sundown. He stopped beside a body bag filled with the remains of Brother Brian.

To the left of the bag was Brother Elliot. He was on his knees, praying with rosary in hand. The Knight was a hard man, covered in scars from many battles fought over the last fifteen years with the order. He had been tested in many ways, but this was the trial that he had been working up to his entire life.

Elliot stopped praying when he noticed Amadeus in front of him. There was fear and sadness in his eyes, but there was no sign that his faith was broken.

"Where did it bite you?"

Elliot lifted up his shredded cloak. The fist-sized bite mark was located on the left side of his chest, inches away from his rib cage. The wound hadn't stopped bleeding, even after an hour. He was impressed that Elliot was still up and moving around.

"You understand what must be done?"

"I understood that the day I first put on this cross, sir." Elliot's military training poked into his speech.

"Are you frightened?"

"No, sir!"

"Good soldier."

Elliot grabbed him by the arm with more strength than he thought he had.

"I want *you* to do it, sir! I want you to save me from damnation!"

"Of course. I almost envy you. Now you fight alongside of our savior." Amadeus stood up and removed his colt .45 from his holster and held it to Elliot's chest. Elliot looked up at him with a sense of peace in his eyes that Amadeus longed for himself.

"Thank you, Grand Master."

He fired two shots into Elliot's chest. His body wiggled and shook violently to the ground. He landed on his back, cross still in his hand. His final expression was that of joy, confidant that all of his suffering over the years would pay off in heaven.

Amadeus was pleased for his Knight. He turned away from the others so that they wouldn't see that he was emotionally moved by Elliot finding his salvation. He needed to focus on the mission at hand.

"We need a clean-up crew here," Amadeus barked from under his hood.

"Already called the order from Philadelphia. They'll be here by chopper within the hour," Dick said, knowing that it would put his boss at ease. Amadeus didn't speak; he just waved to them to stay with him as he walked over to one of the enormous, military style vans. In the back was Father Wood. His arrow wound had been bandaged. A silver collar was fastened around his neck and a silver chain kept him bolted to the floor.

Once Wood saw the three men at the entrance of the van, he momentarily forgot about the chain and jumped to attack. It did its job and choked him back into the corner. A white bandage with a red spot took up a quarter of his chest. His metal cross still hung around his neck.

"And how are you doing tonight, man-beast?" Amadeus taunted.

Father Wood didn't answer him. Amadeus stepped into the van and shut the doors, leaving the two alone together. Dick and Jack stood outside to ensure that no one would interfere with the meeting. Both of them could hear every word uttered inside.

"I don't hate you," Amadeus explained as he removed a small box from out of a little work desk that was decorated with file papers and weapons. Father Wood began to worry over what was in that simple, brown, cardboard box.

"I hate the thing that is inside you. It must be hell to feel this demon in your own soul. You want to be good, you do your best. It's just that you keep hearing these voices inside you demanding blood; these outside forces tempting you to become something unholy. I pity you, as I pity all werewolves."

"Is that what you call pity?" Wood growled. He wanted to transform and rip him apart, but the silver burned into his flesh every time he tried. "You killed men, women, and children out there tonight. What kind of pity is that?" he bellowed.

"It was too late for them. They were lost. They all thought that this was who they were, like it was...normal!" The origin of the town's name suddenly dawned on him. He quietly chuckled to himself at the simplicity of the symbolism.

"You're different aren't you? You know that what you feel is wrong. You want to fight it, but you're too weak."

"You don't know anything about me!" Wood sounded rather defensive. Amadeus removed a file from the box. He opened it up and flipped through a few pages until he found the report marked with a red pen.

"I don't, do I? Here is something dated January 31st, 1966. This was a year before you came to Normal. You confided to your superior that you were fighting 'dark impulses that dwell within.' That's good, by the way. It's very poetic. He made a note of it, thinking that you were a homosexual. He had no idea how bad you truly were."

Father Wood didn't say a thing. He knew that this was true. He did fear what was lurking inside of him. He worried every day that he was unknowingly a soldier in the Devil's army. The people of Normal believed that it was a natural part of them. He had moved here in hopes that he would believe it, too, but he had never stopped praying for strength.

"What do you want?"

"I can save you. I need you to help us find the Divitas. I know that they are looking to drink the blood of a fairy or a succubus. I need to know where they are going. If you help us, I will do everything in God's power to release you from this curse."

Father Wood remained silent. He knew full well that "release you from this curse" meant death. Amadeus understood his anxiety.

"I won't kill you," the grand master assured him. He sounded so sure, that it gave Wood hope that maybe there was another way. He pointed his nose toward the floor. He wanted to be saved, but he didn't feel good about what he needed to do.

"I know of one place." Wood had never felt so dirty. He hoped that this act would wash away those feelings. "It's a place...a go-go bar, really. It's called Neverland. It's a go-go bar where fairies strip and dance."

"How do you know this?"

"I don't know for sure, but sometimes some of the men from the town..." Father Wood was just reminded that these men where now dead. He did his best to keep focused. "In confession, some of the men around town told me they would go there. They'd talk about the fairies. How beautiful they were."

"Really? Where?"

"Franklin Lakes. Vick once tried to talk me into going, right in the middle of confessing about it."

"And the succubus?"

Father Wood just looked blankly at him. He had no idea about a succubus. Amadeus believed him and reached into the box once more.

"That's all right, Father. You can still help us on the second monster." Amadeus pulled out a pair of ripped up t shirts. He held them close to Father Wood's face.

"Here. We found these in the Divitas' room over at the inn. You're going to track them for us." Amadeus was almost ordering him. Father Wood meekly leaned forward and sniffed the clothes. He looked away in shame.

"I can do it. I can find them." Father Wood was not proud of himself, but he felt this was his only way to set things right with God.

Amadeus burst out of the truck. There was much work to do. He took Dick and Jack to one side to plan out their next move. The Knights would split into two teams. Amadeus would take one team to find Neverland and Jack would lead a team to find the succubus.

"Where do you want me, boss?" Dick asked.

"I don't fully trust Roberto. I think he's holding back information. Go back to St. Patrick's and question him and the others again."

"Yes sir," Dick smirked.

Dick didn't hesitate, he had work to do. He went back to his car to radio ahead. He wanted Roberto, Vincenzo, Isabella, and especially Morgan, to be ready when he arrived. Jack and Amadeus watched him hurry off without even saying goodbye to the both of them.

"Before you go and choose your team, Brother Jack, I should ask you something." Amadeus took the young man aside. Jack listened without interruption. The number of Knights gathering bodies and digging up evidence didn't seem to distract the two men.

"Do you know why vampires are so important to the Church?" His question hung in the air for a few brief seconds before Jack tried to answer. It seemed like such an odd thing to bring up at this point.

"Because they drink the blood of the living?" Jack had a number of answers, but this felt like the obvious one to say. Amadeus gave him a broken smile.

"Yes. That is horrible. However, most of these monsters kill. I'm talking about their greatest sin. Why they must be stopped at all costs."

Jack waited impatiently for his answer. He wondered what could be worse than murder.

"Their immortality. All beings die at some point, except the vampire. They take the power out of God's hands. They think that they can make God irrelevant. They seek to make their own world without his word, like he's nothing.

"This is your first time leading a mission. I need you to show them..." Amadeus pulled Jack's sword from his belt. He held the blade close enough for Jack to see his own eyes reflected back at him. "...with this sword, blessed by the Pope himself with God's power. Show them what real fear is."

"I will," Jack swore.

Brad and Beverly were dead. The sun cruelly poked through the corners of the window shades and did it's best to wake them. Brad turned over and pushed his face deeper into his pillow. He didn't want to move.

"Wha...? What time is it?" Beverly moaned.

"I don't know..." Brad slid off the bed and onto the floor. He picked his naked body up onto his knees and crawled over to his clothes. He dug through the pile to find his watch. It was 2:30 pm.

The Joneses managed to stumble downstairs to the kitchen. Phinnaeus and Eleanor were enjoying a cup of tea together. There was something different about Mr. and Mrs. March, but they were too sleepy to figure out what that was.

"Cheerio! Would you like some breakfast?" Eleanor chirped.

"Coffee." Brad and Beverly muttered in unison.

They sat listening to the Marches ramble on about the habits of the local birds. They faded in and out during the whole conversation. Once it was time to leave, Phinnaeus carried their luggage down to their car for them. As Brad was checking out, Eleanor asked him to wish his parents a happy anniversary. Phinnaeus and Eleanor watched the Joneses slowly putter down the road.

"Brilliant couple, I thought," Phinnaeus murmured as he stood next to his wife.

"Well, they left just in time. The next guests are scheduled to arrive in half an hour. Three, under the name Strickland."

CHAPTER EIGHTEEN

Zoe thought she would never meet a person whiter than herself, but Eleanor March proved her wrong. The thin, pale woman watched her sign with zeal in the register book. Eleanor picked it up and read her signature. She was very amused that she had used a pentagram to dot the "I" in her name.

Dominic wondered if Mrs. March was having a muscle spasm, not realizing that she was smiling at the girl. The young witch was excited by the decor of Under a Starry Night. While her eyes were shooting all around the room, taking in every last bit of Victorian furniture and art, she noticed that Lucia had given them the slip.

Dominic knew where she'd gone off to. He spotted her out the window. He excused himself from Zoe and Mrs. March to go and speak to his wife. Lucia was standing out in the middle of a small, neglected graveyard that sat behind the house and overlooked the Paulinskill River. The sparkling sunlight reflecting off the water made her long for the lights and glitter of the disco. All she wanted was to be home again.

"Lucia? Is everything all right?"

"Sure. Look at these graves. Most of them are German names and most died between 1777 and 1780."

"I don't follow you."

"You really should read more. These are Hessian soldiers. They were paid to come over here and fight the Americans for the English during the Revolutionary War."

"Oh." Dominic took his eyes off of her and looked around to the plots and graves. He could see what she was talking about, but he didn't understand what had her so absorbed in the area. Cemeteries made him uncomfortable. One time in a coffin was enough for him.

Lucia thought about how these men had traveled away from their homes. Some accepted the mission for money, others for glory. Whatever their reasons were for joining the fight, they had left someone behind to wait. In many cases, these loved ones had waited forever. She could tell that her husband didn't really care and was simply trying to humor her.

"So, do we have a plan for what to do after we drink some succubus blood? Are we going to find the Knights or do we just wait for them to attack again?" Lucia changed the subject.

"I don't know. Zoe thinks they're based under St. Patrick's, but she's not sure." Dominic sat on top of a fairly solid looking headstone.

Lucia turned away from him once more with her arms folded. He was going to keep talking, but she seemed to be upset about more than the subject at hand.

"What is it?" Dominic was becoming annoyed.

"What?" was all she answered.

"Don't talk to me like I'm stupid! I know when something is really bothering you! Why don't you just come out and say it?"

They were both quiet for a long while. The could hear the breeze brush the long grass on the tombstones and the water ripple. He watched her back tense up, as firm as any of the stones around them.

"Do you feel them?" Lucia asked.

"Feel who? The Knights? The succubus? What?" Dominic's confusion became mixed with concern.

"No! Never mind," she sighed.

"What's troubling you?"

"If you don't know what I'm talking about, then the answer is no."

"Hey!" Zoe walked up to the couple with a terrible sense of timing. The two vampires didn't answer her, but that didn't slow down her excitement.

"I talked to both of the owners. I think she's a succubus and I think her husband is an incubus, too! Isn't that..." Zoe stopped as she passed by one of the grave makers.

"Whoa, boss! Hey, I think this is a Hessian soldier burial ground!" Zoe declared.

Lucia smiled at Dominic as if he was the dumbest man on earth, finally letting out a little giggle. She was thankful for Zoe. The girl allowed her to forget her fears, if only for just a moment. Once she remembered again, she wanted to change the subject. Lucia felt it was best to carry on with the spell and get home as quickly as possible. Dominic let her talk about the soldiers with Zoe, against his better judgment. He looked up to the blue sky and wondered if it would hurt a vampire to pray.

Phinnaeus peeled back a curtain in the dining room to spy on their newest guests. Eleanor watched from over his shoulder. They were very curious about the power they sensed from all three of them.

"What do you suppose they are, Eleanor? Vampires? Werewolves? Witches? Perhaps they're elves?" Phinnaeus proposed.

His wife closed her eyes and took a deep breath. The energy she felt from them sharpened her nipples with excitement. She pressed her breasts against his back and reached around to take hold of his penis.

"I can't distinguish what they are. There are traces of elf, werewolf, and fairy in their blood. Since the Divitas would be rather large to be elves, I'd say they're vampires," Eleanor guessed.

"Vampires? Does it not seem odd that they're out in the daylight?" Phinnaeus asked as he firmly rubbed her right leg. Both were at the edge of sexual climax, yet their faces expressed nothing that would suggest so. They eagerly awaited the chance to feed on such creatures.

"I'm sure of it." Eleanor was positive.

Father Wood hadn't made a sound in over an hour. The sun was about to set on a day of driving all around the state. He sat in the passenger seat next to Brother Paul as he drove the lead car. Jack sat behind them as he held on to the silver chain that kept Wood in place. A black van followed them with another eight Knights who were growing restless as they traveled up I-287 to Franklin Lakes.

Jack had begun to think that they had lost the Divita's trail. He thought they would have to meet up with Amadeus and the other half of the team at Neverland. He hoped that Wood wasn't trying to set them up in some sort of a trap. When they closed in on exit 41B, Father Wood came alive again.

"Here! Here! Stop here!" Father Wood shouted and jolted violently in his seat. He wanted out, but Paul tried to restrain him. Jack saw something sincere in Wood. He asked Paul to back off from their captive.

Father Wood jumped out of the car with Paul and Jack right behind him. He sniffed in the air as if he was plugged into some other world invisible to those watching.

"That way!" Wood declared, pointing down I-80.

Mr. and Mrs. March observed their guests closely throughout the day and into the evening. Lucia sat in the corner of the den and read her tarot cards, never seeming happy with the answers. Dominic and Zoe whispered to each other as they ate their dinner. The Marches tried not to act suspicious, but their curiosity was getting the best of them. Lucia soon caught them staring at her from the kitchen. Eleanor became excited at the power, anger, and fear in the woman's eyes.

"Would you like another cup of tea, Mrs. Divita?" Eleanor quickly recovered.

"No, thank you. I'm done," Lucia answered politely. She then went over to Dominic and Zoe as they were finishing their cheesecake and coffee.

"I'll be upstairs reading, don't stay up too late." She kissed him on the cheek and lightly bit his ear. Phinnaeus studied every curve of Lucia's voluptuous body as she walked away.

"I want her," Phinnaeus quietly told his wife.

"Are you sure you'll be able to handle her?"

"To be intimidated by such a gargantuan woman is a sign of weakness," he answered.

"And you shall have her, as I shall have him. I eagerly anticipate his touch," Eleanor agreed.

"What of the other girl? Zoe?" he asked.

"We can save her for desert." Eleanor watched the girl finish the last piece of cheesecake. Zoe noticed her gaze and smiled back at her, her cheeks still filled with cake. Eleanor nodded out of respect.

Amadeus and his team had searched Franklin Lakes for most of the day. They found the Neverland Gentlemen's Club on Gravity Road. The massive black van that housed the Knights was the only vehicle within miles. The nightclub's small size and modest appearance hardly surprised the Knights; Fairy folk were notorious for stealthy disguises. The sign on the door read "Open at Midnight," but they had no time to waste. The Knights circled the building, hoods pulled over their heads and holding their crosses tightly.

"In God's name, all evil must be gone from this place," they chanted.

Amadeus and Brother Colin were still at work in the back of the van. The grand master handed Colin a five foot long iron beam with leather handles.

"Fairies are a difficult breed to combat. They are powerful tricksters. Prayer and iron are the major weapons that we have. As the others weaken their power with prayer, you will use this battering ram to be the first inside. If we get in, do not forget that these beings were the angels that stood back and did nothing to stop Lucifer when he rebelled against our Lord. This is how they choose to make their time on Earth. As whores. Do not hold back."

"Yes, Grand Master." At six and a half feet tall, Colin was the only Knight that was larger than Amadeus himself. He took hold of the weapon and marched out of the van. He built up a steady pace with each footstep, aiming for the wooden door of the strip bar. The door exploded with a single strike from the mighty Knight.

There was nothing behind the door. No Divitas. No fairies. There wasn't even a building. They found themselves standing in the middle of an empty parking lot. The grand master angrily studied the ground. The building had vanished. The only thing left in the darkness was the sound of fairies giggling.

Eleanor handed Phinnaeus another dish. She washed the dishes while he wiped them and put them away. Dominic and Zoe had retired for the night minutes earlier. It was just after nine in the evening, which gave Mrs. March doubt that they were dealing with vampires.

Once they were finished with the dishes, they climbed the stairs to their bedroom. They could hear the sounds of snoring from both Zoe's and the Divitas' rooms. They were ready. After entering their bedroom, Phinnaeus removed his jacket and began to unbutton his shirt. He then pulled off his boots. They methodically finished undressing and put their clothes away in the closet.

Phinnaeus and Eleanor left their bedroom, nude and holding hands. The door to the Divitas' room opened silently. They could see Dominic and Lucia asleep underneath the covers. The two thin, black shadows quietly slid across the room to the foot of the bed. Mr. and Mrs. March released each other's hands and stood on opposite sides of the bed. They carefully pulled back the spread until it passed the Divitas' feet.

Dominic and Lucia were fully nude and lying on their backs. It was perfect. Eleanor climbed on top of Dominic and Phinnaeus took his place over Lucia. The energy coming off the couple was almost too much and they hadn't even started to drain them yet. Phinnaeus leaned in close to Lucia's face. The natural trance the Marches emitted should have taken affect. He rubbed his cheek against hers and smelled her hair.

Lucia's eyes popped open. Her fanged smile and eyes glowed like those of a wild animal. Phinnaeus was so shocked by this, he raised one eyebrow.

"Like what you see?" Lucia growled.

"Oh, dear." Phinnaeus seemed concerned. Dominic reached up and took Eleanor by the wrists. Zoe pushed the bedroom door shut. She had been standing in the corner the whole time. The Marches were slightly embarrassed to be caught in such a manner. A victim had never woken up during one of their feedings.

"I don't understand. How could she be there when we heard her in the other room?" Eleanor asked. Zoe slipped her notepad into her back pocket and tried not to smile too much.

"Magic!" Dominic answered for Zoe, who waved her hands as if she was a stage magician.

"What is the meaning of this deception?" There was a level of displeasure in Phinnaeus's voice. He acted as if he and his wife were the victims.

Dominic and Lucia hopped off the bed as Zoe took her place beside them. Phinnaeus and Eleanor stood still in the middle of the room, simply holding hands.

"We need your help," Lucia earnestly spoke.

"Help?" Whatever do you mean?" Eleanor took a step in front of her husband. The Divitas were proving to be far more interesting than she'd first thought.

Dominic had planned to do the talking, but his wife had already taken the floor. She'd been different since the morning after the werewolves. He worried that there was something wrong back home. Since they had become vampires, she had always had a stronger mental connection to the children. Dominic chose to stay silent, fearing that knowing would hurt their chances at success.

"Dominic and I are on the run. The Knights of the Silver Cross have chased us out of our home in New York. Zoe is a witch. She has a magic spell that can give us the power to fight them. If you'll help us in this spell, we can rejoin our children. Zoe can be with her true love once again."

"What do you need of us?" Phinnaeus inquired.

"We just need to drink a little of your blood." Lucia was a little worried over how that sounded, but what was said was said.

Mr. and Mrs. March listened very carefully to Lucia's story. They looked at each other for a few seconds without uttering a word. Zoe could swear that they were speaking telepathically, but it was hard to read their faces.

"Very well," Phinnaeus dryly answered.

CHAPTER NINETEEN

Phinnaeus casually glided into his bedroom to put on his scarlet robe and slippers. He then stepped downstairs and scoped out a half cup of brown powder from a cookie jar in the shape of Queen Victoria's head. He exited through the rear of the bed and breakfast to the edge of the cemetery. He poured the contents of the half cup in an "X" formation on a bare patch of ground.

He watched the powder seep into the earth like liquid. He was pleased that the powder he'd bought for protection still worked after so many years of peace and quiet. His joy was cut short as he felt the energies of eleven others watching him. He knew that there wasn't any time to waste.

Five hundred feet away, Brother Jack watched as Phinnaeus entered the house once more. He wondered if the incubus had seen them. He handed Paul the binoculars and asked him what he thought. Phinnaeus seemed creepy enough, but he wasn't sure.

"I tell you, this is where they are! That's their car. I smell all three of them." Father Wood's voice cracked with desperation.

Jack believed him. They had finally caught up with their prey. They needed to act fast. If there was a succubus, she surely would have felt their presence. He ordered his men to watch over Wood as he contacted Amadeus by radio.

"Grand Master? This is Brother Jack."

There was only crackling radio silence. Jack tried again. After a third attempt, he was becoming fearful of what may have happened with the fairies in Franklin Lakes. The Knights and Father Wood anxiously waited to hear Jack speak with his mentor.

"Report." Amadeus's voice finally came through, loud and clear. The others could see the relief in Jack's posture.

"Wood has led us to a house in Stillwater. I believe the targets are inside preparing to drink the blood of a succubus. Should we wait until you can arrive?"

"Negative! If they complete the spell, they will become Master Vampires! You must stop them before it's too late."

"Yes, Grand Master. Before we go, what should we do with Father Wood?"

Father Wood was unable to hear Amadeus's answer. There wasn't anything in Jack's body language to give away what was to be done.

"Thank you. I will," was all that Jack said to the grand master. He shut the radio off and tossed it into the front seat of the sedan.

Father Wood felt a sense of relief as Jack walked over to him. There was an expression of mercy on his face that felt real to the tormented priest. He told Brother Paul to uncuff him and back away. The release of the bonds around his wrists almost made the werewolf cry. It seemed to mirror the release of the bonds that had held his soul for so many years.

"Father Zachery Wood, please drop to your knees," Jack ordered. Wood gladly did so, with his head bent down. Jack lifted his chin so that he could look upon him.

"You can look up at me, Father Wood. You have proven that one can find redemption in the eyes of God, no matter the sin. You have done well."

The blade of the silver katana sword sliced through Father Wood's neck only a moment after it left Jack's sheath. Wood's body clumsily fell to the ground beside his head. The cross still hung around the stump at his shoulders. It was the final image Wood would see. He was again with God. He was forgiven.

"God bless you, Zachery." Jack truly hoped that it was enough to redeem his soul. He slipped the sword back into its place as he turned away from Wood's body. There would be plenty of time to mourn after the Divitas had been dealt with.

When Phinnaeus rejoined his wife, he was disappointed that the Divitas had already put their clothes back on. Dominic was clad in a pair of jeans and one of his ruby-red dress shirts. Lucia wore a black t-shirt and leather pants that hugged her body like a second skin. She finished off the look with a pair of biker boots that she'd bought while in Normal.

"I believe that we should make hast. I can feel those that would do harm to our guests nearby," Phinnaeus told his wife loud enough for the others to hear. This confirmed Lucia's fears that something had happened back home.

Dominic took his wife's hand to let her know that they would get through this together. He knew that she was afraid that the children were in trouble. He could feel their quicker heartbeats, but didn't want to admit it because saying it out loud meant that it was true.

Zoe was obviously unnerved by the news. She worried that Morgan had been caught or killed by the Knights. She thought that if her love was already dead, immortality would feel like a punishment rather than a gift.

Eleanor suggested using the attic to perform the ritual, which sounded good to all involved. They followed the Marches up to the third floor where Phinnaeus pulled a string that unfolded the dusty, wooden steps that led to the attic. Eleanor carefully climbed up the steps, followed by her husband.

"Now, don't be alarmed once you climb up here. We have been so busy of late, we haven't had any time to tidy up the attic," Eleanor politely warned. Zoe went up the steps expecting to see trunks filled with clothes and layers of dust everywhere, but what she saw first were two dried-up corpses. She ducked back out of the room unable to move any farther.

"Get your ass out of my face!" Lucia shouted, causing Zoe to practically jump into the attic. Lucia and Dominic saw what all the fuss was about once they stepped through the opening and noticed the bodies. Lucia was underwhelmed, but her husband was slightly confused.

"I thought you didn't kill anyone?" Dominic asked. Phinnaeus and Eleanor shrugged.

"We don't really. Although we sometimes can get carried away," Eleanor sounded openly embarrassed and didn't wish to discuss the matter any further.

Lucia and Dominic didn't have time to wonder. They began to remove items from the center of the room. They pushed aside trunks, rugs, and a couple of sewing dummies. Mr. and Mrs. March just watched them work with curiosity. They marveled at their passion, feeling that such creatures needed to survive. Zoe cautiously approached the succubus, reading from her notepad.

"Um, hi! Ah...for the spell, we need you to sit in the middle and just let them drink from your arms when the time comes in the ritual."

"Understood. Will it give us pleasure?" Phinnaeus inquired.

"Umm...I don't know. Maybe?" Zoe's answer was good enough for the two of them. They nodded at each other in anticipation.

"There is something else that you need to do. We need you to release your energy at the end, to seal the spell."

Mr. and Mrs. March didn't give her any emotional kind of

response. They simply reached out to the girl. She caressed Zoe's lips with her thumb and he slowly twirled a lock of her hair. It was their way of accepting her requirements. Zoe did her best not to scream at their touch.

The group of Knights watched the old house at the other side of the cemetery. It was dark except for a faint light in the attic window. When they stepped into the middle of the graveyard, the hallowed ground shook under their feet.

"Hold it!" Jack ordered. It was obvious that they were expected.

Hands broke through the dirt all around them. A chorus of groans and cries of pain came from the coffins below. The corpses from a hundred graves pulled themselves free and circled the intruders. The air was instantly polluted with the stink of decay. Most of the rotted bodies that slowly walked toward them were dressed in 18th century military uniforms. Some of the attackers were carrying the rifles that they'd been buried with. They grunted something that sounded German.

"Gehirne! Gehirne! Gehirne!" they muttered.

"Anyone here speak German?" Jack asked the group. Brother Ryan raised his hand. Jack waited for him to translate. Ryan listened carefully and found that they were repeating the same word.

"They're saying 'brains.'" Brother Ryan became nervous, but it hardly surprised any of them. The walking dead moved in closer to their prey. Jack drew his sword.

"Relax. They're only zombies." Jack sliced off the heads of two zombies in front of him. He suggested to the other Knights to use only their swords and save their stakes and bullets for the vampires.

The zombies were hardly a match for the monster hunters. Many of them couldn't walk, much less fight. Some were still armed with their empty rifles and jabbed at the Knights with the bayonet at the end. It did very little. Jack and the Knights almost seemed annoyed as they barely used any effort to hack off their heads. All it did was delay them.

Dominic and Lucia began to drink the blood from the Marches. Phinnaeus became overwhelmed when Lucia's teeth dug in to his flesh. It was every bit as wonderful as he'd hoped it would be. Eleanor never wanted it to end. She wondered if this was what her prey felt as she sucked the energy from their bodies. It was heavenly. She wished that she could give Dominic every last drop from her veins.

The vampires could feel themselves grow stronger with every gulp of blood they swallowed. The spell was working. All of the work that they had done was finally paying off. Their mental abilities were increasing. They could both sense Jack and the Knights breaking into the house and rushing up the stairs. They hoped that Zoe would hurry up and complete the spell before they were discovered. The Marches and the Divitas felt the Knights underneath the attic. Brother Jack pulled the cord and brought down the steps. Lucia released Phinnaeus's wrist.

"Zoe! Finish the fucking spell!" Lucia spat. Before Zoe could give the word to the Marches, Jack and his men opened fire. Zoe ducked away from the flying debris beside Phinnaeus and Eleanor as Dominic and Lucia were hit by dozens of rounds. The gunfire propelled them backwards through the windows.

There were two Knights waiting below who began firing as soon as the Divitas reached the ground. Lucia rose up first, slashing their throats and running off toward the graveyard. The bullet wounds burned with every move, but she had to keeping going. She was halfway through the cemetery when she noticed that Dominic was lagging behind. He had been hit hard. One bullet had exploded near his heart, spreading wooden splinters throughout the inside of his chest.

"Dominic?"

Zoe didn't have a chance to pick herself up off the floor. Brother Paul jerked her to her feet by the back of her shirt. His sword stopped just short of slicing through her neck.

"If you try to cast a spell, it will be the last syllable you'll ever speak!" Paul shouted in her ear.

Mr. and Mrs. March were held at gunpoint. They slowly raised their hands in surrender. Jack didn't stop to give orders. He jumped out the window, landing between the bodies of the Knights that Lucia had just killed. He swore that these would be her last victims.

At the edge of the burial ground, there were the beginnings of a plot. The shovel had been left behind, waiting for the gravedigger to return and finish the job. He kicked it up to his hand and gave it a quick inspection. He pointed it to the ground and broke off the metal head with his foot, leaving a sharp, wood spike at the end. He was ready.

Dominic fell to his knees. The pain cut through his torso like dozens of tiny scissors clipping their way around his insides. Jack wasn't far behind, he would be on them within seconds. Lucia took Dominic's hand in an effort to pull him up. He didn't budge.

"Lucia! I can't! I can't move...you go! You keep going! I'll give you time to escape."

Lucia suddenly couldn't feel the bullets buried deep within her flesh. Numbness overtook her. It was as if the answer to their problems had been there all along and she was now able to see clearly for the first time. She got down on her knees in front of her husband. Dominic's breathing became panicked.

"Lucia, what are you doing? Just run!"

Lucia kissed Dominic. She almost laughed over the blood she smeared across his face. She rubbed it off his chin. He used what was left of his strength to try and push her away, but she wouldn't budge.

"Please! Lucia, please! Just go! Just fucking run! Please! I don't want you to die! Please!"

"I'm tired of running. I'm tired of fighting. I wanted to be happy. I want us to be happy. Do you feel happy?"

"We will! After...all this is. The children! Lucia! They have the children!"

"After we're gone, they'll let them go. They're grownups now. They're safer without us."

Dominic and Lucia heard Jack coming closer. He was preparing to strike. Lucia didn't want to spend their last moments together fighting. She rested her finger on his lips, hoping to hush him up.

"Dominic. I hear him coming. I don't have much time to say this. I love you." Lucia held her husband as they wept together, free of any anger or blame. It was their moment and they didn't wanted to let go ever again.

Jack waited for them to act, but they didn't move. He realized it wasn't a trick. They weren't going to be fighting him this time. He decided not to hold off any longer. Jack ran at them and impaled Lucia in the back with his spear. He had brought it down with enough force to run it through both of the Divitas.

Neither of them screamed, they just caved in together. Jack forced the spear into the earth. He told himself that the vampires were just as much victims as those that they preyed upon, but he still couldn't help smiling.

CHAPTER TWENTY

"Grand Master? It's done," Jack casually reported into his car radio. Three of his men stood by the bodies of Dominic and Lucia in case they recovered. They were still lying on top of each other with the shovel handle stuck through their chests and into the ground. Zoe had been hauled out to the edge of the cemetery, alongside Phinnaeus and Eleanor. The Marches were covered in bruises and debris from the attack.

"Very good, Brother Jack." Amadeus's pride was apparent, even over the static filled radio. He would later need to enact penance for such feelings. Jack could see their captives coming up on his left.

"What of the others?"

"I gave my word to Roberto Divita that I would not personally kill Strickland. Finish the mission as you see fit. Clean up the scene and return home with the vampires' heads."

"Yes, Grand Master." Jack set the radio back on the dashboard. This would be the first clean up under his command. He took a moment to ask God for the strength to carry on and do what must be done.

Paul had placed a gag in Zoe's mouth so she couldn't cast any spells and two other Knights held the Marches with great vigor, even though succubi and incubi weren't known for their fighting abilities.

"What are your orders, Brother Jack?" Paul asked.

"Execute those two." Jack pointed at the Marches and began to walk toward the Divitas bodies. He didn't bother to look back at the scene.

"What about the witch?" Paul shouted out. Jack paused.

"Burn the witch." Jack's voice was free of emotion. He understood fully what it meant to battle these monsters in God's name. He knew that a certain mindset was needed for this work. He had watched Amadeus working and would follow his example. He couldn't look at them and see the people they once were. A Knight needed to remember the type of monsters they had become.

Phinnaeus and Eleanor watched as chairs, tables, and even parts of their porch were broken up and brought out to a bare spot in the yard. Zoe was tied to a tall wooden coat rack that had been planted in the ground, the furniture placed around her.

"They've ruined our porch," Phinnaeus spoke to his wife through telepathy, since the Knights would surely silence him.

"Yes, and they're going to exterminate that charming girl," Eleanor thought back to him.

"I wonder if it's too late to give Mr. and Mrs. Divita our energy?" He asked.

"Perhaps, but I don't think a portion of our strength is enough to resurrect them," Eleanor answered as she heard a gun click behind her head. She took his hand and circled his smooth skin with her thumb.

"What a marvelous idea -- a sacrifice for the love of others. You always were the romantic one."

"Thank you, dear." She squeezed his hand and they both reached out to the Divitas' bodies with their minds. They ignored the two Knights standing behind them, their guns just inches away. The Marches could see Jack standing over the vampires with his sword drawn, ready to strike. Phinnaeus and Eleanor released every bit of energy from their hearts and souls that they had collected over the years. The Knights pulled the triggers and the Marches fell forward onto the ground still holding hands.

As he swung his sword at the Divitas, Jack felt a warm burst of energy and saw a dense mist form along the ground. He felt his sword cut into the earth. The mist was so thick that he was unable to see his handiwork, but it faded away as quickly as it appeared. Dominic and Lucia were gone and Jack knew that his men were in danger.

Paul and Ryan were ready to set the fire as they did their best to block out the whimpering of their prisoner. Paul found the notepad in her back pocket. He was angered by what was written in its pages.

"Is this where you think the answers are? These are lies!" Paul slapped her in the face with the tiny notebook. Ryan removed a lighter from his pants pocket and tossed it over to Paul. He lit the notepad and threw it onto the pile of wood.

The fire slowly built around the terrified witch. The dry wooden furniture crackled as the flames drew closer to her. Her muffled screams did nothing to diminish the awe that the Knights felt in that moment. The fire would cleanse this evil from the world. They were winning their war.

Paul noticed a dewy sensation on his forehead. At first he thought it was sweat from the heat of the fire or from the earlier fight. Then he realized that it was a dense mist, which had rolled in from out of nowhere. The mist formed a cloud that circled and covered Zoe, putting out the fire. The Knights stood in stunned silence until they heard Jack running up from behind them.

"They're alive! They're alive!" Jack yelled.

The Knights pulled their weapons, ready to fire, as the mist grew even thicker. They knew that the vampires could attack from any direction, in any form.

Ryan decided to draw them out. He put his gun to Zoe's face. The weapon didn't stay on her long; it came off with the rest of his arm.

Lucia had reappeared between them. Ryan fell on top of the pile of wood next to the Zoe. Paul and Jack fired in Lucia's direction, but their bullets only passed through more mist.

Jack was grabbed by something above. Dominic, now in his bat form, carried him into the night sky. His fierce grip ripped into the Knight's skin, forcing him to let go of his gun. Jack tried to reach for his sword just as Dominic released him midair. Jack landed on his back, bouncing once before blacking out.

Paul fired again on Lucia. Her black hair twisted and enveloped her until she no longer looked human. Lucia rushed at him in the shape of a half-ton wolf. Her jaws clamped down around his neck, lopping off his head. The five remaining Knights were torn apart by attacks that seemed to come from all directions at once. The vampires were suddenly alone among the mutilated bodies of their hunters.

"That was good! How...?" Lucia needed a second to catch her breath as she transformed back into herself. Dominic had landed, back in his human form, just a few feet from his wife. They could each feel the power that Zoe and Morgan had been talking about before their quest. They were alive again, even though they weren't sure how it had happened.

"Lucia!" Dominic gave his wife a bear-hug that lifted her into the air. He kissed her with more passion than he had in some time. She wanted to pretend to push him away, but his warm touch was too wonderful to deny. She let her mask fall for just a second and smiled at him.

Zoe's muffled voice snapped the vampires out of their daze. Lucia hurried over to Zoe to untie her. She pulled herself out from the pile of half-burnt wood and rested on the front steps of the house. She couldn't speak. She had watched the Knights execute the Marches and nearly burn her at the stake. She needed some time to recover.

"Zoe? Are you okay?" Lucia gently asked, putting her arm around the shaking girl. Zoe flinched. Lucia gave her some space.

Dominic walked over to where Jack had landed to see if the Knight had died from the fall. To his surprise, he was still breathing.

"I think their leader is still alive," Dominic exclaimed.

"Good. Kill him," Lucia said as she looked at what they'd done to Zoe. She had no mercy for any of these men.

"He can tell us where they have the children," Dominic reasoned. He dragged Jack farther away from the others; this Knight needed to survive to deliver a special message.

"Ask your children! You should be able to call out to them!" Zoe sat blinking, as if she had just woken up from a bad dream.

Lucia looked over to the bodies of the Marches. She guessed that they had been able to release their energy to finish the spell. It was a gift that she knew she could never repay. She stripped a pair of cloaks off the dead Knights and covered their bodies.

"Thank you." Lucia closed her eyes and thought of Isabella, Vincenzo, and Roberto. Her mind traveled, past the highways and neighborhoods, into New York. As she feared, the children were a mile under St. Patrick's Cathedral.

"Oh, fuck! Fuck! I knew it! I fucking knew it! They have them!" Lucia screamed. Zoe jumped up and took Lucia by the shoulders. The forceful hold brought Lucia's mind back to her.

"Lucia! Lucia, listen to me! Is Morgan with them? Is she alive?" Zoe desperately asked. Lucia reached out again. Much to her dismay, she was unable to see her.

"I'm sorry, I don't know."

Zoe let go of Lucia started pacing in a tiny, panicked circle. She tried to pull herself together for what was to come. She needed strength to face the possibility that Morgan was already dead. Of all things, a broom sticking out of the still smoking pile of wood gave her the nudge she required.

"Where's Dominic? We've got to make me immortal now!" Zoe pleaded.

"Is there time?"

"Yeah! It only takes a minute!"

"Dominic! Get your ass back over here! Dominic!" Lucia barked. Dominic reappeared from out of the shadows. He was carrying Jack's sword and gun holster.

"What did you do with that butt burglar?" Lucia asked.

"I left him hand cuffed to a grave."

"Is he still alive?"

"Yes." He looked down at his feet.

"Why?" Lucia stomped her foot.

"I had a message for him to deliver."

"Oh yeah, 'cause that so fucking worked the last time!" Lucia moaned.

"Not now! Zoe, how do we do this spell of yours?"

To her dismay, Zoe realized that the spell had been written down in her burnt notebook. She bit her lower lip as she replayed the words in her mind. She tried to pretend that she didn't see Lucia and Dominic's growing impatience. The whole thing came back to her suddenly, causing her to run back into the house and return seconds later with a coffee mug.

"Okay! You each cut yourselves and bleed into this cup and I drink while reciting the incantation." Zoe held out the cup to both of them, like a little beggar. The vampires took one good look at each other, as if to say "what the hell." Dominic and Lucia bit their own wrists and bled into the yellow mug. It was half full when Zoe nodded that it was enough. She took a deep breath before bringing it to her lips.

"With this, I wish to see all that life has to give to me." She then drank the whole cup of master vampire blood. The rich, warm taste burned the walls of her esophagus as the spell quickly took effect. The world began to seem very dark to Zoe. She suddenly couldn't see or hear Dominic and Lucia. She feared that she may have made a mistake with the spell and she had gone blind and deaf. She called out for help just as everything exploded into light. Stars and planets were born before her eyes. She looked down at her own hands to see every atom that had been used to create them. Trees and rivers formed all around her. Life grew from nothing under her feet.

Zoe was a witness to creation. The evolution sped up and the pains of birth started to infect her. She was no longer an observer; the universe was merging with her body and soul. The power peeled away her flesh and bones, turning her inside out. She experienced creation and destruction all at once.

All Dominic and Lucia could see was Zoe falling to her hands and knees. She growled like an animal. Her eyes turned completely black. Light exploded from her mouth as she cried out in Latin, in German, in Hebrew, and in languages that they had never heard before. Lucia stepped behind her husband. For the first time, she was afraid to go near Zoe.

Then, it suddenly stopped. Zoe stood up with a confident expression on her little round face. All of the spells she'd ever written down in her notebook were part of her now. She knew each and every one by heart. A white strip of hair fell down in front of her glasses. She pulled it back, paying it no mind, before spotting the broom among the kindling. She reached out for it and imagined it in her hand. The broom shook itself out of the pile and flew into her grasp.

"Zoe? Are you all right?" Lucia cautiously asked.

"Yes. Let's go." Zoe held her broom skyward and it propelled her into the air. The Divitas followed suit as bats and the three rushed toward New York.

Lucia called out to Isabella with her mind. The girl was sitting on her bed. She had been crying for hours, but suddenly she could hear her mother's voice.

"Isabella! Isabella!" Lucia called out. Isabella bolted upright on her bed, the sudden jolt got Vincenzo's attention. For the first time since being captured, she seemed hopeful.

"Mamma? Is that really you?" she cried out.

"Yes, baby. Tell your brothers that Mamma and Poppa are coming!"

CHAPTER TWENTY ONE

I t was lucky that Joey Paparazzo was hungry. When he got out of bed, he noticed his wife still had a cigarette between her fingers as she was falling fast asleep. He took it and put it out in the ashtray on the night stand. He couldn't believe his wife would be so stupid.

"What the fuck you doing? You nearly burnt the whole house down! Our sons are in the next fucking room!"

She just snored. He waved his hands in disgust. He thought that of all the things he went through in any given week, that this would be the way he would die. He decided to yell at her in the morning, if he was still angry. Right now all he wanted was to see if there was still lunch meat left in the fridge.

When he stepped into the kitchen, he felt a breeze. The back door was open. Someone was inside the house.

He hoped that he could reach the gun in his desk drawer, ten paces from where he stood. He casually walked over to the desk, pretending that he hadn't noticed anything was wrong. Joey opened the top drawer to find the gun was missing. Then he was grabbed from behind by what seemed like the darkness itself.

"You have an appointment to keep, Mr. Paparazzo." a rough voice whispered as a cloth bag was slipped over his head. He was quietly taken out to a waiting car with a gun pressed firmly in his ribs. In the car, a familiar smell of aftershave tipped him off that Frank was in the seat next to him.

"Frank, is that you?"

"Joey? Thank God--" Both Frank and Joey were silenced by a short series of gun butts to their heads. They were ordered to be quiet. The two mobsters guessed that they were being taken by the vampire hunters. If they were right, then they had some questions of their own to ask them.

The trip was brief and it sounded like they had stopped in an underground parking area. They were finally pulled out of the car and thrown into leather seats and told to wait until they were spoken to. They didn't dare test that command. They could both sense the presence of two or more men in the room with them.

A door creaked open and a pair of heavy footsteps echoed in their ears. The air in the room grew noticeably tenser. Their hoods were untied and yanked off. Amadeus sat at a thick, wooden desk before them while Dick leaned on a table against the wall behind him. A huge, antique, wooden cross looked down on them from behind the desk.

"What right you got grabbing us in the middle of--" Joey was struck again. The hit nearly tipped him over, but he was able to catch himself. Frank decided not to say a word. Dick dropped his cowboy hat lower in order to conceal his snickering.

"Greetings, gentlemen. I've called you here for two reasons. First, I have some good news about those vampires you encountered. They have been slain. Their heads are being delivered here as we speak. Dominic and Lucia Divita will no longer hunt the streets of New York City."

Amadeus could tell that this news eased the nerves of the two men. Frank gave the sign of the cross, feeling like this whole ugly business was finally over.

"That is good news! I want to thank you all." Joey got up and put his hand out to shake the grand master's, but he didn't move. Joey knew that there was more to this meeting than a simple update.

"Sit down." Amadeus wasn't going to repeat himself. Joey slowly sat back in his chair.

"The second reason I had you brought here was to confess."

Joey and Frank tried to behave as if they had no idea what he was talking about, but they knew.

"You are both responsible for the beating of a young woman and the death of a man. Both of these people worked at the Inferno." Amadeus then turned his sights on Frank. The mobster sank in his seat from the eye contact. "The night before, you murdered your mistress and her son."

"What? No! That's bullshit! I didn't..." Frank protested.

"How could you pin anything on us?" Joey challenged. He momentarily forgot to fear the priest.

"Your men are Catholic, are they not? You have to confess somewhere. We know what members of your organization have done. I know everything you both have done -- the murders, the cover ups, the adultery. Normally, we wouldn't take action in these matters. This time, I can't look away. I want you both to confess."

A dense mist rolled over the walls of St. Patrick's Cathedral and quickly seeped beneath the doorframes. The mist traveled flat against the floor, going unnoticed as it sneaked past three late-night churchgoers. The mist floated under the secret entrance in the Cardinal's office and down the seemingly endless stairway. The numerous crosses that hung on the walls were meant to keep out any attacking vampires, but they wouldn't work this time.

The cloud went undisturbed until it reached a pair of Knights guarding the lower halls. They instantly recognized what had rolled in before them. They were being invaded.

Brothers Thomas and Charles drew their side arms at the mist and, amazingly, it stopped. Charles quickly took his radio from his belt and began to call to Brother David in the watch room.

"Brother David? It's Brother Charles and Thomas in the west exit hallway. We have an emergency here." Those were the last words Brother David heard.

A large, black wolf jumped out of the mist. It tore Thomas in half with its massive claws. The wolf landed with its back to Charles. He aimed for its head as it transformed into Lucia. He didn't get off the shot. His gun was taken from him. By the time he realized Dominic was there, the vampire had already smashed his skull into the concrete wall behind him.

Zoe watched with a grimace as the Knight slid down to the floor, leaving behind a trail of blood from the impact. She was still feeling ill from merging into mist with the Divitas. She thought she was going to vomit until her belly corrected itself.

"Do you think they got off a warning?" Zoe asked.

"I hope so. I'm tired of sneaking around," Dominic explained.

The words of Amadeus chilled the men to the bone. Joey and Frank had always done what they felt was best of their families, but even they felt guilt over Stacy and her boy. The proud men slumped in their chairs. Frank almost felt relieved that he would have a chance to make good with God.

"Confess? Well, sure. You got a booth in the next room of something?" Joey sheepishly asked. He was confused when Dick began to chuckle. The laughter stopped when Amadeus shot his head back in Dick's direction.

"Booth? No. You're going to confess to the police." Amadeus's words fell like a building on the two men. The air was sucked out of their chests as they waited for the grand master to laugh. He wasn't joking.

"The Church usually looks the other way when it comes to the mafia. It's even made deals and partnerships over the years. I could only sit back and watch as your kind bleed this city dry of money, of lives, of its very soul. As far as I'm concerned, you are just as bad as the vampires. Tonight, that changes. You are going to march into police headquarters and tell them what you have done."

"Or what?" Joey didn't like being told what to do. It hardly mattered that he and Frank were unarmed. He would fight to the death before turning himself in. He only hoped that Frank was just as committed.

Morgan had been unconscious for hours, chained to a brick wall with iron shackles that sucked the strength from her body. She woke with a jolt as a premonition came to her. She scanned the cell, looking for Roberto. He had never left her side.

"Morgan? Morgan!" Roberto held her tight. He had feared that she was fading away.

"They're here! Your parents are here!" She spoke as well as she could with her hoarse voice.

Roberto froze. His parents must have succeeded. He could only sit and wait to see what would happen next. The cell door clanged open and two knights barged in. One lifted Morgan up by the arm as the other unlocked her chains.

"What are you doing?" Neither answered Roberto's question. He stepped in close to them only to be pushed back. The knights began to drag Morgan out of the room, still ignoring him.

"Where are you taking her? I told you everything I know!" Roberto protested. One of the Knights finally looked in his direction.

"We have some questions for her. We'll have her back in a few hours," he barked. Roberto tensed up. He didn't believe the Knight's tale. There was finality in his voice that told a different story.

"Roberto! Roberto! They're going to kill me! Please, Roberto! Don't let them take me!" Morgan cried out.

Roberto met the eyes of the Knight, who stared back with a cold glare. There was true fear in Morgan's cries. Roberto needed to do something. The Knight was momentarily distracted when Brother David's voice echoed through the room over their radio.

"We may have a break-in over at the west exit hallway. I repeat, we may have a break-in over at the west exit hallway!"

Roberto grabbed the arm of the Knight with the radio, planning to turn him around for a punch to the jaw. The Knight was a more talented fighter than he'd hoped. He dodged the swing and put Roberto's arm behind his back instantly. Morgan used her last remaining strength to twist out of the other Knight's hold. She sprang at the two men, knocking them off balance. Roberto took the opportunity to pull the Knight's gun from his holster.

He shot the first Knight in the shoulder, then put another bullet in the leg of the other Knight, who fell just short of grabbing them both. The bullets in their weapons were designed to take down a vampire. The tiny wooden splinters exploded throughout every muscle near their gunshot wounds. Despite the pain, both men reached for their swords, but their captives had already barreled out of the cell. Morgan shut the door, locking the men inside.

The elf fell to her knees, the iron in the shackles still sucking the life from her small, frail body. Roberto spread her wrists apart so that he could shoot the chain. Morgan flung her arms up.

"No! Don't! I lifted his pocket! Here!" She opened up her hand revealing a number of keys on the rusty chain. He unlocked her shackles and realized that one of the others could unlock the door to his sibling's cell.

"Vincenzo! Isabella! Maybe one of these--" Roberto stopped short when he saw her ears wiggle, much like they had on the roof of her building days earlier. She snatched the gun out of his hands and spun around, firing at three Knights that were rounding the corner.

"There is a possible break-in at the west exit on level one. There is also reported gunfire heard in the stockade on level five." The radio alert interrupted Amadeus's stand down. Joey and Frank were more than a little relieved when the fight was put off. Dick stood up from his leaning position. The cowboy's break in character gave the mobsters another reason for concern. Amadeus snatched the microphone from off his desk.

"What do you mean a 'break-in?'" he bellowed.

"Brothers Charles and Thomas are down. It looks like a werewolf." Brother David didn't sound sure. The grand master and Dick made eye contact with each other. They knew what it was; Jack had failed, was possibly even dead. This was the situation that they'd worked so hard to avoid. Both old men had been aching to fight this battle for so long.

"That is negative. What we have is one, possibly two, vampires! Maybe even a witch! I want this base locked down! No one gets in or out!" he shouted as he exited the room. Dick and Brother Matthew were in lock step along side of him.

"Dick! I want you to go down to level five and execute the prisoners. That's why they're here. I want you to disappoint them."

"You got it." Dick was more than pleased to carry out these orders. He took one brief second to brace his hand on Amadeus's shoulder. Neither needed to say it out loud, but they valued each other's friendship. Dick tipped his hat to his grand master and hurried to the stairway.

"Brother Matthew, you're with me." Amadeus felt a small tug at his cloak. It was Joey and Frank. The two had never looked more pitiful to him.

"What about us?" Joey pleaded.

"Stay here. It's the safest place for now." Amadeus turned and raced off without another worry over their welfare. The mobsters quickly shut the door and locked it. Joey massaged his temples, doing his best to make himself feel more at ease. His belly rumbled with apprehension.

"Oh, my God. I can't believe I'm gonna die under a fucking church! All because of you, you fucking mook!" Joey was surprised by his man's silence. He opened his eyes again to see Frank going through Amadeus's desk.

"Hey! Look at this!" Frank had picked the lock on the drawers to find two loaded Colt 45's. "We're not dead yet!" Frank felt like a man once again.

Knights were appearing by the dozen. They fired their weapons and they swung their swords, only to attack mist. Dominic and Lucia ripped and decapitated the Knights, transforming from wolf to bat to mist. The men couldn't get a proper handle on their targets. They were faster than anything they had ever encountered.

Zoe ran behind the others. She was unable to fight by hand, so she allowed her flying broom to do the scraping. She could levitate it by her side and use it to strike at Knights, like a staff being handled by a ghost. One Knight was able to dodge her broom and kicked her to the floor. Before he could plunge his sword into her chest, she raised her hands to him out of fright. Flames shot from her palms, setting the man ablaze.

Zoe's hands were red and warm, but not burnt. They certainly didn't feel like fire had just escaped from them. She watched the man fall to the ground, burning to death. She couldn't believe that she had done that by sheer will. It was quite a shock to her system.

"Zoe!" Lucia yelled twice before the witch noticed her.

"Huh? Yeah!"

"Are you all right?" Lucia offered her hand to lift Zoe up. She was still mesmerized by what she'd done.

"Did you see what I did?"

"Yes. I like this new you. How did you do that?" Lucia was deeply impressed.

"I don't know. I keep realizing new things that I can do. It's like suddenly discovering you can tap dance or something!"

They had cleared what Dominic guessed was the second level under the church. Once the vampires had a moment to breath, they felt out the complex. There were three more floors beneath their feet. The Knights were reorganizing at all sides. They heard their children's heartbeats at the bottom of all of this.

The Divitas and Zoe moved forward down the hall. It opened up into a large room filled with nearly a hundred desks and a clear space at the other end. A twenty-foot-tall wooden cross loomed over the room. There was a flight of stairs on the other side that, most likely, lead farther down to the remaining levels.

Zoe took a half step when Dominic snapped out and grabbed her by the arm. She was startled, but quickly realized what he was sensing. The floor rumbled from the heavy footsteps of forty Knights.

The men took their positions at every corner of the meeting hall. Some had their guns drawn while others had their hands on their swords. All of them waited for the word to strike. Amadeus came into view as he walked out on an overlooking balcony. Dominic guessed it was where he would usually give speeches to his men. He could sense the rage radiating off his wife next to him. Zoe hid behind the vampires with broom in hand.

"You have made a serious mistake. You will never leave this holy place," Amadeus declared.

"We have come for our children and Morgan! Hand them over and we'll only kill you. That's the best offer you'll get from us!" Dominic's fangs grew sharp as he barked his demands.

"Your children are safe. They are free from your abusive clutches."

Lucia noticed that Zoe was whispering something. She listened closer.

"The light, the light, will shield us at this sight," Zoe repeated under her breath. Lucia couldn't contain her excitement over what was to come. She decided just to let the men talk while Zoe warmed up.

On the third repeat of the spell, Zoe began to glow bright yellow and a burst of energy and light exploded from her body. The blast blew the many surrounding Knights off their feet and across the hall. The vampires didn't need any word to attack. Dominic and Lucia went around the room, decapitating Knight after Knight. They didn't give any of them a chance to draw use weapons.

Amadeus had also been knocked to the floor by the protection spell. The two Knights at his side helped him to his feet as he watched the vampires tearing through his men. Lucia and Dominic broke necks and tore off limbs. When they were fired upon, they transformed into mist to dodge the bullets. The battle was one sided.

Zoe choose not to stay and fight. All she wanted was to find Morgan. She ran through the splattering blood and flying body parts to the stairs. More Knights were entering the hall. Some of these men had been asleep and others had been called in from the field to defend the base. The witch removed a tiny switchblade from her back pocket and carefully stuck her own left palm until it drew blood. She circled the blood, forming a pentagram, and recited the spell.

"Guide me below and above to find my true love," Zoe began to feel that Morgan was on the next floor down. This level looked like an endless row of offices. The hallway was clear of anyone else. They all seemed to be busy fighting the Divitas. There wasn't any sign of Morgan. Zoe followed her nose down the hall. A door cracked open after she pasted it. Zoe spun around, hoping to find that Morgan had escaped and was hiding out in one of the rooms.

It wasn't Morgan.

Frank and Joey stepped out of Amadeus's office. Frank instantly recognized her from the first day at the Inferno. The mobster wasn't sure what she had to do with the Divitas, but it didn't really matter to him.

"I know this fat little cunt! She's with them!" Frank shouted. Both men raised their weapons, eager to join the fight against the monsters. Zoe flung out her hands releasing the broom. The broom swatted the gun from Frank's hand and bashed Joey in the head. The blow caused him to spin around into the brick wall. As Zoe turned to run for the stairs, she remembered, too late, that she could make fireballs. A bullet took a small bite out of her right shoulder. Frank had quickly recovered one of the guns.

Zoe swung around in pain. Before she could shoot a fireball in defense, Frank tackled her. He began to pistol whip her, breaking her glasses. He could end this at any second, but he wanted to enjoy it as long as he could.

A spell suddenly came to Zoe. She reached up and smeared the blood from her hand onto his face. The odd gesture stunned him for just a second.

"Inside out! Inside out! Inside out!" Zoe's eyes glowed black as she spoke the words. Frank dropped the gun and jumped away from her. Joey had regained his footing and his gun. He was ready to blast away at Zoe when Frank keeled over.

"Frank! What's wrong? What'd that bitch do to you?" Joey saw the blood on his face, not sure where it had come from.

Frank took hold of his heart. A slight pain became sharper with every second. Something felt like it was ripping apart in his chest. He feared it was a heart attack from all the excitement. He wasn't so lucky. He doubled over and vomited what looked like a thick, charcoal sack. After it had passed, he couldn't breathe. He attempted to speak, but nothing was coming.

"What the fuck is that?" Joey wasn't sure what to make of the sack.

"His lungs," Zoe said quite calmly.

Frank's eyes watered with panic as he continued to gasp for air. Then a rumbling inside was followed by another series of sharp pains. Something else traveled up his throat. He puked up his liver and then his kidneys. Joey could only watch as his friend tried to scream while throwing up blood, bile, and his lower intestines. Frank fell into the mess. Even dead, his stomach gushed from out his mouth.

Joey covered his own mouth. The smell was enough to make him vomit, but he dared not do so. He carefully pushed Frank up to see if he was still alive. The heart sticking out of his mouth was enough of an answer. Joey was angry. He stood up, his gun drawn at Zoe at point blank range.

Zoe's eyes glazed over black. He could see the heat coming from her hands. He decided to run instead of fight. He rushed past a young man and woman, not bothering to see who they were. It was Morgan and Roberto.

Morgan was horrified at the sight of her girlfriend. The woman that she had loved, and wanted to give the gift of everlasting life, didn't resemble the woman that stood before her. Zoe saw Morgan's beautiful face, but her eyes quickly ran down her arm to see her holding hands with Roberto. Zoe was shocked back to normal. Morgan let go of Roberto as she and Zoe ran to each other.

The women embraced as if they hadn't seen each other in years.

They kissed, but there was an emptiness to the kiss. They were happy that they were alive, but each woman knew that they had changed. Sadness underlined what would be their last moment of joy together.

Roberto stayed back, letting them share their time together. He tried not to think about the mess that was unrolled at their feet. He felt that the mobster had probably had it coming, but it also showed him what Zoe had become.

"We need to get going! Zoe, are my parents here?" Roberto didn't wish to butt in. He did his best to be polite. Zoe and Morgan slowly peeled apart, still holding hands. Zoe wiped the tears from her eyes.

"They're upstairs, fighting the Knights."

"How many?" Roberto asked.

"Um...all of them, I think."

"Will you help us find Vincenzo and Isabella?"

More Knights were coming out of the woodwork. Lucia stuck her fingers in the eyes of one Knight as she took hold of his head. She gripped around his sockets and the inside of his mouth as he screamed in pain. One quick tug and she pulled his skull apart.

Seeing this horrified one Knight long enough to distract him while Dominic ripped the row of wooden crosses off of his belt. The vampire struck him and four other Knights in their hearts. There was no room to fly, so Dominic transformed into a wolf and jumped to the balcony where he'd last seen Amadeus. He was no longer there.

"Dominic! I'm going to get the babies!" There were still men to fight, but he wasn't going to argue. He nodded, but she had already transformed into mist and floated down one of the stairways.

The hundred man army that made up the mighty Knights of the Silver

Cross had dwindled to almost nothing. Dominic changed back to his original form and tracked the smell of humans through a narrow passageway that led back to the floor of the meeting hall. Amadeus stood in the middle of the remains of his fallen men. He had removed his cloak. He held his board sword in position.

"Dominic Divita."

"Be careful, don't trip over the bodies," Dominic joked. His opponent wasn't amused.

"Dominic Divita, son of Sergio and Bella Divita, it isn't too late to save your soul."

"What did you say to me?"

"You were a good Catholic until you were lured away by that demon in a woman's skin." The tone of Amadeus's voice was that of stern judgment. It didn't matter to him that Dominic and Lucia had killed most of his Knights. He was still in command.

"What do you know about my parents?" Dominic wasn't prepared for talk of his mother and father.

"I have to say that I'm impressed with your son, Roberto. Despite being raised by a couple of monsters, his faith is unwavering. He told us much. He asked me to save you."

"How do you plan on doing that?" Dominic could hardly see how he was in any position to do anything.

"Because the power of Christ compels you." Amadeus held out his sword, ready to strike.

Dick Walker marched into the cell block where the younger Divitas were being held with two Knights at his side. There was moaning coming from a few cells over -- human moans.

"Go check that out," Dick ordered as he stood by the door to the twins' cell. Brother George didn't hesitate. He carefully opened the door to find the two Knights that Roberto and Morgan had left behind.

"Brother Walker!" he shouted.

"I can see. We don't have time to patch them up!"

The wounded Knights did their best to stand as they were spoken to. Even though pain raced through their bodies, and their wounds were still bleeding heavily, they knew that the mission came first. They waited for Dick's instructions.

"I need you four to block that entry!" Dick turned away from his men and opened the door to the twin's cell. He could see on their faces that they had no illusions about what was to come next. He decided not to even to hide it. Dick opened up his cloak, revealing a pair of Colt 45's and his katana sword. Each weapon was solid silver and featured a detailed image of the cross.

"I won't lie to you kids. It's time. I won't pray for you, but I'll give you a choice. Which way do you want it?"

Vincenzo and Isabella reacted much differently than Dick had counted on. They began to laugh. They knew what was coming down the hall. Dick spun back around to the door when he heard the sound of his men howling in pain echo throughout the cell block. He had less time than he thought.

Dick pulled his guns from his belt and put them to the twins' temples. They didn't even flinch. They just looked back at him with the most mischievous grins he had ever seen. Before he was able to fire, Lucia stepped into the cell. She held the heads of the four other Knights by the hair.

Dick held his stance, unsure if he could get off the shot. He wondered if maybe he could turn and fire on her in time. She released the heads, making four heavy, wet splats at her feet.

"What are you doing with my children?" Lucia coldly asked.

"The way I see it now, you have two choices." Dick spoke with his back to the vampire. He hoped that he could talk his way through this, instead he felt his wrists burn as Lucia snatched the guns from him. His hands went with them. Lucia pushed him away from the twins. She held the guns at him, his own fingers still gripped around the triggers.

"No. I make my own choices." Lucia then realized that she could not only sense the blood in the severed hands, but she could manipulate them as well. With a single thought, the hands pulled the triggers, shooting Dick in the chest. The Knight fell on his back. She dropped the handguns and was on top of him just as quickly. Then he said something that stopped her cold.

"Ursula..." He did his best to get his message out through heavy breathes.

"Ursula misses you..." Dick's last words struck an angry cord in Lucia that had not been reached in years. Her children, her husband, her way of life had been threatened by these men. This was the last thing she wanted to hear.

Lucia unleashed an inhuman scream. She dug her claws deep into his chest, wrapping her fingers around his ribs. She tore open his chest. Vincenzo and Isabella didn't even bother to duck the massive amounts of blood, meat, and bone that flew across the cell. Lucia slashed and pounded at him. She took handfuls of flesh, ripping them free of his body. She continued until there wasn't anything left of his torso.

A strip of blood-matted hair slapped against onto Lucia's cheek. She pushed it back as she stood up from her kill. She was eager to give her children a hug, but she was a mess. Lucia quickly changed into mist and back once more. She was suddenly fresh, without any marks or stains. She broke off the chains that kept Vincenzo and Isabella in place. A sense of optimism washed over all three of them as they held each other tight, even though they still hadn't escaped or found Roberto and Morgan.

"I missed you, Mamma!" Vincenzo exclaimed. Isabella was too

emotional to speak, but her smile was enough. Lucia kissed them. Normally at this age they would have complained about being too old, but they didn't make such comments this time.

"I missed you, too! Where are your brother and Morgan? Are they near?" Lucia panicked when she saw their eyes drop. If she had thought to read their minds, she would have known the truth. Instead, she feared that they were already dead.

"I don't know, Mamma," Vincenzo finally answered.

"Let's find them!" Lucia didn't have to search long. Roberto, Morgan, and Zoe were in the doorway.

Lucia's face lit up at the sight of him. She went to her first born son without any tension from the past, she just wanted to hold him. He could see the icy expressions of his siblings over his mother's shoulder. He wanted to look elsewhere, but elsewhere meant looking at what was left of Dick Walker.

Roberto had seen bodies left by his parents over the years, but this puddle of human waste was hardly recognizable as a man. He could only tell it was Dick from the cowboy boots that still twitched in his presence. A chill swelled from in his belly once he realized that the arms that had created that mess were the same arms that were around him.

"Christ. You do remember him, don't you?" Amadeus took a step closer. The vampire was locked into position. There was something inside him, inside his head, that frozen him to the spot. The giant wooden cross that loomed behind Amadeus seemed to be weighing down on Dominic.

"Never met him." Dominic kept his fangs visible to the grand master.

It didn't intimidate him. Amadeus swung his sword, slashing across Dominic's chest. The cut didn't just tear into his flesh, but his very soul. Amadeus brought his sword on him again, this time, the blade sliced down the middle. The buttons of his shirt popped off, opening up to reveal the cross that Amadeus had just craved into his skin.

"Lying is a sin." Amadeus kicked Dominic in the chest with enough force to fling him over a nearby desk. He lifted the desk, knocking it aside to find the mighty vampire picking himself up.

"You have sinned much. You dishonored your own parents." He picked Dominic up by the throat.

"You have killed countless times. You worship a false god!" Amadeus bashed his face into a metal file cabinet. He threw him to the floor, but was surprised when Dominic took hold of his leg. The vampire lifted him off the ground and propelled him along the wall. Amadeus quickly recovered, just in time to dodge a desk that Dominic threw in his direction. Both men faced stood and each other once again.

"You still remember, Dominic! You don't forget! You never forget! You keep telling yourself that your vampire god will save you. You think you can do whatever you please without any punishment. You can't have God's love and continue with this life of evil! You can say that you deny God, but you know the truth!"

"Fuck you!" Dominic transformed into a wolf as he charged straight for him. Amadeus blocked his fangs and claws with his sword. The two crashed around the room together. The hunter used leverage to flip the massive wolf off of him. Dominic bounced on his back until he was once again on his human feet. By this time, Amadeus was already in midair over him. The sword slashed through his chest, just missing his head.

"You never forget Christ's power! It compels you! Give in! Fear God!" Amadeus struck Dominic again. The blow knocked him to the ground. The vampire got up, only to be hit once more.

"The power of Christ compels you! The power of Christ compels you!" Amadeus shouted as he thrashed him with his sword. Dominic fell to his knees. The grand master stood high over him, ready to deliver one final strike.

"You cannot deny the truth inside your heart! The power of Christ compels you!" Amadeus swung his sword down as if the wrath of God had given strength to his very arms.

Amadeus only chopped through mist. The silver broad sword clanged against the concrete floor. Dominic reformed a foot in front of him. The grand master couldn't believe the power that he sensed from the vampire. The cross that he had sliced into his chest was gone. His eyes were free of fear and guilt.

"Never again." Dominic was reborn. He gave a right cross into Amadeus's chest. The punch broke his ribs, shattered his lungs, and burst his heart. The jolt sent him somersaulting backwards in the air, until he slammed into the wooden cross.

Dominic didn't say anything else. He walked over to the cross to watch his fallen enemy take his final breathes. Amadeus couldn't speak. He simply raised his right hand and pointed to Dominic, as if he was holding a gun, for a brief second before it fell at his side. He fought until the end.

"Poppa!" the twins yelled from the top of the stairs. Isabella and Vincenzo raced to their father. It reminded him of the greetings they used to give him every day as children.

Zoe and Morgan followed, no longer holding hands. Lucia stepped aside, knowing her babies would want to see their poppa. Roberto dragged his heels into the room. The smell of death sickened him. He could no longer stand to see the bodies left behind in his parents' wake.

"Poppa!" was all that Isabella could muster in between her tears. She stopped crying when she felt her father tense up.

He pushed his children to the floor and leapt up to the balcony as an unknown gunman fired at him, missing with every shot. Dominic didn't find a last remaining knight; instead it was a simple, scared little man. He easily took the gun from the frightened man's hand.

"Who the fuck are you?" Dominic was quite confused over this new player. The man didn't answer. He simply cowered at the vampire's feet.

As he stared into his eyes Dominic caught flashes of memories that he quickly realized were not his own. He could hear conversations with Amadeus and Frank. He could see the bodies of an unknown woman and her child. Then he heard a name -- Joey Paparazzo. He couldn't believe his luck. The man that had caused all of this trouble was at his mercy.

"I know who you are, Joey. I'm not going to kill you."

"Yeah?" Joey looked up at him from behind his hands.

He was frightened once more when Dominic grabbed him by the neck and plastered him to the wall. He bit into his own wrist as he forced open Joey's mouth to drink. He held Joey's mouth shut once more, giving him no other choice but to swallow the tiny droplets of blood that had landed on his tongue. The blood was unlike anything he had ever tasted. It was warm and ignited all of his senses. It was better than any alcohol that had ever passed his lips. It was intoxicating.

"Yes! You belong to me. Everything I want, you want, and what I want is to own ten percent of your family's business. We're going to be partners for a long time. Sound good?"

"Yeah..." Joey whimpered.

"Yeah, what?" Dominic tightened his grip around the mobster's esophagus.

"Yeah...Master!"

Roberto looked over the scene but didn't say a word. He just couldn't believe it. He watched Amadeus's blood drip to the floor as his family hugged and cried like there was something to be happy about. He was dead inside. He knew in his heart that his parents were lost.

CHAPTER TWENTY TWO

"Your Holiness! Your Holiness! Brother Jack Cain has just arrived!" the pope's cardinals shouted.

The pope had been waiting on edge since the Vatican had received the message from Cardinal McGinnis twelve hours earlier. The New York order of the Knights of the Silver Cross were reported dead and Jack Cain was the only known survivor.

Jack was escorted to the pope's private study. He was still visibly shaken over his failure to prevent the deaths of his fellow Knights and his mentor. He knelt before the pope, broken. The pope asked him to rise. The old holy man didn't blame him for the disaster. He only felt sorrow for his loss.

"Please, stand up. My poor, brave Knight. You have suffered so much. Tell me what happened." The pope sounded more like a worried father than the leader of the Church.

"Your Holiness, I led a team to stop the vampires and their witch before it was too late. I thought we were successful, but they proved more powerful than we expected. My team was struck down." Jack couldn't continue for the moment. His silence gave the pope cause for concern.

"Your Holiness, Dominic Divita wanted me to give you a message."

"A message?"

"He wanted to propose a truce. You are not to send any more

Knights into New York City. In exchange for your cooperation, the Divita family will keep the vampires and other such monsters in New York City in line. If you don't agree to the terms, the Divita family will kill whatever Knights you send and bring the fight here, to the Vatican." Jack looked away in shame. He felt, just repeating the message, that he had committed a most repulsive sin.

The pope went pale. He sat down behind his desk without giving any sort of answer. This frightened the cardinals in the room. They begged him to say something...anything. He didn't see much choice in the matter but to agree to the terms. This was the first day since he had become pope that he truly hoped that he was infallible.

EPILOGUE

Isabella and Vincenzo both felt their hearts jump when they tasted the first warm drops of their parents' blood slide around in their mouths. Lucia held her daughter carefully as she allowed her to drink the blood from her wrist. Dominic did the same for his son. The living room had been easy to clear for this private ceremony, considering the Knights had thrown every piece of furniture around the room looking for whatever it was they'd been looking for.

Dominic and Lucia's apprehension grew as they felt their children's death rattles evolve from little earthquakes deep inside their chests to tremors that caused them to tremble all over. This was the first time that they had made vampires of their own and doubts as to whether this was going well leaked into their minds. The twins didn't share these fears. Isabella and Vincenzo had never felt so happy, or so safe, as they quickly shed their mortal lives in the arms of those who had given them in the first place.

They didn't speak as they carried their children upstairs and placed them in their own beds. There was much work to be done before the following sunset. The whole event was being treated like a big birthday party.

The living room wasn't the only spot that the Knights had ransacked. Nearly every room of the brownstone had some broken furniture while others had been carefully disassembled. It was easy to see that they hadn't been satisfied with what they'd found. They had even dug up the cellar, hoping to find corpses. None were uncovered.

Dominic and Lucia spend the night cleaning their home. They had hoped to have help, but Roberto hadn't been home since they left St. Patrick's. They had both called his usual hangouts, as well as the disco. He wasn't there. Lucia even tried to contact him with her mind. He didn't answer her, nor did he answer his father. They were becoming worried.

The following morning, the home looked almost livable. The destroyed items were sitting out with the trash, the rest was put back together. Dominic knew that his wife was planning to make the best out of the situation and go on a shopping expedition over the next few days.

The only room that had been left mostly untouched was the kitchen. Zoe arrived early to help cook for the night's celebration. She had come dressed simply, in a white t-shirt and jeans, while carrying something more appropriate for the party. Zoe had baked a chocolate cake in the shape of a coffin. She stood over the cake with the icing bag, unsure of what to write. She had never been to a vampire making party before. She had no idea what someone should say.

"How about 'To Your New Life!'" Dominic's suggestion came from out of nowhere, startling her so much that she squirted a little icing out onto the floor. Zoe took a deep breath to catch herself before reaching for a towel to wipe up the mess. The tension was obvious in her body language. Dominic had noticed it earlier, but he wasn't too sure if he should bring it up.

"Thanks for coming over to help, Zoe."

She blushed, doing her best to seem normal.

"Is Morgan coming later for the party?"

Zoe's shoulders collapsed at the very mention of her former girlfriend's name. She didn't want to talk about Morgan's sudden exit in the middle of the night. Their five-year relationship had ended with an awkward distance rather than an explosive fight. She was still unsure how to react. Morgan had acted so different, so cold. She must have been hiding her true feelings about their relationship for months. Zoe wondered if she'd known all along, that she'd fooled herself into thinking that everything was going to work out for them in the end. She tried to forget the pain, this was Vincenzo and Isabella's night and she didn't wish to ruin it.

"Oh, um...she isn't coming. Is that okay?"

Dominic didn't need to read her mind to know something had happened. He caressed the cheek of his friend. A smile found its way to her lips at his touch. He hadn't taken the time to recognize it before, but he was proud of her. He had watched her evolve over the past couple of weeks in ways than he hadn't expected. There were no words said between the two, anything said would have been redundant.

Dominic's fingers left her cheek and momentary ran through the newly formed white streak in her hair. He released it, allowing it to fall back into place.

"Do you like it?" Zoe sheepishly asked.

"I do. It reminds me of an old friend. Was this because of the spell?" He was happy to talk about something cheerful to break the mood.

"Yeah! It's a side effect. I tried to dye it, but it didn't work. I guess I'll keep it."

Dominic left the kitchen to give Zoe some time alone, only to discover that Lucia was no longer in the house. He reached out to her with his mind. She was out trying to find their son. While he shared her nervousness over his whereabouts, he couldn't think anyone who wanted to get revenge on them so soon. What he felt was most likely, was that Roberto needed time away from the family to reflect.

He went into Roberto's room. The Strigori Bible was missing. It had been taken by the Knights in hopes that it might give them clues on how to defeat him and his wife. Dominic didn't miss it. All he wanted was to hear his son enter from downstairs. He lay down on his son's bed and quickly became fixated on the painted planets and stars on the ceiling. He could see why such vastness fascinated Roberto.

The vampire stared into the painting and wondered if there were other worlds that might be out there in the unknown universe. He asked himself if they had gods or if they'd dismissed them as he had just done. As Dominic was lying there all alone, he decided that he had no idea what was beyond this world and that was okay.

Dominic picked himself up once he could smell the pasta cooking down in the kitchen. Dusk was only a few hours away and he needed to find his wife and son. He reached out with his mind and found Lucia at the Inferno. He pulled out his shoes and Amadeus's sword, wrapped up in newspaper, from the closet and said goodbye to Zoe.

"Zoe? I'm going to the Inferno. I want to hang my new sword in my office while I have a few hours before the children awaken," he casually offered.

"Are you going to be back in time? They're not going to eat me, are they?" Zoe's concern fueled her sauce stirring to a faster degree than what was needed.

"Don't worry! They're still going to be themselves, but we'll be back in time...and stir the sauce slower," he answered.

It wasn't difficult to find his wife. What was challenging was getting her to respond to his call to her. Dominic had not yet mastered this new ability, so to the passersby on the street he looked like some crazy person as he swiftly walked with his eyes closed, mumbling to himself. A secretary sitting on a corner bench watched him as she mindlessly chewed on her sandwich. She was confused. He was too well dressed to be homeless. She decided to stay clear of him anyway.

The Inferno had been closed since Eddie and Susan had gone

missing. Zoe was in the process of locating Susan, and a service at the club was already planned for Eddie. The lights were all off, as if that mattered to a vampire, and a faint sound of crying reverberated throughout the building. It was his wife.

Lucia stood in the middle of the dance floor that she ruled over every night with ease. At this moment she seemed so small, so alone. He asked her what was wrong, but she remained silent. She knew that he was there, she just didn't want to face him. In her hand, she held a piece of paper and the envelope that they'd given Roberto his birthday money in. She had found the envelope in her dressing room, inside it was the money, along with a letter.

"Lucia? Lucia, what is it?" he demanded.

Lucia continued to look away from him. She hushed up her cries and allowed her hair to fall over her face to hide her tears. Her arm sprung up with the items in hand.

He guardedly took them from her shaking hand. Every cent they'd given Roberto was there. Dominic flipped open the crumbled pages of the typed letter.

Mother. Father.

I have done everything I could do to be a good son. You both have not only given me life, but have given up so much for not only me, but Vincenzo and Isabella. I've tried to look past what you've become and what you do. All these years, I blamed Ursula for that. I hoped that one day I could find a way to save you or at least your souls. I buried bodies. I cleaned up your messes. I did all of these sinful acts in honor of you. I told myself that you were both goodhearted, in spite of all these things.

I have been kidding myself.

The truth is that you both died the night Ursula took you. I miss you. I wish I could have you back. I want to throw this letter in a shitcan and run to you and tell you how much I love you.

But, you're dead. I need to remind myself that you are not my Mamma and Poppa. You're monsters that are running around in their bodies. You're nothing more than a pair of soulless cadavers that kill to maintain themselves. Worse yet, you've fooled my brother and sister into following your path into evil.

They're as dead to me as you are.

I hate what you've become. I should have kept quiet, pretended that everything was cool. When the moment was right, I could have chopped off your heads while you rested. I thought about it all last night.

I hate you, "Mother."
You are not the mother I knew. You're now an ugly bitch of a monster that deserves nothing short of damnation. I hate what you've done to father.

I hate you, "Father."
You gave in. You were weak. You let mother tell you what to believe. All to please her, you have turned your back on God, on what was right, and on me. I believed in you. Once again, I was only kidding myself.

In the end, I wasn't strong enough to kill you. I couldn't chop off the head of the father that sat with me every night by the radio until I fell asleep. I couldn't kill the mother that told me stories of her travels across Italy.

Instead, Morgan and I are going to leave you to this Hell you've made for yourselves. I only hope that there will come a day when someone else is strong enough to do what is right.

I hope you're happy.
Roberto

Dominic read and reread the words until he could believe that they truly existed. His son was not only gone, but he hated him as well. His mouth went dry of anything to say. He had no comforting thoughts, no insights, no jokes. The air around him went dense. He reached out to Lucia, only to have his arm swatted back.

"No! Don't touch me!" Lucia cried out. He didn't listen and reached for her again. She pushed back. The envelope floated to the dance floor. He wanted to ask why she didn't want to hold him, but all he gave her was a look of sorrow.

"I can't feel him anymore!" Lucia screamed. Her husband's look of confusion caused her to become even more upset. She began to pound on his chest hard enough to crack his ribs.

"Ah! You fucking idiot! You never notice anything! Try to sense him out!" Her words pushed him to the floor. Dominic sat himself upright and took a deep breath and tried to find his son with his own mind. He could sense Vincenzo and Isabella back at their house. Roberto wasn't there.

"Ever since we were made into vampires, I could feel our children breathing. I could feel their hearts beat next to mine. I never felt lonely. I always knew when they were safe, because they were always right here with me. Didn't you feel that?"

Dominic mournfully nodded.

"Now, it's gone. I feel so dead inside," Lucia's voice cracked with each word. She got down beside him as she brushed aside his tears. She seemed to have gathered enough strength to propose a question or some topic. Dominic hoped that he had enough to answer.

"I'm sorry." Her out of the blue statement snapped him back to reality.

"What?"

"I drove you to this. Didn't I? You would have been happier if you'd never met me."

"No! Lucia? What are you talking about?"

"I drove you away from your family, your life. Your mother was right. I have dragged you down to Hell. You would have been perfectly happy worshiping your God, married to some beautiful woman that followed your every command. Just admit it."

Dominic's tears shook off his face with his sudden laughter. She was perplexed by his reaction. She often wondered why some questions about their relationship made him laugh. He tilted her face up to his own. He wiped the tears racing to her jaw with his thumbs. This powerful woman that loved so fiercely was still terrified of being alone, of being vulnerable.

"Lucia. I made my own choices. I choose to be with you. I choose to be a vampire. I wanted this family. I want nothing more than to be with you. You never believe me. What can I say to make you believe me?"

"Dominic, just shut up and hold me."

More time passed as each of them took turns being the strong one as the other cried over their loss. As the sun began to set outside, their two remaining children were about to be reborn.

Dominic picked himself up off the dance floor as Lucia regained her composure. Instead of insisting on leaving, he put his hand out for her and lifted her up into a dancer's position. The two vampires slowly danced in a fixed circle, clutching each other so that they could feed off each other's strength. Dominic and Lucia both knew that they needed to go, but all they wanted was to dance like this forever.

Author Bio

Justin Cristelli is the writer and creator of the comic book series, *Red Knight*. He is the author of *Caprice and Other Stories* and co-wrote the screenplay for the film version of *Caprice*. He is also known as The Real Manos, a reviewer on You Tube that reviews comics, film, and Mystery Science Theater 3000. He lives with his geeky wife, Lindsay Cristelli, in Norfolk, Virginia.